Otori has been a thrilling addition to the shelves of "crossover" children's fiction . . . Takeo is a kind of Japanese Aragorn, a man of thought and feeling as well as violence . . . *Brilliance of the Moon* provides an unexpectedly thoughtful conclusion to an enthralling and original work of fantasy'
Amanda Craig, *The Times*

'The brutality of the action . . . is balanced by Lian Hearn's delicate, sensitive story-telling. *Brilliance of the Moon* . . . makes a thrilling finale to a fascinating epic'
Sunday Telegraph

'Lian Hearn, one of Pullman's few rivals for quality . . . blood-splashed combat alternates with contemplative stillness and the writing remains extraordinary. Hearn's trilogy ends as it began, virtually pitch-perfect'
Francis Spufford, *Evening Standard*

Praise for *Grass for His Pillow*

'Even better than volume one . . . the beauty, savagery and strangeness of Hearn's gripping tale is heightened by her exquisite, crystalline prose'
Independent on Sunday

'What lifts this thrilling tale is the clarity with which medieval Japan is described'
The Times

'This is history plus mystery, magic, myth and echoes of the Arthurian and other legends, in a saga which I found brilliant and enthralling'
Sunday Telegraph

'The story is entrancing, the writing compelling, the world intoxicating . . . captivating . . . . thralling; this is story-telli
*Watersto

'Quite simply the best story of magic, love, sex, revenge and suspense to have come this way since Philip Pullman'
Amanda Craig, *Independent on Sunday*

'This is a thrilling tale of love, violence, loyalty and betrayal, fast-moving, set in a faraway country long ago, where people and places have exotic names'
Guardian

'It exerts a mesmeric attraction . . . those who fall upon such tales with joy will find it the most compelling novel to have been published this year'
The Times

'I approached this book gingerly, but found it absorbing and strangely comforting, despite the battles, betrayals and torture within its pages . . . Hearn's writing style is brisk yet elegant. Her descriptive passages evoke the beauty of the countryside, providing an effective counterpoint to the vicious power struggles'
Telegraph

'A cross between *Harry Potter* and *Crouching Tiger, Hidden Dragon*, this atmospheric thriller . . . is a heady mix of magic, martial arts and intense, convincing detail'
Georgia Metcalfe, *Daily Mail*

'The story is so tantalizing you'll be grateful for the next two in the trilogy'
B magazine

'Read *Across the Nightingale Floor* by Lian Hearn. This magical novel set in a mythical land similar to medieval Japan is such hot stuff that Universal have snapped up the film rights'
19 magazine

Lian Hearn studied modern languages at Oxford University and worked as a film critic and arts editor in London before settling in Australia. A lifelong interest in Japan led to the study of the Japanese language, many trips to Japan, and culminated in the writing of the Tales of the Otori.

Tales of the Otori

Heaven's Net is Wide

Across the Nightingale Floor
Grass for His Pillow
Brilliance of the Moon

The Harsh Cry of the Heron

Also available in audio download

LIAN HEARN

Brilliance of the Moon

Tales of the Otori

MACMILLAN

First published 2004 by Macmillan

This edition published 2005 by Young Picador
an imprint of Pan Macmillan Ltd
and reissued 2013 by Macmillan Children's Books
a division of Macmillan Publishers Ltd

20 New Wharf Road, London N1 9RR
Basingstoke and Oxford
Associated companies throughout the world

www.panmacmillan.com

ISBN 978-0-330-41350-3

9 8

A CIP catalogue recorded for this book is available from
the British Library.

Typeset by Set Systems
Printed and bound by CPI Group (UK) Ltd, Croydon, CR0 4YY

for B

THE THREE COUNTRIES

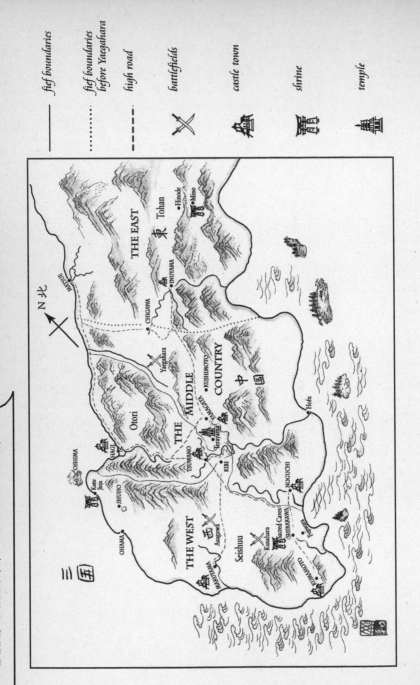

Tales of the Otori

Characters

The Clans

The Otori
(Middle Country; castle town: Hagi)

Otori Shigeru . . . . rightful heir to the clan

Otori Takeshi . . his younger brother, murdered by the Tohan clan

Otori Takeo . . . . (born Tomasu) his adopted son

Otori Shigemori . . . . Shigeru's father, killed at
the battle of Yaegahara (d.)

Otori Ichiro . . . . a distant relative, Shigeru
and Takeo's teacher

Chiyo ⎫
Haruka ⎰ . . . . maids in the household

Shiro . . . . a carpenter

Otori Shoichi . . . . Shigeru's uncle, now lord of the clan

Otori Masahiro . . . . his younger brother

Otori Yoshitomi . . . . Masahiro's son

Miyoshi Kahei ⎫
Miyoshi Gemba ⎰ . . . . brothers, friends of Takeo

Miyoshi Satoru . . . . their father, captain of the
guard in Hagi Castle

Endo Chikara . . . . a senior retainer

Terada Fumifusa . . . . a pirate

Terada Fumio . . . . his son, friend of Takeo

Ryoma . . . . a fisherman, Masahiro's illegitimate son

The Tohan
(The East; castle town: Inuyama)

Iida Sadamu . . . . lord of the clan

Iida Nariaki . . . . his cousin

Ando ⎫
Abe ⎭ . . . . Iida's retainers

Lord Noguchi . . . . an ally

Lady Noguchi . . . . his wife

Junko . . . . a servant in Noguchi Castle

The Seishuu
(an alliance of several ancient families in the West. Main castle towns: Kumamoto and Maruyama)

Arai Daiichi . . . . a warlord

Niwa Satoru . . . . a retainer

Akita Tsutomu . . . . a retainer

Sonoda Mitsuru . . . . Akita's nephew

Maruyama Naomi . . . . head of the Maruyama
domain, Shigeru's lover

Mariko . . . . her daughter

Sachie . . . . her maid

Sugita Haruki . . . . a retainer

Sugita Hiroshi . . . . his nephew

Sakai Masaki . . . . Hiroshi's cousin

Lord Shirakawa . . . . head of the Shirakawa domain

Kaede . . . . his eldest daughter,
Lady Maruyama's cousin

Ai ⎫
Hana ⎭ . . . . his daughters

Ayame
Manami } . . . . maids in the household
Ayako

Amano Tenzo . . . . a Shirakawa retainer

Shoji Kiyoshi . . . . senior retainer to Lord Shirakawa

The Tribe

The Muto Family
Muto Kenji . . . . Takeo's teacher, the Master
Muto Shizuka . . . . Kenji's niece, Arai's mistress
and Kaede's companion

Zenko } . . . . her sons
Taku
Muto Seiko . . . . Kenji's wife
Muto Yuki . . . . their daughter
Muto Yuzuru . . . . a cousin
Kana } . . . . maids
Miyabi

The Kikuta Family
Kikuta Isamu . . . . Takeo's real father (d.)
Kikuta Kotaro . . . . his cousin, the Master
Kikuta Gosaburo . . . . Kotaro's younger brother
Kikuta Akio . . . . their nephew
Kikuta Hajime . . . . a wrestler
Sadako . . . . a maid

The Kuroda Family
Kuroda Shintaro . . . . a famous assassin
Kondo Kiichi . . a Tribe member, warrior and Kaede's retainer

Imai Kazuo . . . . an actor

Kudo Keiko . . . . an actor

Others

Lord Fujiwara. . . . . . . a nobleman, exiled from the capital
Mamoru . . . . his protégé and companion
Ono Rieko. . . . . his first wife's cousin
Murita . . . . a retainer
Dr Ishida. . . . . his physican

Matsuda Shingen . . . . the abbot at Terayama
Kubo Makoto . . . . a monk, Takeo's closest friend

Jin-emon. . . . . a bandit

Jiro. . . . . a farmer's son

Jo-An . . . . an outcaste

Horses

Raku. . . . . grey with black mane and tail.
                    Takeo's first horse, given by him to Kaede
Kyu. . . . . . . black, Shigeru's horse, disappeared in Inuyama
Aoi. . . . . black (half-brother to Kyu)
Ki. Amano's chestnut
Shun. . . . . Takeo's bay. A very clever horse

bold = main characters

(d.) = character died before the start of Book One

Others too, in far-flung villages,
Will no doubt be gazing at this moon
That never asks which watcher claims the night . . .
Loud on the unseen mountain wind,
A stag's cry quivers in the heart,
And somewhere a twig lets one leaf fall

'The Fulling Block (Kinuta)' by Zeami
Translated by Royall Tyler

Foreword

These events took place in the months following the marriage of Otori Takeo and Shirakawa Kaede at the temple at Terayama. This marriage strengthened Kaede's resolve to inherit the domain of Maruyama and gave Takeo the resources he needed to carry out his work of revenge for his adopted father Shigeru and take his place as head of the Otori clan. However, it also enraged Arai Daiichi, the warlord who now controlled most of the Three Countries, and insulted the nobleman Lord Fujiwara, who considered Kaede betrothed to him.

The previous winter, Takeo, under the Tribe's sentence of death, had fled to Terayama, where the detailed records of the Tribe that Shigeru had compiled were given to him, along with the Otori sword Jato. On the way, his life was saved by the outcaste Jo-An, one of the forbidden sect, the Hidden, who took him to a mountain shrine to hear the prophetic words of a holy woman.

Three bloods are mixed in you. You were born into the Hidden but your life has been brought into the open and is no longer your own. Earth will deliver what heaven desires.

Your lands will stretch from sea to sea. But peace comes at the price of bloodshed. Five battles will buy you peace, four to win and one to lose . . .

One

The feather lay in my palm. I held it carefully, aware of its age and its fragility. Yet its whiteness was still translucent, the vermilion tips of the pinions still brilliant.

'It came from a sacred bird, the *houou*,' Matsuda Shingen, the abbot of the temple at Terayama, told me. 'It appeared to your adopted father, Shigeru, when he was only fifteen, younger than you are now. Did he ever tell you this, Takeo?'

I shook my head. Matsuda and I were standing in his room at one end of the cloister around the main courtyard of the temple. From outside, drowning out the usual sounds of the temple, the chanting, and the bells, came the urgent noise of preparations, of many people coming and going. I could hear Kaede, my wife, beyond the gates, talking to Amano Tenzo about the problems of keeping our army fed on the march. We were preparing to travel to Maruyama, the great domain in the West to which Kaede was the rightful heir, to claim it in her name – to fight for it if necessary. Since the end of winter warriors had been making their way to Terayama to join me and I now had close to a thousand men billeted in the temple and in the surrounding villages, not counting the district's farmers who also strongly supported my cause.

Amano was from Shirakawa, my wife's ancestral home, and the most trusted of her retainers, a great horseman and good with all animals. In the days that followed our marriage, Kaede and her woman, Manami, had shown considerable skill in handling and distributing food and equipment. They discussed everything with Amano and had him deliver their decisions to the men. That morning he was enumerating the ox carts and packhorses we had at our disposal. I tried to stop listening, to concentrate on what Matsuda was telling me, but I was restless, eager to get moving.

'Be patient,' Matsuda said mildly. 'This will only take a minute. What do you know about the *houou*?'

I reluctantly pulled my attention back to the feather in my palm and tried to recall what my former teacher Ichiro had taught me when I had been living in Lord Shigeru's house in Hagi. 'It is the sacred bird of legend that appears in times of justice and peace. And it is written with the same character as the name of my clan, Otori.'

'Correct,' Matsuda said, smiling. 'It does not often appear, justice and peace being something of a rarity in these times. But Shigeru saw it and I believe the vision inspired him in his pursuit of these virtues. I told him then that the feathers were tinged with blood, and indeed his blood, his death, still drive both you and me.'

I looked more closely at the feather. It lay across the scar on my right palm where I had burned my hand a long time ago, in Mino, my birthplace, the day Shigeru had saved my life. My hand was also marked with the straight line of the Kikuta, the Tribe family to which I belonged, from which I had run away the previous winter. My inheritance, my past and my future all seemed to be there, held in the palm of my hand.

'Why do you show it to me now?'

'You will be leaving here soon. You have been with us all winter, studying and training to prepare yourself to fulfil Shigeru's last commands to you. I wanted you to share in his vision, to remember that his goal was justice, and yours must be too.'

'I will never forget it,' I promised. I bowed reverently over the feather, holding it gently in both hands, and offered it back to the abbot. He took it, bowed over it and replaced it in the small lacquered box from which he had taken it. I said nothing, remembering all that Shigeru had done for me, and how much I still needed to accomplish for him.

'Ichiro told me about the *houou* when he was teaching me to write my name,' I said finally. 'When I saw him in Hagi last year he advised me to wait for him here but I cannot wait much longer. We must leave for Maruyama within the week.' I had been worrying about my old teacher since the snows had melted, for I knew that the Otori lords, Shigeru's uncles, were trying to take possession of my house and lands in Hagi and that Ichiro continued stubbornly to resist them.

I did not know it, but Ichiro was already dead. I had the news of it the next day. I was talking with Amano in the courtyard when I heard something from far below: shouts of anger, running feet, the trampling of hooves. The sound of horses plunging up the slope was unexpected and shocking. Usually no one came to the temple at Terayama on horseback. They either walked up the steep mountain path or, if unfit or very old, were carried by sturdy porters.

3

A few seconds later Amano heard it too. By then I was already running to the temple gates, calling to the guards.

Swiftly they set about closing the gates and barring them. Matsuda came hurrying across the courtyard. He was not wearing armour, but his sword was in his belt. Before we could speak to each other, a challenge came from the guard house.

'Who dares to ride to the temple gate? Dismount and approach this place of peace with respect!'

It was Kubo Makoto's voice. One of Terayama's young warrior monks, he had become, over the last few months, my closest friend. I ran to the wooden stockade and climbed the ladder to the guard house. Makoto gestured towards the spyhole. Through the chinks in the wood I could see four horsemen. They had been galloping up the hill; now they pulled their heaving, snorting mounts to a halt. They were fully armed, but the Otori crest was clearly visible on their helmets. For a moment I thought that they might be messengers from Ichiro. Then my eyes fell on the basket tied to the bow of one of the saddles. My heart turned to stone. I could guess, only too easily, what was inside such a container.

The horses were rearing and cavorting, not only from the exertion of the gallop, but also from alarm. Two of them were already bleeding from wounds to their hindquarters. A mob of angry men poured from the narrow path, armed with staves and sickles. I recognized some of them: they were farmers from the nearest village. The warrior at the rear made a rush at them, sword flailing, and they fell back slightly but did not disperse, maintaining their threatening stance in a tight half circle.

The leader of the horsemen flung a look of contempt at them and then called towards the gate in a loud voice.

'I am Fuwa Dosan of the Otori clan from Hagi. I bring a message from my lords Shoichi and Masahiro for the upstart who calls himself Otori Takeo.'

Makoto called back, 'If you are peaceful messengers, dismount and leave your swords. The gates will be opened.'

I already knew what their message would be. I could feel blind fury building up behind my eyes.

'There's no need for that,' Fuwa replied scornfully. 'Our message is short. Tell the so-called Takeo that the Otori do not recognize his claims and that this is how they will deal with him and any who follow him.'

The man alongside him dropped the reins on his horse's neck and opened the container. From it he took what I dreaded to see. Holding it by its topknot he swung his arm and threw Ichiro's head over the wall into the temple grounds.

It fell with a slight thud onto the petalled grass of the garden.

I drew my sword, Jato, from my belt.

'Open the gate!' I shouted. 'I am going out to them.'

I leaped down the steps, Makoto behind me.

As the gates opened, the Otori warriors turned their horses and drove them at the wall of men around them, swords sweeping. I imagine they thought the farmers would not dare attack them. Even I was astonished at what happened next. Instead of parting to let them through, the men on foot hurled themselves at the horses. Two of the farmers died immediately, cut in half by the warriors' swords, but then the first horse came down, and its rider fell into the pack around him. The others met a similar fate. They had no chance to use their swordsmanship: they were dragged from their horses and beaten to death like dogs.

Makoto and I tried to restrain the farmers and eventually managed to drive them back from the bodies. We restored calm only by severing the warriors' heads and having them displayed on the temple gates. The unruly army threw insults at them for a while and then retired down the hill, promising in loud voices that if any other strangers dared approach the temple and insult Lord Otori Takeo, the Angel of Yamagata, they would be dealt with in the same way.

Makoto was shaking with rage – and some other emotion that he wanted to talk to me about – but I did not have the time then. I went back inside the walls. Kaede had brought white cloths and water in a wooden bowl. She was kneeling on the ground beneath the cherry trees, calmly washing the head. Its skin was blue-grey, the eyes half closed, the neck not severed cleanly but hacked with several blows. Yet, she handled it gently, with loving care, as if it were a precious and beautiful object.

I knelt beside her, put out my hand and touched the hair. It was streaked with grey, but the face in death looked younger than when I had last seen it, when Ichiro was alive in the house in Hagi, grieving and haunted by ghosts, yet still willing to show me affection and guidance.

'Who is it?' Kaede said in a low voice.

'Ichiro. He was my teacher in Hagi. Shigeru's too.'

My heart was too full to speak further. I blinked away my tears. The memory of our last meeting rose in my mind. I wished I had said more to him, told him of my gratitude and my respect. I wondered how he had died, if his death had been humiliating and agonizing. I longed for the dead eyes to open, the bloodless lips to speak. How irretrievable the dead are, how completely they go from us! Even when their spirits return they do not speak of their own deaths.

I was born and raised among the Hidden, who believe that only those who follow the commandments of the Secret God will meet again in the afterlife. Everyone else will be consumed in the fires of hell. I did not know if my adopted father Shigeru had been a believer but he was familiar with all the teachings of the Hidden and spoke their prayers at the moment of his death, along with the name of the Enlightened One. Ichiro, his adviser and the steward of his household, had never given any such sign – in fact, rather the opposite: Ichiro had suspected from the start that Shigeru had rescued me from the warlord Iida Sadamu's persecution of the Hidden, and had watched me like a cormorant for anything that might give me away.

But I no longer followed the teachings of my childhood and I could not believe that a man of Ichiro's integrity and loyalty was in hell. Far stronger was my outrage at the injustice of this murder and my realization that I now had another death to avenge.

'They paid for it with their lives,' Kaede said. 'Why kill an old man and go to all that trouble to bring his head to you?' She washed away the last traces of blood and wrapped a clean white cloth around the head.

'I imagine the Otori lords want to draw me out,' I replied. 'They would prefer not to attack Terayama; they will run into Arai's soldiers if they do. They must hope to entice me over the border and meet me there.'

I longed for such a meeting, to punish them once and for all. The warriors' deaths had temporarily assuaged my fury, but I could feel it simmering in my heart. However, I had to be patient; my strategy was first to withdraw to Maruyama and build up my forces there. I would not be dissuaded from that.

I touched my brow to the grass, bidding my teacher goodbye. Manami came from the guest rooms and knelt a little way behind us.

'I've brought a box, lady,' she whispered.

'Give it to me,' Kaede replied. It was a small container, woven from willow twigs and strips of red-dyed leather. She took it and opened it. The smell of aloes rose from it. She put the white wrapped bundle inside and arranged the aloes round it. Then she placed the box on the ground in front of her, and the three of us bowed again before it.

A bush warbler called its spring song and a cuckoo responded from deep in the forest, the first I had heard that year.

We held the funeral rites the following day and buried the head next to Shigeru's grave. I made arrangements for another stone, to be erected for Ichiro. I longed to know what had happened to the old woman Chiyo and the rest of the household at Hagi. I was tormented by the thought that the house no longer existed, that it would have been burned: the tea room, the upper room where we had so often sat looking out onto the garden, the nightingale floor, all destroyed, their songs silenced for ever. I wanted to rush to Hagi to claim my inheritance before it was taken from me. But I knew this was exactly what the Otori hoped I would do.

Five farmers died outright and two died later from

their wounds. We buried them in the temple graveyard. Two of the horses were badly hurt, and Amano had them killed mercifully, but the other two were unharmed; one I liked in particular, a handsome black stallion that reminded me of Shigeru's horse, Kyu, and could have been its half-brother. At Makoto's insistence we buried the Otori warriors with full rites, too, praying that their ghosts, outraged at their ignoble deaths, would not linger to haunt us.

That evening the abbot came to the guest room and we talked until late into the night. Makoto and Miyoshi Kahei, one of my allies and friends from Hagi, were also with us; Kahei's younger brother Gemba had been sent ahead to Maruyama to tell the domain's senior retainer Sugita Haruki of our imminent departure. Sugita had assured Kaede the previous winter of his support for her claim. Kaede did not stay with us – for various reasons, she and Makoto were not at ease in each other's presence and she avoided him as much as possible – but I told her beforehand to sit behind the screen so she could hear what was said. I wanted to know her opinion afterwards. In the short time since our marriage I had come to talk to her as I had never talked to anyone in my life. I had been silent for so long, it seemed now I could not get enough of sharing my thoughts with her. I relied on her judgment and her wisdom.

'So now you are at war,' the abbot said, 'and your army has had its first skirmish.'

'Hardly an army,' Makoto said. 'A rabble of farmers! How are you going to punish them?'

'What do you mean?' I replied.

'Farmers are not supposed to kill warriors,' he said. 'Anyone else in your situation would punish them with the utmost cruelty. They would be crucified, boiled in oil, flayed alive.'

'They will be if the Otori get hold of them,' Kahei muttered.

'They were fighting on my behalf,' I said. Privately I thought the warriors had deserved their shameful end, though I was sorry I had not killed them all myself. 'I'm not going to punish them. I'm more concerned with how to protect them.'

'You have let an ogre out,' Makoto said. 'Let's hope you can contain it.'

The abbot smiled into his wine cup. Quite apart from his earlier comments on justice, he had been teaching me strategy all winter and, having heard my theories on the capture of Yamagata and other campaigns, knew how I felt about my farmers.

'The Otori seek to draw me out,' I said to him, as I had said earlier to Kaede.

'Yes, you must resist the temptation,' he replied. 'Naturally your first instinct is for revenge, but even if you defeated their army in a confrontation, they would simply retreat to Hagi. A long siege would be a disaster. The city is virtually impregnable, and sooner or later you would have to deal with Arai's forces at your rear.'

Arai Daiichi was the warlord from Kumamoto who had taken advantage of the overthrow of the Tohan to seize control of the Three Countries. I had enraged him by disappearing with the Tribe the previous year, and now my marriage to Kaede would certainly enrage him further. He had a huge army, and I did not want to be confronted by it before I had strengthened my own.

'Then we must go first to Maruyama, as planned.

But if I leave the temple unprotected, you and the people of the district may be punished by the Otori.'

'We can bring many people within the walls,' the abbot said. 'I think we have enough arms and supplies to hold the Otori off if they do attack. Personally, I don't think they will. Arai and his allies will not relinquish Yamagata without a long struggle and many among the Otori would be reluctant to destroy this place, which is sacred to the clan. Anyway, they will be more concerned with pursuing you.' He paused and then went on: 'You can't fight a war without being prepared for sacrifice. Men will die in the battles you fight, and if you lose, many of them, including you yourself, may be put to death very painfully. The Otori do not recognize your adoption, they do not know your ancestry; as far as they are concerned you are an upstart, not one of their class. You cannot hold back from action because people will die as a result. Even your farmers know that. Seven of them died today, but those who survived are not sad. They are celebrating their victory over those who insulted you.'

'I know that,' I said, glancing at Makoto. His lips were pressed together tightly, and though his face showed no other expression, I felt his disapproval. I was aware yet again of my weaknesses as a commander. I was afraid both Makoto and Kahei, brought up in the warrior tradition, would come to despise me.

'We joined you by our own choice, Takeo,' the abbot went on, 'because of our loyalty to Shigeru and because we believe your cause is just.'

I bowed my head, accepting the rebuke and vowing he would never have to speak to me in that vein again. 'We will leave for Maruyama the day after tomorrow.'

'Makoto will go with you,' the abbot said. 'As you know, he has made your cause his own.'

Makoto's lips curved slightly as he nodded in agreement.

Later that night, around the second half of the hour of the Rat, when I was about to lie down beside Kaede, I heard voices outside, and a few moments later Manami called quietly to us to say that a monk had come with a message from the guard house.

'We have taken a prisoner,' he said when I went to speak to him. 'He was spotted skulking in the bushes beyond the gate. The guards pursued him and would have killed him on the spot, but he called your name and said he was your man.'

'I'll come and talk to him,' I said, taking up Jato, suspecting it could only be the outcaste Jo-An. Jo-An had seen me at Yamagata when I had released his brother and other members of the Hidden into death. It was he who had given me the name of the Angel of Yamagata. Then he had saved my life on my desperate journey to Terayama in the winter. I had told him I would send for him in the spring and that he should wait until he heard from me, but he acted in unpredictable ways, usually in response to what he claimed was the voice of the Secret God.

It was a soft, warm night, the air already holding summer's humidity. In the cedars an owl was hooting. Jo-An lay on the ground just inside the gate. He'd been trussed up roughly, his legs were bent under him, his hands bound behind his back. His face was streaked with dirt and blood, his hair matted. He was moving his lips very slightly, praying soundlessly. Two monks were

12

watching him from a careful distance, their faces twisted in contempt.

I called his name and his eyes opened. I saw relief shine in them. He tried to scrabble into a kneeling position and fell forward, unable to save himself with his hands. His face hit the dirt.

'Untie him,' I said.

One of the monks said, 'He is an outcaste. We should not touch him.'

'Who tied him up?'

'We did not realize then,' the other said.

'You can cleanse yourselves later. This man saved my life. Untie him.'

Reluctantly they went to Jo-An, lifted him up, and loosened the cords that bound him. He crawled forward and prostrated himself at my feet.

'Sit up, Jo-An,' I said. 'Why are you here? I said you were to come when I sent for you. You were lucky not to be killed, turning up here without warning, without permission.'

The last time I'd seen him I'd been almost as shabbily dressed as he was, a fugitive, exhausted and starving. Now I was aware of the robe I wore, my hair dressed in the warrior style, the sword in my belt. I knew the sight of me talking to the outcaste would shock the monks profoundly. Part of me was tempted to have him thrown out, to deny that there was any relationship between us, and to throw him from my life at the same time. If I so ordered the guards, they would kill him immediately with no second thought. Yet I could not do it. He had saved my life; moreover for the sake of the bond between us, both born into the Hidden, I had to treat him not as an outcaste but as a man.

'No one will kill me until the Secret One calls me home,' he muttered, raising his eyes and looking at me. 'Until that time, my life is yours.' There was little light where we stood, just the lamp the monk had brought from the guard house and placed on the ground near us, but I could see Jo-An's eyes burning. I wondered, as I often had before, if he were not alive at all but a visitant from another world.

'What do you want?' I said.

'I have something to tell you. Very important. You'll be glad I came.'

The monks had stepped back out of pollution's way but were still close enough to hear us.

'I need to talk to this man,' I said. 'Where should we go?'

They threw an anguished look at each other and the older man suggested, 'Maybe the pavilion, in the garden?'

'You don't need to come with me.'

'We should guard Lord Otori,' the younger said.

'I'm in no danger from this man. Leave us alone. But tell Manami to bring water, some food and tea.'

They bowed and left. As they crossed the courtyard they started whispering to each other. I could hear every word. I sighed.

'Come with me,' I said to Jo-An. He limped after me to the pavilion, which stood in the garden not far from the large pool. Its surface glittered in the starlight, and every now and then a fish leaped from the water, flopping back with a loud splash. Beyond the pool the greyish white stones of the graves loomed out of the darkness. The owl hooted again, closer this time.

'God told me to come to you,' he said when we were settled on the wooden floor of the pavilion.

'You should not talk so openly of God,' I chided him. 'You are in a temple. The monks have no more love for the Hidden than the warriors.'

'You are here,' he muttered. 'You are our hope and our protection.'

'I'm just one person. I can't protect all of you from the way a whole country feels.'

He was silent for a moment or two. Then he said, 'The Secret One thinks about you all the time, even if you have forgotten him.'

I did not want to listen to this sort of message.

'What do you have to tell me?' I said impatiently.

'The men you saw last year, the charcoal burners, were taking their god back to the mountain. I met them on the path. They told me the Otori armies are out, watching every road around Terayama and Yamagata. I went to look for myself. There are soldiers hidden everywhere. They will ambush you as soon as you leave. If you want to get out, you will have to fight your way through them.'

His eyes were fixed on me, watching my reaction. I was cursing myself for having stayed so long at the temple. I'd been aware all along that speed and surprise were my main weapons. I should have left days before. I had been putting off leaving, waiting for Ichiro. Before my marriage I'd gone out night after night to check the roads around the temple for just such an eventuality. But since Kaede had joined me I could not tear myself away from her. Now I was trapped by my own vacillation and lack of vigilance.

'How many men would you say?'

'Five or six thousand,' he replied.

I had barely a thousand.

'So you'll have to go over the mountain. As you did in the winter. There's a track that goes west. No one's watching it because there's still snow on the pass.'

My mind was racing. I knew the path he meant. It went past the shrine where Makoto had planned to spend the winter before I stumbled in out of the snow on my flight to Terayama. I'd explored it myself a few weeks earlier, turning back when the snow became too deep to wade through. I thought of my forces, men, horses, oxen: oxen would never make it, but men and horses might. I would send them at night, if possible, so the Otori would think we were still in the temple . . . I would have to start at once, consult the abbot immediately.

My thoughts were interrupted by Manami and one of the manservants. The man was carrying a bowl of water. Manami brought a tray with a bowl of rice and vegetables and two cups of twig tea. She set the tray down on the floor, gazing at Jo-An with as much revulsion as if he were a viper. The man's reaction was equally horrified. I wondered briefly whether it would harm me to be seen associating with outcastes. I told them to leave us and they did so quickly, though I could hear Manami's disapproving muttering all the way back to the guest house.

Jo-An washed his hands and face, then joined his hands together to say the first prayer of the Hidden. Even as I found myself responding to the familiar words, a wave of irritation swept over me. He had risked his own life again to bring me this vital news, but I wished he showed more discretion, and my spirits sank at the thought of the liability he might become.

When he had finished eating I said, 'You'd better leave. You have a long journey home.'

He made no response, but sat, head turned slightly sideways, in the listening position I was by now familiar with.

'No,' he said finally. 'I am to go with you.'

'It's impossible. I don't want you with me.'

'God wants it,' he said.

There was nothing I could do to argue him out of it, short of killing him or imprisoning him, and these seemed shabby rewards for his help to me.

'Very well,' I said, 'but you can't stay in the temple.'

'No,' he agreed docilely, 'I have to fetch the others.'

'What others, Jo-An?'

'The rest of us. The ones who came with me. You saw some of them.'

I had seen these men at the tannery by the river where Jo-An worked, and I would never forget the way they had stared after me with burning eyes. I knew they looked to me for justice and protection. I remembered the feather: justice was what Shigeru had desired. I also had to pursue it for the sake of his memory and for these living men.

Jo-An put his hands together again and gave thanks for the food.

A fish leaped in the silence.

'How many are there?' I asked.

'About thirty. They're hiding in the mountains. They've been crossing the border in ones and twos for the last weeks.'

'Isn't the border guarded?'

'There've been skirmishes between the Otori and Arai's men. At the moment there's a stand-off. The borders are all open. The Otori have made it clear they're not challenging Arai or hoping to retake Yamagata. They only want to eliminate you.'

It seemed to be everyone's mission.

'Do the people support them?' I asked.

'Of course not!' he said almost impatiently. 'You know who they support: the Angel of Yamagata. So do we all. Why else are we here?'

I was not sure I wanted their support, but I could not help but be impressed by their courage.

'Thank you,' I said.

He grinned then, showing his missing teeth, reminding me of the torture he had already suffered because of me. 'We'll meet you on the other side of the mountain. You'll need us then, you'll see.'

I had the guards open the gates and said goodbye to him. I watched his slight, twisted shape as he scuttled away into the darkness. From the forest a vixen screamed, a sound like a ghost in torment. I shivered. Jo-An seemed guided and sustained by some great supernatural power. Though I no longer believed in it I feared its force like a superstitious child.

I went back to the guest house, my skin crawling. I removed my clothes and, despite the lateness of the hour, told Manami to take them away, wash and purify them, and then come to the bath house. She scrubbed me all over and I soaked in the hot water for ten or fifteen minutes. Putting on fresh clothes, I sent the servant to fetch Kahei and then to ask the abbot if we might speak with him. It was the first half of the hour of the Ox.

I met Kahei in the passageway, told him briefly what

18

had transpired, and went with him to the abbot's room, sending the servant to fetch Makoto from the temple, where he was keeping the night vigil. We came to the decision that we would move the entire army as soon as possible, apart from a small band of horsemen who would remain at Terayama for a day to fight as a rearguard.

Kahei and Makoto went immediately to the village beyond the gates to rouse Amano and the other men and start packing up food and equipment. The abbot ordered servants to inform the monks, reluctant to sound the temple bell at this hour of night in case we sent a warning to spies. I went to Kaede.

She was waiting for me, already in her sleeping robe, her hair loose down her back like a second robe, intensely black against the ivory material and her white skin. The sight of her, as always, took my breath away. Whatever happened to us, I would never forget this springtime we had had together. My life seemed full of undeserved blessings, but this was the greatest of them.

'Manami said an outcaste came and you let him in and spoke with him.' Her voice was as shocked as her woman's had been.

'Yes, he's called Jo-An. I met him in Yamagata.' I undressed, put on my robe and sat opposite her, knee to knee.

Her eyes searched my face. 'You look exhausted. Come and lie down.'

'I will; we must try and sleep for a few hours. We march at first light. The Otori have surrounded the temple; we are going over the mountain.'

'The outcaste brought you this news?'

'He risked his life to do so.'

19

'Why? How do you know him?'

'Do you remember the day we rode here with Lord Shigeru?' I said.

Kaede smiled. 'I can never forget it.'

'The night before I climbed into the castle and put an end to the suffering of the prisoners hanging on the walls. They were Hidden: have you heard of them?'

Kaede nodded. 'Shizuka told me a little about them. They were tortured in the same way by the Noguchi.'

'One of the men I killed was Jo-An's brother. Jo-An saw me as I came out of the moat and thought I was an angel.'

'The Angel of Yamagata,' Kaede said, slowly. 'When we came back that night the whole town was talking about it.'

'Since then we have met again; our fates seem to be entwined in some way. Last year he helped me get here. I would have perished in the snow but for him. On the way he took me to see a holy woman and she said certain things about my life.'

I had told no one, not even Makoto, not even Matsuda, of the words of the prophetess, but now I wanted to share them with Kaede. I whispered some of them to her: that in me three bloods mingled, I was born into the Hidden but my life was no longer my own, that I was destined to rule in peace from sea to sea, when Earth delivered what Heaven desired. I had repeated these words over and over to myself, and as I've said before, sometimes I believed them and sometimes I did not. I told her that five battles would bring us peace, four to win and one to lose, but I did not tell her what the saint had predicted about my own son: that I would die at his hands. I told myself it was too terrible a burden to lay on her but the truth was I did not want to talk about another secret I had kept from her: that a girl from the Tribe, Muto Kenji's daughter Yuki, was carrying my child.

'You were born into the Hidden?' she said carefully. 'But the Tribe claimed you because of your father's blood. Shizuka tried to explain it to me.'

'Muto Kenji revealed that my father was Kikuta, from the Tribe, when he first came to Shigeru's house. He did not know, though Shigeru did, that my father was also half-Otori.' I had already shown Kaede the records that confirmed this. Shigeru's father, Otori Shigemori, was my grandfather.

'And your mother?' she asked quietly. 'If you feel able to tell me . . .'

'My mother was one of the Hidden. I was raised among them. My family was massacred in our village, Mino, by Iida's men, and they would have killed me then if Shigeru had not rescued me.' I paused and then spoke of what I had hardly allowed myself to think about. 'I had two sisters, little girls. I imagine they were also murdered. They were nine and seven years old.'

'How terrible,' Kaede said. 'I am always afraid for my sisters. I hope we can send for them when we arrive at Maruyama. I hope they are safe now.'

I was silent, thinking of Mino, where we had all felt so safe.

'How strange your life has been,' Kaede went on. 'When I first met you I felt you hid everything. I watched you go away as if into a dark and secret place. I wanted to follow you there. I wanted to know everything about you.'

'I will tell you everything. But let's lie down and rest.'

21

Kaede pulled back the quilt and we lay down on the mattress. I took her in my arms, loosening both our robes so I could feel her skin against mine. She called to Manami to put out the lamps. The smell of smoke and oil lingered in the room after the woman's footsteps had died away.

I knew all the sounds of the temple at night by now: the periods of complete stillness, broken at regular intervals by the soft padding of feet as the monks rose in the darkness and went to pray, the low chanting, the sudden note of a bell. But tonight that regular and harmonious rhythm was disturbed, with sounds of people coming and going all night. I was restless, feeling I should be part of the preparations, yet reluctant to leave Kaede.

She whispered, 'What does it mean, to be one of the Hidden?'

'I was raised with certain beliefs; most I don't hold any more.' As I said this I felt my neck tingle, as if a cold breath had passed over me. Was it really true that I had abandoned the beliefs of my childhood – ones that my family had died for rather than give up?

'It was said that when Iida punished Lord Shigeru it was because he was one of the Hidden – and my kinswoman Lady Maruyama too,' Kaede murmured.

'Shigeru never spoke of it to me. He knew their prayers, and said them before he died, but his last word was the name of the Enlightened One.'

Until today, I had hardly thought of this moment. It had been obliterated by the horror of what had followed, and by my overwhelming grief. Today I had thought of it twice and suddenly for the first time I put together the prophetess's words and Shigeru's. 'It is all one,' she had said. So Shigeru had believed this too. I heard again her wondering laughter and thought I saw him smile at me. I felt that something profound had suddenly been revealed to me, something I could never put into words. My heart seemed to miss a beat in astonishment. Into my silenced mind several images rushed at once: Shigeru's composure when he was about to die, the prophetess's compassion, my own sense of wonder and anticipation the first day I had come to Terayama, the red-tipped feather of the *houou* on my palm. I saw the truth that lay behind the teaching and the beliefs, saw how human striving muddied the clarity of life, saw with pity how we are all subject to desire and to death, the warrior as much as the outcaste, the priest, the farmer, even the emperor himself. What name could I give to that clarity? Heaven? God? Fate? Or a myriad of names like the countless old spirits that men believed dwelled in this land? They were all faces of the faceless, expressions of that which cannot be expressed, parts of a truth but never the whole truth.

'And Lady Maruyama?' Kaede said, surprised by my long silence.

'I think she held strong beliefs, but I never spoke to her about them. When I first met her she drew the sign on my hand.'

'Show me,' Kaede whispered, and I took her hand and traced the sign on her palm.

'Are the Hidden dangerous? Why does everyone hate them?'

'They're not dangerous. They are forbidden to take life, and so they do not defend themselves. They believe everyone is equal in the eyes of their God, and that he will judge everyone after death. Great lords like Iida hate this teaching. Most of the warrior class do. If everyone is equal and God watches everything, it must be wrong to treat the people so badly. Our world would be overthrown from the ground up if everyone thought like the Hidden.'

'And you believe this?'

'I don't believe such a God exists, but I believe everyone should be treated as if they were equal. Outcastes, farmers, the Hidden, should all be protected against the cruelty and greed of the warrior class. And I want to use anyone who is prepared to help me. I don't care if they're farmers or outcastes. I'll take them all into my armies.'

Kaede did not reply; I imagined these ideas seemed strange and repellent to her. I might no longer believe in the God of the Hidden, but I could not help the way their teachings had formed me. I thought of the farmers' action against the Otori warriors at the temple gates. I had approved of that, for I saw them as equals, but Makoto had been shocked and outraged. Was he right? Was I unchaining an ogre that I could never hope to control?

Kaede said quietly, 'Do the Hidden believe women are equal to men?'

'In God's eyes they are. Usually the priests are men, but if there is no man of the right age, the older women become priestesses.'

'Would you let me fight in your army?'

'As skilful as you are, if you were any other woman, I would be glad to have you fight alongside me as we did at Inuyama. But you are the heir to Maruyama. If you were to be killed in battle our cause would be completely lost. Besides, I could not bear it.'

I pulled Kaede close to me, burying my face in her

hair. There was one other thing I had to speak to her about. It concerned another teaching of the Hidden, one that the warrior class find incomprehensible: that it is forbidden to take your own life. I whispered, 'We have been safe here. Once we leave, everything will be different. I hope we can stay together, but there will be times when we will be separated. Many people want me dead, but it will not be until the prophecy is fulfilled and our peaceful country stretches from sea to sea. I want you to promise me that whatever happens, whatever you are told, you will not believe I am dead until you see it with your own eyes. Promise you will not take your own life until you see me dead.'

'I promise it,' she said quietly. 'And you must do the same.'

I made the same vow to her. When she was asleep I lay in the dark and thought about what had been revealed to me. Whatever had been granted to me was not for my sake but for the sake of what I might achieve: a country of peace and justice where the *houou* would not only be seen but would build its nest and raise its young.

Two

We slept a little. I woke while it was still dark to hear from beyond the walls the steady tramping of men and horses filing up the mountain track. I called to Manami and then woke Kaede and told her to dress. I would come back for her when it was time to leave. I also entrusted to her the chest that contained Shigeru's records of the Tribe. I felt I had to have these protected at all times, a safeguard for my future against the death sentence that the Tribe had issued against me and a possible guarantee of alliance with Arai Daiichi, now the most powerful warlord in the Three Countries.

The temple was already feverish with activity, the monks preparing not for the dawn prayers but for a counter-attack on the Otori forces and the possibility of a long siege. Torches sent flickering shadows over the grim faces of men preparing for war. I put on leather armour, laced with red and gold. It was the first time I had worn it with a real purpose. It made me feel older, and I hoped it would give me confidence. I went to the gate to watch my men depart as day broke. Makoto and Kahei had already gone ahead with the vanguard. Plovers and pheasants were calling from the valley. Dew clung to the blades of bamboo grass and to the spring spiders' webs woven between them – webs that were quickly trampled underfoot.

When I returned, Kaede and Manami were both dressed in men's clothes for riding, Kaede wearing the armour, made originally for a page, that I had picked out for her. I had had a sword forged for her, and she wore this in her belt, along with a knife. We quickly ate a little cold food and then returned to where Amano was waiting with the horses.

The abbot was with him, in helmet and leather cuirass, his sword in his belt. I knelt before him to thank him for all he had done for me. He embraced me like a father.

'Send messengers from Maruyama,' he said cheerfully. 'You will be there before the new moon.'

His confidence in me heartened me and gave me strength.

Kaede rode Raku, the grey horse with the black mane and tail that I had given her, and I rode the black stallion we had taken from the Otori warriors, which Amano had called Aoi. Manami and some of the other women who travelled with the army were lifted onto packhorses, Manami making sure the chest of records was strapped behind her. We joined the throng as it wound its way through the forest and up the steep mountain path that Makoto and I had descended the previous year in the first snow. The sky was aflame, the sun just beginning to touch the snowy peaks, turning them pink and gold. The air was cold enough to numb our cheeks and fingers.

I looked back once at the temple, at its broad sloping roofs emerging from the sea of new leaves like great ships. It looked eternally peaceful in the morning sun, with white doves fluttering round the eaves. I prayed it would be preserved just as it was at that moment, that it would not be burned or destroyed in the coming fight.

The red morning sky was true to its threat. Before

long, heavy grey clouds moved in from the west, bringing first showers, then steady rain. As we climbed towards the pass, the rain turned to sleet. Men on horseback did better than the porters, who carried huge baskets on their backs; but as the snow underfoot became deeper, even the horses had a hard time of it. I'd imagined that going into battle would be a heroic affair, the conch shells sounding, the banners flying. I had not imagined it would be this grim slog against no human enemy, just the weather and the mountain, and the aching climb upwards, always upwards.

The horses balked finally and Amano and I dismounted to lead them. By the time we crossed the pass, we were soaked to the skin. There was no room on the narrow track to ride back or ahead to check on my army. As we wound downwards I could see its snake-like shape, dark against the last traces of snow, a huge many-legged creature. Beyond the rocks and scree, now appearing as the rain melted the snow, stretched deep forests. If anyone lay in wait for us there we would be completely at their mercy.

But the forests were empty. The Otori were waiting for us on the other side of the mountain. Once under cover of the trees we caught up with Kahei where he had stopped to give the vanguard a rest. We now did the same, allowing the men to relieve themselves in small groups, and then eat. The damp air filled with the acrid smell of their piss. We had been marching for five or six hours, but I was pleased to see warriors and farmers alike had held up well.

During our halt the rain grew heavier. I was worried about Kaede, after her months of ill-health, but even though she seemed very cold, she did not complain. She ate a little, but we had nothing warm and could not waste

28

time making fires. Manami was uncharacteristically silent, watching Kaede closely and nervously starting at any sound. We pressed on as soon as possible. By my reckoning it was after noon, sometime between the hour of the Goat and that of the Monkey. The slope became less steep and soon the track widened a little, enough so that I could ride along it. Leaving Kaede with Amano, I urged my horse on and cantered down the slope to the head of the army, where I found Makoto and Kahei.

Makoto, who knew the area better than any of us, told me there was a small town, Kibi, not far ahead, on the other side of the river, where we should stop overnight.

'Will it be defended?'

'Only by a small garrison, if at all. There's no castle, and the town itself is barely fortified.'

'Whose land is it?'

'Arai put one of his constables in,' Kahei said. 'The former lord and his sons sided with the Tohan at Kushimoto. They all died there. Some of the retainers joined Arai, the rest became masterless and took to the mountains as brigands.'

'Send men ahead to say we require shelter for the night. Let them explain that we do not seek battle; we are only passing through. We'll see what the response is.'

Kahei nodded, called to three of his men, and sent them on at a gallop while we continued more slowly. Barely an hour later they were back. The horses' flanks were heaving, covered in mud to the stifle, their nostrils red and flared.

'The river is in full flood and the bridge is down,' their leader reported. 'We tried to swim across but the current is too strong. Even if we had made it, the foot soldiers and packhorses never would.'

'What about roads along the river? Where's the next bridge?'

'The eastern road leads through the valley back to Yamagata, straight back to the Otori,' Makoto said. 'The southern one leads away from the river over the range towards Inuyama, but the pass will not be open at this time of year.'

Unless we could cross the river we were trapped.

'Ride forward with me,' I said to Makoto. 'Let's take a look for ourselves.'

I told Kahei to bring the rest of the army forward slowly, except for a rearguard of one hundred men, who were to strike out to the east in case we were already being pursued by that route.

Makoto and I had hardly gone half a mile before I could hear it, the steady sullen groan of a river in flood. Swollen by the melting snow, as inexorable as the season, the spring river poured its yellow-green water across the landscape. As we rode out of the forest through the bamboo groves and into the reed beds, I thought we had come to the sea itself. Water stretched before us as far as the eye could see, dappled by rain, the same colour as the sky. I must have gasped because Makoto said, 'It's not as bad as it looks. Most of it is irrigated fields.'

I saw then the squared pattern of dykes and paths. The rice fields would be boggy but shallow; however, through the middle of them ran the river itself. It was about one hundred feet wide, and had risen over the protective dykes, making it at least twelve feet deep. I could see the remains of the wooden bridge: two piers just showing their dark tops against the swirling water. They looked unspeakably forlorn beneath the drifting rain, like all men's dreams and ambitions laid waste by nature and time.

I was gazing at the river, wondering if we could swim across, reconstruct the bridge, or what in Heaven's name, when above the steady roar of the water I heard the sounds of human activity. Focusing my attention, I thought I could recognize voices, the chink of an axe, then unmistakably the sudden crash of falling timber.

To my right, upstream, the river curved away around a bend, the forest growing closer to the banks. I could see the remnants of what might have been a jetty or loading dock, presumably for taking lumber from the forest to the town. I turned my horse's head and at once began to ride through the fields towards the bend.

'What is it?' Makoto called, following me.

'There's someone there.' I grabbed at Aoi's mane as he slipped and almost lost his footing.

'Come back,' he shouted. 'It's not safe. You can't go alone.'

I heard him unsling his bow and fit an arrow to the cord. The horses plunged and splashed through the shallow water. Some memory was stringing itself together in my mind, of another river, impassable for different reasons. I knew what – whom – I would find.

Jo-An was there, half-naked, soaking wet, with his thirty or more outcastes. They had taken lumber from the jetty, where it had been stranded by the flood, and had felled more trees and cut enough reeds to build one of their floating bridges.

They stopped work when they saw me and began to kneel in the mud. I thought I recognized some of them from the tannery. They were as thin and wretched as ever, and their eyes burnt with the same hungry light. I tried to imagine what it had cost them to abscond with Jo-An out of their own territory, to break all the laws against the felling of trees, on the faint promise that I would bring justice and peace. I did not want to think about the ways they would be made to suffer if I failed them.

'Jo-An!' I called, and he came to the horse's side. It snorted at him and tried to rear, but he took the bridle and calmed it. 'Tell them to keep working,' I said, adding, 'so I am even further in your debt.'

'You owe me nothing,' he replied. 'You owe God everything.'

Makoto rode up alongside, and I found myself hoping he had not heard Jo-An's words. Our horses touched noses and the black stallion squealed and tried to bite the other. Jo-An smacked it on the neck.

Makoto's glance fell on him. 'Outcastes?' he said, disbelieving. 'What are they doing here?'

'Saving our lives. They're building a floating bridge.'

He pulled his horse back a few steps. Beneath his helmet I could see the curl of his lips. 'No one will use it—' he began, but I cut him off.

'They will, because I command it. This is our only way of escape.'

'We could fight our way back to the bridge at Yamagata.'

'And lose all our advantage of speed? Anyway, we would be outnumbered five to one. And we'd have no retreat route. I won't do that. We'll cross the river by the bridge. Go back to the men and bring many of them to work with the outcastes. Let the rest prepare for the crossing.'

'No one will cross this bridge if it is built by outcastes,' he said, and something in his voice, as if he were speaking

32

to a child, enraged me. It was the same feeling I'd had months ago when Shigeru's guards had let Kenji into the garden at Hagi, fooled by his tricks, unaware that he was a master assassin from the Tribe. I could only protect my men if they obeyed me. I forgot Makoto was older, wiser and more experienced than I was. I let the fury sweep over me.

'Do as I command you at once. You must persuade them, or you'll answer to me for it. Let the warriors act as guards while the packhorses and foot soldiers cross. Bring bowmen to cover the bridge. We will cross before nightfall.'

'Lord Otori.' He bowed his head and his horse plunged and splashed away over the rice fields and up the slope beyond. I watched him disappear between the shafts of bamboo, then turned my attention to the outcastes' work.

They were lashing together the lumber they had collected and the trunks they had felled into rafts, each one supported on piles of reeds tied into bundles with cords plaited from tree bark and hemp. As each raft was finished they floated it out into the water and lashed it to the ones already moored in place. But the force of the current kept the rafts pushed into the bank.

'It needs to be anchored to the farther side,' I said to Jo-An.

'Someone will swim across,' he replied.

One of the younger men took a roll of cord, tied it round his waist and plunged into the river. But the current was far too strong for him. We saw his arms flailing above the surface, then he disappeared under the yellow water. He was hauled back, half-drowned.

'Give the rope to me,' I said.

33

Jo-An looked anxiously down the bank. 'No, lord, wait,' he begged me. 'When the men come one of them can swim across.'

'When the men come the bridge must be ready,' I retorted. 'Give me the rope.'

Jo-An untied it from the young man, who was sitting up now, spitting out water, and handed it up to me. I made it fast around my waist and urged my horse forward. The rope slid over his haunches, making him leap; he was in the water almost before he realized it.

I shouted at him to encourage him, and he put one ear back to listen to me. For the first few paces his feet were on the bottom. Then the water came up to his shoulder and he began to swim. I tried to keep his head turned towards where I hoped we would land, but strong and willing as he was, the current was stronger, and we were carried by it downstream towards the remains of the old bridge.

I glanced towards it and did not like what I saw. The current was hurling branches and other debris against the piles, and if my horse were to be caught among them he would panic and drown us both. I felt and feared the power of the river. So did he. Both ears lay flat against his head, and his eyes rolled. Luckily his terror gave him extra strength. He put in one great exertion, striking out with all four feet. We cleared the piles by a couple of arm spans and suddenly the current slackened. We were past the middle. A few moments later the horse found his footing and began to plunge up and down, taking huge steps to try and clear the water. He scrambled up onto firm ground and stood, head lowered, sides heaving, his former exuberance completely extinguished. I slipped from his back and patted his neck, telling him his father must have been a water spirit for him to swim so well. We were both saturated, more like fish or frogs than land animals.

I could feel the pull of the cord around my waist and dreaded it taking me back into the water. I half-crawled, half-scrambled to a small grove of trees at the edge of the river. They stood around a tiny shrine dedicated to the fox god, judging by the white statues, and were submerged to their lower branches by the flood. It lapped at the feet of the statues, making the foxes look as if they floated. I passed the cord around the trunk of the nearest tree, a small maple just beginning to burst into leaf, and started to haul on it. It was attached to a much stronger rope; I could feel its sodden weight as it came reluctantly up out of the river. Once I had enough length on it, I secured it to another, larger tree. It occurred to me that I was probably going to pollute the shrine in some way, but at that moment I did not care what god, spirit or demon I offended as long as I got my men safely across the river.

All the time I was listening. Despite the rain I couldn't believe this place was as deserted as it seemed; it was at the site of a bridge on what seemed to be a well-used road. Through the hiss of the rain and the roar of the river I could hear the mewing of kites, the croaking of hundreds of frogs, enthusiastic about the wet, and crows calling harshly from the forest. But where were all the people?

Once the rope was secure, about ten of the outcastes crossed the river holding on to it. Far more skilled than I, they redid all my knots and set up a pulley system using the smooth branches of the maple. Slowly, laboriously they hauled on the rafts, their chests heaving, their muscles standing out like cords. The river tore at the rafts, resenting their intrusion into its domain, but the men persisted and the rafts, made buoyant and stable by their reed

35

mattresses, responded like oxen and came inch by inch towards us.

One side of the floating bridge was jammed by the current against the existing piles. Otherwise I think the river would have defeated us. I could see the bridge was close to being finished, but there was no sign of Makoto returning with the warriors. I had lost all sense of time, and the clouds were too low and dark to be able to discern the position of the sun, but I thought at least an hour must have passed. Had Makoto not been able to persuade them? Had they turned back to Yamagata as he had suggested? Closest friend or not, I would kill him with my own hands if they had. I strained my ears but could hear nothing except the river, the rain and the frogs.

Beyond the shrine where I stood, the road emerged from the water. I could see the mountains behind it, white mist hanging like streamers to their slopes. My horse was shivering. I thought I should move him around a little to keep him warm, since I had no idea how I would ever get him dry. I mounted and went a little way along the road, thinking also that I might get a better view across the river from the higher ground.

Not far along stood a kind of hovel built from wood and daub and roughly thatched with reeds. A wooden barrier had been placed across the road beside it. I wondered what it was: it did not look like an official fief border post and there did not seem to be any guards.

As I came closer I saw that several human heads were attached to the barrier, some freshly killed, others no more than skulls. I'd barely had time to feel revulsion when, from behind me, my ears caught the sound I'd been waiting for, the tramping of horses and men from the other side of the river. I looked back and saw through the rain the vanguard of my army emerging from the forest and splashing towards the bridge. I recognized Kahei by his helmet. He was riding in the front, Makoto alongside him.

My chest lightened with relief. I turned Aoi back; he saw the distant shapes of his fellows and gave a loud neigh. This was echoed at once by a tremendous shout from inside the hovel. The ground shook as the door was thrown open and the largest man I'd ever seen, larger even than the charcoal burners' giant, stepped out.

My first thought was that he was an ogre or a demon. He was nearly two arm spans tall and as broad as an ox, yet despite his bulk his head seemed far too large, as if the skull bone had never stopped growing. His hair was long and matted, he had a thick, wiry moustache and beard, and his eyes were not human-shaped but round like an animal's. He only had one ear, massive and pendulous. Where the other ear had been a blue-grey scar gleamed through his hair. But his speech when he shouted at me was human enough.

'Hey!' he yelled in his enormous voice. 'What d'you think y'doing on my road?'

'I am Otori Takeo,' I replied. 'I am bringing my army through. Clear the barrier!'

He laughed; it was like the sound of rocks crashing down the side of a mountain. 'No one comes through here unless Jin-emon says they can. Go back and tell your army that!'

The rain was falling more heavily; the day was rapidly losing its light. I was exhausted, hungry, wet and cold. 'Clear the road,' I shouted impatiently. 'We are coming through.'

He strode towards me without answering. He was carrying a weapon but he held it behind his back so I could not see clearly what it was. I heard the sound before I saw his arm move: a sort of metallic clink. With one hand I swung the horse's head around, with the other I drew Jato. Aoi heard the sound, too, and saw the giant's arm lunge outwards. He shied sideways, and the ogre's stick and chain went past my ears, howling like a wolf.

The chain was weighted at one end and the stick to which it was attached had a sickle set in it. I'd never encountered such a weapon before, and had no idea how to fight him. The chain swung again, catching the horse round the right hind leg. Aoi screamed in pain and fear and lashed out. I kicked my feet from the stirrups, slid down on the opposite side from the ogre, and turned to face him. I'd obviously fallen in with a madman who was going to kill me if I did not kill him first.

He grinned at me. To him, I must have looked no larger than the Peach Boy or some other tiny character from a folk tale. I caught the beginning of movement in his muscle and split my image, throwing myself to the left. The chain went harmlessly through my second self. Jato leaped through the air between us and sank its blade into his lower arm, just above the wrist. Ordinarily it would have taken off the hand, but this adversary had bones of stone. I felt the reverberations up into my shoulder, and for a moment I feared my sword would lodge in his arm like an axe in a tree.

Jin-emon made a kind of creaking groan, not unlike the sound of the mountain when it freezes, and transferred the stick to his other hand. Blood was now oozing from his right hand, dark-blackish red in colour, not splashing as you would expect. I went invisible for a moment as the chain howled again, briefly considered retreating to the river, wondering where on earth all my men were when I needed them. Then I saw an unprotected space and thrust Jato up into it and into the flesh that lay there. The wound left by my sword was huge, but again he hardly bled. A fresh wave of horror swept through me. I was fighting something nonhuman, supernatural. Did I have any chance of overcoming it?

On the next swing the chain wrapped itself round my sword. Giving a shout of triumph, Jin-emon yanked it from my hands. Jato flew through the air and landed several feet away from me. The ogre approached me, making sweeping movements with his arms, wise to my tricks now.

I stood still. I had my knife in my belt, but I did not want to draw it in case he swung his chain and ended my life there and then. I wanted this monster to look at me. He came up to me, seized me by the shoulders and lifted me from the ground. I don't know what his plan was – maybe to tear out my throat with his huge teeth and drink my blood. I thought, *He is not my son, he cannot kill me*, and stared into his eyes. They had no more expression than a beast's, but as they met mine I saw them round with astonishment. I sensed behind them his dull malevolence, his brutal and pitiless nature. I realized the power that lay within me and let it stream from me. His eyes began to cloud. He gave a low moan and his grasp slackened as he wavered and crashed to the ground like a great tree under the woodsman's axe. I threw myself sideways, not wanting to end up pinned beneath him, and rolled to where Jato lay, making Aoi who had been circling nervously around us prance and rear again. Sword in hand, I ran back to where Jin-emon had fallen; he was snoring in the deep Kikuta sleep. I tried to raise the huge head to cut it off but its weight was too great, and I did not want to risk damaging the blade of my sword. Instead I thrust Jato into his throat and cut open the artery and windpipe. Even here the blood ran sluggishly. His heels kicked, his back arched, but he did not waken. Eventually his breathing stopped.

I'd thought he was alone, but then a sound came from the hovel and I turned to see a much smaller man scuttling from the door. He shouted something incoherent, bounded across the dyke behind the hut, and disappeared into the forest.

I shifted the barrier myself, gazing on the skulls and wondering whose they were. Two of the older ones fell while I was moving the wood, and insects crawled out from their eye sockets. I placed them in the grass and went back to my horse, chilled and nauseated. Aoi's leg was bruised and bleeding from where the chain had caught it although it did not appear to be broken. He could walk, but he was very lame. I led him back to the river.

The encounter seemed like a bad dream, but the more I pondered it the better I felt. Jin-emon should have killed me – my severed head should now be on the barrier along with the others – but my Tribe powers had delivered me from him. It seemed to confirm the prophecy completely. If such an ogre could not kill me, who could? By the time I got back to the river new energy was flowing through me. However, what I saw there transformed it into rage.

The bridge was in place, but only the outcastes were on the nearer side. The rest of my army were still on the other bank. The outcastes were huddled in that sullen way of theirs that I was beginning to understand as their reaction to the irrationality of the world's contempt for them.

Jo-An was sitting on his haunches, gazing gloomily at the swirling water. He stood when he saw me.

'They won't cross, lord. You'll have to go and order them.'

'I will,' I said, my anger mounting. 'Take the horse, wash the wound and walk him round so he doesn't chill.'

Jo-An took the reins. 'What happened?'

'I had an encounter with a demon,' I replied shortly, and stepped onto the bridge.

The men waiting on the opposite side gave a shout when they saw me but not one of them ventured onto the other end of the bridge. It was not easy to walk on – a swaying mass, partly submerged at times, pulled and rocked by the river. I half ran, thinking as I did so of the nightingale floor that I had run across so lightly in Hagi. I prayed to Shigeru's spirit to be with me.

On the other side Makoto dismounted and grasped my arm. 'Where were you? We feared you were dead.'

'I might well have been,' I said in fury. 'Where were you?' Before he could answer Kahei rode up to us.

'What's the delay for?' I demanded, 'Get the men moving.'

Kahei hesitated. 'They fear pollution from the outcastes.'

'Get down,' I said, and as he slid from his horse's back I let them both feel the full force of my rage. 'Because of your stupidity I nearly died. If I give an order, it must be obeyed at once, no matter what you think of it. If that doesn't suit you, then ride back now, to Hagi, to the temple, to wherever, but out of my sight.' I spoke in a low voice, not wanting the whole army to hear me, but I saw how my words shamed them. 'Now send those with horses who want to swim into the water first. Move the packhorses onto the bridge while the rear is guarded, then the foot soldiers, no more than thirty at a time.'

41

'Lord Otori,' Kahei said. He leaped back in the saddle and galloped off down the line.

'Forgive me, Takeo,' Makoto said quietly.

'Next time I'll kill you,' I said. 'Give me your horse.'

I rode along the lines of waiting soldiers, repeating the command. 'Don't be afraid of pollution,' I told them. 'I have already crossed the bridge. If there is any pollution let it fall on me.' I had moved into a state that was almost exalted. I did not think anything in Heaven or on Earth could harm me.

With a mighty shout, the first warrior rode into the water, and others streamed after him. The first horses were led onto the bridge, and to my relief it held them safely. Once the crossing was underway, I rode back along the line, issuing commands and reassuring the foot soldiers, until I came to where Kaede was waiting with Manami and the other women who accompanied us. Manami had brought rain umbrellas and they stood huddled beneath them. Amano held the horses alongside them. Kaede's face lit up when she saw me. Her hair was glistening with rain, and drops clung to her eyelashes.

I dismounted and gave the reins to Amano.

'What happened to Aoi?' he asked, recognizing this horse as Makoto's.

'He's hurt, I don't know how badly. He's on the other side of the river. We swam across.' I wanted to tell Amano how brave the horse had been, but there was no time now.

'We are going to cross the river,' I told the women. 'The outcastes built a bridge.'

Kaede said nothing, watching me, but Manami immediately opened her mouth to complain.

I put up my hand to silence her. 'There is no alternative. You are to do what I say.' I repeated what I had told the men: that any pollution would fall on me alone.

'Lord Otori,' she muttered, giving the minimum bob of her head and glancing out of the corner of her eye. I resisted the urge to strike her, though I felt she deserved it.

'Am I to ride?' Kaede said.

'No, it's very unstable. Better to walk. I'll swim your horse across.'

Amano would not hear of it. 'There are plenty of grooms to do that,' he said, looking at my soaked, muddy armour.

'Let one of them come with me now,' I said. 'He can take Raku and bring an extra horse for me. I must get back to the other side.' I had not forgotten the man I'd seen scuttling away. If he had gone to alert others of our arrival, I wanted to be there to confront them.

'Bring Shun for Lord Otori,' Amano shouted to one of the grooms. The man came up to us on a small bay horse and took Raku's reins. I said a brief farewell to Kaede, asking her to make sure the packhorse carrying the chest of records made the crossing safely, and mounted Makoto's horse again. We cantered back along the line of soldiers, which was now moving quite quickly onto the bridge. About two hundred were already across, and Kahei was organizing them into small groups, each with its own leader.

Makoto was waiting for me by the water's edge. I gave him his horse back and held Raku while he and the groom rode into the river. I watched the bay horse, Shun. He went fearlessly into the water, swimming strongly and calmly as if it were the sort of thing he did every day. The groom returned over the bridge and took Raku from me.

While they swam across, I joined the men on the floating bridge.

They scrambled across like the rats in Hagi harbour, spending as little time on the soggy mass as possible. I imagined few of them knew how to swim. Some of them greeted me, and one or two touched me on the shoulder as if I would ward off evil and bring good luck. I encouraged them as much as I could, joking about the hot baths and excellent food we'd get in Maruyama. They seemed in good spirits, though we all knew that Maruyama lay a long way ahead.

On the other side I told the groom to wait with Raku for Kaede. I mounted Shun. He was on the small side, and not a handsome horse, but there was something about him I liked. Telling the warriors to follow, I rode ahead with Makoto. I particularly wanted bowmen with us, and two groups of thirty were ready. I told them to conceal themselves behind the dyke and wait for my signal.

Jin-emon's body still lay by the barrier, and the whole place was silent, apparently deserted.

'Was this something to do with you?' Makoto said, looking with disgust at the huge body and the display of heads.

'I'll tell you later. He had a companion who got away. I suspect he'll be back with more men. Kahei said this area was full of bandits. The dead man must have been making people pay to use the bridge; if they refused he took their heads.'

Makoto dismounted to take a closer look. 'Some of these are warriors,' he said, 'and young men too. We should take his head in payment.' He drew his sword.

'Don't,' I warned. 'He has bones of granite. You'll damage the blade.'

He gave me an incredulous look and did not say anything, but in one swift movement slashed across the neck. His sword snapped with an almost human sound. There were gasps of astonishment and dread from the men around us. Makoto gazed at the broken blade in dismay, then looked shamefaced at me.

'Forgive me,' he said again. 'I should have listened to you.'

My rage ignited. I drew my own sword, my vision turning red in the old, familiar way. How could I protect my men if they did not obey me? Makoto had ignored my advice in front of these soldiers. He deserved to die for it. I almost lost control and cut him down where he stood, but at that moment I heard the sound of horses' hooves in the distance, reminding me I had other, real enemies.

'He was a demon, less than human,' I said to Makoto. 'You had no way of knowing. You'll have to fight using your bow.'

I made a sign to the men around us to be silent. They stood as if turned to stone; not even the horses moved. The rain had lessened to a fine drizzle. In the fading misty light we looked like an army of ghosts.

I listened to the bandits approach, splashing through the wet landscape, and then they appeared out of the mist, over thirty horsemen and as many on foot. They were a motley, ragged band, some obviously masterless warriors with good horses and what had once been fine armour, others the riff-raff left behind after ten years of war: escapees from harsh masters on estates or in silver mines, thieves, lunatics, murderers. I recognized the man who'd fled from the hovel; he was running at the stirrup of the leading horse. As the band came to a halt, throwing up mud and spray, he pointed to me and screamed, again something unintelligible.

The rider called, 'Who is it who murdered our friend and companion, Jin-emon?'

I answered, 'I am Otori Takeo. I am leading my men to Maruyama. Jin-emon attacked me for no reason. He paid for it. Let us through or you will pay the same price.'

'Go back to where you came from,' he replied with a snarl. 'We hate the Otori here.'

The men around him jeered. He spat on the ground and swung his sword above his head. I raised my hand in signal to the bowmen.

Immediately the sound of arrows filled the air; it is a fearful noise, the hiss and clack of the shafts, the dull thunk as they hit living flesh, the screams of the wounded. But I had no time to reflect on it then, for the leader urged his horse forward and galloped towards me, his sword arm stretched above his head.

His horse was bigger than Shun, and his reach longer than mine. Shun's ears were forward, his eyes calm. Just before the bandit struck, my horse made a leap to the side and turned almost in mid-air so I could slash my adversary from behind, opening up his neck and shoulder as he hit out vainly at where I had been.

He was no demon or ogre but all too human. His human blood spurted red. His horse galloped on while he swayed in the saddle, and then he fell suddenly sideways to the ground.

Shun, meanwhile, still completely calm, had spun back to meet the next attacker. This man had no helmet and Jato split his head in two, spattering blood, brains and bone. The smell of blood was all around us, mixed with rain and mud. As more and more of our warriors came up to join the fray, the bandits were completely overwhelmed. Those who still lived tried to flee, but we rode after them and cut them down. Rage had been rising steadily in me all day and had been set alight by Makoto's disobedience; it found its release in this brief, bloody skirmish. I was furious at the delay that these lawless, foolish men had caused us, and I was deeply satisfied that they had all paid for it. It was not much of a battle but we won it decisively, giving ourselves a taste of blood and victory.

We had three men dead and two others wounded. Later four deaths by drowning were reported to me. One of Kahei's companions, Shibata from the Otori clan, knew a little about herbs and healing, and he cleaned and treated the wounds. Kahei rode ahead to the town to see what he could find in the way of shelter, at least for the women, and Makoto and I organized the rest of the force to move on more slowly. He took over command while I went back to the river where the last of the men were crossing the floating bridge.

Jo-An and his companions were still huddled by the water's edge. Jo-An stood and came to me. I had a moment's impulse to dismount and embrace him, but I did not act on it and the moment passed.

I said, 'Thank you, and thanks to all your men. You saved us from disaster.'

'Not one of them thanked us,' he remarked, gesturing at the men filing past. 'Lucky we work for God, not for them.'

'You're coming with us, Jo-An?' I said. I did not want them to return across the river, facing who knew what penalties for crossing the border, cutting down trees, helping an outlaw.

He nodded. He seemed exhausted, and I was filled

with compunction. I did not want the outcastes with me – I feared the reaction of my warriors and knew the friction and grumbling their presence would cause – but I could not abandon them here.

'We must destroy the bridge,' I said, 'lest the Otori follow us over it.'

He nodded again and called to the others. Wearily they got to their feet and began to dismantle the cords that held the rafts in place. I stopped some of the foot soldiers, farmers who had sickles and pruning knives, and ordered them to help the outcastes. Once the ropes were slashed, the rafts gave way. The current immediately swept them into the midstream, where the river set about completing their destruction.

I watched the muddy water for a moment, called my thanks again to the outcastes and told them to keep up with the soldiers. Then I went to Kaede.

She was already mounted on Raku, in the shelter of the trees around the fox shrine. I noticed quickly that Manami was perched on the packhorse with the chest of records strapped behind her, and then I had eyes only for Kaede. Her face was pale but she sat straight-backed on the little grey, watching the army file past with a slight smile on her lips. In this rough setting she, whom I had mainly seen restrained and subdued in elegant surroundings, looked happy.

As soon as I saw her, I was seized by the fiercest desire to hold her. I thought I would die if I did not sleep with her soon. I had not expected this and I was ashamed of how I felt. I thought I should have been concerned with her safety instead; moreover I was the leader of an army; I had a thousand men to worry about. My aching desire for my wife embarrassed me and made me almost shy of her.

She saw me and rode towards me. The horses whickered at each other. Our knees touched. As our heads bent towards each other I caught her jasmine scent.

'The road's clear now,' I said. 'We can ride on.'

'Who were they?'

'Bandits, I suppose.' I spoke briefly, not wanting to bring the blood and the dying into this place where Kaede was. 'Kahei has gone ahead to find you somewhere to sleep tonight.'

'I'll sleep outside if I can lie with you,' she said in a low voice. 'I have never felt freedom before, but today, on the journey, in the rain, in all its difficulties, I have felt free.'

Our hands touched briefly, then I rode on with Amano, talking to him about Shun. My eyes were hot and I wanted to conceal my emotion.

'I've never ridden a horse like him before. It's as if he knows what I'm thinking.'

Amano's eyes creased as he smiled. 'I wondered if you would like him. Someone brought him to me a couple of weeks ago; my guess is he was either stolen or picked up after his owner was killed. I can't imagine anyone getting rid of him voluntarily. He's the smartest horse I've ever known. The black's more showy – good for making an impression – but I know which one I'd rather be on in a fight.' He grinned at me. 'Lord Otori is lucky with horses. Some people are. It's like a gift; good animals come to you.'

'Let's hope it augurs well for the future,' I replied.

We passed the hovel. The dead were laid out in rows along the dyke. I was thinking that I should leave some men to burn or bury the corpses when there was a disturbance ahead, and one of Kahei's men came through on his horse, shouting at the soldiers to let him pass, calling my name.

'Lord Otori!' he said, reining in his horse just in front of us. 'You're wanted up ahead. Some farmers have come to speak with you.'

Ever since we'd crossed the river, I'd been wondering where the local people were. Even though the rice fields were flooded, there was no sign of them having been planted. Weeds choked the irrigation channels, and though in the distance I could see the steep thatched roofs of farmhouses, no smoke rose from them and there was no sign nor sound of human activity. The landscape seemed cursed and empty. I imagined that Jin-emon and his band had intimidated, driven away or murdered all the farmers and villagers. It seemed news of his death had travelled fast and had now brought some of them out from hiding.

I cantered up through the file. The men called out to me, seeming cheerful; some were even singing. They were apparently unworried by the coming night, apparently had complete faith in my ability to find them food and shelter.

At the front of the army Makoto had called a halt. A group of farmers were squatting on their heels in the mud. When I reached them and dismounted, they threw themselves forward.

Makoto said, 'They've come to thank us. The bandits have been terrorizing this area for nearly twelve months. They've been unable to plant this spring for fear of them. The ogre killed many of their sons and brothers, and many of their women have been abducted.'

'Sit up,' I said to them. 'I am Otori Takeo.'

They sat up, but as soon as I spoke my name they bowed again. 'Sit up,' I repeated. 'Jin-emon is dead.'

Down they went again. 'You may do with his body what you wish. Retrieve your relatives' remains and bury them honourably.' I paused. I wanted to ask them for food, but feared they had so little I would be condemning them to death by starvation once we had moved on.

The oldest among them, obviously the head man, spoke hesitantly. 'Lord, what can we do for you? We would feed your men, but they are so many . . .'

'Bury the dead and you owe us nothing,' I replied. 'But we must find shelter tonight. What can you tell us about the nearest town?'

'They will welcome you there,' he said. 'Kibi is an hour or so away on foot. We have a new lord, one of Lord Arai's men. He has sent warriors against the bandits many times this year, but they have always been defeated. The last time, his two sons were killed by Jin-emon, as was my eldest son. This is his brother, Jiro. Take him with you, Lord Otori.'

Jiro was a couple of years younger than I was, painfully thin but with an intelligent face beneath the rain-streaked dirt.

'Come here, Jiro,' I said to him, and he got to his feet and stood by the bay's head. It smelled him carefully as if inspecting him. 'Do you like horses?'

He nodded, too overwhelmed by my addressing him directly to speak.

'If your father can spare you, you may come with me to Maruyama.' I thought he could join Amano's grooms.

'We should press on now,' Makoto said at my elbow.

'We have brought what we could,' the farmer said, and made a gesture to the other men. They lowered their sacks and baskets from their shoulders and took out scant offerings of food: cakes made from millet, fern shoots and

51

other wild greens cut from the mountain, a few tiny salted plums and some withered chestnuts. I did not want to take them, but I felt to refuse would be to dishonour the farmers. I organized two soldiers to gather up the food and bring the sacks with them.

'Bid your father farewell,' I said to Jiro, and saw the older man's face working suddenly to fight back tears. I regretted my offer to take the boy, not only because it was one more life to be responsible for but also because I was depriving his father of his help in restoring the neglected fields.

'I'll send him back from the town.'

'No!' both father and son exclaimed together, the boy's face reddening.

'Let him go with you,' the father pleaded. 'Our family used to be warriors. My grandparents took to farming rather than starve. If Jiro serves you maybe he can become a warrior again and restore our family name.'

'He would do better to stay here and restore the land,' I replied. 'But if it is truly what you want, he may come with us.'

I sent the lad back to help Amano with the horses we had acquired from the bandits, telling him to come back to me when he was mounted. I was wondering what had happened to Aoi whom I had not set eyes on since I'd left him with Jo-An; it seemed like days ago. Makoto and I rode knee by knee at the head of our tired but cheerful army.

'It's been a good day, a good start,' he said. 'You have done exceptionally well, despite my idiocy.'

I remembered my earlier fury against him. It seemed to have evaporated completely now.

'Let's forget it. Would you describe that as a battle?'

'For unfledged men it was a battle,' he replied. 'And a victory. Since you won it, you can describe it however you like.'

Three left to win, one to lose, I thought and then almost immediately wondered if that was how a prophecy worked. Could I choose to apply it how it pleased me? I began to see what a powerful and dangerous thing it was: how it would influence my life whether I believed it or not. The words had been spoken to me, I had heard them, I would never be able to wipe them from my memory. Yet I could not quite commit myself to believing in them blindly.

Jiro came trotting back on Amano's own chestnut Ki. 'Lord Amano thought you should change horses, and sent you his. He doesn't think he can save the black horse. It needs to rest its leg, and won't be able to keep up. And no one here can afford to keep a creature that can't work.'

I felt a moment of sorrow for the brave and beautiful horse. I patted Shun's neck. 'I'm happy with this one.'

Jiro slid from the chestnut's back and took Shun's reins. 'Ki's better looking,' he remarked.

'You should make a good impression,' Makoto said dryly to me.

We changed horses, the chestnut snorting through his nose and looking as fresh as if he'd just come from the meadow. Jiro swung himself up onto the bay, but as soon as he touched the saddle, Shun put his head down and bucked, sending him flying through the air. The horse regarded the boy in the mud at his feet in surprise, almost as though thinking, *What's he doing down there?*

Makoto and I found it far funnier than it really was and roared with laughter. 'Serves you right for being rude about him,' Makoto said.

To his credit, Jiro laughed too. He got to his feet and apologized gravely to Shun, who then allowed him to mount without protest.

The boy lost some of his shyness after that and began to point out landmarks on the road, a mountain where goblins lived, a shrine whose water healed the deepest wounds, a roadside spring that had never dried up in a thousand years. I imagined that, like me, he'd spent most of his childhood running wild on the mountain.

'Can you read and write, Jiro?' I asked.

'A little,' he replied.

'You'll have to study hard to become a warrior,' Makoto said with a smile.

'Don't I just need to know how to fight? I've practised with the wooden pole and the bow.'

'You need to be educated as well otherwise you'll end up no better than the bandits.'

'Are you a great warrior, sir?' Makoto's teasing encouraged Jiro to become more familiar.

'Not at all! I'm a monk.'

Jiro's face was a picture of amazement. 'Forgive me for saying so, but you don't look like one!'

Makoto dropped the reins on his horse's neck and took off his helmet, showing his shaven head. He rubbed his scalp and hung the helmet on the saddle bow. 'I'm relying on Lord Otori to avoid any more combat today!'

After nearly an hour we came to the town. The houses around it seemed to be inhabited and the fields looked better cared for, the dykes repaired and the rice seedlings planted out. In one or two of the larger houses, lamps were lit, casting their orange glow against torn screens. Others had fires burning in the earthen-floored kitchens;

the smell of food wafting from them made our stomachs growl.

The town had once been fortified, but recent fighting had left the walls broken in many places, the gates and watchtowers destroyed by fire. The fine mist softened the harsh outlines of destruction. The river that we had crossed flowed along one side of the town; there was no sign of a bridge but there had obviously once been a thriving boat trade, though now more boats seemed damaged than whole. The bridge where Jin-emon had set up his toll barrier had been this town's lifeline and he'd all but strangled it.

Kahei was waiting for us at the ruins of the main gateway. I told him to stay with the men while I went on into the town with Makoto and Jiro and a small guard.

He looked concerned. 'Better that I go, in case there is some trap,' he suggested, but I did not think this half-ruined place offered any danger, and I felt it wiser to ride up to Arai's constable as if I expected his friendship and cooperation. He would not refuse to help me to my face, whereas he might if he thought I had any fear of him.

As Kahei had said, there was no castle, but in the centre of the town on a slight hill was a large wooden residence whose walls and gates had recently been repaired. The house itself looked run-down but relatively undamaged. As we approached, the gates were opened and a middle-aged man stepped out, followed by a small group of armed men.

I recognized him at once. He had been at Arai's side when the Western Army rode into Inuyama, and had accompanied Arai to Terayama. Indeed he had been in the room when I had last seen Arai. Niwa, his name was, I recalled. Was it his sons who had been killed by Jin-emon? His face had aged and held fresh lines of grief.

I reined in the chestnut horse and spoke in a loud voice. 'I am Otori Takeo, son of Shigeru, grandson of Shigemori. I intend no harm to you or your people. My wife, Shirakawa Kaede, and I are moving our army to my wife's domain at Maruyama, and I ask for your help in providing food and lodging overnight.'

'I remember you well,' he said. 'It's been a while since we last met. I am Niwa Junkei. I hold this land by order of Lord Arai. Are you now seeking an alliance with him?'

'That would give me the greatest pleasure,' I said. 'As soon as I have secured my wife's domain, I will go to Inuyama to wait on his lordship.'

'Well, a lot seems to have changed in your life,' he replied. 'I believe I am in your debt; news on the wind is that you killed Jin-emon and his bandits.'

'It is true that Jin-emon and all his men are dead,' I said. 'We have brought back the warriors' heads for proper burial. I wish I had come earlier to spare you your grief.'

He nodded, his lips compressed into a line so thin that it looked black, but he did not speak of his sons. 'You must be my guests,' he said, trying to infuse some energy into his tired voice. 'You are very welcome. The clan hall is open to your men: it's been damaged but the roof still stands. The rest may camp outside the town. We will provide such food as we can. Please bring your wife to my house; my women will look after her. You and your guard will of course also stay with me.' He paused and then said bitterly, abandoning the formal words of courtesy, 'I am aware that I am only offering you what you would otherwise take. Lord Arai's orders have always been to detain you. But I could not protect this district against a gang of bandits. What hope would I have against an army the size of yours?'

'I am grateful to you.' I decided to ignore his tone, attributing it to grief. But I wondered at the scarcity of troops and supplies, the obvious weakness of the town, the impudence of the bandits. Arai must barely hold this country; the task of subduing the remnants of the Tohan must be taking up all his resources.

Niwa provided us with sacks of millet and rice, dried fish and soybean paste, and these were distributed to the men along with the farmers' offerings. In their gratitude the townspeople welcomed the army and gave what food and shelter they could. Tents were erected, fires lit, horses fed and watered. I rode around the lines with Makoto, Amano and Jiro, half appalled at my own lack of knowledge and experience, half amazed that in spite of it my men were settled down for the first night of our march. I spoke to the guards Kahei had set and then to Jo-An and the outcastes who had camped near them. An uneasy alliance seemed to have grown up between them.

I was inclined to watch all night too – I would hear an approaching army long before anyone else – but Makoto persuaded me to go back and rest for at least part of the night. Jiro led Shun and the chestnut away to Niwa's stables, and we went to the living quarters.

Kaede had already been escorted there and had been given a room with Niwa's wife and the other women of the household. I was longing to be alone with her, but I realized there would be little chance of it. She would be expected to sleep in the women's room, and I would be with Makoto and Kahei, several guards, and probably next door to Niwa and his guards too.

An old woman, who told us she had been Niwa's wife's wet nurse, led us to the guest room. It was spacious and well proportioned, but the mats were old and stained and the walls spotted with mildew. The screens were still open: on the evening breeze came the scent of blossom and freshly wet earth, but the garden was wild and untended.

'A bath is ready, lord,' she said to me and led me to the wooden bath house at the further end of the veranda. I asked Makoto to keep guard and told the old woman to leave me alone. No one could have looked more harmless, but I was not taking any risks. I had absconded from the Tribe; I was under their sentence of death; I knew only too well how their assassins could appear under any guise.

She apologized that the water would not be very hot, and grumbled about the lack of firewood and food. It was in fact barely lukewarm, but the night was not cold, and just to scrub the mud and blood off my body was pleasure enough. I eased myself into the tub, checking out the day's damage. I was not wounded, but I had bruises I had not noticed getting. My upper arms were marked by Jin-emon's steel hands – I remembered that all right – but there was a huge bruise on my thigh already turning black; I had no idea what had caused it. The wrist that Akio had bent backwards so long ago at Inuyama and that I'd thought had healed, was aching again, probably from the contact with Jin-emon's stone bones. I thought I would strap a leather band around it the following day. I let myself drift for a few moments and was on the point of falling asleep when I heard a woman's tread outside; the door slid open and Kaede stepped in.

I knew it was her, by her walk, by her scent. She said, 'I've brought lamps. The old woman said you must have

sent her away because she was too ugly. She persuaded me
to come instead.'

The light in the bath house changed as she set the
lamps on the floor. Then her hands were at the back of my
neck, massaging away the stiffness.

'I apologized for your rudeness but she said that where
she grew up the wife always looked after the husband in
the bath, and that I should do the same for you.'

'An excellent old custom,' I said trying not to groan
aloud. Her hands moved to my shoulders. The overwhelming desire I'd felt for her came flooding back
through me. Her hands left me for a moment and I heard
the sigh of silk as she untied her sash and let it fall to the
ground. She leaned forward to run her fingers across my
temples and I felt her breasts brush the back of my neck.

I leaped from the bath and took her in my arms. She
was as aroused as I was. I did not want to lay her down
on the floor of the bath house. I lifted her and she
wrapped her legs around me. As I moved into her I felt the
rippling beginnings of her climax. Our bodies merged into
one being, imitating our hearts. Afterwards we did lie
down, though the floor was wet and rough, clinging to
each other for a long time.

When I spoke it was to apologize. I was ashamed again
of the strength of my desire. She was my wife; I'd treated
her like a prostitute. 'Forgive me,' I said. 'I'm sorry.'

'I wanted it so badly,' Kaede said in a low voice. 'I was
afraid we would not be together tonight. I should ask your
forgiveness. I seem to be shameless.'

I pulled her close to me, burying my face in her hair.
What I felt for her was like an enchantment. I was afraid
of its power, but I could not resist it and it delighted me
more than anything else in life.

'It's like a spell,' Kaede said, as though she read my mind. 'It's so strong I can't fight it. Is love always like this?'

'I don't know. I've never loved anyone but you.'

'I am the same.' When she stood her robe was soaked. She scooped water from the bath and washed herself. 'Manami will have to find me a dry robe from somewhere.' She sighed. 'Now I suppose I have to go back to the women. I must try to talk to poor Lady Niwa who is eaten up by grief. What will you talk about with her husband?'

'I'll find out what I can about Arai's movements and how many men and domains he controls.'

'It's pitiful here,' Kaede said, 'Anyone could take over this place.'

'Do you think we should?' The thought had already occurred to me when I'd heard Niwa's words at the gate. I also scooped water from the tub, washed myself, and dressed.

'Can we afford to leave a garrison here?'

'Not really. I think part of Arai's problem may be that he took too much land too fast. He has spread himself very thin.'

'I agree,' Kaede said, pulling her robe round her body and tying the sash. 'We must consolidate our position at Maruyama and build up our supplies. If the land there is as neglected as it is here, and was at my home, we'll have trouble feeding our men once we get there. We need to be farmers before we can be warriors.'

I gazed at her. Her hair was damp, her face soft from love-making. I had never seen a being as beautiful as she was, but beneath all that she had a mind like a sword. I found the combination and the fact that she was my wife unbearably erotic.

She slid the door open and stepped into her sandals. She dropped to her knees. 'Good night, Lord Takeo,' she said in a sweet, coy voice, quite unlike her own, rose lithely, and walked away, her hips swaying beneath the thin, wet robe.

Makoto sat outside, watching her, a strange look on his face, maybe disapproving, maybe jealous.

'Take a bath,' I told him, 'though the water's half cold. Then we must join Niwa.'

Kahei returned to eat with us. The old woman helped Niwa serve the food; I thought I caught a smirk on her face as she placed the tray before me, but I kept my eyes lowered. By now I was so hungry, it was hard not to fall on the food and cram it in fistfuls into my mouth. There was little enough of it. Later the women came back with tea and wine and then left us. I envied them, for they would be sleeping close to Kaede.

The wine loosened Niwa's tongue, though it did not improve his mood; rather, it made him more melancholy and tearful. He had accepted the town from Arai, think-ing it would make a home for his sons and grandsons. Now he had lost the first and would never see the second. His sons had not even, in his mind, died with honour on the battlefield, but had been murdered shamefully by a creature who was barely human.

'I don't understand how you overcame him,' he said, sizing me up with a look that verged on scornful. 'No offence, but both my sons were twice your size, older, more experienced.' He drank deeply, then went on: 'But then, I could never understand how you killed Iida, either. There was that rumour about you after you disappeared, of some strange blood in you that gave you special powers. Is it a sort of sorcery?'

I was aware of Kahei tensing beside me. Like any warrior he took immediate offence at the suggestion of sorcery. I did not think Niwa was being deliberately insulting; I thought he was too dulled by grief to know what he was saying. I made no reply. He continued to study me but I did not meet his gaze. I was starting to long for sleep; my eyelids were quivering, my teeth aching.

'There were a lot of rumours,' Niwa went on. 'Your disappearance was a considerable blow to Arai. He took it very personally. He thought there was some conspiracy against him. He had a long-term mistress – Muto Shizuka. You know her?'

'She was a maid to my wife,' I replied, not mentioning that she was also my cousin. 'Lord Arai himself sent her.'

'She turned out to be from the Tribe. Well, he'd known that all along, but he hadn't realized what it meant. When you went off apparently to join the Tribe – or so everyone was saying – it brought a lot of things to a head.'

He broke off, his gaze becoming more suspicious. 'But you presumably know all this already.'

'I heard that Lord Arai intended to move against the Tribe,' I said carefully. 'But I have not heard of the outcome.'

'Not very successful. Some of his retainers – I was not among them – advised him to work with the Tribe, as Iida did. Their opinion was that the best way to control them was to pay them. Arai didn't like that: he couldn't afford it for a start, and it's not in his nature. He wants things to be cut and dried and he can't stand to be made a fool of. He thought Muto Shizuka, the Tribe, even you, had hoodwinked him in some way.'

'That was never my intention,' I said. 'But I can see how my actions must have looked to him. I owe him an apology. As soon as we are settled at Maruyama I will go to him. Is he at Inuyama now?'

'He spent the winter there. He intended to return to Kumamoto and mop up the last remnants of resistance there, move eastwards to consolidate the former Noguchi lands, and then pursue his campaign against the Tribe, starting in Inuyama.' He poured more wine for us all and gulped a cupful down. 'But it's like trying to dig up a sweet potato: there's far more underground than you think and no matter how carefully you try to lift it pieces break off and begin to put out shoots again. I flushed out some members here; one of them ran the brewery, the other was a small-scale merchant and money lender. But all I got were a couple of old men, figureheads, no more. They took poison before I could get anything out of them; the rest disappeared.'

He lifted the wine cup and stared morosely at it. 'It's going to split Arai in two,' he said finally. 'He can handle the Tohan; they're a simple enemy, straightforward, and the heart mostly went out of them with Iida's death. But trying to eradicate this hidden enemy at the same time – he's set himself an impossible task, and he's running out of money and resources.' He seemed to catch what he was saying and went on quickly, 'Not that I'm disloyal to him. I gave him my allegiance and I'll stand by that. It's cost me my sons though.'

We all bowed our heads and murmured our sympathy.

Kahei said, 'It's getting late. We should sleep a little if we are to march again at dawn.'

'Of course.' Niwa got clumsily to his feet and clapped his hands. After a few moments the old woman, lamp in hand, came to show us back to our room. The beds were already laid out on the floor. I went to the privy and then walked in the garden for a while to clear my head from the wine. The town was silent. It seemed I could hear my men breathing deeply in sleep. An owl hooted from the trees around the temple, and in the distance a dog barked. The gibbous moon of the fourth month was low in the sky; a few wisps of cloud drifted across it. The sky was misty, with only the brightest stars visible. I thought about all Niwa had told me. He was right: it was almost impossible to identify the network that the Tribe had set up across the Three Countries. But Shigeru had done so, and I had his records.

I went to the room. Makoto was already asleep. Kahei was talking to two of his men who had come to keep guard. He told me he had also put two men to watch the room where Kaede slept. I lay down, wished she was next to me, briefly considered sending for her, then fell into the deep river of sleep.

Three

For the next few days our march to Maruyama continued without event. The news of Jin-emon's death and the defeat of his bandits had gone ahead of us and we were welcomed because of it. We moved quickly, during short nights and long days, making the most of the favourable weather before the full onset of the plum rains.

As we travelled, Kaede tried to explain to me the political background of the domain that was to become hers. Shigeru had already told me something of its history, but the tangled web of marriages, adoptions, deaths, which might have been murders, jealousy, and intrigue was mostly new to me. It made me marvel anew at the strength of Maruyama Naomi, the woman Shigeru had loved, who had been able to survive and rule in her own right. It made me regret her death, and his, all the more bitterly, and strengthened my resolve to continue their work of justice and peace.

'Lady Maruyama and I talked a little together on a journey like this,' Kaede said. 'But we were riding in the opposite direction, towards Tsuwano where we met you. She told me women should hide their power and be carried in the palanquin lest the warlords and warriors crush them. But here I am riding beside you, on Raku, in freedom. I'll never go in a palanquin again.'

It was a day of sun and showers, like the fox's wedding

in the folk tale. A sudden rainbow appeared against a dark grey cloud; the sun shone bravely for a few moments; rain fell silver. Then the clouds swept across the sky, sun and rainbow vanished, and the rain had a cold, harsh sting to it.

Lady Maruyama's marriage had been intended to improve relations between the Seishuu and the Tohan. Her husband was from the Tohan and was related to both the Iida and the Noguchi families. He was much older than she was, had been married before, and already had grown children. The wisdom of an alliance through such an encumbered marriage had been questioned at the time, not least by Naomi, who, although only sixteen, had been brought up in the Maruyama way to think and speak for herself. However, the clan desired the alliance, and so it was arranged. During Lady Maruyama's life her stepchildren had caused many problems. After her husband died they had contested the domain – unsuccessfully. Her husband's only daughter was the wife of a cousin of Iida Sadamu, Iida Nariaki, who, we learned on the way, had escaped the slaughter at Inuyama and had fled into the West, from where it seemed he now intended to make a new claim on the domain. The Seishuu clan lords were divided. Maruyama had always been inherited through the female line, but it was the last domain that clung to a tradition that affronted the warrior class. Nariaki had been adopted by his father-in-law before Lady Maruyama's marriage, and was considered by many to be legal heir to his wife's property.

Naomi had been fond of her husband and grieved genuinely when he died after four years, leaving her with a young daughter and a baby son. She was determined her daughter would inherit her estate. Her son died mysteriously, some said poisoned, and in the years that followed the battle of Yaegahara, the widowed Naomi attracted the attention of Iida Sadamu himself.

'But by that time she had met Shigeru,' I said, wishing I knew where and how. 'And now you are her heir.' Kaede's mother had been Lady Maruyama's cousin and Kaede was the closest living female relative to the former head of the clan for Lady Maruyama's daughter, Mariko, had died with her mother in the river at Innyama.

'If I am allowed to inherit,' Kaede replied. 'When her senior retainer Sugita Haruki came to me late last year he swore the Maruyama clan would support me, but Nariaki may have already moved in.'

'Then we will drive him out.'

On the morning of the sixth day we came to the domain border. Kahei halted his men a few hundred paces before it, and I rode forward to join him.

'I was hoping my brother would have met us before now,' he said quietly.

I had been hoping the same. Miyoshi Gemba had been sent to Maruyama before my marriage to Kaede to convey the news of our imminent arrival. But we had heard nothing from him since. Apart from my concerns for his safety, I would have liked some information about the situation in the domain before we entered it – the whereabouts of Iida Nariaki, the feelings in the town towards us.

The barrier stood at a crossroads. The guard post was silent, the roads on all sides deserted. Amano took Jiro and they rode off to the south. When they reappeared Amano was shouting.

'A large army has been through: there are many hoof prints and horse droppings.'

'Heading into the domain?' I called.

'Yes!'

Kahei rode closer to the guard post and shouted, 'Is anyone there? Lord Otori Takeo is bringing his wife, Lady Shirakawa Kaede, heir to Lady Maruyama Naomi, into her domain.'

No answer came from the wooden building. A wisp of smoke rose from an unseen hearth. I could hear no sound, other than the army behind me, the stamping of restless horses, the breathing of a thousand men. My skin was tingling. I expected at any moment to hear the hiss and clack of arrows.

I rode Shun forward to join Kahei. 'Let's take a look.'

He glanced at me, but he'd given up trying to persuade me to stay behind. We dismounted, called to Jiro to hold the horses' reins, and drew our swords.

The barrier itself had been thrown down and crushed in the rush of men and horses that had trampled over it. A peculiar silence hung around the place. A bush warbler called from the forest, its song startlingly loud. The sky was partly covered with large grey clouds, but the rain had ceased again and the breeze from the south was mild.

I could smell blood and smoke on it. As we approached the guard house we saw the first of the bodies just inside the threshold. The man had fallen across the hearth and his clothes were smouldering. They would have burnt if they had not been soaked with blood from where his belly had been slashed open. His hand still gripped his sword but the blade was clean. Behind him lay two others, on their backs; their clothes were stained with their own last evacuations, but not with blood.

'They've been strangled,' I said to Kahei. It chilled me, for only the Tribe use garrottes.

He nodded, turning one over to look at the crest on his back. 'Maruyama.'

'How long since they died?' I asked, looking round the room. Two of the men had been taken completely by surprise, the third stabbed before he could use his sword. I felt fury rise in me, the same fury I'd felt against the guards in Hagi when they'd let Kenji into the garden or when I'd slipped past them, fury at the dullness of ordinary men who were so easily outwitted by the Tribe. They'd been surprised while they'd been eating, killed by assassins before any of them could get away to carry a warning of the invading army.

Kahei picked up the tea kettle from where it had been sent flying. 'Barely warm.'

'We must catch up with them before they reach the town.'

'Let's get moving,' Kahei said, his eyes bright with anticipation.

But as we turned to go I caught a fresh sound, coming from a small storeroom behind the main guard post. I made a sign to Kahei to keep silent and went to the door. Someone was behind it, trying to hold his breath but definitely breathing, and shivering, and letting the breath out in what was almost a sob.

I slid the door and entered in one movement. The room was cluttered with bales of rice, wooden boards, weapons, farming implements.

'Who's there? Come out!'

There was a scuttling noise and a small figure burst out from behind the bales and tried to slide between my legs. I grabbed it, saw it was a boy of ten or eleven years, realized he held a knife, and wrenched his fingers apart until he cried out and dropped it.

He wriggled in my grasp, trying not to sob.

'Stand still! I'm not going to hurt you.'

'Father! Father!' he called.

I pushed him in front of me into the guard room. 'Is one of these your father?'

His face had gone white, his breath came raggedly, and there were tears in his eyes, but he still struggled to control himself. There was no doubt he was a warrior's son. He looked at the man on the floor whom Kahei had pulled from the fire, took in the terrible wound and the sightless eyes, and nodded.

Then his face went green. I pulled him through the door so he could vomit outside.

There'd been a little tea left in the kettle. Kahei poured it into one of the unbroken cups and gave it to the boy to drink.

'What happened?' I said.

His teeth were chattering but he tried to speak normally, his voice coming out louder than he'd intended. 'Two men came through the roof. They strangled Kitano and Tsuruta. Someone else slashed the tethers and panicked the horses. My father ran after them, and when he came back inside the men cut him open with their knives.'

He fought back the sob. 'I thought they'd gone,' he said. 'I couldn't see them! They came out of the air and cut him open.'

'Where were you?'

'I was in the storeroom. I hid. I'm ashamed. I should have killed them!'

70

Kahei grinned at the fierce little face. 'You did the right thing. Grow up and kill them then!'

'Describe the men to me,' I said.

'They wore dark clothes. They made no sound at all. And they did that trick so that you could not see them.' He spat and added, 'Sorcery!'

'And the army that came through?'

'Iida Nariaki of the Tohan, together with some Seishuu. I recognized their crests.'

'How many?'

'Hundreds,' he replied. 'They took a long time to go past. But it's not so long since the last ones rode through. I was waiting until I thought they had all gone. I was about to come out when I heard you, so I stayed hidden.'

'What's your name?'

'Sugita Hiroshi, son of Hikaru.'

'You live in Maruyama?'

'Yes, my uncle, Sugita Haruki, is chief retainer to the Maruyama.'

'You'd better come with us,' I said. 'Do you know who we are?'

'You are Otori,' he said, smiling for the first time, a wan feeble smile. 'I can tell by your crests. I think you are the ones we have been waiting for.'

'I am Otori Takeo and this is Miyoshi Kahei. My wife is Shirakawa Kaede, heir to this domain.'

He dropped to his knees. 'Lord Otori. Lord Miyoshi's brother came to my uncle. They are preparing men because my uncle is sure Iida Nariaki will not let Lady Shirakawa inherit without a fight. He's right, isn't he?'

Kahei patted him on the shoulder. 'Go and say good-bye to your father. And bring his sword. It must be yours now. When the battle is won we will bring him to Maruyama and bury him with honour.'

This is the upbringing I should have had, I thought, watching Hiroshi come back holding the sword, which was almost as long as he was. My mother had told me not to tear the claws off crabs, not to hurt any living creature, but this child had been taught since birth to have no fear of death or cruelty. I knew Kahei approved of his courage: he had been raised in the same code. Well, if I did not have ruthlessness by now, after my training in the Tribe, I would never get it. I would have to pretend it.

'They drove off all our horses!' Hiroshi exclaimed as we walked past the empty stables. He was shaking again, but with rage, I thought, not fear.

'We'll get them back, and more,' Kahei promised him. 'You go with Jiro, and stay out of trouble.'

'Take him back to the women and tell Manami to look after him,' I said to Jiro as I took Shun from him and remounted.

'I don't want to be looked after,' the boy announced when Kahei lifted him onto the back of Jiro's horse. 'I want to go into battle with you.'

'Don't kill anyone by mistake with that sword,' Kahei said, laughing. 'We're your friends, remember!'

'The attack must have come as a complete surprise,' I said to Makoto, after telling him briefly what we'd learned. 'The guard house was hardly manned.'

'Or maybe the Maruyama forces were expecting it and pulled back all their available men to ambush them or attack on more favourable ground,' he replied. 'Do you know the land between here and the town?'

'I've never been here.'

'Has your wife?'

I shook my head.

'Then you'd better get that boy back. He may be our only guide.'

Kahei shouted to Jiro, who had not gone far. Hiroshi was delighted to be brought back again and he knew a surprising amount about the terrain and the fortification of the town. Maruyama was a hill castle; a sizeable town lay on the slopes and at the foot of the rounded hill on which the castle was built. A small, fast-flowing river supplied the town with water and fed a network of canals, kept well stocked with fish; the castle had its own springs. The outer walls of the town had formerly been kept in good repair and could be defended indefinitely, but since Lady Maruyama's death and the confusion that had followed Iida's downfall, repairs had not been kept up and guards were few. In effect, the town was divided between those who supported Sugita and his championship of Kaede, and those who thought it more practical to bend before the wind of fate and accept the rule of Iida Nariaki and his wife, whose claim, they said, also had legitimacy.

'Where is your uncle now?' I asked Hiroshi.

'He has been waiting a little way from the town with all his men. He did not want to go too far from it, in case it was taken over behind his back. So I heard my father say.'

'Will he retreat into the town?'

The boy's eyes narrowed in an adult way. 'Only if he absolutely has to, and then he would have to fall back to the castle, for the town can no longer be defended. We are very short of food; last year's storms destroyed much of the harvest, and the winter was unusually hard. We could not stand a long siege.'

'Where would your uncle fight if he had the choice?'

'Not far from the town gate this road crosses a river, the Asagawa. There's a ford; it's almost always shallow but sometimes there's a flash flood. To get to the ford, the road goes down into a steep ravine and then up again. Then there's a small plain, with a favourable slope. My father taught me you could hold up an invading army there. And with enough men you could outflank them and box them in the ravine.'

'Well spoken, Captain,' Kahei said. 'Remind me to take you with me on all my campaigns!'

'I only know this district,' Hiroshi said, suddenly bashful. 'But my father taught me that in war one must know the terrain above everything.'

'He would be proud of you,' I said. It seemed our best plan would be to press on and hope to trap the forces in front of us in the ravine. Even if Sugita had pulled back into the town we could take the attacking army by surprise, from behind.

I had one more question for the boy. 'You said it's possible to outflank an army in the ravine. So there's another route between here and the plain?'

He nodded. 'A few miles further to the north there is another crossing. We rode that way a few days ago to come here; after a day of heavy rain there was a sudden flood through the ford. It takes a little longer, but not if you gallop.'

'Can you show Lord Miyoshi the way?'

'Of course,' he said, looking up at Kahei with eager eyes.

'Kahei, take your horsemen and ride with all speed that way. Hiroshi will show you where to find Sugita. Tell him we are coming and that he is to keep the enemy bottled up in the ravine. The foot soldiers and farmers will come with me.'

'That's good,' Hiroshi said approvingly. 'The ford is full of boulders; the footing is not really favourable to war horses. And the Tohan will think you are weaker than you are and underestimate you. They won't expect farmers to fight.'

I thought, *I should be taking lessons in strategy from him*.

Jiro said, 'Am I to go with Lord Miyoshi too?'

'Yes, take Hiroshi on your horse, and keep an eye on him.'

The horsemen rode away, the hoofs echoing across the broad valley.

'What hour is it?' I asked Makoto.

'About the second half of the Snake,' he replied.

'Have the men eaten?'

'I gave orders to eat quickly while we were halted.'

'Then we can move on right away. Start the men now; I'll ride back and tell the captains and my wife. I'll join you when I've spoken to them.'

He turned his horse's head, but before he moved off he gazed briefly at the sky, the forest, and the valley.

'It's a beautiful day,' he said quietly.

I knew what he meant: a good day to die. But neither he nor I was destined to die that day, though many others were.

I cantered back along the line of resting men, giving the orders to move on and telling their leaders our plan. They got to their feet eagerly, especially when I told them who our main enemy was; they shouted mightily at the prospect of punishing the Tohan for the defeat at

Yaegahara, the loss of Yamagata, and the years of oppression.

Kaede and the other women were waiting in a small grove of trees, Amano as usual with them.

'We are going into battle,' I said to Kaede. 'Iida Nariaki's army crossed the border ahead of us. Kahei has ridden around the side of them, where we hope he will meet up with his brother and Lord Sugita. Amano will take you into the forest where you must stay until I come for you.'

Amano bowed his head. Kaede looked as if she were going to speak, but then she too inclined her head. 'May the all-merciful one be with you,' she whispered, her eyes on my face. She leaned forward slightly and said, 'One day I will ride into battle beside you!'

'If I know you are safe I can give all my concentration to the fight,' I replied. 'Besides, you must protect the records.'

Manami said, her face drawn with anxiety, 'A battle-field is no place for a woman!'

'No,' Kaede replied. 'I would only be in the way. But how I wish I had been born a man!'

Her fierceness made me laugh. 'Tonight we will sleep in Maruyama!' I told her.

I kept the image of her vivid, courageous face in my mind all day. Before we left the temple Kaede and Manami had made banners, the Otori heron, the white river of the Shirakawa, and the hill of the Maruyama, and we unfurled them now as we rode through the valley. Even though we were going into battle, I still checked out the state of the countryside. The fields looked fertile enough, and should already have been flooded and planted, but the dykes were broken and the channels clogged with weeds and mud.

Apart from the signs of neglect, the army ahead of us had stripped the land and farms of whatever they could find. Children cried by the roadside, houses burned, and here and there dead men lay, killed casually, for no reason, their bodies left where they'd fallen.

From time to time when we passed a farm or hamlet, the surviving men and boys came out to question us. Once they learned that we were pursuing the Tohan and that I would allow them to fight, they joined us eagerly, swelling our ranks by about a hundred.

About two hours later, when it was well past noon, maybe coming into the hour of the Goat, I heard from ahead the sounds I had been listening for: the clash of steel, the whinnying of horses, the shouts of battle, the cries of the wounded. I made a sign to Makoto and he gave the order to halt.

Shun stood still, ears pricked forwards, listening as attentively as I did. He did not whinny in response as though he knew the need for silence.

'Sugita must have met them here, as the boy said,' Makoto murmured. 'But can Kahei have reached him already?'

'Whoever it is, it is a major battle,' I replied.

The road ahead disappeared downhill into the ravine. The tops of the trees waved their new green leaves in the spring sunshine. The noise of battle was not so great that I could not also hear birdsong.

'The bannermen will ride forward with me,' I said.

'You should not go ahead. Stay in the centre where it is safer. You will be too easy a target for bowmen.'

'It is my war,' I replied. 'It's only right that I should be the first to engage in it.' The words may have sounded calm and measured; in truth I was tense, anxious to begin the fight and anxious to end it.

'Yes, it is your war, and every one of us is in it because of you. All the more reason for us to try and preserve you!'

I turned my horse and faced the men. I felt a surge of regret for those who would die, but at least I had given them the chance to die like men, to fight for their land and families. I called to the bannermen and they rode forward, the banners streaming in the breeze. I looked at the white heron and prayed to Shigeru's spirit. I felt it possess me, sliding beneath my skin, aligning itself with my sinews and bones. I drew Jato and the blade flashed in the sun. The men responded with shouts and cheers.

I turned Shun and put him into a canter. He went forward calmly and eagerly, as though we were riding together through a meadow. The horse to my left was over-excited, pulling against the bit and trying to buck. I could feel all the muscular tension in the rider's body as he controlled the horse with one hand while keeping the banner erect in the other.

The road darkened as it descended between the trees. The surface worsened, as Hiroshi had predicted, the soft, muddy sand giving way to rocks, then boulders, with many potholes gouged out by the recent floods. The road itself would have turned into a river every time it rained.

We slowed to a trot. Above all the sounds of battle I could hear the real river. Ahead of us a bright gap in the foliage showed where the road emerged from under the trees to run along its bank for a few hundred feet before the ford. Silhouetted against the brightness were dark shapes, like the shadows against paper screens that amuse children, writhing and clashing in the contortions of slaughter.

I had thought to use bowmen first, but as soon as I saw the conflict ahead I realized they would kill as many allies as enemies. Sugita's men had driven the invading army back from the plain and were pushing them foot by foot along the river. Even as we approached some were trying to break ranks and flee; they saw us and ran back in the other direction, shouting to alert their commanders.

Makoto had raised the conch shell and now blew into it, its haunting, eerie note echoing from the wall of the ravine on the far side of the river. Then the echo itself was echoed as a reply came from way ahead, too far away for us to see the man blowing it. There was a moment of stillness, the moment before the wave breaks, and then we were among them and the fight had begun.

Only the chroniclers writing afterwards can tell you what happens in battle, and then they usually tell only the tale of the victor. There is no way of knowing when you are locked in the midst of it which way the fighting is going. Even if you could see it from above, with eagle's eyes, all you would see would be a quilt of pulsating colour, crests and banners, blood and steel – beautiful and nightmarish. All men on the battlefield go mad: how else could we do the things we do and bear to see the things we see?

I realized immediately that our skirmish with the bandits had been nothing. These were the hardened troops of the Tohan and the Seishuu, well armed, ferocious, cunning. They saw the heron crest and knew at once who was at their rear. To revenge Iida Sadamu by killing me was the instant goal of half their army. Makoto had been being sensible when he'd suggested I stay protected in the centre.

I'd fought off three warriors, only saved from the third by Shun's sense of timing, before my friend caught up with me. Wielding his stave like a lance he caught a fourth man under the chin, knocking him from the saddle. One of our farmers leaped on the fallen warrior and severed his head with his sickle.

I urged Shun forward. He seemed instinctively to find a path through the crush, always turning at the right moment to give me the advantage. And Jato leaped in my hand, as Shigeru had once said it would, until it streamed with blood from the point to the hilt.

There was a thick knot of men around Makoto and me as we fought side by side, and I became aware of another similar cluster ahead. I could see the Tohan banner fluttering above it. The two clusters surged and swirled as men rose and fell around them, until they were so close I could see my counterpart in the centre of the other.

I felt a rush of recognition. This man wore black armour, with a horned helmet the same as Iida Sadamu had worn when I had looked up at him from beneath his horse's feet in Mino. Across his breast gleamed a string of gold prayer beads. Our eyes met above the sea of struggling men, and Nariaki gave a shout of rage. Wrenching at his horse's head and urging it forward, he broke through the protective circle around him and rode at me.

'Otori Takeo is mine!' he yelled. 'Let no one touch him but me!' As he repeated this over and over again, the men attacking me fell back a little and we found ourselves face to face a few paces apart.

I make it sound as if there was time to think it all through, but in reality there was none. These scenes return to me in flashes. He was in front of me; he shouted again insultingly, but I barely heard the words. He dropped the reins on his horse's neck and lifted his sword with both hands. His horse was bigger than Shun, and he, like Iida, much larger than me. I was watching the sword for the moment it began to move, and Shun was watching it too.

The blade flashed. Shun jumped sideways and the sword hit only air. The impetus of the huge blow dislodged the rider momentarily. As he fell awkwardly against his horse's neck, it bucked, enough to unseat him further. He had to either fall or drop his sword. Sliding his feet free of the stirrups, he held the horse's mane with one hand and with surprising agility swung himself to the ground. He fell onto his knees but still held the sword. Then he leaped to his feet and in the same movement rushed at me with a stroke that would have taken off my leg, if Shun had stood still long enough for it to connect.

My men pressed forward and could easily have overcome him.

'Stay back!' I shouted. I was determined now to kill him myself. I was possessed by fury like nothing I had ever known, as different from the cold murders of the Tribe as day is from night. I let the reins fall and leaped from Shun's back. I heard him snort behind me and knew he would stand as still as a rock until I needed him again.

I stood facing Iida's cousin as I'd wished I'd faced Iida himself. I knew Nariaki despised me, and with reason: I did not have his training or his skills, but in his scorn I saw his weakness. He rushed forward, the sword whirling: his plan was to try to cut me down with his longer reach. I suddenly saw myself in the hall at Terayama, practising with Matsuda. I saw Kaede's image as I had seen it then, she was my life and my strength. *Tonight we will sleep in*

Maruyama, I promised her again, and the same move came to me.

Black blood, I thought, maybe I even shouted it aloud to Nariaki. *You have it and I have it. We are of the same class.* I felt Shigeru's hand within my own. And then Jato bit home and Iida Nariaki's red blood was spraying my face.

As he fell forwards onto his knees Jato struck again, and his head bounced at my feet, his eyes still full of fury, his lips snarling.

That scene remains engraved in my memory, but little else does. There was no time to feel fear, no time to think at all. The moves I'd been taught by Shigeru and by Matsuda came to my sword through my arm but not by my conscious will. Once Nariaki was dead, I turned to Shun. Blinking the sweat from my eyes, I saw Jo-An at his head; the outcaste held my enemy's horse too.

'Get them out of the way,' I shouted. Hiroshi had been right about the terrain. As the Tohan and Seishuu troops were driven back and we advanced, the crush intensified. Terrified horses stumbled in holes, breaking their legs, or were forced up against boulders, unable to go forwards or back, panicking.

Jo-An scrambled like a monkey onto Shun's back and forced his way through the milling men. From time to time I was aware of him, moving through the battle, taking riderless, panic-stricken animals to the forest. As he'd said, there are many tasks in a battle besides killing.

Soon I could see the Otori and Maruyama banners ahead of us, and I saw the Miyoshi crest too. The army between us was trapped. They continued to fight savagely but they had no way out and no hope.

I don't think one of them escaped alive. The river

foamed red with their blood. After it was all over and silence had descended, the outcastes took care of the bodies and laid them out in rows. When we met up with Sugita we walked along the lines of the dead, and he was able to identify many of them. Jo-An and his men had already taken charge of dozens of horses. Now they stripped the dead of their weapons and armour and arranged to burn the corpses.

The day had passed without my noticing time. It must have been the Hour of the Dog; the battle had lasted five or six hours. Our armies had been roughly equal: a little under two thousand men on each side. But the Tohan had lost all of theirs, while we had less than a hundred dead and two hundred wounded.

Jo-An brought Shun back to me and I rode with Sugita into the forest where Kaede had been waiting. Manami had managed to set up camp with her usual efficiency and had lit a fire and boiled water. Kaede knelt on a carpet beneath the trees. We could see her figure through the silver grey trunks of the beeches, cloaked by her hair, her back straight. As we drew nearer I saw that her eyes were closed.

Manami came to meet us, her eyes bright and red-rimmed. 'She has been praying,' she whispered. 'She has sat like that for hours.'

I dismounted and called her name. Kaede opened her eyes and joy and relief leaped into her face. She bowed her head to the ground, her lips moving in silent thanks. I knelt before her and Sugita did likewise.

'We have won a great victory,' he said. 'Iida Nariaki is dead and nothing now will stop you taking possession of your domain at Maruyama.'

'I am immensely grateful to you for your loyalty and courage,' she said to him and then turned to me.

'Are you hurt?'

'I don't think so.' The frenzy of battle was fading and I was aching all over. My ears were ringing and the smell of blood and death that clung to me was nauseating me. Kaede looked unattainably clean and pure.

'I prayed for your safety,' she said, her voice low. Sugita's presence made us awkward with each other.

'Take some tea,' Manami urged us. I realized my mouth was completely dry, my lips caked with blood.

'We are so dirty,' I began, but she put the cup in my hand and I drank it gratefully.

It was past sunset and the evening light was clear and tinged with blue. The wind had dropped and birds were singing their last songs of the day. I heard a rustle in the grass and looked up to see a hare cross the clearing in the distance. I drank the tea and looked at the hare. It gazed back at me with its large wild eyes for many moments before it bounded away. The tea's taste was smoky and bitter.

Two battles lay behind us, three ahead, if the prophecy was to be believed: *two now to win and one to lose.*

Four

One month earlier, after Shirakawa Kaede had left with the Miyoshi brothers to go to the temple guest house at Terayama, Muto Shizuka had set out for the secret village of her Tribe family, hidden in the mountains on the far side of Yamagata. Kaede had wept when they said farewell to each other, had pressed money on Shizuka and insisted she take one of the packhorses and send it back when she could, but Shizuka knew she would be quickly forgotten once Kaede was with Takeo.

Shizuka was deeply uneasy about leaving Kaede and about the impetuous decision to marry Takeo. She rode silently, brooding on the madness of love and the disaster the marriage would be to them. She had no doubt they would marry: now that fate had brought them together again, nothing would stop them. But she feared for them once Arai heard the news. And when her thoughts turned to Lord Fujiwara, a chill came over her despite the spring sunshine. She knew he could only be insulted and out-raged and she dreaded what he might do in revenge.

Kondo rode with her, his mood no better than hers. He seemed distressed and annoyed at being dismissed so sud-denly. Several times he said, 'She could have trusted me! After all I've done for her! I swore allegiance to her, after all. I would never do anything to harm her.'

Kaede's spell has fallen on him too, Shizuka thought.

He's been flattered by her reliance on him. She turned to him so often; now she will turn to Takeo.

'It was Takeo's order that we leave,' she told him. 'He is right. He cannot trust any one of us.'

'What a mess,' Kondo said gloomily. 'Where shall I go now, I wonder? I liked it with Lady Shirakawa. The place suited me.' He threw his head back and sniffed.

'The Muto family may have new instructions for both of us,' Shizuka replied shortly.

'I'm getting on,' he grumbled. 'I wouldn't mind settling down. I'll make way for the next generation. If only there were more of them!'

He turned his head and gave her his ironic smile. There was something in his look that unsettled her, some warmth behind the irony. In his guarded way he was making some kind of advance to her. Ever since he'd saved her life on the road to Shirakawa the previous year, a tension had existed between them. She was grateful to him and had at one time thought she might sleep with him, but then the affair had begun with Dr Ishida, Lord Fujiwara's physician, and she had wanted no one but him.

Though, she thought ruefully, that was hardly being practical. Kaede's marriage to Takeo would effectively remove her from Ishida for ever. She had no idea how she could ever meet the doctor again. His farewells had been warm; he had pressed her to return as soon as possible, had even gone so far as to say he would miss her, but how could she return to him if she was no longer in Kaede's service and part of her household? Their affair had been conducted with great secrecy thus far but if Fujiwara were to hear of it, she feared for the physician's safety.

The thought of never seeing the kind and intelligent man again cast her down utterly. *I am as bad as Kaede,* she thought. *Truly, you never reach the age when you escape being scorched by love.*

They passed through Yamagata and travelled another twenty miles to a village where they stayed the night. Kondo knew the innkeeper; they might even have been related, though Shizuka did not care enough to find out. As she feared, he made it clear that he wanted to sleep with her, and she saw the disappointment in his eyes when she pleaded exhaustion, but he did not press her or force her as he might have done. She felt grateful, and then annoyed with herself for so feeling.

However, the next morning after they had left the horses at the inn and begun the steep climb on foot into the mountains, Kondo said, 'Why don't we get married? We'd make a good team. You've got two boys, haven't you? I could adopt them. We're not too old to have more children together. Your family would approve.'

Her heart sank at the thought, especially as she knew her family probably would approve.

'You're not married?' It seemed surprising, given his age.

'I was married when I was seventeen, to a Kuroda woman. She died several years ago. We had no children.'

Shizuka glanced at him, wondering if he grieved for her.

He said, 'She was a very unhappy woman. She was not completely sane. She had long periods when she was tormented by horrible imaginings and fears. She saw ghosts and demons. She was not so bad when I was with her, but I was frequently ordered to travel. I worked as a spy for my mother's family, the Kondo, who had adopted me. On one long trip away I was delayed by bad weather. When I did not return at the expected time she hanged herself.'

For the first time his voice lost its irony. She perceived his real grief and found herself suddenly, unexpectedly moved by him.

'Maybe she was taught too harshly,' he said. 'I've often wondered what we do to our children. In many ways it was a relief to have none.'

'When you're a child it's like a game,' Shizuka said. 'I remember being proud of the skills I had and despising other people for not having them. You don't question the way you're brought up; that's just how it is.'

'You are talented; you are the Muto masters' niece and grandchild. Being Kuroda, in the middle, is not so easy. And if you don't have natural talents the training is very difficult.' He paused and went on quietly, 'Possibly she was too sensitive. No upbringing can completely eradicate a person's essential character.'

'I wonder. I'm sorry for your loss.'

'Well, it was a long time ago. But it certainly made me question a lot of things I'd been taught. Not that I tell most people. When you're part of the Tribe, you're obedient, that's all there is to it.'

'Maybe if Takeo had been brought up in the Tribe he would have learned obedience as we all do,' Shizuka said, as if thinking aloud. 'He hated being told what to do and he hated being confined. So, what do the Kikuta do? Give him to Akio for training as if he were a two-year-old. They've only themselves to blame for his defection. Shigeru knew how to handle him from the start. He won his loyalty. Takeo would have done anything for him.' *As we all would have done*, she found herself thinking and tried to suppress it. She had many secrets concerning Lord Shigeru that only the dead knew, and she was afraid Kondo might discern them.

'What Takeo did was quite considerable,' Kondo said, 'if you believe all the stories.'

'Are you impressed, Kondo? I thought nothing impressed you!'

'Everyone admires courage,' he replied. 'And, like Takeo, I am also of mixed blood, from both the Tribe and the clans. I was raised by the Tribe until I was twelve and then I became a warrior on the surface, a spy beneath. Maybe I understand something of the conflict he must have gone through.'

They walked in silence for a while; then he said, 'Anyway, I think you know I am impressed by you.'

He was less guarded today, more open in his feeling towards her. She was acutely aware of his desire and, once she had pitied him, less able to resist it. As Arai's mistress or as Kaede's maid she had had status and the protection status gave but now nothing was left to her apart from her own skills and this man who had saved her life and would not make a bad husband. There was no reason not to sleep with him, so after they stopped to eat, around noon, she let him lead her into the shade of the trees. The smell of pine needles and cedar was all around them, the sun warm, the breeze soft. A distant waterfall splashed, muted. Everything spoke of new life and spring. His love-making was not as bad as she'd feared, though he was rough and quick compared with Ishida.

Shizuka thought, *If this is what is to be I must make the best of it.*

And then she thought, *What's happened to me? Have I suddenly got old? A year ago I would have given a man like Kondo short shrift, but a year ago I still thought I was Arai's. And so much has happened since then, so much intrigue, so many deaths: losing Shigeru and Naomi, pretending all the time I did not care; barely able to weep, not even when the father of my children tried to have me murdered, not even when I thought Kaede would die . . .*

It was not the first time that she had felt sickened by the constant pretence, the ruthlessness, the brutality. She thought of Shigeru and his desire for peace and justice, and of Ishida, who sought to heal, not to kill, and felt her heart twist with more pain than she would have thought possible. *I am old,* she thought. *Next year I will turn thirty.*

Her eyes went hot and she realized she was about to weep. The tears trickled down her face, and Kondo, mistaking them, held her more closely. Her tears lay wet between her cheek and his chest, forming a pool on the vermilion and sepia pictures that were tattooed on his body.

After a while she stood up and went to the waterfall. Dipping a cloth into the icy water, she washed her face, then cupped her hands to drink. The forest around her was silent apart from the croaking of spring frogs and the first tentative cicadas. The air was already cooling. They must hasten if they were to reach the village before nightfall.

Kondo had already picked up their bundles and slung them onto the pole. Now he lifted it to his shoulder.

'You know,' he said as they walked on, raising his voice so she could hear him, for she, knowing the path, was in front, 'I don't believe you would hurt Takeo. I don't think it would be possible for you to kill him.'

'Why not?' she said, turning her head. 'I've killed men before!'

'I know your reputation, Shizuka! But when you speak of Takeo your face softens as if you pity him. And I don't believe you would ever bring grief to Lady Shirakawa because of the strength of your affection for her.'

'You see everything! You know everything about me! Are you sure you're not a fox spirit?' She wondered if he had discerned her affair with Ishida and prayed he would not speak of it.

'I have Tribe blood in my veins too,' he returned.

'If I am far from Takeo, I will not be torn two ways,' she said. 'The same goes for you.' She walked on for a while in silence and then spoke abruptly, 'I suppose I do pity him.'

'Yet people say you are ruthless.' His voice had recovered its hint of mockery.

'I can still be moved by suffering. Not the sort people bring on themselves through their own stupidity, but the suffering that is inflicted by fate.'

The slope steepened and she felt her breath catch. She did not speak until it lessened again but she was thinking of the threads that bound her life with Takeo and Kaede, and with the destiny of the Otori.

There was room on the path now for two, and Kondo came up alongside her.

'Takeo's upbringing among the Hidden, his adoption into the warrior class by Shigeru, and the demands of the Tribe seem irreconcilable elements in his life,' Shizuka said finally. 'They will tear him apart. And now this marriage will arouse more hostility against him.'

'I don't suppose he'll live for long. Sooner or later someone will catch up with him.'

'You never know,' she replied, pretending a lightness she did not feel. 'Perhaps it would not be possible for me, or anyone else, to kill him – because we would never get near him.'

'Two attempts were made on his way to Terayama,' Kondo said. 'They both failed and three men died.'

'You did not tell me that!'

'I suppose I didn't want to alarm Lady Shirakawa and make her ill again. But with every death the rage against him grows stronger. It's not a way I would like to live.'

No, Shizuka thought, *nor would any of us. We would like to live without intrigue and suspicion. We would like to sleep deeply at night, not listening for every unfamiliar sound, fearing the knife through the floor, the poison in the meal, the unseen archer in the forest. At least for a few weeks I can feel safe in the secret village.*

The sun was beginning to set, sending brilliant rays between the cedars and turning their trunks black. The light spilled extravagantly across the forest floor. For the last few minutes Shizuka had been aware that they were being followed.

It must be the children, she thought, and remembered with a flash of clarity how she had honed her own skills as a child in this very area. She knew every rock, every tree, every contour of the land.

'Zenko! Taku!' she called. 'Is that you?'

One stifled giggle was the only reply. She thought she heard footsteps; loose rocks fell somewhere in the distance. The children were taking the quick way home, running up the ridge and down again, while she and Kondo followed the winding path. She smiled and tried to shake off her dark mood. She had her sons; she would do whatever seemed best for them. And she would follow her grandparents' advice. Whatever they told her to do, she would do. There was a certain comfort in obedience and, as Kondo said, it meant everything to the Tribe. Again, she tried not to think of her own deep disobedience in the past and hoped it would remain buried with the dead.

They left the main path and, clambering over a pile of boulders, followed a smaller one that wound through a craggy ravine. At the far end it made one more twist and began to descend into the valley. Shizuka stopped for a moment; the view never failed to enchant her, the hidden valley in the middle of the rugged mountain country was so surprising. Through the slight haze made up of mist rising from the stream and smoke from hearth fires they could look down on the small collection of buildings, but by the time they had followed the path through the fields the houses stood above them, protected by a strong wooden wall.

The gate, however, was open, and the men guarding it greeted Shizuka cheerfully.

'Hey! Welcome home!'

'Is this how you greet visitors now? Very casual; suppose I was a spy?'

'Your sons already told us you were coming,' one of the guards replied. 'They saw you on the mountain.'

A sweet relief ran through her. She had not realized until this moment the depth of her constant anxiety for them. But they were alive and healthy.

'This is Kondo . . .' she broke off, realizing she did not know his given name.

'Kondo Kiicihi,' he said. 'My father was Kuroda Tetsuo.'

The guards' eyes narrowed as they registered the name, placed him in the Tribe hierarchy, and summed him up by appearance as well as by history. They were cousins or nephews of hers: she had grown up with them, spending months on end with her grandparents, sent there for

93

training while she was still a child. When they were boys she had competed with them, studied and outwitted them. Then her life had led her back to Kumamoto and to Arai.

'Be careful of Shizuka!' one of them now warned Kondo. 'I'd sooner sleep with a viper.'

'You've got more chance,' she retorted.

Kondo said nothing but glanced at her, one eyebrow raised, as they walked on.

From outside, the village buildings looked like ordinary farmhouses, with steep-pitched thatch roofs and faded cedar beams. Farming tools, firewood, sacks of rice and reed stalks were all stacked away neatly in the sheds at the end of the buildings. The outer windows were barred with wooden slats and the steps were made from rough-hewn mountain stone. But, within, the houses held many secrets: hidden passageways and entrances, tunnels and cellars, false cupboards and floors which could conceal the whole community if necessary. Few knew of the existence of this secret village, and even fewer found their way here, yet the Muto family were always ready for attack. And here they trained their children in the ancient traditions of the Tribe.

Shizuka felt an involuntary thrill at the memory of it. Her heartbeat quickened. Nothing since then, not even the fight at Inuyama Castle, came anywhere near the intense excitement of those childhood games.

The main house lay in the centre of the village, and at its entrance her family were already waiting to greet her: her grandfather with her two sons and, to her surprise and pleasure, next to the old man, her uncle, Muto Kenji.

'Grandfather, Uncle,' she greeted them demurely, and was about to introduce Kondo when the younger boy ran to her excitedly and threw his arms round her waist.

'Taku!' his older brother rebuked him, and then said, 'Welcome, Mother. It's been such a long time since we saw you.'

'Come here and let me look at you,' she said, delighted by their appearance. They had both grown and had lost their childhood chubbiness. Zenko had turned twelve at the beginning of the year, and Taku ten. Even the younger boy had strength and hardness in his muscles, and they both had direct, fearless eyes.

'He is growing like his father,' Kenji said, clapping Zenko on the shoulder.

It was true, Shizuka thought, gazing on her older son. He was the image of Arai. Taku, she thought, had more of a Muto look, and he, unlike his brother, bore the straight line of his Kikuta relatives across his palms. The sharp hearing and other skills might already be manifesting themselves. But she would find out more about that sort of thing later.

Kondo, meanwhile, had knelt before the two Muto masters, telling them his name and parentage.

'He is the one who saved my life,' Shizuka said. 'You may have heard: there was an attempt to murder me.'

'You are not the only one,' Kenji said, catching her eye, as if to silence her, and indeed she did not want to say too much in front of the boys. 'We'll talk about it later. I'm glad to see you.'

A maid came with water to wash the dust from the travellers' feet.

Shizuka's grandfather said to Kondo, 'You are very welcome and we are deeply grateful to you. We met a long time ago; you were only a child, you probably don't remember. Please, come and eat.'

As Kondo followed the old man inside, Kenji murmured

to Shizuka, 'But what has happened? Why are you here? Is Lady Shirakawa all right?'

'Nothing has changed your fondness for her, I see,' Shizuka replied. 'She has joined Takeo in Terayama. I expect they will marry soon – against all my advice, I might add. It is a disaster for them both.'

Kenji sighed quietly. She thought she saw a slight smile on his face. 'A disaster probably,' he said, 'but one ordained by fate.'

They stepped inside the house. Taku had run ahead to tell his great-grandmother to bring wine and cups, but Zenko walked quietly next to Kondo.

'Thank you for saving my mother's life, sir,' he said formally. 'I am in your debt.'

'I hope we will get to know each other and be friends,' Kondo replied. 'Do you like hunting? Maybe you can take me out on the mountain. I've eaten no meat for months.'

The boy smiled and nodded. 'Sometimes we use traps and, later in the year, falcons. I hope you will still be here then.'

He is a man already, Shizuka thought. *If only I could protect him, if only they both could stay children for ever.*

Her grandmother came with the wine. Shizuka took it from her and served the men. Then she went with the old woman to the kitchen, breathing in deeply, savouring all the familiar smells. The maids, cousins of hers, welcomed her with delight. She wanted to help with the food as she always had, but they would not let her.

'Tomorrow, tomorrow,' her grandmother said. 'Tonight you can be the honoured guest.'

Shizuka sat on the edge of the wooden step that led from the earthen-floored kitchen to the main part of the house. She could hear the murmur of the men talking, the higher voices of the boys, Zenko's already breaking.

'Let's drink a cup together,' her grandmother said, chuckling. 'We didn't expect you, but you're all the more welcome for that. What a jewel, isn't she?' she appealed to the maids who readily agreed.

'Shizuka is prettier than ever,' Kana said. 'More like the boys' sister than their mother.'

'And she's got a good-looking man in tow as usual,' laughed Miyabi. 'Did he really save your life? It's like something out of a story.'

Shizuka smiled and drank the wine in a gulp, happy for the moment to be home, listening to the sibilant dialect of her relatives as they pressed her for gossip and news.

'They say Lady Shirakawa is the most beautiful woman in the Three Countries,' Kana said. 'Is it true?'

Shizuka downed another cup, feeling the warmth of the wine hit her stomach and send its cheerful message through her body.

'You've no idea how beautiful,' she replied. 'You say I'm pretty. Well, men look at me and want to sleep with me, but they look at Shirakawa Kaede and despair. They can't bear the fact that such beauty exists and they will never possess it. I tell you, I was far prouder of her looks than of my own.'

'They say she bewitches people,' Miyabi said, 'And whoever desires her dies.'

'She's bewitched your uncle,' the old woman cackled. 'You should hear him talk about her.'

'Why did you leave her?' Kana asked, deftly dropping vegetables sliced as thin as paper into the steamer.

'She's been bewitched herself by love. She's joined Otori Takeo, the Kikuta boy who's caused so much trouble. They are determined to marry. He sent me and Kondo away because the Kikuta have issued an edict against him.'

Kana yelped as she steamed her fingers by mistake.

'Ah, what a shame,' Miyabi sighed. 'They're both doomed, then.'

'What do you expect?' Shizuka retorted. 'You know the punishment for disobedience.' But the corners of her own eyes grew hot as if she were about to weep.

'Come, come,' her grandmother said. She seemed more gentle than Shizuka remembered. 'You've had a long journey. You're tired. Eat and get your strength back. Kenji will want to talk to you tonight.'

Kana spooned rice from the cooking pot into a bowl and heaped vegetables on top of it. They were the spring vegetables of the mountain, burdock, fern shoots and wild mushrooms. Shizuka ate where she was, sitting on the step, as she so often had when she was a child.

Miyabi asked delicately, 'I have to prepare the beds but – where is the visitor to sleep?'

'He can go with the men,' Shizuka replied through a mouthful of rice. 'I will be up till late with my uncle.'

If they slept together in her family home, it would be as good as announcing their marriage. She was not sure yet; she would do nothing without seeking Kenji's advice.

Her grandmother patted her on the hand, her eyes bright and happy, and poured them both another cup of wine. When the rest of the meal was ready and the girls had taken the trays of food to the men, the old woman got to her feet.

'Take a walk with me. I want to go to the shrine. I'll make an offering in thanks for your safe return.'

She took rice balls, wrapped in a cloth, and a small

flask of wine. Next to Shizuka she seemed to have shrunk, and she walked more slowly, grateful for her grand-daughter's arm to lean on.

Night had fallen. Most people were inside, eating the evening meal or preparing for sleep. A dog barked at the door of one house and bounded towards them but was called back by a woman, who then shouted a greeting to them.

From the thick grove that surrounded the shrine, owls were hooting and Shizuka's sharp ears caught the high squeaking of bats.

'Can you still hear them?' her grandmother said, peering at the fleeting shapes. 'And I can barely see them! That's the Kikuta in you.'

'My hearing is nothing special,' Shizuka said. 'I wish it were.'

A stream ran through the grove and fireflies glowed along the bank.

The gates loomed before them, vermilion red in the faint light. They passed beneath them and washed their hands and rinsed their mouths at the fountain. The cistern was of blue-black stone, and a dragon forged from iron kept guard over it. The mountain spring water was icy cold and pure.

Lamps burned in front of the shrine, but it seemed deserted. The old woman placed her offerings on the wooden pedestal in front of the statue of Hachiman, the god of war. She bowed twice, clapped her hands three times, and repeated this ritual three times. Shizuka did the same and found herself praying for the god's protection, not for herself or for her family, but for Kaede and Takeo in the wars that would certainly engulf them. She was almost ashamed of herself and was glad no one could read her thoughts – no one but the god himself.

Her grandmother stood staring upwards. Her face seemed as ancient as the carved statue and as full of numinous power. Shizuka felt her strength and her endurance, and was moved by love and reverence for her. She was glad she had come home. The old people had the wisdom of generations; maybe some of that wisdom would be transferred to her.

They remained motionless for a few moments, and then there was a bustle of sound, a door sliding open, footsteps on the veranda. The shrine priest came towards them, already in his evening clothes.

'I didn't expect anyone so late,' he said. 'Come and drink a cup of tea with us.'

'My granddaughter is back.'

'Ah, Shizuka! It's been a long time. Welcome home.'

They sat with the priest and his wife for a while, chatting casually, catching up with the gossip of the village. Then her grandmother said, 'Kenji will be ready for you now. We must not keep him waiting.'

They walked back between the darkened houses, now mostly silent. People slept early at this time of year and rose early to start the spring work, preparing the fields and planting. Shizuka recalled the days she had spent as a young woman, ankle-deep in the rice fields, planting the seedlings, sharing her youth and fertility with them, while traditional songs were chanted by the older women on the banks. Was she too old to take part in the spring planting now?

If she married Kondo, would she be too old to have another child?

The girls were cleaning up the kitchen and scouring

the dishes when they returned. Taku was sitting where Shizuka had sat earlier, his eyes closing, his head nodding.

'He has a message for you,' Miyabi laughed. 'Wouldn't give it to anyone but you!'

Shizuka sat down beside him and tickled his cheek. 'Messengers can't fall asleep,' she teased.

'Uncle Kenji is ready to talk to you now,' Taku said importantly, and then spoiled the effect by yawning. 'He's in the living room with Grandfather, and everyone else has gone to bed.'

'Where you should be,' Shizuka said, pulling him into her arms. She hugged him tightly and he relaxed against her like a little boy, nuzzling his head into her breasts. After a few moments he began to wriggle and said in a muffled voice, 'Don't keep Uncle Kenji waiting, Mother.'

She laughed and released him. 'Go to bed.'

'Will you still be here in the morning?' He yawned again.

'Of course!'

He gave her a sweet smile. 'I'll show you everything I've learned since I last saw you.'

'Your mother will be astonished,' Miyabi said.

Shizuka walked with her younger son to the women's room, where he still slept. Tonight she would have him next to her, hear his childish breathing through the night, and wake in the morning to see the relaxed limbs and the tousled hair. She had missed that so much.

Zenko slept in the men's room now; she could hear his voice questioning Kondo about the battle of Kushimoto, where he had fought with Arai. She heard the note of pride in the boy's voice when he mentioned his father's name. How much did he know of Arai's campaign against the Tribe, of his attempt on her life?

What will happen to them? she thought. *Will their mixed blood be as destructive to them as Takeo's?*

She said goodnight to Taku, walked through the room and slid the door open to the next room, where her uncle and grandfather sat waiting for her. She knelt before them, touching her brow to the matting. Kenji smiled and nodded, saying nothing. He looked at his father and raised his eyebrows.

'Well, well,' the old man said. 'I must leave you two together.'

As Shizuka helped him to his feet, she was struck by how much he, too, had aged. She walked with him to the door, where Kana was waiting to help him get ready for bed.

'Goodnight, child,' he said. 'What a relief it is to have you here in safety in these dark days. But how long will we be safe anywhere?'

'Surely he's being overly pessimistic,' she said to her uncle as she returned. 'Arai's rage will subside. He'll realize he cannot eradicate the Tribe and that he needs spies like any other warlord. He'll come to terms with us.'

'I agree. No one sees Arai as a problem in the long term. It would be easy enough to lie low until he's calmed down, as you say. But there is another matter that could be far more serious. It seems Shigeru left us an unexpected legacy. The Kikuta believe he kept records of our networks and members and that these records are now in Takeo's possession.'

Her heart stopped in her throat. It seemed to her that she had brought the past to life just by thinking about it.

'Is it possible?' she replied, trying to respond normally.

'The Kikuta master, Kotaro, is convinced of it. At the end of last year he sent Takeo to Hagi, with Akio, to locate the records and bring them back. It seems Takeo went to Shigeru's house, saw Ichiro and then got away from Akio somehow and headed for Terayama. He evaded and killed two agents and an Otori warrior on the way.'

'An Otori warrior?' Shizuka repeated stupidly.

'Yes, the Kikuta are stepping up their contacts with the Otori, both in alliance against Arai and to eliminate Takeo.'

'And the Muto?'

Kenji grunted. 'I have not made a decision yet.'

Shizuka raised her eyebrows and waited for him to go on.

'Kotaro is assuming the records were being looked after at the temple, which in hindsight seems obvious to me. That wicked old Matsuda never gave up plotting despite becoming a priest, and he and Shigeru were very close. I think I can even recall the chest Shigeru carried them in. I can't imagine how I overlooked it. My only excuse is that I had other things on my mind at that time. The Kikuta are furious with me and I'm left looking like an idiot.' He grinned ruefully. 'Shigeru outfoxed me, me who they used to call the Fox!'

'That explains the edict against Takeo,' Shizuka said. 'I thought it was for disobedience. It seemed fierce, but it didn't surprise me. When I heard he was working with Akio I knew there would be trouble.'

'My daughter said so too. She sent a message to me while Takeo was still in our house in Yamagata. There was some incident: he outwitted my wife and escaped for a night, nothing major, and he came back by morning, but Yuki wrote then that he and Akio would end up killing each other. Akio very nearly did die, by the way. Muto

Yuzuru's men pulled him out of the river, half drowned and half frozen.'

'Takeo should have finished him off,' Shizuka couldn't help saying.

Kenji smiled without mirth. 'I'm afraid that was my first reaction too. Akio claimed he tried to prevent Takeo from getting away, but I learned later from Yuki that he was already under instructions to kill him, once the whereabouts of the records had been discovered.'

'Why?' Shizuka said, 'What good does his death do to them?'

'It's not a simple situation. Takeo's appearance has disturbed a lot of people, especially among the Kikuta. His lack of obedience and his recklessness don't help.'

'The Kikuta sound so extreme, whereas you always seemed to give Takeo a lot of leeway,' Shizuka said.

'It was the only way to handle him. I learned that as soon as I got to Hagi. He's got good instincts, he'll do anything for you if you win his loyalty, but you can't force him. He'll break rather than give in.'

'Must be a Kikuta trait,' Shizuka murmured.

'Maybe.' Kenji sighed deeply and stared into the shadows. He did not speak for a while, then said, 'For the Kikuta everything is black and white; you obey or you die, the only cure for stupidity is death, all the things they're brought up to believe.'

If the Kikuta ever find out my part in all this they will kill me, Shizuka thought. *I dare not tell Kenji either.* 'So now Takeo is not only lost to the Tribe, but holds information with which he can destroy us?'

'Yes, and that information will buy him an alliance with Arai sooner or later.'

'He will never be allowed to live,' Shizuka said with renewed sorrow.

'He's survived so far. It's proved harder than the Kikuta thought it would be to get rid of him.' Shizuka thought she detected a note of rueful pride in her uncle's voice. 'And he has the knack of surrounding himself with devoted followers. Half the Otori clan's young warriors have already crossed the border to join him in Terayama.'

'If he and Kaede marry, as I am sure they will,' Shizuka said, 'Arai will be enraged. It may take more than Shigeru's records to placate him.'

'Well, you know Arai better than anyone. There's also the question of his sons, and of you. I haven't told the boys that their father ordered your death, but they're sure to find out sooner or later. It won't bother Taku, he's Tribe through and through, but Zenko idolizes his father. He's not going to be as talented as Taku, and in many ways it would be better for him to be raised by Arai. Is there any possibility of it?'

'I don't know,' Shizuka said. 'The more land he conquers the more sons he will want, I would imagine.'

'We should send someone to him to see how he's reacting – to Takeo's marriage, to the Otori – and how he feels towards the boys. What about Kondo? Shall I send him?'

'Why not?' Shizuka replied, with a certain relief.

'Kondo seems fond of you. Will you marry him?'

'He wants it,' she said. 'I told him I had to ask your advice. But I would like more time to think about it.'

'No need to rush into anything,' Kenji agreed. 'You can give him your answer when he returns.' His eyes gleamed with some emotion that she could not read. 'And I can decide what action to take.'

Shizuka said nothing, but she studied Kenji's face in

the lamplight, trying to make sense of all the pieces of information he had given her, trying to decipher the unspoken as much as the spoken. She felt he was glad to be able to share these concerns with her and guessed he had not told anyone else, not even his own parents. She was aware of the great affection he had had for Shigeru and still held for Takeo and could imagine the conflict that having to collaborate in Takeo's death would cause him. She had never known him, or any other Tribe member, to speak so openly of divisions between the masters.

If the Muto and the Kikuta families were to fall out, could the Tribe survive? It seemed an even greater danger to her than anything Arai or Takeo might do.

'Where is your daughter now?' she asked.

'As far as I know, she is in one of the secret Kikuta villages north of Matsue.' Kenji paused and then said quietly, almost painfully, 'Yuki was married to Akio at the beginning of the year.'

'To Akio?' Shizuka could not help exclaiming.

'Yes, poor girl. The Kikuta insisted and there was no way I could refuse them. There had been talk of a match between them ever since they were both children. I had no rational grounds for withholding my consent anyway, just the irrational sentiments of the father of an only child. My wife did not share these. She was strongly in favour, especially as Yuki was already pregnant.'

Shizuka was astonished. 'With Akio's child?'

He shook his head. She had never before seen her uncle unable to speak like this.

'Not Takeo's?'

He nodded. The lamps flickered; the house lay silent.

Shizuka could think of nothing to say in response. All she could think of was the child Kaede had lost. She seemed to hear again the question Kaede had asked her in the garden at Shirakawa, *Would they have taken the child as they took Takeo?* That the Tribe should have a child of Takeo's seemed like something supernatural to her, the cruel workings of fate that humans cannot hope to escape, turn and twist as they might.

Kenji took a deep breath and went on, 'She became infatuated with Takeo after the incident at Yamagata, and took his side strongly against the Kikuta master and me. As you might imagine, I myself was in considerable anguish over the decision to kidnap Takeo in Inuyama before the assassination attempt on Iida. I betrayed Shigeru. I don't think I will ever forgive myself for the part I played in his death. For years I considered him my closest friend. However, for the sake of unity within the Tribe, I did as the Kikuta desired and delivered Takeo to them. But between you and me, I would have been happy to have died at Inuyama if that could have erased the shame I felt. I have not spoken of this to anyone except you.

'Of course the Kikuta are delighted to have the child. It will be born in the seventh month. They hope it will inherit the skills of both its parents. They blame Takeo's upbringing for all his defects; they intend to raise this child themselves from birth—'

He broke off. The silence in the room deepened. 'Say something, niece, even if it's only that it serves me right!'

'It is not for me to judge you for anything you have done,' she replied in a low voice. 'I am sorry for all you must have suffered. I am amazed at the way fate plays with us like pieces on a board.'

'Do you ever see ghosts?'

'I dream of Lord Shirakawa,' she admitted. After a

107

long pause she added, 'You know that Kondo and I brought about his death to preserve Kaede and her child.'

She heard the hiss of his breath, but he did not speak and after a few moments she continued. 'Her father was out of his mind, on the point of violating and then killing her. I wanted to save her life and the child's. But she lost it anyway and nearly died. I don't know if she remembers what we did, and I would not hesitate to do the same thing again; but for some reason, perhaps because I have never spoken of it to anyone, not even Kondo, it haunts me.'

'If it was to save her life, I'm sure your action was justified,' he replied.

'It was one of those moments when there was no time to think. Kondo and I acted instinctively. I had never killed a man of such high rank before. It seems like a crime to me.'

'Well, my betrayal of Shigeru also seems like a crime. He visits me in dreams. I see him as he looked when we brought him up out of the river. I drew the hood from his face and asked him to forgive me, but he only had strength to speak to Takeo. Night after night he comes to me.' There was another long silence.

'What are you thinking of?' she whispered. 'You would not split the Tribe?'

'I must do what seems best for the Muto family,' he replied. 'And the Kikuta have my daughter and will soon have my grandchild. Obviously these are my first obligation. But I swore to Takeo when I first met him that while I was alive he would be safe. I will not seek his death. We'll wait and see which way he jumps. The Kikuta want the Otori to provoke him and lure him into battle. They've been concentrating all their attention on Hagi and

108

Terayama.' He hissed through his teeth. 'I suppose poor old Ichiro will be their first target. But what do you think Takeo and Kaede will do once they're married?'

'Kaede is determined to inherit Maruyama,' Shizuka replied. 'I imagine they will move south as soon as possible.'

'Maruyama has only a few Tribe families,' Kenji said. 'Takeo will be safer there than anywhere.' He was silent, wrapped in his thoughts. Then he smiled slightly. 'Of course, we can only blame ourselves for the marriage. We brought them together; we encouraged them even. Whatever can have possessed us?'

Shizuka recalled suddenly the training hall in Tsuwano, heard the clash of the wooden poles, the rain pouring down outside, saw their faces young and vivid, on the threshold of passion. 'Perhaps we felt sorry for them. They were both pawns being used in a conspiracy wider than either of them suspected, both likely to die before they had begun to live.'

'Or perhaps you are right and we were the pawns, moved by the hand of fate,' her uncle replied. 'Kondo can leave tomorrow. Stay here for the summer. It will be good to talk about these things with you. I have deep decisions to make that will affect many generations to come.'

Five

The first weeks in Maruyama were spent as Kaede had predicted, in restoring the land. Our welcome was warm and seemingly wholehearted, but Maruyama was an extensive domain with many hereditary retainers and a large body of elders who were as opinionated and conservative as most old men. My reputation as Shigeru's avenger stood me in good stead, but the usual rumours surfaced about how I had achieved it: my doubtful origins, the hint of sorcery. My own Otori warriors were completely loyal and I trusted Sugita, his family, and the men who had fought alongside him, but I had my suspicions of many of the others, and they were equally suspicious of me.

Sugita was delighted by our marriage and confided in me what he had once said to Kaede – that he believed I might unite the Three Countries and bring peace. But the elders generally were surprised by it. No one dared say anything to my face, but from hints and whispered conversations I soon gathered that a marriage to Fujiwara had been expected. It did not bother me particularly – I had no idea then of the extent of the nobleman's power and influence – but like everything else that summer it added to my sense of urgency. I had to move against Hagi; I had to take over the leadership of the Otori clan. Once I had gained what was legally mine and had my base in Hagi, no one would dare question or challenge me.

In the meantime my wife and I became farmers, riding out every day with Sugita, inspecting fields, woods, villages, and rivers, ordering repairs, clearing away dead trees, pruning, and planting. The land was well surveyed and the taxation system sound and not unjust. The domain was rich, although neglected, and its people hardworking and enterprising. They needed very little encouragement to return to the level of activity and prosperity they had enjoyed under Lady Naomi.

The castle and residence were also somewhat neglected, but as Kaede set about restoring them they quickly regained the beauty created by Naomi. The matting was replaced, screens repainted, wooden floors polished. In the garden stood the tea room built by Naomi's grandmother that she had told me about the first time I had met her in Chigawa. She had promised me that one day we would drink tea there together, and when the redecoration of the simple rustic building was completed and Kaede prepared tea I felt that the promise had been fulfilled, even though Naomi herself was no longer alive.

I was conscious of Naomi's spirit, and Shigeru's, with us at all times. As the abbot had said in Terayama, in Kaede and me they seemed to have the chance to live again. We would achieve everything they had dreamed of but had been thwarted in. We placed tablets and offerings in a small shrine deep within the residence, and prayed before it every day for guidance and help. I had a profound sense of relief that I was finally carrying out Shigeru's last requests to me, and Kaede seemed happier than she had ever been before.

It would have been a time of great joy, celebrating

victory and seeing the land and the people begin to flourish again, had it not been for the darker work I felt compelled to undertake, a work that gave me no pleasure at all. Sugita tried to tell me there were no Tribe members in the castle town, so well hidden were they and so secret their operations. But I knew better, for Shigeru had chronicled them all, and I had not forgotten the men Hiroshi had described, who had appeared out of the air, clad in dark clothes, and killed his father. We had found no such bodies among the dead at Asagawa. They had survived the battle and would now be stalking me.

Of the families listed in the records, most were Kuroda and Imai, a few of the richer merchants Muto. There were very few Kikuta this far to the west, but the one existing family maintained their customary authority over the others. I clung to the words of the prophecy that had told me that only my own son could kill me, but even though by day I might believe it I still was alert to every sound, slept lightly at night, ate only food that Manami had prepared or supervised.

I had heard nothing of Yuki and did not know if her child was born or if it was a boy. Kaede continued to bleed regularly throughout the summer, and though I knew she was disappointed not to conceive a child, I could not help feeling a certain relief. I longed for children of our own but I feared the complications they would bring. And what would I do if Kaede bore me a son?

How to deal with the Tribe was a problem that constantly exercised my mind. The first week I was in the town I sent messages to the Kikuta and Muto families informing them that I wished to consult with them and they were to wait on me the following day. That night there was an attempt to break into the residence and steal the records. I woke to hear someone in the room, perceived his barely visible form, challenged him, and pursued him to the outer gates, hoping to take him alive. He lost invisibility as he leaped over the wall and was killed by the guards on the other side before I could prevent it. He was dressed in black and tattooed like Shintaro, the assassin who had tried to kill Shigeru in Hagi. I placed him as one of the Kuroda family.

I sent men the next morning to the Kikuta house and had everyone in it arrested. Then I waited to see who would keep the appointment with me. Two old Muto men turned up, wily and slippery. I gave them the option of leaving the province or renouncing their Tribe loyalties. They said they would have to speak with their children. Nothing happened for two days; then a hidden bowman tried to shoot me as I rode with Amano and Sugita in a remote country area. Shun and I heard the sound together and evaded the arrow; we hunted down the bowman, hoping to get information from him, but he took poison. I thought he might have been the second man Hiroshi had seen, but I had no way of knowing for sure.

By this time I had run out of patience. I thought the Tribe were playing with me, suspecting I would never have the ruthlessness to deal with them. I had all the adults in the Kikuta family I had taken hanged and that night sent patrols to fifty or more houses, with orders to kill everyone in them except children. I hoped to spare the lives of the young ones, but the Tribe poisoned their own children rather than give them to me. The old men came back to me, but my offer had expired. The only choice they were given now was between poison or the sword. They both took poison on the spot.

A few fled from the province. I did not have the

113

resources to track them down. Most sat tight, concealed in secret rooms as I had once been or in hidden villages in the mountains. No one would have been able to ferret them out except me, who knew everything about them and had been trained by them in their own ways. I was privately sickened by my own ruthlessness and horrified that I was massacring families just as my own had been massacred, but I saw no alternative and I do not think I was cruel. I gave them swift deaths; I did not crucify them or burn them alive or hang them upside down by the heels. My aim was to eradicate an evil, not to terrorize the people.

It was not a popular measure with the warrior class, who had benefited from the services of these merchants, had been supplied with soy products and wine, had borrowed money and occasionally taken advantage of the other, darker trade of murder. It added to their mistrust of me. I tried to keep them busy training men and maintaining the borders while I supervised the recovery of the economy. I'd dealt the merchant class a terrible blow by removing its Tribe component, but on the other hand I'd taken all their assets for the domain itself and had set a great deal of wealth, previously tied up by them, circulating through the system. For two weeks it seemed we would be faced with a shortage of essential goods before winter, but then we uncovered a group of enterprising peasants who, fed up with the extortion of the Tribe, had been distilling and fermenting on a small scale in secret and who knew enough about the process to take over production. We provided the money to set them up in the Tribe's former premises, and in return took sixty parts out of a hundred for the domain treasury. This promised to be so lucrative a practice, it seemed we would need to take no more than thirty parts from the rice harvest which in turn made us popular with the farmers and villagers.

I distributed the Tribe's other lands and assets to those who had come with me from Terayama. One small hamlet on the banks of a river was given over to the outcastes, who immediately set about tanning the skins taken from the dead horses. I was relieved that this group who had helped me so much was now settled peacefully, but my protection of them baffled the elders and increased their suspicions.

Every week a few more Otori warriors turned up to join me. The main Otori army that had tried to surround me at Terayama had pursued me as far as the river we had crossed on the outcastes' bridge, and was still encamped there, controlling the roads between Yamagata, Inuyama, and the West and, apparently, giving Arai a few anxieties too.

I joined Kaede most afternoons in the tea room, where, together with Makoto and the Miyoshi brothers, we discussed strategy. My main fear was that if I stayed where I was for too long, I would be encircled by the Otori to the north and Arai to the southeast. I knew Arai was likely to return to his own town, Kumamoto, during the summer. I could not hope to fight on two fronts. We decided that now was a good time to send Kahei and Gemba to Arai to try to make peace of some kind for however short a period. I was aware I had very little to bargain with: our brief alliance against Iida, Shigeru's legacy and the records of the Tribe. On the other hand, I had enraged him by my earlier disappearance and insulted him by my marriage, and for all I knew, his anger against the Tribe might already have been tempered by expediency.

I had no illusions about peace with the Otori. I could

not negotiate with Shigeru's uncles and they would never abdicate in my favour. The clan was already so divided that it was for all intents in a state of civil war. If I attacked their main force, even if we were victorious, they would simply fall back to Hagi, where they could easily hold us off until winter itself defeated us. Despite the recovery of the Maruyama domain, we did not have the resources for a long siege at such a distance from our home base.

I'd escaped from the Otori army by using the out-castes, whom no one else had dreamed of approaching, and now I began to wonder how I might take them by surprise again. When I thought of the city, I saw it lying in the cup of the bay, so defensible on its landward side, so open to the sea. If I could not get to Hagi by land, might I not be able to go by water?

Troops that could be transported rapidly by sea: I knew of no warlord who had such a force. Yet history tells us that hundreds of years ago a huge army sailed from the mainland and would have been victorious had the Eight Islands not been saved by a storm sent from Heaven. My thoughts kept turning to the boy who'd been my friend in Hagi, Terada Fumio, who had fled with his family to the island of Oshima. Fumio had taught me about ships and sailing, he had taught me to swim, and he had hated Shigeru's uncles as much as I did. Could I turn him into an ally now?

I did not speak openly of these ideas, but one night, after the others had retired, Kaede – who watched me all the time and knew all my moods – said, 'You are thinking of attacking Hagi in some other way?'

'When I lived there I became friendly with the son of a family, the Terada, who had been fishermen. The Otori lords raised the taxation of their catch to such an extent that they took their boats and moved to Oshima – it's an island off the north-west coast.'

'They became pirates?'

'Their markets were closed to them; it was impossible to live by fishing alone. I'm thinking of paying them a visit. If the Terada have enough resources and are willing to help me, it would be possible to take Hagi by sea. But it must be done this year, and that means I must go before the typhoons begin.'

'Why do you have to go yourself?' Kaede asked. 'Send a messenger.'

'Fumio will trust me, but I don't think his family will talk to anyone else. Now that the rains are over, Kahei and Gemba must go at once to Inuyama. I'll go with a few men, Makoto, Jiro maybe.'

'Let me come with you,' Kaede said.

I thought of the complexities of travelling with my wife, of bringing one woman at least to accompany her, of finding suitable accommodation . . .

'No, stay here with Sugita. I don't want us both to be absent from the domain at the same time. Amano must stay here too.'

'I wish I were Makoto,' she said, 'I am jealous of him.'

'He is jealous of you,' I said lightly. 'He thinks I spend far too much time talking to you. A wife is for one thing, providing heirs. Everything else a man should look for in his comrades.'

I had been joking, but she took me seriously. 'I should give you a child.' Her lips were pressed together and I saw her eyes moisten with tears. 'Sometimes I am afraid I will never conceive again. I wish our child had not died.'

'We will have other children,' I said. 'All girls, all as

beautiful as their mother.' I took her in my arms. It was a warm, still night, but her skin felt cold and she was shivering.

'Don't go,' she said.

'I will only be away a week at most.'

The next day the Miyoshi brothers set out for Inuyama to plead my cause with Arai, and the day after, I left with Makoto for the coast. Kaede was still upset and we parted with a slight coolness between us. It was our first disagreement. She wanted to come with me; I could have let her, but I did not. I did not know how long it would be or how much we would both suffer before I saw her again.

Still, I rode out cheerfully enough with Makoto, Jiro and three men. We went in unmarked travelling clothes so we could move swiftly and without formalities. I was happy to be leaving the castle town for a while and happy, too, to be able to set aside the ruthless work I'd undertaken to eradicate the Tribe. The plum rains had ended, the air was clear, the sky deep blue. Along the road we saw signs everywhere of the land's gradual return to prosperity. The rice fields were brilliant green, the harvest would be brought in; this winter, at least, no one would starve.

Makoto was silent and reserved in Kaede's presence, but when we were alone together we talked as only the closest friends can. He had seen me at my weakest and my most vulnerable, and I trusted him as I trusted no one else. I opened my heart to him, and, apart from Kaede, only he knew of my constant expectation of attack from the Tribe and my deep dislike of what I had to do to eradicate them. The only thing that pained him about me was the depth of my love for Kaede. He was jealous, perhaps, though he tried to hide it; but, over and above that, he thought there was something unnatural about it: it was not seemly for a man to feel such passion for his wife. He did not speak of it, but I read the disapproval in his expression.

He had taken Jiro under his wing with his usual unobtrusive thoughtfulness and found the time to teach him writing as well as training with the pole and spear. Jiro proved quick to learn. He seemed to grow several inches over the summer and began to fill out, too, now that he was eating properly. Occasionally, I suggested that he return to his family in Kibi and help with the harvest there, but he begged to be allowed to stay, swearing he would serve either myself or Makoto for the rest of his life. He was typical of most of the farmers' sons who had come to fight for me: quick-witted, courageous, strong. We armed them with long spears and fitted them out with leather armour, dividing them into units of twenty men, each with its own leader. Any who showed the right aptitude we trained as bowmen. I counted them among my greatest assets.

On the afternoon of the third day we came to the coast. It was not as bleak as around Matsue; indeed, on that late summer day, it looked beautiful. Several steep-sided islands rose abruptly from a tranquil sea whose colour was deep blue, almost indigo. The breeze ruffled the surface into triangular waves like knife blades. The islands seemed uninhabited, with nothing breaking the solid green of the pines and cedars that clung to them.

Far in the distance, just visible in the haze, we could make out the bulky shape of Oshima, the cone of its volcano hidden in the clouds. Beyond it, out of sight, lay the city of Hagi.

'Presumably that's the dragon's lair,' Makoto said. 'And how do you intend to approach it?'

From the cliff where our horses stood, the road led

down to a small bay where there was a fishing village – a few hovels, boats pulled up on the shingle, the gates of a shrine to the sea god.

'We could take a boat from there,' I said doubtfully, for the place looked deserted. The fires that the fishermen burn to get salt from seawater were no more than piles of black and charred logs, and there was no sign of movement.

'I've never been in a boat,' Jiro exclaimed, 'except across the river!'

'Nor have I,' Makoto muttered to me as we turned the horses' heads towards the village.

The villagers had already seen us and gone into hiding. As we approached the hovels they tried to run away. The beauty of the place was deceptive; I'd seen many impoverished people throughout the Three Countries, but these were far and away the poorest and the most wretched. My men ran after one of them who was stumbling across the shingle, carrying a child of about two years. They caught up with him easily, hampered as he was by his son, and dragged them both back. The child was wailing but the father had the look of a man beyond grief or fear.

'We are not going to hurt you or take anything from you,' I said. 'I'm looking for someone to go with me to Oshima.'

He glanced up at me, disbelief written in his face. One of the men holding him cuffed him hard.

'Speak when his lordship questions you!'

'His lordship? Being a lord won't save him from Terada. You know what we call Oshima? The entrance to hell.'

'Hell or not, I have to go there,' I replied. 'And I'll pay for it.'

'What good is silver to us?' he said, bitterly. 'If anyone knows I have silver, they'll kill me for it. I'm only alive because I have nothing left worth stealing. Bandits have already taken my wife and my daughters. My son was not weaned when they kidnapped his mother. I nursed him on rags dipped in water and brine. I chewed fish and fed him from my own mouth like a sea bird. I cannot leave him to go with you to certain death at Oshima.'

'Then find us someone who will take me,' I said. 'When we return to Maruyama we'll send soldiers to destroy the bandits. The domain now belongs to my wife, Shirakawa Kaede. We will make this place safe for you.'

'Doesn't matter who it belongs to, your lordship will never return from Oshima.'

'Take the child,' Makoto ordered the men angrily, saying to the fisherman, 'He will die unless you obey!'

'Take him!' the man shrieked. 'Kill him! I should have done so myself. Then kill me and my suffering will be over.'

Makoto leaped from his horse to seize the child himself. It clung to its father's neck like a monkey, sobbing noisily.

'Leave them,' I said, dismounting, too, and giving the reins to Jiro. 'We cannot force them.' I studied the man, taking care not to meet his gaze; after his first quick glance he did not look at me again. 'What food do we have?'

Jiro opened the saddlebags and brought out rice wrapped in kelp and flavoured with pickled plums, and dried fish.

'I want to talk to you alone,' I said to the man. 'Will you and the child sit down and eat with me?'

He swallowed hard, his gaze fixed on the food. The

121

child smelled the fish and turned its head. It held out one hand towards Jiro.

The father nodded.

'Let him go,' I said to the men and took the food from Jiro. Outside one of the hovels was an upturned boat. 'We'll sit there.'

I walked towards it and the man followed. I sat and he knelt at my feet, bowing his head. He placed the child on the sand and pushed its head down too. It had stopped sobbing, but sniffed loudly from time to time.

I held out the food and whispered the first prayer of the Hidden over it, watching the man's face all the time.

His mouth formed words. He did not take the food. The child reached out for it, beginning to wail again. The father said, 'If you are trying to trap me, may the Secret One forgive you.' He said the second prayer and took the rice ball. Breaking it into pieces, he fed it to his son. 'At least my child will have tasted rice before he dies.'

'I am not trying to trap you.' I handed him another rice ball, which he crammed into his mouth. 'I am Otori Takeo, heir to the Otori clan. But I was raised among the Hidden and my childhood name was Tomasu.'

'May he bless and keep you,' he said, taking the fish from me. 'How did you pick me?'

'When you said you should have killed yourself and your son, your eyes flickered upwards as if you were praying.'

'I have prayed many times for the Secret One to take me to him. But you know it is forbidden for me to kill myself or my son.'

'Are you all Hidden here?'

'Yes, for generations, since the first teachers came from the mainland. We've never been persecuted for it as such.

122

The lady of the domain who died last year used to protect us. But bandits and pirates grow bolder and more numerous all the time, and they know we cannot fight back.'

He broke off a piece of fish and gave it to the child. Holding it in his fist the boy stared at me. His eyes were red-rimmed and sticky, his face filthy and streaked with tears. He suddenly gave me a small, wavering smile.

'As I told you, my wife inherited this domain from Lady Maruyama. I swear to you we will clear it of all bandits and make it safe for you. I knew Terada's son in Hagi and I need to speak to him.'

'There's one man who may help you. He has no children, and I've heard he's been to Oshima. I'll try to find him. Go to the shrine. The priests ran away, so there's no one there, but you can use the buildings and leave your horses and men there. If he's willing to take you, he'll come to you tonight. It's half a day's sailing to Oshima and you'll need to leave on the high tide – morning or evening, I'll leave that to him.'

'You won't regret helping us,' I said.

For the first time a smile flickered across his face. 'Your lordship may regret it once you get to Oshima.'

I stood and began to walk away. I'd gone no more than ten paces when he called to me, 'Sir! Lord Otori!'

When I turned he ran to me, the child toddling after him, still sucking on the fish. He said awkwardly, 'You will kill then?'

'Yes,' I said, 'I have killed and I will kill again, even if I am damned for it.'

'May he have mercy on you,' he whispered.

The sun was setting in a blaze of vermilion, and long shadows lay across the black shingle. Seabirds called in harsh mournful voices like lost souls. The waves sucked and dragged at the stones with a heavy sighing.

The shrine buildings were decaying, the timbers coated in lichen, rotting away beneath the moss-covered trees, which had been twisted into grotesque shapes by the north winds of winter. Now, though, the night was windless, oppressive and still, the sighing of the waves echoed by the shrill of cicadas and the whine of mosquitoes. We let the horses graze in the unkempt garden and drink from the ponds. These were empty of fish, which had all been eaten long since; a solitary frog croaked forlornly and occasionally owls hooted.

Jiro made a fire, burning green wood to keep the insects away, and we ate a little of the food we'd brought with us, rationing ourselves since we obviously would not find anything to eat here. I told the men to sleep first; we would wake them at midnight. I could hear their voices whispering for a while and then their breathing became even.

'If this man doesn't show up tonight, what then?' Makoto asked.

'I believe he will come,' I replied.

Jiro was silent by the fire, his head rolling forward as he fought sleep.

'Lie down,' Makoto told him, and when the boy had fallen into the sudden slumber of his age, he said quietly to me, 'What did you say to tame the fisherman?'

'I fed his child,' I replied. 'Sometimes that's enough.'

'It was more than that. He was listening to you as though you spoke the same language.'

I shrugged. 'We'll see if this other fellow turns up.'

Makoto said, 'It is the same with the outcaste. He dares approach you as if he has some claim on you, and speaks to you almost as an equal. I wanted to kill him for his insolence at the river, but you listened to him and he to you.'

'Jo-An saved my life on the road to Terayama.'

'You even know his name,' Makoto said. 'I have never known an outcaste by name in my entire life.'

My eyes were stinging from the smoky fire. I did not reply. I had never told Makoto that I'd been born into the Hidden and raised by them. I had told Kaede but no one else. It was something I'd been brought up never to speak of and maybe the only teaching I still obeyed.

'You've talked about your father,' Makoto said. 'I know he was of mixed Tribe and Otori blood. But you never mention your mother. Who was she?'

'She was a peasant woman from Mino. It's a tiny village in the mountains on the other side of Inuyama, almost on the borders of the Three Countries. No one's ever heard of it. Perhaps that's why I have a strong bond with outcastes and fishermen.'

I tried to speak lightly. I did not want to think about my mother. I had travelled so far from my life with her, and from the beliefs I had been raised in, that when I did think of her it made me uneasy. Not only had I survived when all my people had died but I no longer believed in what they had died for. I had other goals now – other, far more pressing concerns.

'Was? She's no longer alive?'

In the silent, neglected garden, the fire smoking, the sea sighing, a tension grew between us. He wanted to know my deepest secrets; I wanted to open my heart to him. Now that everyone else slept and only we were awake in this eerie place, maybe desire also crept in. I was always aware of his love for me; it was something I had come to count on, like the loyalty of the Miyoshi brothers, like my love for Kaede. Makoto was a constant in my world. I needed him. Our relationship might have changed since the night he had comforted me at Terayama, but at this moment I remembered how lonely and vulnerable I had been after Shigeru's death, how I had felt I could tell him anything.

The fire had died down so I could barely see his face but I was aware of his eyes on me. I wondered what he suspected; it seemed so obvious to me that I thought at any moment he would come out with it himself.

I said, 'My mother was one of the Hidden. I was brought up in their beliefs. She and all my family, as far as I know, were massacred by the Tohan. Shigeru rescued me. Jo-An and this fisherman are also from the Hidden. We . . . recognize each other.'

He said nothing. I went on, 'I'm trusting you to tell no one.'

'Did our abbot know?'

'He never mentioned it to me, but Shigeru may have told him. Anyway, I am no longer a believer. I've broken all the commandments, particularly the commandment not to kill.'

'Of course I will never repeat it. It would do you irreparable harm among the warrior class. Most of them thought Iida was justified in his persecution of them, and not a few emulated him. It explains many things about you that I did not understand.'

'You, as a warrior and a monk, a follower of the Enlightened One, must hate the Hidden.'

'Not hate so much as feel baffled by their mysterious beliefs. I know so little about them and what I do know is probably distorted. Maybe one day we'll discuss it when we are at peace.'

I heard in his voice an effort to be rational, not to hurt me. 'The main thing I learned from my mother was compassion,' I said, 'Compassion and an aversion to cruelty. But my teaching since then has all been to eradicate compassion and reinforce ruthlessness.'

'These are the requirements of government and war,' he replied. 'That is the path fate leads us along. At the temple we are also taught not to kill, but only saints at the end of their active life can aspire to that. To fight to defend yourself, to avenge your lord, or to bring justice and peace is no sin.'

'So Shigeru taught me.'

There was a moment of silence when I thought he would reach out to me. To be honest, I would not have recoiled. I felt a sudden longing to lie down and be held by someone. I might even have made the slightest of movements towards him. But he was the one who withdrew. Rising to his feet he said, 'Get some sleep. I'll watch for a while and wake the men shortly.'

I stayed close to the fire to keep the mosquitoes away but they still whined around my head. The sea continued its ceaseless surge and ebb on the shingle. I was uneasy about what I had revealed, about my own faithlessness, and about what Makoto would now think of me. Childishly, I would have liked him to reassure me that it made no difference. I wanted Kaede. I feared I would disappear into the dragon's lair at Oshima and never see her again.

Sleep finally came. For the first time since my mother's death I dreamed vividly of her. She stood in front of me, outside our house in Mino. I could smell food cooking and heard the chink of the axe as my stepfather cut firewood. In the dream I felt a rush of joy and relief that they were after all still alive. But there was a scrabbling noise at my feet and I could feel something crawling over me. My mother looked down with empty, surprised eyes. I wanted to see what she was looking at and followed her gaze. The ground was a black, heaving mass of crabs, their shells ripped from their backs. Then the screaming began, the sound I'd heard from another shrine, a lifetime away, as a man was torn apart by the Tohan.

I knew the crabs were going to tear me apart as I had torn the shells from them.

I woke up in horror, sweating. Makoto was kneeling beside me. 'A man has come,' he said. 'He will speak only to you.'

The feeling of dread was heavy on me. I did not want to go with this stranger to Oshima. I wanted to return at once to Maruyama, to Kaede. I wished I could send someone else on what was most likely a fool's errand. But anyone else would probably be killed by the pirates before any message could be delivered. Having come this far, having been sent this man who would take me to Oshima and the Terada, I could not turn back.

The man was kneeling behind Makoto. I was unable to see much of him in the dark. He apologized for not coming earlier, but the tide was not right until the second half of the hour of the Ox, and with the moon nearly full he thought I would prefer to go at night rather than wait for the afternoon tide. He seemed younger than the fisherman who'd sent him to me, and his speech was more refined and better educated, making him hard to place.

Makoto wanted to send at least one of the men with me, but my guide refused to take anyone else, saying his boat was too small. I offered to give him the silver before we left, but he laughed and said there was no point handing it over to the pirates so easily; he would take it when we returned, and if we did not return, someone else would come for it.

'If Lord Otori does not return there will be no payment but the blade,' Makoto said grimly.

'But if I die, my dependents deserve some compensation,' he returned. 'These are my conditions.'

I agreed to them, overriding Makoto's misgivings. I wanted to get moving, to shake off the dread left by the dream. My horse Shun whickered to me as I left with the man. I'd charged Makoto to look after him with his life. I took Jato with me and, as usual, hidden under my clothes the weapons of the Tribe.

The boat was pulled up just above the high-water mark. We did not speak as we went to it. I helped him drag it into the water and jumped in. He pushed it further out and then leaped in himself, sculling from the stern with the single oar. Later I took the oar while he hoisted a small square sail made of straw. It gleamed yellow in the moonlight, and amulets attached to the mast jingled in the off-shore wind, which, together with the flow of the tide, would carry us to the island.

It was a brilliant night, the moon almost full throwing a silver track across the unruffled sea. The boat sang its song of wind and wave, the same song I remembered from the boats I'd been in with Fumio in Hagi. Something of the freedom and the illicit excitement of those nights came back to me now, dispelling the net of dread that the dream had caught me in.

Now I could see the young man standing at the end of

the boat quite clearly. His features looked vaguely familiar; yet, I did not think we had ever met before.

'What's your name?'

'Ryoma, sir.'

'No other name?'

He shook his head and I thought he was not going to say any more. Well, he was taking me to Oshima; he did not have to talk to me as well. I yawned and pulled my robe closer round me. I thought I might as well sleep for a while.

Ryoma said, 'If I had another name it would be the same as yours.'

My eyes snapped open and my hand went to Jato, for my first thought was that he meant Kikuta – that he was another of their assassins. But he did not move from the stern of the boat and went on calmly but with a trace of bitterness. 'By rights I should be able to call myself Otori, but I have never been recognized by my father.'

His story was a common enough one. His mother had been a maid at Hagi Castle, twenty years or so earlier. She had attracted the attention of the youngest Otori lord, Masahiro. When her pregnancy had been discovered, he claimed she was a prostitute and the child could be anyone's. Her family had no alternative but to sell her into prostitution; she became what she had been called and lost all chance of her son ever being recognized. Masahiro had plenty of legitimate sons and had no interest in any others.

'Yet, people say I resemble him,' he said. By now the stars had faded and the sky had paled. Day was breaking with a fiery sunrise as red as the previous night's sunset. I realized, now that I could see him properly, why he'd looked familiar. He had the Otori stamp on his features just as I did, marred like his father's by a slightly receding chin and cowed eyes.

'There is a likeness,' I said. 'So we are cousins.'

I did not tell Ryoma, but I recalled all too clearly Masahiro's voice when I had overheard him say: *If we were to adopt all our illegitimate children . . .* His son intrigued me; he was what I would have been but for the slightest divergences in our paths. I had been claimed by both sides of my ancestry, he by neither.

'And look at us,' he said. 'You are Lord Otori Takeo, adopted by Shigeru and rightful heir to the domain, and I am not much better than an outcaste.'

'You know something of my history, then?'

'My mother knows everything about the Otori,' he said with a laugh. 'Besides, you must know your own fame.'

His manner was strange, ingratiating and familiar at the same time. I imagined his mother had spoiled him, bringing him up with unrealistic expectations and false ideas about his status, telling him stories about his relatives, the Otori lords, leaving him proud and dissatisfied, ill-equipped to deal with the reality of his life.

'Is that why you agreed to help me?'

'Partly. I wanted to meet you. I've worked for the Terada; I've been to Oshima many times. People call it the entrance to hell, but I've been there and survived.' His voice sounded almost boastful, but when he spoke again it was with a note of pleading. 'I hoped you might help me in return.' He glanced at me. 'Are you going to attack Hagi?'

I was not going to tell him too much in case he was a spy. 'I think it's general knowledge that your father and his older brother betrayed Lord Shigeru to Iida. I hold them responsible for his death.'

He grinned then. 'That's what I hoped. I have a score to settle with them too.'

'With your own father?'

'I hate him more than I would have thought it possible to hate any man,' he replied. 'The Terada hate the Otori too. If you move against them, you may find allies at Oshima.'

This cousin of mine was no fool; he knew very well what my errand was. 'I'm in your debt for taking me there,' I said. 'I've incurred many debts in seeking to avenge Shigeru's death fully, and when I hold Hagi I'll repay them all.'

'Give me my name,' he said. 'That's all I want.'

As we approached the island he told me how he went there from time to time, taking messages and snippets of information about expeditions to the mainland or shipments of silver, silk and other precious goods between the coastal towns.

'The Terada can do no more than irritate the Otori,' he said, 'but between you maybe you can destroy them.'

I neither agreed nor disagreed with him but tried to change the subject, asking him about the fisherman and how he came to know him.

'If you mean, do I believe the nonsense he does, the answer is no!' he said. He caught my look and laughed. 'But my mother does. It's quite widespread among prostitutes. Perhaps it consoles them for their wretched lives. And besides, they should know if anyone does that all men are the same under their trappings. I don't believe in any god or any life beyond this one. No one's punished after death. That's why I want to see them punished now.'

The sun had burned off the mist and the island's cone shape was now clearly visible, looming up out of the ocean, smoke rising from it. The waves broke white against the grey-black cliffs. The wind had strengthened and drove us skimming over the swell. The tidal race past the island quickened. I felt my stomach heave as we sped down the face of a huge green billow and up the other side. I stared upwards towards the craggy island and took a couple of deep breaths. I did not want to be seasick when I faced the pirates.

Then we rounded the headland and came into the lee. Ryoma shouted to me to take the oar as the sail fluttered and sagged. He untied it and let it fall, then sculled the boat through the calmer water towards the sheltered port.

It was a natural deepwater harbour, with stone walls and breakwaters constructed around it. My heart lifted at the sight of the fleet of vessels moored there, ten or twelve at least, sturdy and seaworthy, capable of carrying dozens of men.

The port was guarded by wooden forts at each end, and I could see men inside at the arrow slits, bows no doubt trained on me. Ryoma waved and shouted, and two men emerged from the nearer fort. They did not wave back, but as they walked towards us one of them nodded perfunctorily in recognition.

As we approached the quayside he shouted, 'Hey, Ryoma, who's the passenger?'

'Lord Otori Takeo,' Ryoma called back importantly.

'Is that so? Your brother, is he? Another of your mother's mistakes?'

Ryoma took the boat up to the wharf skilfully enough and held it steady while I disembarked. The two men were still chuckling. I did not want to start a brawl, but I was not going to let them insult me and get away with it.

'I am Otori Takeo,' I said. 'No one's mistake. I am here to speak to Terada Fumio and his father.'

'And we're here to keep people like you away from them,' said the larger guard. His hair was long, his beard as thick as a northerner's, his face scarred. He waved his sword in my face and grinned. It was all too easy; his arrogance and stupidity made him immediately vulnerable to the Kikuta sleep. I held his gaze, his mouth dropped open, and his grin turned to a gasp of astonishment as his eyes rolled back and his knees buckled. He was a heavy man and he went down heavily, striking his head on the stones.

The other slashed out at me at once with his sword, but it was exactly the move I had expected and I'd already split myself and drawn Jato. As his sword went uselessly through my image, I struck it, twisted it and sent it flying out of his hand.

'Please tell Terada I am here,' I said.

Ryoma had fastened the boat and was on the quayside. He picked up the man's sword. 'This is Lord Otori, you idiot. The one all the stories are about. You're lucky he didn't strike you dead on the spot.'

Other men had come running from the fort. They all now dropped to their knees.

'Forgive me, lord. I didn't mean to offend you,' the guard stammered, his eyes wide at what he no doubt thought was sorcery.

'Luckily for you I'm in a good mood,' I said. 'But you insulted my cousin. I think you should apologize to him.'

With Jato pointed at his throat the man did so, causing Ryoma to smirk with satisfaction.

'What about Teruo?' the guard said, gesturing at his unconscious companion.

'He won't come to any harm. When he wakes up he'll have learned better manners. Now, be so good as to inform Terada Fumio of my arrival.'

Two of them hurried away while the rest returned to the fort. I sat down on the quay wall. A tortoiseshell tom-cat who had watched the whole encounter with interest came and sniffed at the recumbent man, then jumped onto the wall next to me and began to wash itself. It was the fattest cat I'd ever seen. Seafaring men are reputed to be superstitious; no doubt they believed the cat's colouring made it lucky, so they pampered it and fed it well. I wondered if they took it with them on their voyages.

I stroked the cat and looked around. Behind the port lay a small village, and halfway up the hill behind it was a substantial wooden building, part house and part castle. It would have a fine view of the coast and the sea-lanes all the way to the city of Hagi. I couldn't help admiring the position and construction of the place and could understand why no one had been able to expel the pirates from their lair.

I saw the men hurry up the mountain path and heard their voices as they reported their message at the gates of the residence. Then I caught the familiar sound of Fumio's voice, a little deeper and more mature but with the same excited cadence that I remembered. I stood and walked to the end of the quay. The cat jumped down and followed me. By now quite a crowd had gathered, hostile and suspicious. I kept my hand near my sword, and hoped the cat's presence would reassure them. They stood watching me curiously, most of them as tense as I was, while Ryoma kept them informed of my identity. 'This is Lord Otori

Takeo, Lord Shigeru's son and heir, who killed Iida.' Every now and then he added, almost to himself, 'He called me cousin.'

Fumio came running down the hill. I'd been worried about my reception but it was as warm as I could have hoped. We embraced like brothers. He looked older, had grown a moustache, and had filled out through the shoulders – in fact he seemed as well fed as the cat – but his mobile face and lively eyes were unchanged.

'You came alone?' he asked, standing back and studying me.

'This man brought me.' I indicated Ryoma who had dropped to the ground at Fumio's approach. Whatever his pretensions, he knew where the real power lay. 'I cannot stay long; I hope he will take me back again tonight.'

'Wait here for Lord Otori,' Fumio told him, and then as we began to walk away he called off-handedly to the guards, 'Give him something to eat.'

And don't tease him, I wanted to add, but was afraid of shaming him more. I hoped they would treat him better now but doubted it. He was the sort that invited ridicule, doomed always to be a victim.

'I imagine you've come for a purpose,' Fumio said, striding up the hill. He'd lost none of his energy and stamina. 'We'll bathe and eat, then I'll take you to my father.'

No matter how urgent my mission, the lure of hot water was more pressing. The fortified house had been built around a string of pools where water bubbled from the rocks. Even without its violent inhabitants, Oshima, the entrance to hell, would have been a ferocious place. The volcano smoked above us, the air smelled of sulphur, and steam rose from the surface of the pools, where boulders loomed like the petrified dead.

We undressed and slid into the scalding water. I've never been in hotter. I thought my skin would be stripped from me. After the first agonizing moment the sensation was indescribable. It washed away the days of riding and sleeping rough, the night-time boat trip. I knew I should be on my guard – a boyhood friendship was not much of a basis for trust – but at that moment anyone could have assassinated me and I would probably have died happy.

Fumio said, 'We've had news of you from time to time. You have been busy since we last met. I was very sorry to hear of Lord Shigeru's death.'

'It was a terrible loss, not only for me but for the clan. I am still pursuing his murderers.'

'Iida is dead, though?'

'Yes, Iida has paid but it was the Otori lords who planned Shigeru's death and who betrayed him to Iida.'

'You intend to punish them? You can count on the Terada if you do.'

I told him briefly about my marriage to Kaede, our journey to Maruyama and the forces under our command.

'But I must return to Hagi and take up my inheritance there. The Otori lords will not give it to me peacefully, so I'll take it from them by force. And I prefer it that way for then I will destroy them too.'

Fumio smiled and raised his eyebrows. 'You have changed since I knew you first.'

'I have been forced to.'

We left the hot water, dressed and were served food in one of the house's many rooms. It was like a store house, a treasure trove of valuable and beautiful objects, all presumably stolen from merchant ships: ivory carvings, celadon vases, brocade fabric, gold and silver bowls, tiger and leopard skins. I had never been in a room like it, so many precious things displayed but with none of the restraint and elegance that I was used to in the residences of the warrior class.

'Take a closer look at them,' Fumio said when we'd finished eating. 'I'll go and speak to my father. If there's anything that appeals to you, take it. My father acquires them but they mean nothing to him.'

I thanked him for the offer but I had no intention of taking anything back with me. I sat quietly waiting for his return, outwardly relaxed but on my guard. Fumio's welcome had been affectionate but I had no idea what other alliances the Terada might have; for all I knew they might have an understanding with the Kikuta. I listened, placing everyone in the house, trying to identify voices, accents – though I had long since realized that if I was walking into a trap, I had little chance of escaping. I had truly come alone into the dragon's lair.

I had already placed Terada – the dragon himself – towards the back of the house. I'd heard his voice issuing orders, demanding tea, a fan, wine. The voice was rough, full of energy, like Fumio's, often passionate and also often angry, but sometimes revealing an underlying humour. I would not underestimate Terada Fumifusa. He had escaped the rigid hierarchy of the clan system, defied the Otori, and made his name one of the most feared in the Middle Country.

Finally, Fumio returned for me and led me to the back of the house, to a room like an eagle's nest, perched high above the village and the port, facing towards Hagi. In the distance I could just make out the familiar line of the ranges behind the town. The sea was still and calm, streaked like silk, indigo coloured, the waves forming a snowy fringe around the rocks. An eagle floated below, no bigger than a lark.

I had never been in a room like it. Even the top floor of the tallest castle was not this high or this open to the elements. I wondered what happened when the autumn typhoons came racing up the coast. The building was sheltered by the curve of the island; to construct something like this spoke of an immense pride as great as any warlord's.

Terada sat on a tiger skin facing the opened windows. Next to him on a low table were maps and charts, what looked like records of shipping and a tube not unlike a bamboo flute. A scribe knelt at one end of the table, ink stone in front of him, brush in hand.

I bowed low to Terada and spoke my name and parentage. He returned the bow, which was courteous, for if anyone held power in this place it was undoubtedly he.

'I have heard a lot about you from my son,' he said. 'You are welcome here.' He gestured to me to come and sit at his side. As I moved forward, the scribe touched his head to the ground and stayed there.

'I hear you dropped one of my men without laying a finger on him. How did you do it?'

'He used to do it to dogs when we were boys,' Fumio put in, sitting cross-legged on the floor.

'I have some talents like that,' I said. 'I did not want to hurt him.'

'Tribe talents?' Terada demanded. I had no doubt he'd made use of them himself and knew perfectly well what they might be.

I inclined my head slightly.

His eyes narrowed and his lips pouted. 'Show me what you do.' He reached out and whacked the scribe on the head with his fan. 'Do it to this man.'

'Forgive me,' I said. 'Whatever small talents I have are not to be demonstrated as tricks.'

'Unnh,' he grunted, staring at me. 'You mean you won't perform on demand?'

'Lord Terada has put it exactly.'

There was a moment's uneasy silence, then he chuckled. 'Fumio warned me I wouldn't be able to boss you around. You inherited more than the Otori look; you have their pig-headedness too. Well, I've not much use for magic – unless it's the sort that anyone can wield.' He picked up the tube and placed its end against one eye, closing the other. 'This is my magic,' he said, and handed the tube to me. 'What do you think of this?'

'Put it to your eye,' Fumio said, grinning.

I held it gingerly, trying to sniff it unobtrusively in case it was poisoned.

Fumio laughed. 'It's safe!'

I squinted through the tube and couldn't help gasping. The distant mountains, the town of Hagi, seemed to have leaped towards me. I took the tube away from my eye and they were back where they were before, hazy and indistinct. The Terada, father and son, were both chuckling now.

'What is it?' I said. It did not look or feel like something magic. It had been made by the hands of men.

'It's a sort of glass, carved like a lentil. It makes objects larger and brings the distant close,' Terada said.

'Is it from the mainland?'

'We took it from a mainland ship and they have long had similar inventions there. But I believe this one was made in a distant country by the barbarians of the south.' He leaned forward and took it from me, looked through it himself, and smiled. 'Imagine countries and people who can make such things. We think we are the whole world here on the Eight Islands, but sometimes I think we know nothing about anything.'

'Men bring reports of weapons that kill from a huge distance with lead and fire,' Fumio said. 'We are trying to find some for ourselves.' He gazed out of the window, his eyes filled with restless yearning for that vast world beyond. I imagined confinement to the island was like imprisonment to him.

Something about the strange artefact before me and the weapons of which he spoke filled me with a sense of foreboding. The height of the room, the sheer drop to the rocks below, my own tiredness, made my head reel for a moment. I tried to breathe deeply, calmly, but I could feel cold sweat break out on my forehead and prickle in my armpits. I foresaw that alliance with the pirates would both increase their strength and open the way to a flood of new things that would change completely the society I was struggling to establish myself in. The room had gone silent. I could hear the subdued sounds of the household around me; the beat of the eagle's wings, the distant hiss of the sea, the voices of the men at the port. A woman was singing quietly as she pounded rice, an old ballad of a girl who fell in love with a fisherman.

The air seemed to shimmer like the sea below, as though a veil of silk had been slowly withdrawn from the face of reality. Many months ago Kenji had told me that once all men had the skills that now only the Tribe retained – and among them only a handful of individuals like myself. Soon we would vanish, too, and our skills

141

would be forgotten, overtaken by the technical magic that the Terada so desired. I thought of my own role in eradicating those skills, thought of the Tribe members I'd already destroyed, and felt a searing pang of regret. Yet, I knew I was going to make a pact with the Terada. I would not recoil now. And if the far-seeing tube and the weapons of fire would help me, I would not hesitate to use them.

The room steadied. My blood flowed again. No more than a few moments had passed. Terada said, 'I believe you have a proposal to make. I would be interested to hear it.'

I told him I thought Hagi could only be taken from the sea. I outlined my plan to send half my army as a decoy to tie up the Otori forces on the river bank while transporting the other half by ship and attacking the castle itself. In return for help from the Terada I would reinstate them in Hagi and keep a permanent fleet of warships under their command. Once peace was restored, the clan would finance expeditions to the mainland for the exchange of learning and trade.

'I know the strength and influence of your family,' I concluded. 'I cannot believe that you will stay here in Oshima for ever.'

'It is true that I would like to return to my family home,' Terada replied. 'The Otori confiscated it, as you know.'

'It will be returned to you,' I promised.

'You are very confident,' he exclaimed, snorting with amusement.

'I know I can succeed with your help.'

'When would you make this attack?'

Fumio glanced at me, his eyes bright.

'As soon as possible. Speed and surprise are among my greatest weapons.'

'We expect the first typhoons any day now,' Terada said. 'That's why all our ships are in port. It will be over a month before we can put to sea again.'

'Then we'll move as soon as the weather clears.'

'You're no older than my son,' he said. 'What makes you think you can lead an army?'

I gave him details of our forces and equipment, our base at Maruyama and the battles we had already won. His eyes narrowed and he grunted, saying nothing for a while. I could read in him both caution and the desire for revenge. Finally he smacked his fan on the table, making the scribe flinch. He made a deep bow to me and spoke more formally than he had until now. 'Lord Otori, I will help you in this endeavour and I'll see you instated in Hagi. The house and family of Terada swear it to you. We give you our allegiance, and our ships and men are yours to command.'

I thanked him with some emotion. He had wine brought and we drank to our agreement. Fumio was elated; as I found out later, he had reasons of his own for wanting to return to Hagi, not least the girl he was to marry. The three of us ate the midday meal together, discussing troops and strategy. Towards the middle of the afternoon Fumio took me to the port to show me the ships.

Ryoma had been waiting on the quay, the tomcat sitting next to him. He greeted us effusively and followed me as closely as a shadow as we went on board the nearest ship and Fumio showed me around it. I was impressed by its size and capacity and the way the pirates had fortified it with walls and shields of wood. It was fitted with huge canvas sails as well as many oars. The plan that had been a vague idea in my head suddenly became real.

We arranged that Fumio would send word to Ryoma as soon as the weather was favourable. I would begin moving my men north at the next full moon. The boats would come for us at the shrine, Katte Jinja, and would bring us to Oshima. We would make the assault on the city and the castle from there.

'Exploring Hagi at night – it'll be just like old times,' Fumio said, grinning.

'I can't thank you enough. You must have pleaded my cause with your father.'

'There was no need; he could see all the advantages of an alliance with you and he recognizes you as the rightful heir to the clan. But I don't think he would have agreed if you had not come in person, alone. He was impressed. He likes boldness.'

I had known I must come in that fashion, but the knowledge weighed on me. So much to achieve, only I to achieve it, only I to hold together my patchy alliance.

Fumio wanted me to stay longer, but I was now more eager than ever to get back to Maruyama, to start preparations, to forestall at all costs an attack by Arai. Besides, I did not trust the weather. The air was unnaturally still and the sky had clouded over with a solid leaden colour, black-tinged on the horizon.

Ryoma said, 'If we leave soon we'll have the help of the tide again.'

Fumio and I embraced on the quayside and I stepped down into the little boat. We waved farewell and cast off, letting the tide carry us away from the island.

Ryoma kept gazing anxiously at the leaden sky, and with reason, for we were barely half a mile from Oshima when the wind began to pick up. Within a few moments it was blowing hard, driving a stinging rain into our faces. We could make no headway against it with the oar, and as soon as we tried to put the sail up it was ripped from our hands.

Ryoma shouted, 'We'll have to turn back.'

I could not argue, though my spirits sank in despair at the thought of further delay. He managed to turn the fragile boat with the oar. The swell was getting heavier with every minute, great green waves that loomed above us and flung us upwards only to drop us as if into a chasm. We must both have gone as green as the waves, and on the fourth or fifth drop we both vomited at the same time. The slight acrid smell seemed painfully feeble against the huge backdrop of wind and water.

The gale was blowing us towards the port, and we both struggled with the oar to guide the boat into the entrance. I did not think we would make it; I thought the force of the storm would drive us out into the open sea, but the sudden shelter in the lee of the land gave us a moment's grace to steer behind the breakwater. But even here we were not out of danger. The water inside the harbour was being churned like a boiling vat. Our boat was driven towards the wall, sucked back, and then thrown against it with a sickening smack.

It tipped over; I found myself struggling under water, saw the surface above me, and tried to swim upwards to it. Ryoma was a few feet from me. I saw his face, mouth open, as if he were calling for help. I caught hold of his clothes and dragged him up. We surfaced together. He took a great gasp of air and began to panic, flailing his arms and then grabbing me and almost strangling me. His weight took me underwater again. I could not free myself.

I knew I could hold my breath for a long time, but sooner or later even I, with all my Tribe skills, had to breathe air. My head started to pound and my lungs ached. I tried to free myself from his grip, tried to reach his neck so I could disable him long enough to get us both out of this. I thought clearly, *He is my cousin, not my son,* and then, *Maybe the prophecy was wrong!*

I could not believe I was going to die by drowning. My vision was clouding, alternately black and filled with white light, and I felt an agonizing pain in my head.

I am being pulled into the next world, I thought, and then my face burst through the surface and I was taking great gulps of air.

Two of Fumio's men were in the water with us, attached by ropes to the quay. They had swum down to us and dragged us both up by the hair. They pulled us up onto the stones where we both vomited again, mostly sea water. Ryoma was in a worse state than I was. Like many sailors and fishermen, he did not know how to swim and had a terrible fear of drowning.

The rain was lashing down by now, completely obliterating the distant shore. The pirates' boats grunted and groaned as they were rocked together. Fumio was kneeling beside me.

'If you can walk now, we'll get inside before the worst of the storm.'

I got to my feet. My throat ached and my eyes stung but I was otherwise unhurt. I still had Jato in my belt, and my other weapons. There was nothing I could do against the weather, but I was filled with anger and anxiety.

'How long will it last?'

'I don't think it's a real typhoon, probably just a local storm. It could blow itself out by morning.'

Fumio was too optimistic. The storm blew for three days, and for two more the seas were too heavy for Ryoma's little boat. It needed repairs anyway, which took four days to complete after the rain stopped. Fumio wanted to send me back in one of the pirates' ships, but I did not want to be seen in it or with them, fearing to reveal my strategy to spies. I spent the days restlessly, uneasy about Makoto – would he wait for me, would he return to Maruyama, would he abandon me altogether, now that he knew I was one of the Hidden, and go back to Terayama? – and even more anxious about Kaede. I had not meant to stay away from her for so long.

Fumio and I had the opportunity to have many conversations, about ships and navigation, fighting at sea, arming sailors, and so on. Followed everywhere by the tortoiseshell cat, who was as curious as I was, I inspected all the ships and weapons they had and was even more impressed by their power. And every night, while from below came the noise of the sailors gambling and their girls dancing and singing, we talked until late with his father. I came to appreciate even more the old man's shrewdness and courage, and I was glad he was going to be my ally.

The moon was past the last quarter when we finally set out on a calm sea in the late afternoon to take advantage of the evening tide. Ryoma had recovered from his near drowning and at my request had been received in the Terada residence on our last night and had eaten with us. The old pirate's presence had silenced him completely, but I knew he had felt the honour and been pleased by it.

There was enough wind to put up the new yellow canvas sail that the pirates had made for us. They had also given us fresh charms to replace the ones lost when the boat was damaged, as well as a small carving of the sea god, who they said obviously had us under his special protection. The charms sang in the wind, and as we sped past the southern side of the island there was a distant rumble like an echo, and a small gust of black smoke and ash rushed upwards from the crater. The slopes of the island were shrouded in steam. I gazed at it for a long time, thinking the local people were right when they nicknamed it the entrance to hell. Gradually it dwindled and faded, until the lilac mist of evening came up off the sea and hid it completely.

We made the greater part of the crossing before nightfall, luckily, for the mist turned into solid cloud and when darkness came it was complete. Ryoma alternated between bursts of chattiness and long, brooding silences. I could do little more than trust him and take turns with him at the oar. Long before the dark shape of the land loomed ahead of us, I'd heard the change in the note of the sea, the sucking of the waves on the shingle. We came ashore at the exact spot we had disembarked from, and Jiro was waiting on the beach next to a small fire. He leaped to his feet when the boat scraped on the stones, and held it while I jumped out.

'Lord Otori! We'd given up hope. Makoto was about to return to Maruyama to report you missing.'

'We were delayed by the storm.' I was filled with relief that they were still here, that they had not deserted me.

Ryoma was exhausted but he did not want to leave the boat, nor would he rest till daylight. I guessed, despite his earlier boasting, he was afraid; he wanted to return to his home in the dark without anyone knowing where he'd been. I sent Jiro back to the shrine to fetch the silver we had promised him and whatever food we could spare.

When we returned we would have to secure the coastline before we embarked, which would mean clearing it of bandits. I told Ryoma to expect us as soon as the weather settled.

He had become awkward again. I felt he wanted assurances and promises from me that I was not able to give. I thought I had disappointed him in some way. Perhaps he'd expected me to recognize him legally on the spot and take him with me to Maruyama, but I did not want to saddle myself with another dependent. On the other hand I could not afford to antagonize him. I was relying on him as a messenger and I needed his silence. I tried to impress on him the necessity of utter secrecy, and hinted that his future status would depend on it. He swore he would tell no one and took the money and the food from Jiro with expressions of profound gratitude. I thanked him warmly – I was truly grateful to him – but I couldn't help feeling that an ordinary fisherman would have been easier to deal with and more trustworthy.

Makoto, deeply relieved at my safe return, had accompanied Jiro back down to the beach and as we walked to the shrine I told him of the success of my journey, listening all the while to the faint splash of the oar as Ryoma rowed away in the darkness.

Six

W hen Takeo left for the coast, and the Miyoshi brothers for Inuyama, Kaede saw the excitment and anticipation on their faces and was filled with resentment at being left behind. In the days that followed she was plagued by fears and anxieties. She missed her husband's physical presence more than she would have thought possible; she was jealous of Makoto being allowed to accompany him when she was not; she feared for Takeo's safety and was angry with him at the same time.

His quest for revenge is more important to him than I am, she thought often. *Did he marry me just to further his plans of revenge?* She believed he loved her deeply, but he was a man, a warrior, and if he had to choose, she knew he would choose revenge. *I would be the same if I were a man,* she told herself. *I cannot even give him a child: what use am I as a woman? I should have been born a man. May I be allowed to return as one!*

She told no one of these thoughts. Indeed, there was no one in whom she could confide. Sugita and the other elders were polite, even affectionate, to her but seemed to avoid her company. She kept herself busy all day, overseeing the household, riding out with Amano, and making copies of the records that Takeo had entrusted to her. After the attempted theft she'd thought it would be a wise precaution and she hoped it would help her understand the ferocity of Takeo's campaign against the Tribe and the anguish it had caused him. She herself had been disturbed by the slaughter, and also by the piles of dead after the battle at Asagawa. It took so long to raise a man and life was extinguished so easily. She feared retribution, both from the living and from the dead. Yet, what else could Takeo do when so many were conspiring to kill him?

She, too, had killed, had had men killed on her orders. Had losing her child been punishment for her own actions? Her desires were changing; now she was moved to protect and to nurture, to create life, not to destroy it. Was it possible to hold on to her domain and rule it without violence? She had many hours of solitude to think about these things.

Takeo had said he would be back within a week; the time passed, he did not return, and her anxiety grew. There were plans and decisions that needed to be made about the domain's future but the elders continued to be evasive and every suggestion she made to Sugita was greeted by a deep bow and the advice to wait until her husband returned. Twice she tried to summon the elders for a council meeting, but one by one they pleaded indisposition.

'It's remarkable that everyone is sick on the same day,' she said tartly to Sugita. 'I had no idea that Maruyama was so unhealthy for old people.'

'Be patient, Lady Kaede,' he said. 'Nothing needs to be decided before Lord Takeo's return, and that will be any day now. He may have urgent commands for the men; they must be kept in readiness for him. All we can do is wait for him.'

Her irritation was compounded by the realization that,

even though it was her domain, everyone still deferred to Takeo. He was her husband and she must defer to him, too; yet, Maruyama and Shirakawa were hers and she should be able to act in them as she wished. Part of her was shocked that Takeo had gone to make an alliance with pirates. It was like his association with outcastes and farmers, there was something unnatural about it. She thought it must all come from being born into the Hidden. This knowledge that he had shared with her both attracted and repelled her. All the rules of her class told her that her blood was purer than his and that by birth she was of higher rank. She was ashamed of this feeling and tried to suppress it, but it niggled at her and the longer he was away, the more insistent it became.

'Where is your nephew?' she said to Sugita, wanting distraction. 'Send him to me. Let me look at someone under the age of thirty!'

Hiroshi was hardly better company, equally resentful at being left behind. He had hoped to go to Inuyama with Kahei and Gemba.

'They don't even know the road,' he grumbled. 'I would have shown them everything. I have to stay here and study with my uncle. Even Jiro was allowed to go with Lord Otori.'

'Jiro is much older than you,' Kaede said.

'Only five years. And he's the one who should be studying. I already know far more letters than he does.'

'That's because you started earlier. You should never despise people because they haven't had your opportunities.' She studied him; he was a little small for his age, but strong and well put together; he would be a handsome man. 'You are about the same age as my sister,' she said.

'Does your sister look like you?'

'People say so. I think she is more beautiful.'

'That couldn't be possible,' he said quickly, making her laugh. His face coloured slightly. 'Everyone says Lady Otori is the most beautiful woman in the Three Countries.'

'What have they seen?' she retorted. 'In the capital, in the emperor's court, there are women so lovely men's eyes shrivel up when they look at them. They are kept behind screens lest the whole court go blind.'

'What do their husbands do?' he said doubtfully.

'They have to wear blindfolds,' she teased, and threw a cloth that lay next to her over his head. She held him playfully for a few moments, then he twisted away from her. She saw he was ruffled; she had treated him like a child and he wanted to be a man.

'Girls are lucky, they don't have to study,' he said.

'But my sister loves to study and so do I. Girls should learn to read and write just the same as boys. Then they can help their husbands, as I am helping mine.'

'Most people have scribes to do that sort of thing, especially if they can't write themselves.'

'My husband can write,' she said swiftly, 'but like Jiro he started learning later than you.'

Hiroshi looked horrified. 'I didn't mean to say anything against him! Lord Otori saved my life and revenged my father's death. I owe everything to him, but . . .'

'But what?' she prompted, uncomfortably aware of some shadow of disloyalty.

'I'm only telling you what people say,' Hiroshi said. 'They say he is strange. He mixes with outcastes; he lets farmers fight; he has started a campaign against certain merchants that no one understands. They say he cannot

153

have been brought up as a warrior and they wonder what his upbringing was.'

'Who says it? The townspeople?'

'No, people like my family.'

'Maruyama warriors?'

'Yes, and some say he is a sorcerer.'

She could hardly be surprised; these were exactly the things that worried her about Takeo; yet, she was outraged that her warriors should be so disloyal to him.

'Maybe his upbringing was a little unusual,' she said, 'but he is heir to the Otori clan by blood and by adoption, as well as being my husband. No one has the right to say anything against him.' She would find out who it was and have them silenced. 'You must be my spy,' she said to Hiroshi. 'Report to me anyone who gives the slightest sign of disloyalty.'

After that Hiroshi came to her every day, showed her what he had learned in his studies, and told her what he heard among the warrior class. It was nothing definite, just whispers, sometimes jokes, maybe no more than the idle chatter of men with not enough to occupy themselves. She resolved to do nothing about it for the time being but to warn Takeo when he returned.

The time of the great heat began, and it was too sultry to ride outside. Since Kaede could take no decisions till Takeo's return, and since she expected him every day, she spent most of her time kneeling at the lacquer writing table, copying the Tribe records. The doors to the residence were all opened to catch the least breeze, and the sound of insects was deafening. Her preferred room looked out over pools and a waterfall; through the azalea bushes she could see the silver-weathered tea house. Every day she promised herself that she would make tea there for Takeo that night, and every day she was disappointed. Sometimes kingfishers came to the pools and the flash of blue and orange would distract her momentarily. Once a heron alighted outside the veranda and she thought it was a sign that he would be back that day, but he did not come.

She let no one see what she was writing, for she quickly realized the importance of the records. She was amazed at what Shigeru had uncovered, and wondered if someone within the Tribe had acted as his informant. She concealed the original records and the copies in a different place every night and tried to commit as much as possible to memory. She became obsessed with the idea of the secret network, watched for signs of them everywhere, trusted no one, even though Takeo's first work at Maruyama had been to purge the castle household. The range of the Tribe daunted her; she did not see how Takeo would ever escape them. Then the thought would come to her that they had already caught up with him, that he was lying dead somewhere and she would never see him again.

He was right, she thought. *They must all be killed; they must be rooted out, for they seek to destroy him. And if they destroy him, they destroy me.*

The faces of Shizuka and Muto Kenji often rose before her mind's eye. She regretted the trust she had placed in Shizuka and wondered how much of Kaede's life her companion had revealed to others in the Tribe. She had thought that both Shizuka and Kenji had been fond of her; had all that affection been feigned? They had nearly died together in Inuyama Castle; did that count for nothing? She felt betrayed by Shizuka, but at the same time she missed her badly and wished she had someone like her to confide in.

Her monthly bleeding came, bringing her renewed disappointment and placing her in seclusion for a week. Not even Hiroshi visited her. When it was over the copying was finished, too, and she became even more restless. The Festival of the Dead came and went, leaving her filled with sorrow and regrets for the departed. The work on the residence that had gone on all summer was completed, and the rooms looked beautiful, but they felt empty and unlived in. Hiroshi asked one morning, 'Why isn't your sister here with you?' and on a sudden impulse she said, 'Shall we ride to my house and fetch her?'

There had been a week of leaden skies, as if a typhoon were threatening, but then the weather had suddenly cleared and the heat had abated a little. The nights were cooler and it seemed a perfect time to travel. Sugita tried to dissuade her, and even the elusive elders appeared one by one to argue against it, but she ignored them. Shirakawa was only two or three days away. If Takeo came home before she returned he might ride and join her. And the journey would stop her from fretting all day long.

'We can send for your sisters,' Sugita said. 'It is an excellent idea; I should have thought of it myself. I will go to escort them.'

'I need to see my household,' she replied. Now that the idea was in her head she could not relinquish it. 'I have not spoken to my men since my marriage. I should have gone weeks ago. I must check on my land and see that the harvest will be brought in.'

She did not tell Sugita but she had another reason for the journey, one that had lain in her mind all summer. She would go to the sacred caves of the Shirakawa, drink the river's elemental water and pray to the goddess for a child.

'I will be away only a few days.'

'I am afraid your husband will not approve.'

'He trusts my judgment in all things,' she replied. 'And, after all, didn't Lady Naomi often travel alone?'

Because he was accustomed to receiving orders from a woman she was able to overcome his misgivings. She chose Amano to go with her as well as a few of her own men who had accompanied her since she had left in the spring for Terayama. After some consideration she took none of her women with her, not even Manami. She wanted to go quickly, on horseback, without the formalities and dignity that she would have to put up with if she travelled openly. Manami pleaded and then sulked, but Kaede was adamant.

She rode Raku, refusing even to take a palanquin with her. Before she left she had planned to hide the copies of the records below the floor of the tea room, but the hints of disloyalty still worried her, and in the end she could not bear to leave them where anyone might find them. She decided to take both sets with her, already thinking she might hide the originals somewhere in her house at Shirakawa. After much pleading, Hiroshi was allowed to accompany her and she took him to one side and made him promise not to let the chests out of his sight on the journey. And at the last moment she took the sword Takeo had given her.

Amano managed to persuade Hiroshi to leave his father's sword behind, but the boy brought a dagger and his bow as well as a small fiery roan horse from his family's stables that played up all the first day, causing the men endless amusement. Twice it wheeled round and bolted, heading for home, until the boy brought it under control and caught up with them, blue-faced with rage but otherwise undaunted.

157

'He's a nice-looking creature, but green,' Amano said. 'And you make him tense. Don't grip so hard. Relax.'

He made Hiroshi ride alongside him; the horse settled down and the next day gave no problems. Kaede was happy to be on the road. As she had hoped, it kept her from brooding. The weather was fine, the country in the full flush of harvest, the men cheerful at the prospect of seeing their homes and families after months away. Hiroshi was a good companion, full of information about the land they passed through.

'I wish my father had taught me as much as yours taught you,' she said, impressed by his knowledge. 'When I was your age I was a hostage in Noguchi castle.'

'He made me learn all the time. He would not allow me to waste a moment.'

'Life is so short and fragile,' Kaede said. 'Perhaps he knew he would not see you grow up.'

Hiroshi nodded and rode in silence for a while.

He must miss his father, but he will not show it, she thought, and found herself envying the way he had been taught. *I will have my children brought up that way; girls as well as boys will be taught everything and will learn to be strong.*

On the morning of the third day they crossed the Shirakawa River and entered her family's domain. It was shallow and easily fordable, the swift white water swirling between rocks. There was no barrier at the border; they were beyond the jurisdiction of the great clans and in the region of smaller land-holders where neighbours were either involved in petty stand-offs or had formed amicable alliances among themselves. Nominally these warrior families paid allegiance to Kumamoto or Maruyama but they did not move to the castle towns, preferring to live on and farm their own lands, on which they paid very little tax to anyone.

'I've never crossed the Shirakawa before,' Hiroshi said as the horses splashed through. 'This is the furthest I've been from Maruyama.'

'So now it's my turn to instruct you,' she said, taking pleasure in pointing out the landmarks of her country. 'I will take you to the source of the river later, to the great caves, only you will have to wait outside.'

'Why?' he demanded.

'It's a sacred place for women. No men are allowed to set foot in there.'

She was eager to get home now and they did not linger on the way, but she was studying everything: the look of the land, the progress of the harvest, the condition of oxen and children. Compared with a year ago when she had returned with Shizuka things had improved, but there were still many signs of poverty and neglect.

I abandoned them, she thought guiltily. *I should have come home before.* She thought of her tempestuous flight to Terayama in the spring: she seemed to have been another person, bewitched.

Amano had sent two of the men ahead, and Shoji Kiyoshi, the domain's senior retainer, was waiting for her at the gate of her house. He greeted her with surprise and, she thought, coolness. The household women were lined up in the garden, but there was no sign of her sisters or Ayame.

Raku whinnied, turning his head towards the stables and the water meadows where he had run in the winter. Amano came forward to help her dismount. Hiroshi slid from the roan's back and it tried to kick the horse next to it.

159

'Where are my sisters?' Kaede demanded, brushing aside the women's murmured greetings.

No one answered. A shrike was calling insistently from the camphor tree by the gate, grating on her nerves.

'Lady Shirakawa . . .' Shoji began.

She spun to face him. 'Where are they?'

'We were told . . . you sent instructions for them to go to Lord Fujiwara.'

'I did no such thing! How long have they been there?'

'Two months at least.' He glanced at the horsemen and the servants. 'We should speak in private.'

'Yes, at once,' she agreed.

One of the women ran forward with a bowl of water. 'Welcome home, Lady Shirakawa.'

Kaede washed her feet and stepped onto the veranda. Unease was beginning to creep through her. The house was eerily quiet. She wanted to hear Hana and Ai's voices; she realized how much she had missed them.

It was a little after noon. She gave instructions for the men to be fed, the horses watered, and both to be kept ready in case she needed them. She took Hiroshi to her own room and told him to stay there with the records while she spoke to Shoji. She was not hungry at all, but she arranged for the women to bring food to the boy. Then she went to her father's old room and sent for Shoji.

The room looked as if someone had just walked out of it. There was a brush lying on the writing table. Hana must have gone on with her studies even after Kaede's departure. She picked up the brush and was staring at it dully when Shoji tapped on the door.

He entered and knelt before her, apologizing. 'We had no idea it was not your wish. It seemed so likely. Lord Fujiwara himself came and spoke to Ai.'

She thought she detected insincerity in his voice. 'Why did he invite them? What did he want with them?' Her voice was trembling.

'You yourself often went there,' Shoji replied.

'Everything has changed since then!' she exclaimed. 'Lord Otori Takeo and I were married at Terayama. We have established ourselves at Maruyama. You must have heard of this.'

'I found it hard to believe,' he replied. 'Since everyone thought you were betrothed to Lord Fujiwara and were to marry him.'

'There was no betrothal!' she said in fury. 'How dare you question my marriage!'

She saw the muscles round his jaw tense and realized he was as angry as she was. He leaned forward. 'What are we to think?' he hissed. 'We hear of a marriage that is undertaken with no betrothal, no permission asked or given, none of your family present. I am glad your father is already dead. You killed him by the shame you brought on him but at least he is spared this fresh shame—'

He broke off. They stared at each other, both shocked by his outburst.

I'll have to take his life, Kaede thought in horror. *He cannot speak to me like that and live. But I need him: who else can look after things here for me?* Then the fear came to her that he might try and take the domain from her, using his anger to mask ambition and greed. She wondered if he had taken control of the men she and Kondo had gathered together in the winter; if they would obey him now. She wished Kondo were there, then realized that she could trust the Tribe man even less than her father's senior retainer. No one could help her. Struggling to hide her apprehension, she continued to stare at Shoji until he lowered his eyes.

He regained control of himself, wiping the spittle from his mouth. 'Forgive me. I have known you since you were born. It is my duty to speak to you, even though it pains me.'

'I will forgive you this time,' she said. 'But it is you who shame my father, through disrespect to his heir. If you ever speak to me in that fashion again I will order you to slit your belly.'

'You are only a woman,' he said, trying to placate her but enraging her further. 'You have no one to guide you.'

'I have my husband,' she said shortly. 'There is nothing you or Lord Fujiwara can do to alter that. Go to him now and say my sisters are to come home at once. They will return with me to Maruyama.'

He left immediately. Shocked and restless, she could not sit quietly and wait for his return. She called to Hiroshi and showed him the house and garden while she checked all the repairs that she had had done in the autumn. The crested ibises in their summer plumage were feeding on the banks of the rice fields, and the shrike continued to scold them as they trespassed into its territory. Then she told him to fetch the chests of records and, carrying one each, they made their way upstream along the Shirakawa, or White River, to where it emerged from under the mountain. She would not hide them where Shoji might find them; she would entrust them to no human. She had decided to give them to the goddess.

The holy place calmed her, as always, but its ageless, sacred atmosphere awed her rather than lifted her spirits. Below the huge arch of the cave's entrance the river flowed slowly and steadily in deep pools of green water, belying its name, and the twisted shapes of the calcified rocks gleamed like mother of pearl in the half light.

The old couple who maintained the shrine came out to greet her. Leaving Hiroshi in the company of the man, Kaede went forward with his wife, each of them carrying one of the chests.

Lamps and candles had been lit inside the cavern, and the damp rock glistened. The roar of the river drowned out all other noise. They stepped carefully from stone to stone, past the giant mushroom, past the frozen waterfall, past heaven's stairway – all shapes made by the limy water – until they came to the rock shaped like the goddess, from which drops fell like tears of mother's milk.

Kaede said, 'I must ask the goddess to protect these treasures for me. Unless I myself come for them, they must stay here with her for ever.'

The old woman nodded and bowed. Behind the rock a cave had been hollowed out, well above the highest level of the river. They climbed up to it and placed the chests in it. Kaede noticed that it contained many other objects that had been given to the goddess. She wondered about their history and what had happened to the women who had placed them there. There was a damp, ancient smell. Some of the objects were decaying; some had already rotted. Would the records of the Tribe rot away here hidden under the mountain?

The air was cold and clammy, making her shiver. When she put the chest down, her arms felt suddenly empty and light. She was seized by the knowledge that the goddess knew her need – that her empty arms, her empty womb, would be filled.

She knelt before the rock and scooped up water from

the pool that had gathered at its base. As she drank she prayed almost wordlessly. The water was as soft as milk.

The old woman, kneeling behind her, began to chant a prayer so ancient that Kaede did not recognize the words, but its meaning washed over her and mingled with her own longing. The rock shape had no eyes, no features, yet she felt the benign gaze of the goddess upon her. She remembered the vision she had had at Terayama and the words that had been spoken to her: *Be patient; he will come for you.*

She heard the words clearly again, and for a moment they puzzled her. Then she understood them to mean, *he would come back. Of course he will. I will be patient*, she vowed again. *As soon as my sisters are here, we will go to Maruyama at once. And when Takeo returns, I will conceive a child. I was right to come here.*

She felt so strengthened by the visit to the caves that at the end of the afternoon she went to the family temple to pay her respects to her father's tomb. Hiroshi came with her, as did one of the women of the house, Ayako, who carried offerings of fruit and rice and a bowl of smoking incense.

His ashes lay buried among the graves of her ancestors, the Shirakawa lords. Beneath the huge cedars it was gloomy and cool. The wind soughed in the branches, carrying the *min-min* of cicadas. Over the years earthquakes had shifted the columns and pillars, and the ground heaved upwards as if the dead were trying to escape.

Her father's grave was still intact. Kaede took the offerings from Ayako and placed them in front of the stone. She clapped her hands and bowed her head. She dreaded hearing or seeing his spirit; yet, she wanted to placate it. She could not think calmly about his death. He had wanted to die but had been unable to find the courage to kill himself. Shizuka and Kondo had killed him: did that constitute murder? She was aware, too, of the part she had played, the shame she had brought on him; would his spirit now demand some payment?

She took the bowl of smouldering incense from Ayako and let the smoke waft over the tomb and over her own face and hands to purify her. She put the bowl down and clapped again three times. The wind dropped, the crickets fell silent and in that moment she felt the earth tremble slightly beneath her. The landscape quivered. The trees shook.

'An earthquake!' Hiroshi exclaimed behind her as Ayako gave a cry of fear.

It was only a small tremor, and no more followed, but Ayako was nervous and jittery on the way home.

'Your father's spirit spoke to you,' she murmured to Kaede. 'What did he say?'

'He approves of everything I have done,' she replied with a confidence she was far from feeling. In fact the tremor had shocked her. She feared her father's angry, embittered ghost and felt it attacked all she had experienced in the sacred caves at the goddess's feet.

'May heaven be praised,' Ayako said, but her lips tightened and she continued to give Kaede anxious glances all evening.

'By the way,' Kaede asked her as they ate together, 'where is Sunoda, Akita's nephew?' This young man had come with his uncle the previous winter and she had made him remain in her household as a hostage, in Shoji's care. She was beginning to think she might have need of him now.

'He was allowed to return to Inuyama,' Ayako said.

'What?' Shoji had relinquished her hostage? She could not believe the extent of his treachery.

'His father was said to be ill,' Ayako explained.

So her hostage was gone, diminishing her power further.

It was already dusk before she heard Shoji's voice outside. Hiroshi had gone with Amano to his house to meet his family and sleep there, and Kaede had been waiting in her father's room, going through the records of the estate. She could see many signs of mismanagement, and when it was obvious Shoji had returned alone, her rage against her father's senior retainer grew even more fierce.

When he came to her Ayako followed him, bringing tea, but Kaede was too impatient to drink it.

'Where are my sisters?' she demanded.

He drank the tea gratefully before replying. He looked hot and tired. 'Lord Fujiwara is glad of your return,' he said. 'He sends you his greetings and asks that you will call on him tomorrow. He will send his palanquin and an escort.'

'I have no intention of calling on him,' she retorted, trying not to lose her temper. 'I expect my sisters to be returned to me tomorrow and after that we will leave for Maruyama as soon as possible.'

'I am afraid your sisters are not there,' he said.

Her heart plunged to her belly. 'Where are they?'

'Lord Fujiwara says Lady Shirakawa is not to be alarmed. They are perfectly safe and he will tell her where they are when she visits him tomorrow.'

'You dare to bring me such a message?' Her voice sounded thin and unconvincing to her own ears.

Shoji inclined his head. 'It gives me no pleasure. But

Lord Fujiwara is who he is; I cannot defy or disobey him, nor, I believe, can you.'

'They are hostages then?' she said in a low voice.

He did not answer directly but merely said, 'I'll give orders for your journey tomorrow. Shall I accompany you?'

'No!' she cried. 'And if I am to go I will ride. I will not wait for his palanquin. Tell Amano I will ride my grey and he is to come with me.'

For a moment she thought he would argue with her, but then he bowed deeply and aquiesced.

After he had gone, her thoughts were in turmoil. If she could not trust Shoji who of the domain's men could she trust? Were they trying to trap her? Surely even Fujiwara would not dare. She was married now. At one moment she thought she should return immediately to Maruyama; the next she realized Ai and Hana were in someone else's possession and she understood what it meant to have hostages held against her.

So must my mother and Lady Naomi have suffered, she thought. *I must go to Fujiwara and bargain with him for them. He has helped me before. He will not turn completely against me now.*

Next she began to worry about what to do with Hiroshi. It had seemed like the safest of journeys; yet, she could not help feeling that she had brought him into danger. Should he ride with her to Lord Fujiwara's or should she send him home as quickly as possible?

She rose early and sent for Amano. She dressed in the simple travelling clothes she had worn on the journey, even though she could hear Shizuka's voice in her head: *You can't appear before Lord Fujiwara on horseback like a warrior.* Her own better judgment told her to delay a few days, to send messages and gifts and then to travel in his palanquin with his escort, dressed perfectly for him, presented like the flawless treasures he prized. Shizuka, even Manami, would have advised her so. But her impatience was too great. She knew she would never endure the waiting and the inactivity. She would meet Lord Fujiwara once more, would find out where her sisters were and what he wanted, and would then go immediately back to Maruyama, back to Takeo.

When Amano came she sent the women away so she could speak privately with him, and quickly explained the situation.

'I have to go to Lord Fujiwara's, but to tell you the truth I am anxious about his intentions. We may need to leave quickly and return to Maruyama at speed. Be ready for it, and make sure the men and horses are prepared.'

His eyes narrowed. 'There will be no fighting, surely?'

'I don't know. I am afraid they will try to detain me.'

'Against your will? It's impossible!'

'It's unlikely, I know, but I am uneasy. Why were my sisters taken away if not to force me in some way?'

'We should leave at once,' he said, young enough not to be cowed by the nobleman's rank. 'Let your husband talk to Lord Fujiwara with the sword.'

'I am afraid of what will be done to my sisters. I must at least find out where they are. Shoji says we cannot defy Fujiwara, and I suppose he is right. I will have to go and speak with him. But I will not go into the house. Do not let them take me inside.'

Amano bowed. Kaede went on, 'Should Hiroshi be sent home? I wish I had not brought him; I have the burden of his safety on me now too.'

'There is safety in numbers,' Amano said. 'He should

168

stay with us. And, anyway, if there is to be trouble, we can ill spare the men to escort him back. I will die before any harm comes to him or you.'

She smiled, grateful for his loyalty. 'Then let us leave with no more delay.'

The weather had changed again. The clarity and coolness of the last few days had given way to a renewed oppressiveness. It was humid and still, the sort of day that heralded the typhoons of late summer. The horses were sweating and restless, Hiroshi's roan more unsettled than ever.

Kaede wanted to talk to Hiroshi, to warn him of the possible dangers that lay ahead, to make him promise not to get involved in any fighting; but the horse was too fidgety, and Amano made the boy ride in front with him, lest the roan upset Raku as well. She could feel the sweat running down inside her clothes. She hoped she would not arrive red in the face and soaked. She was already half-regretting the rashness of her decision. But, as always, riding made her feel more powerful. She had made the journey only in the palanquin before, never able to look out on the landscape from behind the silk curtains and oiled paper screens that had enclosed her. Now she was able to absorb the beauty of the scenery, the richness of farmland and forest, the grandeur of the distant mountains, range after range, each slightly paler than the one in front, fading until they merged into the sky.

No wonder Lord Fujiwara did not want to leave this beautiful place. His image, seductive and intriguing, rose before her eyes. She remembered how he had always seemed to like and admire her. She could not believe he would harm her. But her senses were heightened with some apprehension. *Is this how it feels to ride into battle,* she wondered, *life never seeming more beautiful nor more fleeting, to be grasped and flung away in one and the same breath?*

She put her hand on the sword in her belt, reassured by the feel of the hilt.

They were only a few miles from the gates of Fujiwara's residence when they saw dust on the road ahead, and out of the haze trotted the palanquin bearers and horsemen sent by the nobleman to fetch her. Their leader spotted the silver river crest on Amano's surcoat and drew rein to greet him. His gaze swept over Kaede and then his neck muscles corded as his eyes snapped back to her in astonishment.

'Lady Shirakawa!' He gasped and shouted to the bearers, 'Down! Down!'

They dropped the palanquin and knelt in the dust. The horsemen dismounted and stood with bowed heads. They appeared submissive, but she saw immediately that they outnumbered her men two to one.

'I am on my way to visit his lordship,' she said. She recognized the retainer but could not recall his name. He was the man who had always come to escort her to Lord Fujiwara's in the past.

'I am Murita,' he said. 'Would Lady Shirakawa not prefer to be carried?'

'I will ride,' she said shortly. 'We are so close now.'

His lips were compressed into a thin line. *He disapproves*, she thought, and glanced at Amano and Hiroshi, who were now alongside her. Amano's face gave nothing away, but there was a flush of blood beneath Hiroshi's skin.

Are they embarrassed for me? Am I shaming myself

and them? Kaede straightened her back and urged Raku forward.

Murita sent two of his men ahead, increasing her sense of unease about the reception that awaited them, but she could think of nothing to do but ride onwards.

The horses felt her anxiety. Raku sidestepped a little, ears pricked, eyes rolling and Hiroshi's horse threw its head in the air and tried to buck. The boy's knuckles were white on the reins as he brought it under control.

When they came to the residence, the gates were open and armed guards stood inside the courtyard. Amano dismounted and came to help Kaede from Raku's back.

'I will not get down until Lord Fujiwara comes,' she said boldly. 'I do not intend to stay.'

Murita hesitated, unwilling to take such a message.

'Tell him I am here,' she pressed.

'Lady Shirakawa.' He bowed his head and dismounted, but at that moment Lord Fujiwara's young companion, Mamoru, the actor, came from the house and knelt in front of her horse.

'Welcome, lady,' he said. 'Please come inside.'

She was afraid that if she did she would never come out. 'Mamoru,' she said curtly, 'I will not go inside. I have come to find out where my sisters are.'

He stood then and came to the right side of her horse, stepping between her and Amano. He, who had rarely looked directly at her, now seemed to be trying to meet her gaze.

'Lady Shirakawa,' he began, and she heard something in his voice.

'Remount,' she said to Amano and he obeyed her instantly.

'Please,' Mamoru said quietly, 'it's best if you comply.

I beg you. For your sake, for the sake of your men, the boy . . .'

'If Lord Fujiwara will not come to speak to me and will not tell me what I want to know, I have no further business here.'

She did not see who gave the order. She was aware only of some look that flashed between Mamoru and Murita.

'Ride!' she cried to Amano, and tried to turn Raku's head, but Murita was holding the bridle. She leaned forward, drawing her sword and urging the horse to rear. He shook his head free from the man's grip and went up on his hind legs, striking out with his forefeet. She struck downwards at Murita and saw the blade slice against his hand. He cried out in fury, pulling out his own sword. She thought he would kill her, but he grabbed at the bridle again, wrenching the horse's head down. She felt something plunge and flail behind her: it was Hiroshi's horse, panicking. Mamoru was plucking at her clothes, calling out to her, begging her to surrender. Beyond him she could see Amano. His sword was drawn, but before he could use it an arrow struck him in the chest. She saw the look of shock come into his eyes, then blood began to bubble with each breath and he fell forward.

'No!' she screamed. Murita, at the same moment, in frustrated rage, thrust his sword upwards into Raku's exposed chest. The horse screamed, too, in pain and fear and his bright blood began to gush. As he faltered, legs swaying, head sinking, Murita caught Kaede and tried to drag her from his back. She struck out at him once more but the horse was falling, taking her down, and her blow had no strength in it. Murita caught her wrist and effortlessly twisted the sword from her hand. Saying nothing he half dragged, half carried her to the house.

'Help me! Help me!' she called, twisting her head round, trying to look back at her men, but the swift, ferocious assault had left them all dead or dying. 'Hiroshi!' she screamed, and heard hoofs pounding. The last thing she saw before Murita carried her inside was the roan bolting, carrying the boy away against his will. It was the slightest grain of comfort.

Murita searched her for other weapons, finding her knife; his hand was bleeding freely and rage made him rough. Mamoru ran before them opening doors, as he took her to the guest rooms. When he released her she fell to the ground, sobbing with rage and grief.

'Raku! Raku!' she wept, as grief-stricken as if the horse had been her child. Then she wept for Amano and the others whom she had led to their death.

Mamoru knelt beside her, babbling, 'I'm sorry, Lady Shirakawa. You must submit. No one is going to hurt you. Believe me, we all love and honour you here. Please calm yourself.'

When she only wept more desperately he said to the maids, 'Send for Dr Ishida.'

A few minutes later she was aware of the physician's presence. He knelt beside her and she raised her head, pushing aside her hair and gazing at him with stricken eyes.

'Lady Shirakawa—' he began, but she interrupted him.

'My name is Otori. I am married. What is this outrage? You will not let them keep me here. You will tell them to let me go at once.'

'I wish I could,' he said in a low voice. 'But we all lead

173

our lives here according to his lordship's will not our own.'

'What does he want from me? Why has he done this? He has abducted my sisters, murdered my men!' The tears poured anew down her face. 'He did not need to kill my horse.' She was racked by sobs.

Ishida told the maids to fetch herbs from his house and bring hot water. Then he examined her gently, looking in her eyes and feeling her pulse.

'Forgive me,' he said, 'but I must ask you if you are carrying a child.'

'Why must you know that? It is nothing to do with you!'

'His lordship's intention is to marry you. He considers that you were betrothed to him. He had already sought the emperor's permission, as well as Lord Arai's.'

'We were never betrothed,' Kaede sobbed. 'I am married to Otori Takeo.'

Ishida said gently, 'I can't discuss these things with you. You will see his lordship directly. But as your physician I must know if you are pregnant.'

'What if I am?'

'Then we will get rid of it.'

When Kaede cried out in grief, he said, 'Lord Fujiwara is already making great concessions to you. He could have you put to death for your infidelity. He will forgive you and marry you, but he will not give his name to another man's child.'

She made no response other than renewed sobbing. The maid returned with the herbs and tea kettle and Ishida brewed the infusion.

'Drink it,' he told Kaede. 'It will calm you.'

'Suppose I refuse?' she said, sitting abruptly and

snatching the bowl from him. She held it out at arm's length as though she would pour it onto the matting. 'Suppose I refuse all food and drink? Will he marry a corpse?'

'Then you condemn your sisters to death – or worse,' he said. 'I'm sorry, I take no pleasure in the situation, nor am I proud of my part in it. All I can do is be utterly truthful with you. If you submit to his lordship's will you will preserve your honour and their lives.'

She gazed at him for a long moment. Slowly she brought the cup to her lips. 'I am not pregnant,' she said, and drained it.

Ishida sat with her while her senses began to numb, and when she was calm, he told the maids to take her to the bath house and wash the blood from her.

By the time she was bathed and dressed, the infusion had dulled her grief and the brief murderous episode seemed like something she had dreamed. In the afternoon she even slept a little, hearing as if from another country the chanting of the priests lifting the pollution of death from the house and restoring it to its peace and harmony. When she woke and found herself in the familiar room, she forgot for a moment the past months and thought, *I am at Fujiwara's. How long have I stayed here? I must call Shizuka and ask her.*

Then she remembered but with no intensity, just a dull knowledge of what had been snatched so violently from her.

It was twilight, the cool ending to a long, heavy day. She could hear the soft footsteps of the servants and their whispered voices. A maid came to the room with a tray of food. Kaede picked at it listlessly but the smell of food sickened her and she soon called for it to be taken away.

The maid returned with tea. She was followed into the room by another woman, middle aged, with small sharp eyes and a severe look, obviously not a servant from her elegant clothes and refined manner. She bowed to the ground before Kaede and said, 'I am Ono Rieko, a cousin of Lord Fujiwara's late wife. I spent many years in her ladyship's household. His lordship sent for me to make the preparations for the wedding ceremony. Please accept me with kindness.' She bowed her head formally to the floor again.

Kaede felt an instinctive dislike for the woman before her. Her appearance was not unpleasing – she could not imagine Fujiwara suffering any person around him who was not attractive – but she sensed both self-pride and mean-spiritedness in her character.

'Do I have any choice?' she said coldly.

Rieko gave a little trill of laughter as she sat up. 'I am sure Lady Shirakawa will change her mind about me. I am only a very ordinary person but there may be things I can advise you on.' She began to pour the tea saying, 'Dr Ishida wants you to have a cup of this now. And as it is the first night of the moon, Lord Fujiwara will come shortly to welcome you, and view the new moon with you. Drink your tea and I'll make sure your hair and dress are appropriate.'

Kaede took a sip of tea and then another, trying not to gulp it down for she was terribly thirsty. She was calm and could barely feel anything; yet, she was aware of the slow thudding of blood behind her temples. She dreaded meeting him, dreaded the power he had over her. It was the power that men held over women everywhere, in every aspect of their lives. She must have been mad to think she could fight it. She remembered all too clearly Lady Naomi's words: *I must appear a defenceless woman, otherwise these warriors will crush me.*

Now they were crushing her. Shizuka had warned her that her marriage would enrage the elders of her class – that it would never be permitted. But if she had listened and done what she was told, she would never have had the months with Takeo. The thought of him now was so freshly painful, even with the calming tea, that she laid it away in the secret recesses of her heart, as hidden as the records of the Tribe in the sacred caves.

She became aware that Rieko was studying her closely. She turned her face away and took another sip of tea.

'Come, come, Lady Shirakawa,' Rieko said briskly. 'You must not brood. You are about to make a brilliant marriage.' She came a little closer, shuffling forward on her knees. 'You are as beautiful as they say, apart from being too tall, but your skin has a tendency to sallowness, and that heavy look does not become you. Your beauty is your greatest asset: we must do all we can to preserve it.'

She took the cup and set it on the tray. Then she unloosened Kaede's hair from the ties that held it back and began to comb it out.

'How old are you?'

'Sixteen,' Kaede replied.

'I thought you were older, twenty at least. You must be the type that ages rapidly. We'll have to watch that.' The comb raked across Kaede's scalp, bringing tears of pain to her eyes.

Rieko said, 'It must be very difficult to dress your hair; it is very soft.'

'I usually tie it back,' Kaede said.

'It is the fashion in the capital to wear it piled on the head,' Rieko said, tugging in a way that intentionally hurt. 'Thicker, coarser hair is more desirable.'

Whereas sympathy and understanding might have released Kaede's grief, Rieko's unkindness steeled her, making her determined never to break down, never to show her feelings. *I slept in ice,* she thought. *The goddess speaks to me. I will discover power of some sort here and use it, until Takeo comes for me.* He would come, she knew, or die in the attempt, and when she saw his lifeless corpse she would be freed from her promise and she would join him in the shadows of the afterworld.

In the distance dogs began barking suddenly and excitedly, and a moment later the house shook in a tremor, longer and a little more severe than the previous day's.

Kaede felt what she always felt: shock, amazement that the earth could quiver like fresh bean curd, and a sort of elation that nothing was fixed or certain. Nothing lasted for ever, not even Fujiwara and his house full of treasures.

Rieko dropped the comb and struggled to her feet. The maids came running to the door.

'Come outside quickly,' Rieko cried, her voice alarmed.

'Why?' Kaede said. 'The quake will not be a big one.'

Rieko had already left the room. Kaede could hear her ordering the maids to extinguish all the lamps, almost shrieking at them in her panic. Kaede remained where she was, listening to the running feet, the raised voices, the barking dogs. After a few moments she took up the comb and finished combing out her hair. Since her head ached she left it loose.

The robe they had dressed her in earlier seemed quite

suitable for moon viewing: it was dove grey, embroidered with bush clover and pale lemon warblers. She wanted to look at the moon, to be bathed in its silvery light, and to be reminded of how it came and went in the heavens, disappeared for three days and then returned.

The maids had left the doors to the veranda open. Kaede stepped out and knelt on the wooden floor, gazing towards the mountain, recalling how she had sat here with Fujiwara, wrapped in bearskins as the snow fell.

Another slight tremor came but she felt no fear. She saw the mountain tremble against the pale violet sky. The dark shapes of the garden trees were swaying, though there was no wind, and birds, disturbed, were calling as if it were dawn.

Slowly their calls subsided and the dogs fell quiet. The thin golden sickle of the new moon hung next to the evening star just above the peaks. Kaede closed her eyes.

She smelled Fujiwara's fragrance before she heard him. Then she caught the tread of feet, the rustle of silk. She opened her eyes.

He stood a few feet away from her, staring at her with the rapt, covetous look that she remembered so well.

'Lady Shirakawa.'

'Lord Fujiwara.' She returned his gaze for longer than she should before slowly prostrating herself until her brow touched the floor.

Fujiwara stepped onto the veranda, followed by Mamoru, who was carrying carpets and cushions. Not until the nobleman was seated did he give Kaede permission to sit up. He reached out and touched the silk robe.

'It's very becoming. I thought it would be. You gave

poor Murita quite a shock when you turned up on horse-back. He nearly speared you by mistake.'

She thought she would faint from the fury that suddenly erupted through the herb-induced tranquillity. That he should allude so lightly, jokingly, to the murders of her men, of Amano, who had known her since she was a child . . .

'How dare you do this to me?' she said, and heard Mamoru's gasp of shock. 'I was married three months ago to Otori Takeo at Terayama. My husband will punish you—' She broke off, trying to regain control.

'I thought we would enjoy the moon before we talked,' he replied, showing no response to the insulting way she had spoken. 'Where are your women? Why are you here alone?'

'They ran when the earth shook,' she replied shortly.

'Were you not afraid?'

'I have nothing to be afraid of. You have already done the worst anyone can do to me.'

'It seems we are to talk now,' he said. 'Mamoru, bring wine and then see that we are undisturbed.'

He looked meditatively at the moon without speaking for the next few minutes until Mamoru came back. When the young man had retired into the shadows again, Fujiwara indicated that Kaede should pour the wine. He drank and said, 'Your marriage to the person who calls himself Otori Takeo has been set aside. It was undertaken without permission and has been ruled invalid.'

'By whose authority?'

'Lord Arai, your own senior retainer Shoji, and myself. The Otori have already disowned Takeo and declared his adoption illegal. The general opinion was that you should die for your disobedience to Arai and your infidelity to me, especially when your involvement in Iida's death became more widely known.'

'We had an agreement that you would share my secrets with no one,' she said.

'I thought we had an agreement that we would marry.'

She could make no response without insulting him further, and his words had in fact frightened her. She was all too aware that he could order her death on a moment's whim. No one would dare either to disobey such an order or to judge him afterwards.

He went on: 'You are aware of my high regard for you. I was able to effect something of a transaction with Arai. He agreed to spare you if I married you and kept you in seclusion. I will support his cause with the emperor in due course. In return I sent your sisters to him.'

'You gave them to Arai? They are in Inuyama?'

'I believe it's quite common to hand women over as hostages,' he returned. 'Arai was incensed, by the way, when you dared to keep Akita's nephew as your hostage. It could have been a good move, but you threw all that away when you acted so rashly in the spring. All it achieved, then, was to offend Arai and his retainers further. Arai was your champion before. It was very fool-hardy to treat him so badly.'

'I know now that Shoji betrayed me,' she said bitterly. 'Akita's nephew should never have been allowed to go home.'

'You mustn't be harsh on Shoji.' Fujiwara's voice was bland and calm. 'He was doing what he thought right for you and your family. As are we all. I would like our marriage to take place as soon as possible: I think before the end of the week. Rieko will instruct you in your dress and behaviour.'

She felt despair descend on her like the hunter's net over the wild duck. 'All men involved with me have died except my lawful husband, Lord Otori Takeo. Aren't you afraid?'

'Common talk is that it is men who desire you who die; I feel no more desire for you than I ever did. I do not want more children. Our marriage is to save your life. It will be in name only.' He drank again and replaced the cup on the floor. 'It would be appropriate now to express your gratitude.'

'I am to be just one of your possessions?'

'Lady Shirakawa, you are one of the few people I have shared my treasures with – the only woman. You know how I like to keep them away from the eyes of the world, wrapped up, hidden.'

Her heart quailed. She said nothing.

'And don't think Takeo will come and rescue you. Arai is determined to punish him. He is mounting a campaign against him now. The domains of Maruyama and Shirakawa will be taken in your name and given to me as your husband.' He let his gaze cover her as if he would drink in every drop of her suffering. 'His desire for you has indeed been his downfall. Takeo will be dead before winter.'

Kaede had studied Fujiwara throughout the previous winter and knew all the changing expressions of his face. He liked to think he was impassive, his feelings always perfectly controlled, but she had grown adept at reading him. She heard the note of cruelty in his voice, and caught the taste of pleasure on his tongue. She had heard it before when he spoke Takeo's name. She had thought him almost infatuated with Takeo when she had told him her secrets when the snow lay thick on the ground and icicles as long as men's legs hung from the eaves. She had seen the gleam of desire in his eye, the slight slackening of his mouth, the way his tongue swelled around the name. Now she realized that the nobleman desired Takeo's death. It would give him pleasure and set him free from his obsession. And she had no doubt that her suffering would heighten his pleasure.

At that moment she resolved two things: She would show him nothing, and she would live. She would submit to his will so that he had no excuse to kill her before Takeo came for her, but she would never give either him or the devil woman he'd assigned to her the satisfaction of seeing how deeply she suffered.

She allowed her eyes to fill with contempt as she looked at Fujiwara, and then she gazed past him at the moon.

The marriage took place a few days later. Kaede drank the infusions that Ishida brewed, thankful for the numbness they brought her. She was resolved to have no feelings, to be like ice, remembering how long ago it was that Takeo's gaze had plunged her into the deep, cold sleep. She did not blame Ishida or Mamoru for the part they played in her imprisonment, for she knew they were bound by the same rigid code she was, but she swore Murita would pay for the murder of her men and her horse, and she came to loathe Rieko.

She watched herself go through the rituals as if she were a doll or a puppet manipulated on a stage. Her family were represented by Shoji and two of her retainers: one she knew was a brother of Hirogawa, the man she had

had executed by Kondo when he had refused to serve her, the day of her father's death. *I should have taken the lives of his whole family*, she thought bitterly. *I spared them only to make an enemy of them.* There were other men there, of high rank, who she imagined must have been sent by Arai. They did not acknowledge her in any way and she was not told their names. It made her realize all too clearly her new position: no longer mistress of a domain, her husband's ally and equal, but second wife to a nobleman, with no other life than what he saw fit to allow her.

It was an elaborate ceremony, far more lavish than her wedding at Terayama. The prayers and chanting seemed to go on endlessly. The incense and bells made her head swim, and when she had to exchange the ritual three cups of wine three times with her new husband, she feared she would faint. She had eaten so little all week, she felt like a wraith.

The day was unnaturally oppressive and still. Towards evening it began to rain heavily.

She was taken from the shrine by palanquin, and Rieko and the other women undressed and bathed her. They rubbed creams into her skin and perfumed her hair. She was clad in night robes, more sumptuous than those she usually wore in the day. Then she was taken to new apartments, in the deep interior of the residence, ones she had never seen before nor even known existed. They had been newly decorated. The beams and bosses glowed with gold leaf, the screens had been painted with birds and flowers and the straw matting was fresh and sweet smelling. The heavy rain made the rooms dim, but dozens of lamps burned in ornately carved metal stands.

'All this is for you,' Rieko said, a note of envy in her voice.

Kaede did not reply. She wanted to say, *For what purpose, seeing that he will never lie with me?* – but what business was this of Rieko's? Then the thought came to her: maybe he intended to, just once, as he had with his first wife to conceive his son. She began to tremble with revulsion and fear.

'You don't need to be afraid,' Rieko sneered. 'It's not as if you don't know what to expect from marriage. Now, if you were, as you should be, a virgin . . .'

Kaede could not believe that the woman dared to speak to her in such a manner and in front of the servants.

'Tell the maids to leave us,' she said. And when they were alone, 'If you insult me again I shall see that you are dismissed.'

Rieko laughed her empty trilling laugh. 'I don't think my lady quite understands her situation. Lord Fujiwara will never dismiss me. If I were you I would be more afraid for my own future. If you transgress in any way – if your behaviour is anything less than what is expected of Lord Fujiwara's wife – *you* may find *yourself* dismissed. You think you are brave and that you would have the courage to take your own life. Let me tell you, it is harder than it seems. When it comes to the point, most women fail. We cling to life, weak things that we are.' She picked up a lamp and raised it so the light fell on Kaede's face. 'You have probably been told all your life that you are beautiful, but you are less beautiful now than you were a week ago, and in a year you will be less beautiful still. You have reached your peak; from now on your beauty will fade.'

She held the lamp a little closer. Kaede could feel the scorch of the flame on her cheek.

'I could scar you now,' Rieko hissed. 'You would be turned out of the house. Lord Fujiwara will only keep you

185

while you please his eye. After that the only place for women like you is the brothel.'

Kaede stared back without flinching. The flame flickered between them. Outside the wind was rising and a sudden gust shook the building. Far in the distance, as if from another country, a dog was howling.

Rieko laughed again and placed the lamp on the floor. 'So it is not for your ladyship to speak of dismissing me. But I expect you are overwrought. I will forgive you. We must be good friends as his lordship desires. He will come to you soon. I will be in the next room.'

Kaede sat perfectly still, listening to the rising wind. She could not help thinking about her wedding night with Takeo, the feel of his skin against hers, his lips against the back of her neck when he lifted away the weight of her hair, the pleasure he brought to her whole body before he entered her and they became one person. She tried to keep the memories at bay, but desire had taken hold of her and it threatened to melt her icy numbness.

She heard footsteps outside and held herself rigid. She had vowed not to give her feelings away, but she was sure her aching body would somehow betray her.

Leaving his servants outside, Fujiwara stepped into the room. Kaede immediately bowed to the ground before him, not wanting him to see her face, but the act of submission itself made her tremble more.

Mamoru came in behind the nobleman, carrying a small carved chest made of paulownia wood. He placed it on the ground, bowed deeply and crawled backwards to the door of the adjoining room.

'Sit up, my dear wife,' Lord Fujiwara said, and as she did so she saw Rieko pass a wine flask through the door to Mamoru. The woman bowed and crept out of sight but not, Kaede knew, out of earshot.

Mamoru poured wine and Fujiwara drank, gazing at Kaede with rapt attention. The young man passed a cup to her and she raised it to her lips. The taste was sweet and strong. She took only the smallest sip. It seemed that everything conspired to set her body on fire.

'I don't believe she has ever looked so lovely,' Lord Fujiwara remarked to Mamoru. 'Note how suffering has brought out the perfect shape of her face. The eyes have a deeper expression and the mouth is moulded like a woman's now. It will be a challenge to capture that.'

Mamoru bowed without replying.

After a short silence Fujiwara said, 'Leave us alone,' and when the young man had gone, he picked up the chest and rose to his feet.

'Come,' he said to Kaede.

She followed him like a sleepwalker. Some unseen servant slid open the screen at the rear of the room and they stepped into another chamber. Here beds had been spread out with silk-covered quilts and wooden pillow blocks. The room was scented with a heavy fragrance. The screens closed and they were alone together.

'There is no need to be unduly alarmed,' Fujiwara said. 'Or perhaps I have misjudged you and it will be disappointment you feel.'

She felt for the first time the sting of his contempt. He had read her clearly, had discerned her desire. A wave of heat swept over her.

'Sit down,' he said.

She sank to the ground, keeping her eyes lowered. He also sat, placing the chest between them.

'We must pass a little time together. It's only a formality.'

Kaede did not reply, not knowing what to say.

'Speak to me,' he ordered. 'Tell me something interesting or amusing.'

It seemed a complete impossibility. Finally she said, 'May I ask Lord Fujiwara a question?'

'You may.'

'What am I to do here? How am I to spend my days?'

'Doing whatever it is that women do. Rieko will instruct you.'

'May I continue my studies?'

'I think educating a girl was something of a mistake. It does not seem to have improved your character. You may read a little – K'ung Fu-Tzu, I suggest.'

The wind gusted more strongly. Here in the centre of the house they were protected from its full force, but even so, the beams and pillars shook and the roof creaked.

'May I see my sisters?'

'When Lord Arai has finished his campaign against the Otori, we may go to Inuyama in a year or so.'

'May I write to them?' Kaede said, feeling fury build within her that she should have to beg for such favours.

'If you show Ono Rieko your letters.'

The lamp flames flickered in the draught and the wind moaned outside in an almost human voice. Kaede thought suddenly of the maids she'd slept alongside at Noguchi Castle. On wild, stormy nights, when the wind kept everyone awake, they would scare each other more with ghost stories. Now she felt she could hear the same ghostly voices she'd imagined then in the many-tongued speech of the wind. The maids' stories were all of girls like themselves who'd been killed unjustly or had died for love, who had been abandoned by their lovers, betrayed by their husbands, murdered by their overlords. Their angry, jealous ghosts cried out for justice from the world of the shades. She shivered a little.

'You are cold?'

'No, I was thinking of ghosts. Maybe one touched me. The wind is strengthening. Is it a typhoon?'

'I believe so,' he replied.

Takeo, where are you? she thought. *Are you out somewhere in this weather? Are you thinking of me at this moment? Is it your ghost that hangs behind me, making me shiver?*

Fujiwara was watching her. 'One of the many things I admire about you is that you show no fear. Not in the earthquake, not in a typhoon. Most women are thrown into a panic by these things. Of course, that does seem more feminine, and your boldness has taken you too far. You must be protected from it.'

He must never know how afraid I am of hearing of their death, she thought. *Takeo most, but also Ai and Hana. I must never show it.*

Fujiwara leaned forward slightly and with one pale, long-fingered hand indicated she should look at the chest.

'I have brought a wedding gift for you,' he said, opening the lid and lifting out an object wrapped in silk. 'I don't expect you are familiar with these curiosities. Some are of great antiquity. I have been collecting them for years.'

He placed it on the floor in front of her. 'You may look at it when I have left you.'

Kaede eyed the package warily. His tone warned her that he was enjoying some kind of cruel teasing at her

189

expense. She had no idea what it might be: a small statue, perhaps, or a flask of perfume.

She raised her eyes to his face and saw the slight smile play on his lips. She had no weapons and no defences against him except her beauty and her courage. She gazed past him, serene and immobile.

He stood and wished her goodnight. She bowed to the floor as he left. The wind shook the roof and the rain lashed against it. She could not hear his footsteps as he walked away: it was as if he disappeared into the storm.

She was alone, though she knew Rieko and the maids were waiting in the adjoining rooms. She let her gaze fall on the deep purple silk and after a few moments picked it up and unwrapped the object inside.

It was an erect male member, carved from some reddish, silky wood, cherry perhaps, and perfect in every detail. She was both repelled and fascinated by it, as no doubt Fujiwara had known she would be. He would never touch her body, he would never sleep with her, but he had read her awakened desire, and with this perverse gift he was both despising and tormenting her.

Tears sprang into her eyes then. She rewrapped the carving and placed it back in the box. Then she lay down on the mattress in her marriage chamber and wept silently for the man she loved and desired.

Seven

'I feared I would have to report your disappearance to your wife,' Makoto said as we made our way through the darkness to the shrine. 'I dreaded it more than any battle I have ever faced.'

'I was afraid you would have deserted me,' I replied.

'I hope you know me better than that! It would have been my duty to tell Lady Otori, but I was going to leave Jiro here with horses and food and return as soon as I had spoken to her.' He added in a low voice, 'I would never desert you, Takeo; you must know that.'

I felt ashamed of my doubts and did not share them with him.

He called to the men who were keeping guard and they shouted in reply.

'Are you all awake?' I said, for usually we shared the night watch and slept in turns.

'None of us felt like sleep,' he replied. 'The night is too still and heavy. The recent storm, the one that delayed you, came up out of nowhere. And for the last couple of days we've had the feeling there is someone spying on us. Yesterday, Jiro went to look for wild yams in the forest and saw someone lurking in the trees. I thought the bandits the fisherman mentioned might have got word of our presence and were checking out our strength.'

We'd been making more noise than a team of oxen as we stumbled along the overgrown path. If anyone was spying on us, they would have no doubt of my return.

'They're probably afraid we're competition,' I said. 'As soon as we get back with more men we'll get rid of them, but the six of us can't take them on now. We'll leave at first light and hope they don't ambush us on the road.'

It was impossible to tell what hour it was or how long it would be till dawn. The old shrine buildings were full of strange noises, creaks from the timber, rustles in the thatch. Owls called all night from the woods, and once I heard a pad of feet: a wild dog, perhaps, or maybe even a wolf. I tried to sleep but my mind was full of all those who wanted to kill me. It was quite possible that we had been traced here and the delay made it even more likely. The fisherman – Ryoma even – might have let slip something about my trip to Oshima, and I knew only too well that the Tribe's spies were everywhere. Quite apart from the edict they had issued against me, many of them would now feel bound by blood feuds to avenge their relatives.

Though by day I might believe in the truth of the prophecy, as always in the early hours of the morning I found it less comforting. I was inching towards achieving my goal; I could not bear the thought of dying before I'd succeeded. But with so many arrayed against me, was I as much of a lunatic as Jo-An to believe I could overcome them?

I must have dozed off, for when I next opened my eyes the sky was light grey and birds were starting to sing. Jiro was still asleep next to me, breathing deeply and evenly like a child. I touched his shoulder to wake him and he opened his eyes, smiling. Then as he returned from the other world I saw disappointment and grief spring into his face.

'Were you dreaming?' I said.

'Yes. I saw my brother. I was so glad he was alive after all. He called to me to follow him and then walked away into the forest behind our house.' He made a visible effort to master his emotions and got to his feet. 'We're leaving right away, aren't we? I'll go and get the horses ready.'

I thought of the dream I had had about my mother and wondered what the dead were trying to tell us. In the dawn light the shrine looked more ghostly than ever. It was a bitter, hostile place and I could not wait to leave it.

The horses were fresh after the days of rest, and we rode fast. It was still hot and oppressive, with grey clouds and no wind. I looked back at the beach as we went up the cliff path, wondering about the fisherman and his remaining child, but there was no sign of life from the hovels. We were all jumpy. My ears were alert to every sound, straining to hear above the pounding of the horses' feet and the creak and jingle of the harnesses as well as the dull roaring of the sea.

At the top of the cliff I halted for a moment and gazed out towards Oshima. It was hidden in the mist, but a heavy crown of clouds showed where it lay.

Jiro had stopped alongside me, the others riding on into the forest ahead. There was a moment of silence, and in that moment I heard the unmistakable sound, somewhere between a creak and a sigh, of a bowstring being drawn.

I shouted out a warning to Jiro and tried to reach him to push him down, but Shun leaped sideways, almost unseating me, and I found myself clinging to his neck. Jiro turned his head and looked towards the forest. The arrow passed whistling above me and struck him in the eye.

He let out a cry of shock and pain; his hands went to his face and then he fell forwards onto his horse's neck. The horse neighed in alarm, bucked a little, and tried to take off after its companions in front, its rider swinging helplessly from side to side.

Shun stretched out his neck and went snaking across the ground towards the shelter of the trees. Ahead, Makoto and the guards had turned. One of the men rode forwards and managed to grab the panicked horse by the bridle.

Makoto lifted Jiro from the saddle, but by the time I reached them the boy had died. The arrow had penetrated right through his head, shattering the back of the skull. I dismounted, cut off the bolt, and drew out the shaft. The arrow was massive and fletched with eagle feathers. The bow that had sent it must have been huge, the sort that solitary bowmen use.

I was filled with almost unbearable anguish. The shot had been meant for me. If I had not heard it and evaded it, Jiro would not be dead. Mad rage erupted in me. I would kill his murderer or die myself.

Makoto said in a whisper, 'It must be an ambush. Let's take shelter and see how many there are.'

'No, this was meant for me,' I replied, as quietly. 'This is the work of the Tribe. Stay here; take cover. I'm going after him. There will be only one – two at the most.' I did not want the men with me. Only I could move silently and invisibly, only I had the skills to get close to this assassin.

'Come when I call you; I want to take him alive.'

Makoto said, 'If there's only one, rather than take cover we'll ride on. Give me your helmet; I'll ride Shun. We may be able to confuse him. He'll follow us and you can come on him from behind.'

I did not know how far this deception would work or how close the bowman was. He would have seen the arrow miss me. He would guess I'd be after him. But if my men rode ahead, at least they would not be hindering me. The bowman might be anywhere in the forest by now, but I reckoned I could move faster and more silently than he could. As the horses trotted off with their sad burden, I went invisible and ran up the slope, threading my way between the trees. I did not think the bowman would have stayed in the place from which he had sent the fatal arrow; I figured he would have moved in a south-westerly direction to cut us off where the road turned back to the south. But even if he was still watching us, unless he had supreme Tribe skills, he would not know where I was now.

Before long I heard the sounds of a man breathing and the slight pressure of a foot on the soft earth. I stopped and held my own breath. He passed within ten paces of me without seeing me.

It was Kikuta Hajime, the young wrestler from Matsue, with whom I had trained. I had last seen him at the wrestlers' stable when I had left for Hagi with Akio. I had imagined then that he had thought he would never see me again. But Akio had not been able to kill me as he had planned, and now Hajime had been sent against me. The huge bow was slung over his shoulder; he moved, like most heavy men, balanced on the outside of his feet and, despite his weight, swiftly and silently. Only my ears could have discerned him.

I followed him towards the road where I could hear the horses ahead of us, moving at a swift canter as if in flight. I even heard one of the guards shout to Makoto to ride faster, addressing him as Lord Otori, making me grin bitterly at the deception. My quarry and I went at speed up the slope and down again and came out on a rocky outcrop that gave a good vantage point over the road beneath.

Hajime planted his feet firmly on the rock and took the bow from his shoulder. He set the arrow in the cord; I heard him take a deep breath as he drew it back: the muscles stood out on his arms and rippled across his neck. In close combat with him I wouldn't stand a chance. I could probably get him with Jato if I took him from behind, but I'd have to be sure to kill him with the first blow, and I wanted to take him alive.

He stood motionless, waiting for his target to appear from under the trees. I could barely hear his breathing now. I knew the technique he was using and I was familiar enough with the training he'd undergone to recognize his total concentration. He was one with the bow, with the arrow. It was probably a magnificent sight, but all I was aware of was my desire to see him suffer and then die. I tried to calm my rage. I had only a few moments to think.

I still carried on me my Tribe weapons, among them a set of throwing knives. I was no expert with them, but they might answer my purpose now. I had dried and oiled them after my soaking in the pirates' harbour; they slipped silkily from their holster. As the horses approached below, I ran, still invisible, out from my hiding place, throwing the knives as I went.

The first two sailed past him, breaking his concentration and making him turn towards me. He was looking over my head with the same puzzled expression he'd worn in the training hall when I had used invisibility there. It made me want to laugh and pained me beyond words at one and the same time. The third knife caught him on the cheek, its many points making blood flower immediately. He took an involuntary step backwards and I saw he was right on the brink. I threw the next two knives directly at his face and came back to visibility right in front of him. Jato sprang into my hand. He threw himself backwards to avoid the blow and went over the edge, falling heavily almost under the horses' feet.

He was winded by the fall and bleeding from cheek and eyes, but it still took the five of us more than a brief struggle to subdue him. He did not utter a sound, but his eyes burned with rage and malevolence. I had to decide whether to kill him on the spot or drag him back to Maruyama, where I would devise a slow death for him that might assuage my grief for Jiro.

Once Hajime was trussed up and unable to move, I drew Makoto aside to ask his advice. I could not get out of my head the memory of how Hajime and I had trained together; we had almost been friends. Such was the code of the Tribe that it transcended any personal liking or loyalty. Didn't I already know that from my own experience, from Kenji's betrayal of Shigeru? Yet I was shocked by it all over again.

Hajime called to me, 'Hey, Dog!'

One of the guards kicked him. 'How dare you address Lord Otori in that fashion?'

'Come here, Lord Otori,' the wrestler sneered. 'I have something to tell you.'

I went to him.

'The Kikuta have your son,' he said. 'And his mother is dead.'

'Yuki is dead?'

'Once the boy was born, they made her take poison. Akio will raise him alone. The Kikuta will get you. You betrayed them; they will never let you live. And they have your son.'

He made an almost animal-like snarl and, extending his tongue out to its fullest length, clamped his teeth down through it, biting it off. His eyes were wild with pain and rage; yet, he did not make another sound. He spat out his tongue and a gush of blood followed it. It filled his throat, choking him. His powerful body arched and struggled, fighting the death his will imposed on it as he drowned in his own blood.

I turned away, sickened, and saddened beyond belief. My rage had abated. In its place was a leaden heaviness, as if the sky had fallen into my soul. I ordered the men to drag him into the forest, cut off his head and leave his body for the wolves and foxes.

Jiro's body we took with us. We stopped at a small town along the coast, Ohama, where we held the burial service at the local shrine and paid for a stone lantern to be erected for him beneath the cedars. We donated the bow and arrows to the shrine, and I believe they still hang there, up under the rafters along with the votive pictures of horses, for the place was sacred to the horse goddess.

Among the pictures are my horses. We had to stay in the town for nearly two weeks, first to conduct the

funeral ceremonies and cleanse ourselves from the pollution of death, and then for the Festival of the Dead. I
borrowed an ink stone and brushes from the priest and
painted Shun's picture on a slab of wood. Into it I
believe I put not only my respect and gratitude for the
horse that had saved my life again but also my grief for
Jiro, for Yuki, for my life that seemed to lead me only
into witnessing the deaths of others. And maybe my
longing for Kaede, whom I missed with physical pain as
grief set alight my desire for her.

I painted obsessively: Shun, Raku, Kyu, Aoi. It was a
long time since I had painted, and the brush in my hand,
the cool wash of the ink had a calming effect on me. As
I sat alone in the tranquil temple, I allowed myself to
fantasize that this was my whole life. I had retired from
the world and spent my days painting votive pictures for
pilgrims. I recalled the words of the abbot at Terayama
on my first visit there so long ago with Shigeru: *Come
back when this is all over. There will be a place for you
here.*

Will it ever be over? I asked, as I had then.

Often I found tears spring to my eyes. I grieved for
Jiro and for Yuki, for their short lives, for their devotion
to me, which I had not deserved, for their murders on
my account. I longed to avenge them, but the brutality
of Hajime's suicide had repelled me. What endless cycle
of death and revenge had I initiated? I recalled all that
Yuki and I had experienced together and bitterly regretted . . . what? That I had not loved her? Maybe I had not
loved her with the passion I felt for Kaede, but I had
desired her, and the memory of it made me ache with
desire all over again and weep again for her lithe body
now stilled for ever.

I was glad the solemnities of the Festival of the Dead gave me the chance to say farewell to her spirit. I lit candles for all the dead who had gone before me and asked them for their forgiveness and their guidance. It was a year since I had stood on the bank of the river at Yamagata with Shigeru and we had sent our little flaming boats adrift on the current; a year since I had spoken Kaede's name, seen her face come alight and known that she loved me.

Desire tormented me. I could have lain with Makoto and so eased it, as well as comforted him in his grief, but though I was often tempted, something held me back. During the day while I painted for hours I meditated on the past year and all I had done in it, my mistakes and the pain and suffering they had inflicted on those around me. Apart from my decision to go with the Tribe, all my mistakes, I came to realize, sprang from uncontrolled desire. If I had not slept with Makoto his obsession would not have led him to expose Kaede to her father. If I had not slept with her she would not have nearly died when she lost our child. And if I had not slept with Yuki she would still be alive and the son that would kill me would never have been born. I found myself thinking of Shigeru, who had resisted marrying and puzzled his household by his abstinence because he had vowed to Lady Maruyama that he would lie with no one but her. I knew of no other man who had made such a vow, but the more I thought about it the more I wanted to emulate him in this as in everything I did. Kneeling silently before the horse-headed Kannon, I made a vow to the goddess that all my love, physical and emotional, from now on would be given only to Kaede, to my wife.

Our separation had made me realize anew how much

I needed her, how she was the fixed point that steadied and strengthened my life. My love for her was the antidote to the poison that rage and grief had sent through me; like all antidotes I kept it well hidden and well guarded.

Makoto, as grief stricken as I, also spent long hours in silent meditation. We hardly spoke during the day, but after the evening meal we often talked until far into the night. He, of course, had heard Hajime's words to me and tried to ask me about Yuki, about my son, but at first I could not bear to speak of either of them. However, on the first night of the festival after we returned from the shore we drank a little wine together. Relieved that the coolness between us seemed to have vanished and trusting him completely as I trusted no other man, I felt I should tell him the words of the prophecy.

He listened carefully as I described the ancient blind woman, her saintly appearance, the cave, the prayer wheel and the sign of the Hidden.

'I have heard of her,' he said. 'Many people aspiring to holiness go to seek her but I have never known anyone else who has found the way.'

'I was taken by the outcaste, Jo-An.'

He was silent. It was a warm, still night, and all the screens stood open. The full moon poured its light over the shrine and the sacred grove. The sea roared on the shingle beach. A gecko crossed the ceiling, its tiny feet sucking at the beams. Mosquitoes whined and moths fluttered around the lamps. I extinguished the flames so they would not burn their wings: the moon was bright enough to light the room.

Makoto said finally, 'Then I must accept that he is favoured by the Enlightened One, as you are.'

201

'The saint told me, "*It is all one*",' I said. 'I did not understand at the time, but later at Terayama I remembered Shigeru's words just before his death, and the truth of what she said was revealed to me.'

'You cannot put it into words?'

'No, but it is true, and I live my life by it. There are no distinctions between us: our castes as much as our beliefs are illusions that come between us and truth. It is how heaven deals with all men, and how I must too.'

'I followed you because of my love for you and because I believe in the justice of your cause,' he said, smiling. 'I did not realize you were to be my spiritual advisor too!'

'I know nothing of spiritual matters,' I said, suspecting he was laughing at me. 'I have abandoned the beliefs of my childhood and I cannot take on any others in their place. All religious teachings seem to me to be made up half of deep truth and half of utter madness. People cling to their beliefs as if they could be saved by them, but beyond all the teachings there is a place of truth where it is all one.'

Makoto laughed. 'You seem to have more insight in your ignorance than I after years of study and debate. What else did the saint say to you?'

I repeated the words of the prophecy to him. '*Three bloods are mixed in you. You were born into the Hidden but your life has been brought into the open and is no longer your own. Earth will deliver what Heaven desires. Your lands will stretch from sea to sea. Five battles will buy your peace, four to win and one to lose.*'

I paused at that point, not certain whether to go on.

'Five battles?' Makoto said. 'How many have we fought?'

202

'Two, if we count Jin-emon and the bandits.'

'So that was why you asked if that fight could be called a battle! Do you believe it all?'

'Most of the time. Should I not?'

'I would believe anything I heard from her if I had the good fortune to kneel at her feet,' Makoto said quietly. 'Was there anything more?'

'*Many must die*,' I quoted, '*but you yourself are safe from death, except at the hands of your own son*.'

'I am sorry,' he said with compassion. 'That is a terrible burden for any man to bear, especially you who have such a strong bond with children. I imagine you long to have your own sons.'

It touched me that he knew my character so well. 'When I thought Kaede was lost to me for ever, when I first went to the Tribe, I slept with the girl who helped me bring Shigeru out of Inuyama. Her name was Yuki. It was she who took his head to the temple.'

'I remember her,' Makoto said quietly. 'Indeed I'll never forget her arrival and the shock her news caused us.'

'She was Muto Kenji's daughter,' I said, with renewed sorrow for Kenji's loss. 'I cannot believe the Tribe used her so. They wanted to get a child, and once it was born they killed her. I regret it bitterly and I should not have done it, not only because of my son but because it was the cause of her death too. If it is to be my son who kills me, it will be only what I deserve.'

'All young people make mistakes,' Makoto said. 'It is our fate to have to live with their consequences.' He reached out and clasped my hand. 'I am glad you told me all this. It confirms many things I feel about you, that you have been chosen by Heaven and are protected to a certain extent until your goals are achieved.'

'I wish I were protected from sorrow,' I said.

'Then you would indeed reach enlightenment,' he replied dryly.

The full moon brought a change in the weather. The heat lessened and the air cleared. There was even a hint of autumn in the coolness of the mornings. Once the festival was over my spirits lifted a little. Other words of the abbot came to me, reminding me that my followers, all those who supported me, did so of their own free will. I had to set my grief aside and take up my cause again so that their deaths would not be in vain. And the words Shigeru had spoken to me in a small village called Hinode, on the far side of the Three Countries, also returned to me.

Only children weep. Men and women endure.

We made plans to move on the following day, but that afternoon there was a slight earth tremor, just enough to set the wind chimes ringing and make the dogs howl. In the evening there was another, stronger one. A lamp was knocked over in a house up the street from where we were lodging, and we spent most of the night helping the townspeople contain the ensuing fire. As a result, we were delayed another few days.

By the time we left I was mad with impatience to be with Kaede again. It made me hurry towards Maruyama, rising early and pushing the horses till late at night under the waning moon. We were silent mostly; Jiro's presence was too sharply missed to allow the light-hearted banter with which we had ridden out, and

I had a vague sense of apprehension that I could not rid myself of.

It was well into the hour of the Dog when we reached the town. Most of the houses were already darkened and the castle gates were barred. The guards greeted us warmly but they could not dispel my unease. I told myself that it was just that I was tired and irritable after the tedious journey. I wanted a hot bath, something decent to eat, and to sleep with my wife. However, her woman, Manami, met me at the entrance to the residence, and as soon as I saw her face I knew something was wrong.

I asked her to tell Kaede I had returned, and she fell to her knees.

'Sir . . . Lord Otori . . .' she stammered, 'she has gone to Shirakawa to bring her sisters here.'

'What?' I could not believe what I was hearing. Kaede had gone off on her own, without telling me or asking me? 'How long ago? When is she expected back?'

'She left shortly after the Festival.' Manami looked as if she would burst into tears. 'I don't want to alarm your lordship but I expected her before now.'

'Why did you not go with her?'

'She would not allow it. She wanted to ride, to go quickly so she would be back before your return.'

'Light the lamps and send someone to fetch Lord Sugita,' I said, but it seemed he had already heard of my return and was on his way.

I walked into the residence. I thought I could still smell Kaede's fragrance on the air. The beautiful rooms with their hangings and painted screens were all as she had designed them; the memory of her presence was everywhere.

Manami had told the maids to bring lamps, and their shadowy forms moved silently through the rooms. One of them approached me and whispered that the bath was ready for me, but I told her I would speak with Sugita first.

I went into Kaede's favourite room and my gaze fell on the writing table where she knelt so often to copy the records of the Tribe. The wooden box that held them always stood alongside the table; it was not there. I was wondering if she had hidden it or taken it with her when the maid announced Sugita's arrival.

'I entrusted my wife to you,' I said. I was beyond rage, just cold to the depths of my being. 'Why did you allow her to leave?'

He looked surprised at the question. 'Forgive me,' he said. 'Lady Otori insisted on going. She took plenty of men with her, led by Amano Tenzo. My nephew Hiroshi went too. It was a pleasure trip, to see her family home and bring her sisters here.'

'Then why has she not returned?' It seemed harmless enough: maybe I was overreacting.

'I am sure she will be back tomorrow,' Sugita said. 'Lady Naomi made many such journeys; the domain is used to their mistress travelling in this fashion.'

The maid brought tea and food, and we talked briefly of my journey while I ate. I had not told Sugita exactly what I'd had in mind in case it all came to nothing, and I did not go into details now but merely said that I was working out a long-term strategy.

There was no word from the Miyoshi brothers and no reports on what either Arai or the Otori were up to. I felt as if I were wandering in half darkness. I wanted to talk to Kaede and I hated this lack of information. If only I had a network of spies working for me . . . I found myself wondering as I had before if it would be possible to find talented children, Tribe orphans if such children existed, and bring them up for my own purposes. I thought of my son with a strange longing. Would he have a combination of Yuki's talents and mine?

If he did, they would be used against me.

Sugita said, 'I hear young Jiro died.'

'Yes, sadly. He was struck by an arrow that was ˎ intended for me.'

'What a blessing your lordship escaped!' he exclaimed. 'What happened to the assassin?'

'He died. It will not be the last attempt. It is the work of the Tribe.' I wondered how much Sugita knew about my Tribe blood, what rumours had been circulating about me during my absence. 'By the way, my wife was copying something for me. What happened to the box and the scrolls?'

'She never let them out of her sight,' he replied. 'If they are not here, she must have taken them with her.'

I did not want to show my concern so I said no more. Sugita left me and I took a bath, calling to one of the maids to come and scrub my back, wishing Kaede would suddenly appear as she had at Niwa's house, and then remembering, almost unbearably, Yuki. When the maid had left me, I soaked in the hot water thinking about what I was going to tell Kaede, for I knew I must share the prophecy about my son with her, yet I could not imagine how I would frame the words.

Manami had spread out the beds and was waiting to extinguish the lamps. I asked her about the records box and she gave me the same answer as Sugita.

Sleep was a long time coming. I heard the first

roosters crow and then fell into a heavy slumber just as day was breaking. When I woke, the sun was well up and I could hear the sounds of the household all around me.

Manami had just come in with breakfast and was fussing over me and telling me to rest after such a long and tiring journey when I heard Makoto's voice outside. I told Manami to bring him in but he called to me from the garden, not bothering to undo his sandals.

'Come at once. The boy, Hiroshi, has returned.'

I stood so quickly that I knocked the tray and sent it flying. Manami exclaimed in shock and started to pick the things up. Roughly, I told her to leave them and bring my clothes.

When I was dressed I joined Makoto outside.

'Where is he?'

'At his uncle's house. He's not in very good shape.' Makoto gripped my shoulder. 'I'm sorry; the news he brings is terrible.'

My immediate thought was of the earthquake. I saw again the flames that we had fought to extinguish and imagined Kaede caught in them, trapped in her burning house. I stared at Makoto, saw the pain in his eyes, and tried to form the unspeakable words.

'She is not dead,' he said quickly. 'But Amano and all the men, it seems, were slaughtered. Only Hiroshi escaped.'

I could not imagine what had happened. No one would dare harm Kaede in either Maruyama or Shirakawa lands. Had the Tribe kidnapped her to strike at me?

'It was Lord Fujiwara,' Makoto said. 'She is in his house.'

We ran across the main bailey, through the castle gates, down the slope and over the bridge into the town. Sugita's house lay immediately opposite. A small crowd had gathered outside, staring silently. We pushed through them and entered the garden. Two grooms were endeavouring to persuade an exhausted horse to get to its feet. It was a pretty roan colour, its flanks darkened by sweat. Its eyes rolled in its head and froth came from its mouth. I did not think it would ever get up again.

'The boy rode day and night to get here,' Makoto said, but I hardly heard him. Even more than usual I was acutely aware of every detail around me: the shine of the wooden floors from within the house, the fragrance of the flowers placed in alcoves, bird song in the garden shrubs. Inside my head a dull voice was repeating, *Fujiwara?*

Sugita came out at our approach, his face ashen. There was nothing he could say to me. He looked like a man who had already decided to end his life, a shell of what he'd been the night before.

'Lord Otori . . .' he said, faltering.

'Is the boy hurt? Can he talk?'

'You had better come and speak to him.'

Hiroshi lay in a room at the back of the house. It gave onto a small green garden; I could hear a stream flowing through it. It was cooler here than in the main rooms, and the bright morning glare was tempered by shady trees. Two women knelt beside the boy, one wiping his face and limbs with a damp cloth. The other held a tea bowl from which she was trying to persuade him to drink.

They both stopped what they were doing and bowed to the ground when we came in. Hiroshi turned his head, saw me and tried to sit.

'Lord Otori,' he whispered and despite himself his eyes filled with tears. Struggling to control them, he said, 'I'm sorry. I'm sorry. Forgive me.'

I pitied him. He was trying so hard to be a warrior, trying so hard to live by the warrior's strict code. I knelt beside him and gently laid my hand on his hair. He still wore it dressed like a child's; he was years away from his coming-of-age day yet he tried to act like a man.

'Tell me what happened.'

His eyes were fixed on my face but I did not return his gaze. He spoke in a quiet, steady voice as though he had been rehearsing his account over and over on the long ride home.

'When we came to Lady Otori's house, the retainer, Lord Shoji – don't trust him, he betrayed us! – told the lady that her sisters were visiting Lord Fujiwara. She sent him to bring them back, but he returned saying they were no longer there but the lord would tell Lady Shirakawa – he would only call her that – where they were if she visited him. We went the next day. A man called Murita came to meet us. As soon as Lady Otori rode through the gate she was seized. Amano, who was at her side, was killed at once. I didn't see any more.'

His voice tailed off and he took a deep breath. 'My horse bolted. I could not control him. I should have taken a quieter horse but I liked this one because he was so beautiful. Amano rebuked me for it; he said he was too strong for me. I wouldn't listen. I couldn't defend her.'

Tears began to pour down his cheeks. One of the women leaned over and wiped them away.

Makoto said gently, 'We must be grateful to your horse. He certainly saved your life, and if you hadn't escaped we would never have known what had happened.'

I tried to think of something to say to comfort Hiroshi, but there was no comfort.

'Lord Otori,' he said, trying to get up. 'I'll show you the way. We can go and get her back!'

The effort was too much for him. I could see his eyes begin to glaze over. I took him by the shoulders and made him lie down. Sweat was mingling with the tears now, and he was trembling all over.

'He needs to rest but he becomes agitated and tries to get up,' Sugita said.

'Look at me, Hiroshi.' I leaned over him and let my eyes meet his. Sleep came to him at once. His body relaxed and his breathing evened.

The women could not help gasping, and I caught the look that flashed between them. They seemed to shrink away from me, averting their heads and taking great care not to brush against my clothes.

'He'll sleep for a long time,' I said. 'It's what he needs. Tell me when he wakes up.'

I got to my feet. Makoto and Sugita also rose, looking at me expectantly. Inwardly, I was reeling with outrage, but the numbing calm of shock had descended on me.

'Come with me,' I said to Sugita. I really wanted to speak with Makoto alone, but I did not want to risk leaving Sugita. I was afraid he would slit his own belly, and I could not afford to lose him. The Maruyama clan's first loyalty was to Kaede, not to myself; I did not know how they would react to this news. I trusted Sugita more than the rest of them and felt that if he stayed loyal, so would they.

We walked back across the bridge and up the hill to the castle. The crowd outside had increased, and armed men were appearing in the streets. There was an atmosphere of unrest – not really panic or even alarm, just a host of unruly people milling, exchanging rumours, readying themselves for some unexpected action. I had to make decisions quickly before the situation caught fire and burned out of control.

Once we were inside the gates, I said to Makoto, 'Prepare the men. We'll take half our warriors and ride at once against Fujiwara. Sugita, you must stay here and hold the town. We'll leave two thousand men with you. Stock the castle against siege. I will leave tomorrow at first light.'

Makoto's face was drawn and his voice anxious. 'Don't do anything hasty. We have no idea where Arai is. You could be simply riding into a trap. To attack Lord Fujiwara, a man of his rank and status, will only turn opinion against you. It may be best not to react immedi—'

I cut him off. 'It's impossible for me to wait. I will do nothing except bring her back. Start at once.'

We spent the day in frantic preparation. I knew I was right to act immediately. The first reaction of the Maruyama people was fury and outrage. I wanted to take advantage of that. If I delayed I would seem halfhearted, seeming to accept others' opinion of my legitimacy. I was all too aware of the risks I was taking, and knew I was following one act of rashness with

212

another, but I could not conceive of any other way of acting.

At the end of the afternoon I told Sugita to summon the elders. Within the hour they were all assembled. I informed them of my intentions, warned them of the consequences and told them I expected their complete loyalty to myself and my wife. None of them made any objections – I think my anger was too strong for that – but I was uneasy about them. They were of the same generation as Fujiwara and Arai and were formed by the same code. I trusted Sugita, but with Kaede gone, could he keep them loyal while I was absent?

Then I called for Shun and went out for a ride on him to clear my head, stretch his legs before taking him on another hard journey and look at the state of the land.

About half the rice harvest was in, the farmers working day and night to get the rice cut before the weather changed. Those I spoke to were anxious, forecasting an imminent typhoon, citing the halo round the last full moon, the migrating geese, their own aching bones. I organized Sugita's warriors to lend a hand in strengthening the dykes and banks against floods; no doubt they would complain, but I hoped the sense of crisis would override their pride.

Finally I found myself, only half intentionally, on the edge of the hamlet where the outcastes had settled. The usual smell of tanning hides and fresh blood hung over it. Some men, Jo-An among them, were skinning a dead horse. I recognized the bright roan colour; it was Hiroshi's, the one I'd seen dying that morning. I called to Jo-An and dismounted, giving the reins to one of the grooms who'd ridden out with me. I went and stood by the river bank and Jo-An came and crouched by the water, washing the blood from his hands and arms.

'You've heard the news?'

He nodded, glanced at me, and said, 'What will you do?'

'What *should* I do?' I wanted some word from some god. I wanted to hear another prophecy, one that included Kaede, that bound our futures together. I would follow it blindly.

'There are three more battles,' Jo-An said. 'One to lose and two to win. Then you will rule in peace, from sea to sea.'

'With my wife?'

He looked away across the water. Two white egrets were fishing near the weir. There was a flash of orange and blue as a kingfisher swooped from a willow. 'If you are to lose one battle, you should lose it now,' he said.

'If I lose my wife none of it matters to me,' I said. 'I would kill myself.'

'That is forbidden to us,' he replied quickly. 'God has his plan for your life. All you have to do is follow it.'

When I did not reply, he went on, 'It matters to us who have left everything for you. It matters to those in the Otori lands who suffer now. We can bear war if peace comes from it. Don't abandon us.'

Standing by the peaceful river in the evening light I thought that if I did not get her back my heart would break utterly. A grey heron came flying slowly over the surface of the water, just above its own reflection. It folded its huge wings and landed with the slightest of splashes. It turned its head towards us, watching us, then, satisfied that we posed no danger to it, began to stalk silently through the shallows.

My real goal was to avenge Shigeru's death completely and take up my inheritance. Then the prophecy would be fulfilled. But it was impossible for me to let anyone take Kaede from me without resistance. I could do nothing but go after her, even if it meant throwing away everything I had struggled for.

I bade farewell to Jo-An and rode back to the castle. Word had come that Hiroshi was awake and improving in health. I asked for him to be brought to me shortly. While I was waiting I searched the residence for the box of records but found no trace of it. It was yet another source of concern. I feared it might have been stolen, which would mean the Tribe had penetrated the castle once and could do so again.

Hiroshi came to me just before nightfall. He was pale, with dark hollows under his eyes, but otherwise he had made a swift recovery. Physically and mentally he was as tough as a full-grown man. I questioned him about every detail of the journey and made him describe the terrain around Shirakawa and Fujiwara's residence. He told me how Raku had been killed, and the news saddened me deeply. The grey, black-maned horse was the first I had mastered, a link with Shigeru and my brief life as his son in Hagi. Raku had been my gift to Kaede when I had nothing else to give her, and he had brought her to Terayama.

I'd sent everyone else away so I could speak in private to Hiroshi, and now I told him to move closer.

'Promise you will tell no one what we speak of next.'

'I swear it,' he said, adding impulsively, 'Lord Otori,

215

I already owe you my life. I'll do anything to help rescue Lady Otori.'

'We will rescue her,' I said. 'I leave tomorrow.'

'Take me with you,' he begged.

I was tempted to but I did not think he was well enough. 'No, you are to stay here.'

He looked as if he would protest, but thought better of it and bit his lip.

'The records my wife was copying – did she take them with her?'

He whispered, 'We took both the originals and the copies. We hid them at Shirakawa in the sacred caves.'

I blessed Kaede in my heart for her wisdom and foresight. 'Does anyone else know this?'

He shook his head.

'And you could find them again?'

'Of course.'

'You must never tell anyone where they are. Some day we will make a trip together to retrieve them.'

'Then we can punish Shoji,' he said gleefully. After a moment he added, 'Lord Otori, may I ask you something?'

'Certainly.'

'The day my father died, the men who killed the guards made themselves unseen in some way. Can you do that?'

'Why do you ask? Do you think I can?'

'The women in the room today were saying that you were a sorcerer – forgive me. But you can do many strange things, like making me sleep.' He looked at me frowning. 'It was no ordinary sleep; I saw vivid dreams and understood things I'd never known before. If you can make yourself invisible, will you teach me how?'

'Some things cannot be taught,' I said. 'They are talents that are born in you. You already have many skills and you have had the best of upbringings.'

Something I said made his eyes suddenly fill with tears. 'They told me Jiro was dead.'

'Yes, he was killed by an assassin who was aiming at me.'

'And you killed the assassin?'

'I had him put to death, but he was already dying. He bit off his own tongue.'

Hiroshi's eyes gleamed. I wanted to explain something of my pain at Hajime's death and Jiro's, my revulsion at the endless cycle of bloodshed and revenge, but I did not think this warrior's son would be capable of understanding it, even after the Kikuta sleep, and I wanted to ask something else of him.

'Do many people believe I am a sorcerer?'

'Some whisper about it,' he admitted. 'Mostly women, and idiots.'

'I am afraid of disloyalty in the castle. That's why I want to leave you here. If you think there is any danger that Maruyama will side with Arai when I am gone, send word to me.'

Hiroshi stared at me. 'No one here would be disloyal to Lord Otori.'

'I wish I could be as certain.'

'I'll ride and find you myself,' he promised.

'Just make sure you take a quiet horse,' I told him.

I sent him back to his uncle's house and ordered food to be brought. Makoto returned with a report on the preparations; everything was ready for our early departure. However, after the meal he tried again to dissuade me.

'It's utter madness,' he said. 'I won't say another word after tonight and I'll go with you, but to attack a nobleman whose betrothed you stole . . .'

'We were legally married,' I said. 'He is the one who has committed an act of madness.'

'Didn't I warn you at Terayama how such a marriage would be viewed by the world? It was your own rashness that has led to this, and it will lead to your downfall if you persist in it.'

'Can you be sure you weren't motivated by jealousy then as you are now? You've always resented my love for Kaede.'

'Only because it will destroy you both,' he replied quietly. 'Your passion blinds you to everything. You were in the wrong. It would be better to submit to that and try to make your peace with Arai. Don't forget he is probably holding the Miyoshi brothers as hostages. Attacking Lord Fujiwara will only enrage him further . . .'

'Don't give me such advice!' I said in fury. 'Submit to having my wife taken from me? The whole world would despise me. I would rather die!'

'We probably all will,' he replied. 'I am sorry I have to say these things to you, Takeo, but it is my duty to. However, I have told you many times that your cause is mine and I will follow you no matter what you choose to do.'

I was too angry to continue talking to him. I told him I wanted to be alone and called to Manami. She came in, her eyes red with weeping, removed the food trays and spread out the bed. I took a bath, thinking it might be the last for some time. I did not want to stop being angry for when my rage abated, grief and something worse – apprehension – took its place. I wanted to stay in the intense, dark mood of my Kikuta side that made me fearless. One of Matsuda's teachings came into my mind: *If one fights desperately, he will survive. If he tries to survive, he will die.*

The time had come to fight desperately, for if I lost Kaede, I lost everything.

Manami was even more distressed in the morning, sobbing uncontrollably as she said goodbye and setting off the other maids too. But the mood among the men and in the streets was cheerful, with many townspeople flocking out to shout and wave at us as we rode past. I took only warriors, mainly the Otori and the others who had been with me since Terayama, leaving the farmers to finish bringing in the harvest and to protect their own houses and the town. Most of the Maruyama men stayed to defend the castle, but a few came with us to act as guides and scouts.

I had about five hundred warriors on horseback and perhaps another five hundred bowmen, some mounted and some on foot. The rest were foot soldiers armed with poles and spears. There was a train of packhorses, as well as porters, carrying provisions. I was proud of how quickly my army had been mustered and equipped.

We had not gone far and were about to ford the Asagawa, where we had inflicted such a huge defeat on Iida Nariaki, when I became aware that Jo-An and a handful of outcastes were following us. After the river we took the south road towards Shirakawa. I had never travelled on that road before, but I knew it would take us two days at least to reach Kaede's home and Makoto had told me Fujiwara's residence lay a short distance further to the south.

When we stopped for the midday meal, I went to

speak to Jo-An, aware as I did so of the glances the men sent in my direction. I set my ears to catch any comments, determined I would punish anyone who muttered anything, but no one dared.

Jo-An prostrated himself at my feet and I told him to sit up. 'Why have you come?'

He gave a smile that was more like a grimace, showing his broken teeth. 'To bury the dead.'

It was a chilling reply, and one I did not want to hear.

'The weather is changing,' Jo-An went on, gazing at a mass of high cloud spreading like horses' tails across the sky from the west. 'A typhoon is coming.'

'Don't you have any good news for me?'

'God always has good news for you,' he replied. 'I am to remind you of that afterwards.'

'Afterwards?'

'After the battle you lose.'

'Maybe I won't lose it!' Indeed I could not imagine it, with my men so fresh and eager and my own rage burning so powerfully within me.

Jo-An said no more but his lips moved silently, and I knew he was praying.

Makoto also seemed to be praying as we rode on, or was in that state of meditation that monks achieve. He looked serene and withdrawn, as if he had already cut his ties with this world. I hardly spoke to him, as I was still angry with him, but we rode side by side as we had so often done before. Whatever his doubts about this campaign, I knew he would not leave me, and little by little, soothed by the rhythm of the horses' feet, my rage against him abated.

The sky gradually clouded over with a darker tinge on the horizon. It was unnaturally still. We made camp that night outside a small town; in the early hours of the morning it began to rain. By midday it was a downpour, slowing our progress and dampening our spirits. Still, I kept telling myself, there was no wind. We could cope with a little rain. Makoto was less optimistic, fearing we would be held up at the Shirakawa, which was prone to sudden flooding in this weather.

But we never got to the Shirakawa. As we neared the limits of the Maruyama domain I sent scouts ahead. They returned in the late afternoon to say they had spotted a medium-size force, perhaps twelve or fifteen hundred strong, setting up camp on the plain ahead. The banners were Seishuu but they had also seen Lord Fujiwara's crest.

'He has come out to meet us,' I said to Makoto. 'He knew what my reaction would be.'

'He almost certainly is not here in person,' Makoto replied. 'But he would be able to command any number of allies. As I feared, they have set a trap for you. Your reaction would not be hard to guess.'

'We will attack them at dawn.' I was relieved the army was so small. I was not at all intimidated by Fujiwara; what I feared was a confrontation with Arai and some of the thirty thousand men he had under arms. The last I'd heard of Arai was that he was at Inuyama, far away in the east of the Three Countries. But I'd had no news of his activities all summer; he could be back in Kumamoto for all I knew, less than a day's journey from Shirakawa.

I questioned the scouts closely about the terrain. One of them, Sakai, knew the area well, having grown up there. He considered it to be a fair battle ground, or would be in better weather. It was a small plain, flanked

221

to the south and east by mountain ranges but open on the other sides. There was a pass to the south, through which our enemies had presumably come, and a broad valley led away to the north, eventually to the coast road. The road we had travelled on from Maruyama joined this valley a couple of miles before the first rocky outcrops of the plain.

There was little water in these uplands, which was why they were uncultivated. Horses grazed on their wild grasses and were gathered together once a year in the autumn. In early spring the grass was burned off. Sakai told me that Lady Maruyama used to come hawking here when she was younger, and we saw several eagles hunting for food before the sun set.

The valley at our rear reassured me. If we should need it, it was a way of retreat. I did not plan to retreat and I did not want to have to fall back to the castle town. My aim was only to go forward, to crush whoever stood in my way, regain my wife, and wipe out the terrible insult of her abduction. However, I had been taught by Matsuda never to advance without knowing how I would retreat, and for all my rage I was not going to sacrifice my men unnecessarily.

No night ever seemed so long. The rain lessened a little, and by dawn it was no more than drizzle, raising my spirits. We rose in the dark and began to march as soon as it was light, unfurling the Otori banners but not yet sounding the conches.

Just before the end of the valley I ordered a halt. Taking Sakai with me, I went on foot, under cover of the trees, to the edge of the plain. It stretched away to the south-east in a series of small rounded hillocks covered in long grass and wild flowers, broken by outcrops of strangely shaped grey-white rocks, many of them splashed with yellow and orange lichen.

The rain had made the ground beneath our feet muddy and slippery and mist hung in swathes above the plain. It was hard to see more than a couple of hundred paces; yet, I could hear our enemy clearly: the neighing of horses, the shouts of men, the creaking and jingling of harnesses.

'How far did you go last night?' I whispered to Sakai.

'Just over the first ridge; not much further than this. Their scouts were also about.'

'They must know we're here. Why haven't they attacked already?' I would have expected them to ambush us at the head of the valley; the sounds I heard were those of an army in readiness but not on the move.

'Perhaps they don't want to give up the advantage of the slope,' he suggested.

It was true that the slope was in their favour, but it was not particularly steep and gave no huge advantage. The mist bothered me more, as it was impossible to see exactly how many men we faced. I crouched in silence for a few moments, listening. Beyond the drip of the rain and the sighing of the trees I could hear both armies equally . . . or could I? From the enemy the noise seemed to grow in volume like the surge of the sea.

'You saw fifteen hundred at the most?'

'Closer to twelve hundred,' Sakai replied. 'I'd bet on it.'

I shook my head. Maybe the weather, sleeplessness, apprehension, were causing me unnecessary alarm. Maybe my hearing was playing tricks on me. However, when we returned to the main force, I called Makoto and the captains and told them I feared we might be hopelessly outnumbered, in which case we would immediately retreat on the signal from the conch shell.

'Do we pull back to Maruyama?' Makoto asked.

This had been one of my plans, but I needed an alternative. It was what my enemies would expect me to do, and for all I knew they might have already attacked the castle town, in which case I would find myself truly trapped. I took Makoto aside and said, 'If Arai has come out against us, too, we cannot stand and fight. Our only hope is to retreat to the coast and get the Terada to transport us to Oshima. If we start to retreat, I want you to ride ahead and find Ryoma. He must arrange it with Terada Fumio.'

'They'll say I was the first to flee,' he protested. 'I would prefer to stay by your side.'

'There is no one else I can send. You know Ryoma and you know the way. Anyway, we will probably all be in flight.'

He looked at me curiously then. 'Do you have a premonition about this encounter? Is this the battle we lose?'

'Just in case it is, I want to preserve my men,' I replied. 'I've lost so much, I can't afford to lose them too. After all, there are still two to win!'

He smiled; we clasped hands briefly. I rode back to the head of the troops and gave the signal to advance.

The mounted bowmen rode forward, followed by the foot soldiers, with warriors on horseback on either flank. As we came out from the valley, at my signal the bowmen split into two groups and moved to either side.

I ordered the foot soldiers to halt before they came into range of the opposing archers.

Their forces loomed out of the mist. I sent one of the Otori warriors forward. He bellowed in a huge voice, 'Lord Otori Takeo is moving through this country! Allow him to pass or be prepared to die!'

One of their men shouted back, 'We are commanded by Lord Fujiwara to punish the so-called Otori! We'll have his head and yours before noon!'

We must have seemed a pitiful force to them. Their foot soldiers, over-confident, began to stream down the slope with their spears held ready. At once our bowmen let fly and the enemy ran into a hail of arrows. Their bowmen retaliated but we were still beyond their range, and our horsemen swept up through the foot soldiers and against the archers before they could set arrow to cord again.

Then our foot soldiers surged forward and drove them back up the slope. I knew my men were well-trained but their ferocity surprised even me. They seemed unstoppable as they rushed forward. The enemy began to pull back, faster than I'd expected, and we raced after them, swords drawn, slashing and cutting at the retreating men.

Makoto was on my right side, the conch-shell blower on my left as we crested the hill. The plain continued its undulating roll towards the distant range in the east. But instead of a small army in retreat, we were faced with a far more daunting sight. In the dip between the small hills was another army, a huge one, Arai's Western Army, its banners flying, its men prepared.

'Blow the conch!' I shouted to the man alongside me. I should have believed my own ears all along. He placed the shell to his lips and the mournful sound rang across the plain, echoing back from the hills.

'Go!' I yelled to Makoto, and he turned his horse with difficulty and urged it into a gallop. It fought the bit, not wanting to leave its fellows, and Shun whinnied to it. But in a few moments we had all turned and were racing after Makoto back to the valley.

I'd been proud of my men's attack, but I was even prouder of them at that moment in the misty autumn dawn when they obeyed the orders instantly and began to retreat.

The swiftness of our turn around took our enemy by surprise. They had counted on us tearing down the slope after them, where they and Arai's men would cut us to pieces. In the first encounter we had inflicted greater casualties, and for a while their advance was hampered by the fallen dead and by the confusion surrounding both armies. About this time the rain began to fall more heavily again, turning the ground underfoot to slippery mud, which favoured us as we were nearly into the valley with its rockier floor.

I was in the rear, urging the men forward and from time to time turning to fight off our closest pursuers. Where the valley narrowed I left two hundred of my best warriors with orders to hold out as long as they could, buying time for the main force to get away.

We rode all that day, and by the time night fell we had outstripped our pursuers, but with casualties and the rearguard we had left behind, we were barely half the number we had been. I let the men rest for a couple of hours, but the weather was worsening and, as I'd feared, the wind was picking up. So we continued through the night and the next day, hardly eating, hardly resting, occasionally fighting off small bands of horse-men who caught up with us, pushing desperately on towards the coast.

That night we were in striking distance of Maruyama, and I sent Sakai on ahead to see what the situation was in the town. Because of the worsening weather he was of the opinion that we should retreat there, but I was still reluctant to commit myself to a long siege, and still uncertain as to who the town would side with. We halted for a while, ate a little and rested the horses. I was beyond exhaustion, and my memories of that time are cloudy. I knew I was facing total defeat – had already been defeated. Part of me regretted not dying in battle in my desperate attempt to rescue Kaede; part of me clung to the prophecy, believing it would still be fulfilled; and part of me simply wondered what I was doing, sitting like a ghost in the temple where we had taken shelter, my eyelids aching and my whole body craving sleep.

Gusts of wind howled round the pillars, and every now and then the roof shook and lifted as if about to fly away. No one spoke much; an air of resigned defiance hung over everyone: we had not quite crossed over to the land of the dead, but we were on our way there. The men slept, apart from the guards, but I did not. I would not sleep until I had brought them to safety. I knew we should be moving on soon – should march again most of the night – but I was reluctant to rouse them before they were rested.

I kept saying to myself, 'Just a few more minutes, just until Sakai returns,' and then finally I heard the sound of hooves through the wind and the downpour: not one horse, I thought, but two.

I went to the veranda to peer out into the dark and the rain and saw Sakai and behind him Hiroshi sliding from the back of an old, bony horse.

Sakai called, 'I met him on the road just outside the town. He was riding out to find you! In this weather!' They were cousins of some sort, and I could hear the note of pride in his voice.

'Hiroshi!' I said, and he ran to the veranda, undoing his sopping sandals and dropping to his knees.

'Lord Otori.'

I pulled him inside out of the rain, gazing at him in astonishment.

'My uncle is dead and the town has surrendered to Arai's men,' he said in fury. 'I can't believe it! Almost as soon as you'd left the elders decided: my uncle took his own life rather than agree. Arai's men arrived early this morning and the elders caved in at once.'

Even though I'd half expected this news, the blow was still bitter, made worse by the death of Sugita who had supported Kaede so loyally. Yet I was relieved I had followed my instincts and still had my retreat route to the coast. But now we had to move at once. I called to the guards to rouse the men.

'Did you ride all this way to tell me?' I said to Hiroshi.

'Even if all Maruyama desert you I will not,' he said. 'I promised you I'd come; I even chose the oldest horse in the stable!'

'You would have done better to stay at home. My future is looking dark now.'

Sakai said in a low voice, 'I am ashamed too. I thought they would stand by you.'

'I can't blame them,' I said. 'Arai is vastly more

powerful and we have always known Maruyama cannot sustain a long siege. Better to surrender right away, spare the people and save the harvest.'

'They expect you to retreat to the town,' Hiroshi said. 'Most of Arai's men are waiting for you at the Asagawa.'

'Then maybe there will be fewer in pursuit of us,' I said. 'They won't expect me to move towards the coast. If we ride day and night we can get there in a couple of days.' I turned to Sakai. 'There's no point in a child like Hiroshi disobeying his own clan and throwing his life away on a lost cause. Take him back to Maruyama. I release him and you from any obligation to me.'

They both refused adamantly to leave me, and there was no time to argue. The men were awake and ready. It was still raining heavily but the wind had dropped a little, renewing my hope that the worst of the storm was over. It was too dark to go at more than an ox's pace. The men in front carried torches that showed the road, but often the rain dimmed them to smoke. We followed blindly.

There are many tales of the Otori, many ballads and chronicles about their exploits, but none has captured the imagination more than this desperate and doomed flight across the country. We were all young, with the energy and madness of young men. We moved faster than anybody could have believed, but it was not fast enough. I rode always at the rear, urging my men forward, not letting anyone fall behind. The first day we fought off two attacks from our rear, gaining precious time for our main force to go forward. Then the pursuit seemed to die away. I imagine no one thought we would keep going, for it was clear by now that we were riding into the whirling heart of the storm.

The storm was covering our flight, but I knew that if it grew any worse all hope of escaping by boat was gone. On the second night Shun was so tired he could hardly lift one foot after the other. As he plodded along I dozed on his back, sometimes dreaming that the dead rode alongside me. I heard Amano call to Jiro and heard the boy reply, laughing cheerfully. Then it seemed to me that Shigeru rode next to me and I was on Raku. We were going to the castle in Hagi, as we had on the day of my adoption. I saw Shigeru's enemy, the one-armed man Ando, in the crowd and heard the treacherous voices of the Otori lords. I turned my head to cry out to Shigeru to warn him and saw him as I had last seen him alive on the river bank at Inuyama. His eyes were dark with pain, and blood ran from his mouth.

'Do you have Jato?' he said as he had said then.

I snapped awake. I was so wet I felt I had become a river spirit that breathed water instead of air. In front of me my army moved like ghosts. But I could hear the crash of the surf, and when dawn came it showed us the windswept coast.

All the off-shore islands were obliterated by heavy sheets of rain, and with every moment the wind grew stronger. It was howling like a tormented demon when we came to the cliffs where Hajime had lain in wait for me. Two pines had been uprooted and lay across the road. We had to lift them out of the way before we could get the horses through.

I went to the front then and led the way to the shrine of Katte Jinja. One of the buildings had lost its roof, and thatch was blowing around the garden. But Makoto's horse was tethered in what remained of the building, back turned to the wind, head bowed, alongside another stallion that I did not recognize. Makoto himself was inside the main hall with Ryoma.

I knew it was hopeless before they said anything. In fact I was amazed that Makoto had made it at all. That he had found Ryoma seemed like a miracle. I embraced them both, enormously grateful for their loyalty. I discovered later that Ryoma had been told by Fumio to come and wait for me with the message that they would meet me as soon as the weather cleared.

We had not failed through any lack of foresight, courage or endurance. We had been defeated in the end by the weather, by the great forces of nature, by fate itself.

'Jo-An also is here,' Makoto said. 'He took one of the loose horses and followed me.'

I had hardly thought of Jo-An during our flight to the coast, but I was not surprised to find him here. It was as if I had expected him to appear again in the almost supernatural way he turned up in my life. But at that moment I did not want to talk to him. I was too tired to think of anything beyond gathering the men inside the shrine buildings, protecting the horses as much as possible and salvaging what remained of our soaked provisions. After that, there was nothing any of us could do but wait for the typhoon to blow itself out.

It took two days. I woke on the night of the second day and realized I'd been dragged out of sleep by silence. The wind had dropped and, though the eaves still dripped, it was no longer raining. All around me men slept like the dead. I got up and went outside. The stars were as bright as lamps and the air clean and cold. I went to look at the horses. The guards greeted me in low voices.

'Weather's cleared up,' one said cheerfully, but I knew it was too late for us.

I walked on into the old graveyard. Jo-An appeared like a ghost in the ruined garden. He peered up into my face.

'Are you all right, lord?'

'I have to decide now whether to act like a warrior or not,' I said.

'You should be thanking God,' he replied. 'Now that the lost battle is done with, the rest are for you to win.'

I had said the same to Makoto, but that was before the wind and rain had dealt with me. 'A true warrior would slit his belly now,' I said, thinking aloud.

'Your life is not your own to take. God still has his plan for you.'

'If I don't kill myself, I will have to surrender to Arai. He is on my heels, and there is no way the Terada can reach us before he does.'

The night air was beautiful. I heard the muffled whisper of an owl's wings and a frog croaked from the old pond. The crash of the waves on the shingle was abating.

'What will you do, Jo-An? Will you return to Maruyama?' I hoped uneasily that the outcastes would be well treated when I was no longer there to protect them. With the country in turmoil, they would be more vulnerable than ever, turned on as scapegoats, denounced by villagers, persecuted by warriors.

He said, 'I feel very close to God. I think he will call me to him soon.'

I did not know how to reply to this.

Jo-An said, 'You released my brother from his suffering in Yamagata. If it comes to it, will you do the same for me?'

'Don't say such things,' I replied. 'You have saved my life; how can you ask me to take yours?'

'Will you? I am not afraid of dying but I am afraid of the pain.'

'Go back to Maruyama,' I urged him. 'Take the horse you came on. Stay away from the highways. I will send for you if I can. But you know, Arai is likely to take my life. We will probably never meet again.'

He gave his characteristic slight smile.

'Thank you for all you have done for me,' I said.

'Everything that has happened between us is part of God's plan. You should thank *him*.'

I went with him to the horse lines and spoke to the guards. They watched in disbelief as I loosened the stallion's rope and Jo-An leaped onto its back.

After he had trotted off into the darkness, I lay down again but did not sleep. I thought about Kaede and how much I loved her. I thought about my extraordinary life. I was glad I had lived it the way I had, despite all my mistakes. I had no regrets except for those who had died before me. Dawn came as bright and perfect as any I'd ever seen. I washed as best I could and dressed my hair, and when my ragged army awoke, I ordered them to do the same. I called for Ryoma, thanked him for his service and asked if he would wait at least until he heard of my death and take the news to Fumio at Oshima. Then I gathered the men together and spoke to them.

'I am going to surrender to Lord Arai. In return, I trust he will spare your lives and accept your service. I thank you for your loyalty. No one has been better served than I.'

I told them to wait in the shrine under the command of their captains and asked Makoto, Sakai and Hiroshi to come with me. Makoto carried the Otori banner and Sakai the Maruyama. Both were torn and streaked with mud. The horses were stiff and slow, but as we rode the sun came up and warmed them a little. A string of wild ducks flew overhead and a stag barked in the forest. Across the water we could see the clouds above Oshima; apart from them, the sky was a clear, deep blue.

We passed the fallen pines. The storm had gouged out the road around them and undermined the cliff where Hajime had stood. Boulders had tumbled down in a small landslide, and as the horses picked their way around them I thought of the young wrestler. If his arrow had found its mark, Jiro would still be alive – and so would many others. I thought of Hajime's body, lying unburied not far away: he would soon have his revenge.

We had not gone far when I heard ahead the rapid tramping of horses. I held up my hand and the four of us halted. The horsemen came at a trot, a group of about a hundred, two bannermen carrying Arai's crest at their head. When they saw us in the road they stopped abruptly.

Their leader rode forward. He was wearing full armour and an elaborate helmet decorated with a crescent moon.

I was thankful for the warmth of the sun, for I was no longer cold and could speak firmly. 'I am Otori Takeo. This is Sugita Hiroshi, nephew of Lord Sugita of Maruyama. I ask you to spare his life and return him safely to his clan. Sakai Masaki is his cousin and will accompany him.'

Hiroshi said nothing. I was proud of him.

The leader inclined his head slightly which I took to mean agreement. 'I am Akita Tsutomu,' he said. 'My orders are to bring Lord Otori to Lord Arai. He wishes to speak with you.'

'I am prepared to surrender to Lord Arai,' I said, 'on condition that he spare the lives of my men and take them into his service.'

'They may accompany you if they come peacefully.'

'Send some of your men with Kubo Makoto,' I said. 'He will tell them to surrender without a fight. Where is his lordship?'

'Not far from here. We sat out the typhoon in Shuho.'

Makoto left with most of the warriors, and Sakai, Hiroshi and I rode on in silence with Akita.

Eight

Spring had moved into summer; the planting was finished. The plum rains began; the seedlings grew and turned the fields brilliant green. The rain kept Shizuka inside, where she watched it cascading from the eaves while she helped her grandmother plait sandals and rain capes from rice straw and tend the silkworms in the airy lofts. Sometimes she went to the weaving shed and spent an hour or two at the looms. There was always work to do, sewing, dyeing, preserving, cooking, and she found the routine tasks calming. Though she was relieved to lay aside the roles she had played and glad to be with her family and her sons, often a strange depression took hold of her. She had never been fearful, but now she was troubled by anxiety. She slept badly, woken by the slightest sound; when she slept, she dreamed of the dead.

Kaede's father often came to her, fixing his sightless eyes on her. She went to the shrine to make offerings, hoping to placate his spirit, but nightmares still troubled her. She missed Kaede, missed Ishida, longed for Kondo to come back with news of them, and dreaded his return at the same time.

The rains ended and the hot humid days of high summer followed. Melons and cucumbers ripened and were pickled with salt and herbs. Shizuka often roamed the mountains gathering wild mushrooms, mugwort to make moxa with, bugle and madder for dyes, and the other, deadlier harvest from which Kenji prepared poison.

She watched her sons and the other children at their training, half marvelling as the Tribe skills awoke in them. They slipped in and out of sight, and sometimes she saw the trembling, indistinct shape as they learned to use the second self.

Her older son, Zenko, was less skilled than his brother. He was only a year or so away from manhood, and his talents should have been developing rapidly. But Shizuka could see he was more interested in horses and the sword: he took after his father. Would Arai want to own him now? Or would he still seek to protect his legitimate son by removing the illegitimate?

Zenko concerned her more than Taku. It was already obvious that Taku was going to be highly skilled; he would stay with the Tribe and rise high in it. Kenji had no sons, and Taku might even be master of the Muto family one day. His talents were precocious: invisibility came naturally to him and his hearing was sharp; with the onset of puberty it might even become like Takeo's. He had loose limbs like hers and could fold himself into the smallest of spaces and stay hidden for hours on end. He liked to play tricks on the maids, hiding in an empty pickling barrel or a bamboo basket and jumping out to surprise them like the mischievous tanuki in stories.

She found herself comparing her younger son with Takeo. If her cousin had had the same upbringing, if the Kikuta had known about him from birth, he would have been one of the Tribe, like her children, like herself, ruthless, obedient, unquestioning . . .

Except, she thought, *I am questioning. I don't even think I'm obedient any more. And what happened to my ruthlessness? I will never kill Takeo or do anything to hurt Kaede. They can't make me. I was sent to serve her and I came to love her. I gave her my complete allegiance and I won't take it back. I told her at Inuyama that even women could act with honour.*

She thought again of Ishida and wondered if gentleness and compassion were contagious and she had caught them from him. And then she thought of the other deeper secret she held within her. Where had her obedience been then?

The Festival of the Weaver Star fell on a rainy night. The children were dismayed, for the clouded sky meant that the magpies could not build a bridge across Heaven for the princess to meet her lover. She would miss their one meeting and be separated from him for another year.

Shizuka took it as a bad omen, and her depression increased.

Occasionally messengers came from Yamagata and beyond. They brought news of Takeo's marriage to Kaede, their flight from Terayama, the outcastes' bridge and the defeat of Jin-emon. The maids marvelled at what seemed to them like something from an ancient legend and made up songs about it. Kenji and Shizuka discussed these events at night, both torn by the same mixture of dismay and unwilling admiration. Then the young couple and their army moved into Maruyama and news of them dwindled, though reports came from time to time of Takeo's campaign against the Tribe.

'It seems he has learned ruthlessness,' her uncle said to her, but they did not discuss it further. Kenji had other preoccupations. He did not speak of Yuki again, but when the seventh month passed and no news had come of her, the whole household entered a time of waiting. Everyone was anxious for this Muto child, the master's first

238

grandchild, who had been claimed by the Kikuta and would be brought up by them.

One afternoon just before the Festival of the Dead, Shizuka walked up to the waterfall. It was a day of oppressive heat with no wind and she sat with her feet in the cool water. The cascade was white against the grey rocks and the spray caught rainbows. Cicadas droned in the cedars, rasping her nerves. Through their monotonous sound she heard her younger son approaching, though she pretended not to; just at the last moment, when he thought he would surprise her, she reached out and caught him behind the knees. She pulled him into her lap.

'You heard me,' he said, disappointed.

'You were making more noise than a wild boar.'

'I was not!'

'Maybe I have something of the Kikuta hearing,' she teased him.

'I have that.'

'I know. And I think it will become even sharper as you grow older.' She opened his palm and traced the line that ran straight across it. 'You and I have the same hands.'

'Like Takeo,' he said with pride.

'What do you know about Takeo?' she said, smiling.

'He's Kikuta too. Uncle Kenji told us about him: how he can do things no one else can do, even though he was impossible to teach, Uncle says.' He paused for a moment and then said in a small voice, 'I wish we didn't have to kill him.'

'How do you know that? Did Uncle tell you that too?'

'I heard it. I hear lots of things. People don't know I'm there.'

'Were you sent to find me?' she asked, reminding

herself to share no secrets in her grandparents' house without checking where her son was first.

'Not exactly. No one told me to come, but I think you should go home.'

'What's happened?'

'Aunt Seiko came. She is very unhappy. And Uncle . . .' He broke off and stared at her. 'I have never seen him like that before.'

Yuki, she thought at once. She stood quickly and pulled on her sandals. Her heart was pounding, her mouth dry. If her aunt had come, it could only be bad news – the worst.

Her fears were confirmed by the pall of mourning that seemed to have settled over the whole village. The guards' faces were pale, and there were no smiles or banter. She did not stop to question them but hurried to her grandparents' house. The women of the village had already gathered, leaving fires unlit and the evening meal uncooked. She pushed her way through them as they muttered words of sympathy and condolence. Inside, her aunt, Kenji's wife, knelt on the floor next to her grandmother, surrounded by the household women. Her face was drawn, her eyes red, her body shaking with deep sobbing.

'Aunt!' Shizuka knelt before her and bowed deeply. 'What happened?'

Seiko took her hand and gripped it hard but could not speak.

'Yuki passed away,' her grandmother said quietly.

'And the baby?'

'The baby is well; it's a boy.'

'I am so sorry,' Shizuka said. 'Childbirth . . .'

Her aunt was racked by even fiercer sobs.

'It was not childbirth,' the old woman said, putting her arms around Seiko and rocking her like a child.

'Where is my uncle?'

'In the next room, with his father. Go to him. Maybe you can comfort him.'

Shizuka rose and went quietly to the next room, feeling her eyes grow hot with unshed tears.

Kenji sat unmoving next to his father in the dim room. All the shutters were closed and it was stifling. The old man had tears trickling down his face; every now and then he raised his sleeve to wipe them away, but her uncle's eyes were dry.

'Uncle,' she whispered.

He did not move for a while. She knelt silently. Then he turned his head and looked at her.

'Shizuka,' he said. His eyes went bright as tears sprang into them but did not fall. 'My wife is here; did you see her?'

She nodded.

'Our daughter is dead.'

'It's terrible news,' she said. 'I am so sorry for your loss.' The phrases seemed useless and empty of meaning.

He did not say anything else. Eventually she dared to ask, 'How did it happen?'

'The Kikuta killed her. They made her take poison.' He spoke as if he did not believe his own words.

Shizuka herself could not believe them. Despite the heat she felt chilled to the bone. 'Why? How could they do such a thing?'

'They did not trust her to keep the child from Takeo or to bring him up to hate his father.'

She had thought nothing could shock her about the

Tribe, but this revelation made her heart nearly stop beating and her voice disappear.

'Who knows, perhaps they also wanted to punish me,' he said. 'My wife blames me: for not going after Takeo myself, for knowing nothing of Shigeru's records, for spoiling Yuki when she was a child.'

'Don't speak of these things now,' she said. 'You cannot blame yourself.'

He was staring into the distance. She wondered what he was seeing.

'They did not have to kill her,' he said. 'I will never forgive them for that.' His voice broke and though his face was clenched the tears fell then.

The Festival of the Dead was celebrated with more than usual solemnity and grief. Food was placed at the mountain shrines and bonfires lit on the peaks to light the way back to the world of the dead. Yet, the dead seemed reluctant to return. They wanted to stay with the living and remind them over and again of the ways they had died and their need for remorse, for revenge.

Kenji and his wife brought no comfort to each other, unable to draw close in their grief, each blaming the other for Yuki's death. Shizuka spent many hours with each of them, unable to give them any consolation but her presence. Her grandmother brewed calming teas for Seiko, and the woman slept long and often, but Kenji would take nothing to dull his pain, and Shizuka often sat with him until late at night, listening to him talk about his daughter.

'I brought her up like a son,' he said one night. 'She was so talented. And fearless. My wife thinks I gave her too much freedom. She blames me for treating her like a boy. Yuki became too independent; she thought she could do anything. In the end, Shizuka, she's dead because she was a woman.' After a moment he added, 'Probably the only woman I've ever really loved.' In an unexpected gesture of affection he reached out and touched her arm. 'Forgive me. I am of course very fond of you.'

'As I am of you,' she replied. 'I wish I could ease your grief.'

'Well, nothing can ease it,' he said. 'I will never get over it. I must either follow her into death or live with it as we all must live with grief. In the meantime . . .' He sighed deeply.

The rest of the household had retired. It was a little cooler, and the screens stood open to catch the slight breeze that now and then crept down the mountain. A single lamp burned at Kenji's side. Shizuka moved slightly so she could see something of his face.

'What?' she prompted.

He seemed to change the subject. 'I sacrificed Shigeru to the Kikuta for the sake of unity. Now they have taken my daughter from me too.' Again he fell silent.

'What do you plan to do?'

'The boy is my grandchild – the only one I'll ever have. I find it hard to accept that he's lost to the Muto completely. I imagine his father will have a certain interest in him, too, if I know Takeo. I said before that I would not seek Takeo's death; that's partly why I've been hiding out here all summer. Now I will go further: I want the Muto family to come to an agreement with him, to make a truce.'

'And go against the Kikuta?'

'I will never do anything in agreement with them again. If Takeo can destroy them, I will do everything in my power to help him.'

She saw something in his face and knew he was hoping Takeo would give him the revenge he craved. 'You will destroy the Tribe,' she whispered.

'We are already destroying ourselves,' he said bleakly. 'Moreover, everything is changing around us. I believe we are at the end of an era. When this war is over, whoever is the victor will rule over the whole of the Three Countries. Takeo wants to gain his inheritance and punish Shigeru's uncles, but whoever leads the Otori, Arai will have to fight them: either the Otori clan must conquer or they must be utterly defeated and wiped out, for there will be no peace while they simmer on the border.'

'The Kikuta seem to be favouring the Otori lords against Takeo?'

'Yes, I've heard Kotaro himself is in Hagi. I believe in the long run, despite his apparent strength, Arai will not succeed against the Otori. They have a certain legitimacy to claim the Three Countries, you know, because of their ancestral link with the emperor's house. Shigeru's sword, Jato, was forged and given in recognition of that, hundreds of years ago.'

He fell silent and a slight smile curved his lips.

'But the sword found Takeo. It did not go to Shoichi or Masahiro.' He turned to her and the smile deepened. 'I'm going to tell you a story. You may know that I met Shigeru at Yaegahara. I was about twenty-five; he must have been nineteen. I was working as a spy and secret messenger for the Noguchi, who were allies of the Otori then. I already knew that they would change sides during the battle and turn on their former allies, giving the victory to Iida and causing the deaths of thousands of men. I've always been detached from the rights and wrongs of our trade, but the depths of treachery fascinate me. There is something appalling about the realization of betrayal that I like to observe. I wanted to see Otori Shigemori's face when the Noguchi turned on him.

'So, for this rather base motive, I was there in the thick of the battle. Most of the time I was invisible. I have to say, there was something intensely exciting about being in the midst of the fray, unseen. I saw Shigemori; I saw the expression on his face when he realized all was lost. I saw him fall. His sword, which was well known and which many desired, flew from his hands at the moment of death and fell at my feet. I picked it up. It took on my invisibility and seemed to cleave to my hand. It was still warm from its master's grip. It told me that I had to protect it and find its true owner.'

'It spoke to you?'

'That's the only way I can describe it. After Shigemori died, the Otori went into a state of mad desperation. The battle raged for another couple of hours, which I spent looking for Shigeru. I knew him: I'd seen him once before, a few years earlier, when he was training in the mountains with Matsuda. It wasn't until the fighting was over that I came upon him. By then Iida's men were searching for him everywhere. If he could be declared dead in battle it would be convenient for everyone.

'I found him by a small spring. He was quite alone and was preparing to take his own life, washing the blood from his face and hands and scenting his hair and beard with perfume. He had taken off his helmet and loosened his armour. He seemed as calm as if he were about to bathe in the spring.

'The sword said to me, "This is my master," so I called

to him, "Lord Otori!" and when he turned I let him see me and held the sword out to him.

'"Jato," he greeted it, took the sword in both hands, and bowed deeply. Then he looked at the sword and looked at me and seemed to come out of the trance he was in.

'I said something like, "Don't kill yourself," and then, as if the sword spoke through me, "Live and get revenge," and he smiled and leaped to his feet, the sword in his hand. I helped him get away and took him back to his mother's house in Hagi. By the time we got there we had become friends.'

'I often wondered how you met,' Shizuka said. 'So you saved his life.'

'Not I but Jato. This is the way it goes from hand to hand. Takeo has it because Yuki gave it to him in Inuyama. And because of her disobedience then the Kikuta started to distrust her.'

'How strange are the ways of fate,' Shizuka murmured.

'Yes, there is some bond between us all that I cannot fight. It's mainly because Jato chose Takeo, through my daughter, that I feel we must work with him. Apart from that, I can keep my promise never to harm him and maybe make amends for the role I played in Shigeru's death.' He paused and then said in a low voice, 'I did not see the look on his face when Takeo and I did not return that night in Inuyama, but it is the expression he wears when he visits me in dreams.'

Neither of them said anything for a few moments. A sudden flash of lightning lit the room, and Shizuka could hear thunder rolling in the mountains. Kenji went on, 'I hope your Kikuta blood will not take you from us now.'

'No, your decision is a relief to me because it means I

can keep faith with Kaede. I'm sorry, but I would never have done anything to hurt either of them.'

Her admission made him smile. 'So I have always thought. Not only because of your affection for Kaede: I know how strong your feelings were for both Shigeru and Lady Maruyama and the part you played in the alliance with Arai.' Kenji was looking at her closely. 'Shizuka, you did not seem completely surprised when I told you about Shigeru's records. I have been trying to deduce who his informant in the Tribe might have been.'

She was trembling despite herself. Her disobedience – treachery, to give it its true name – was about to be disclosed. She could not imagine what the Tribe would do to her.

'It was you, wasn't it?' Kenji went on.

'Uncle,' she began.

'Don't be alarmed,' he said quickly. 'I will never speak of it to another soul. But I would like to know why.'

'It was after Yaegahara,' she said. 'As you know, I gave the information to Iida that Shigeru was seeking alliances with the Seishuu. Shigeru confided in Arai and I passed the information on. It was because of me that the Tohan triumphed, because of me that ten thousand died on the battlefield and countless others afterwards from torture and starvation. I watched Shigeru in the years following and was filled with admiration for his patience and fortitude. He seemed to me to be the only good man I had ever met, and I had played a leading part in his downfall. So I resolved to help him, to make amends. He asked me many things about the Tribe and I told him everything I could. It was not hard to keep it secret – it was what I had been trained to do.' She paused and then said, 'I am afraid you will be very angry.'

247

He shook his head. 'I should be, I suppose. If I had found out any time before this I would have had to order your punishment and death.' He was gazing at her with admiration. 'Truly you have the Kikuta gift of fearlessness. In fact I am glad you did what you did. You helped Shigeru, and now that legacy protects Takeo. It may even make amends for my own betrayal.'

'Will you go to Takeo now?' she asked.

'I was hoping to have a little more news. Kondo should return soon. Otherwise, yes, I will go to Maruyama.'

'Send a messenger, send me. It's too dangerous to go yourself. But will Takeo trust anyone from the Tribe?'

'Maybe we will both go. And we will take your sons.'

She gazed steadily at him. A mosquito was whining near her hair but she did not brush it away.

'They will be our guarantee to him,' Kenji said quietly.

Lightning flashed again; the thunder was closer. Suddenly rain began to fall heavily. It poured from the eaves and the smell of wet earth sprang from the garden.

The storm lashed the village for three or four days. Before Kondo returned, another message came, from a Muto girl who worked in Lord Fujiwara's residence in the south. It was brief and tantalizing, telling them none of the details they wanted to know, written in haste, and apparently in some danger, saying only that Shirakawa Kaede was in the house and was married to Fujiwara.

'What have they done to her now?' Kenji said, shaken out of his grief by anger.

'We always knew the marriage with Takeo would be opposed,' Shizuka said. 'I imagine Fujiwara and Arai have arranged this between them. Lord Fujiwara wanted to marry her before she left in the spring. I'm afraid I encouraged her to become close to him.'

She pictured Kaede imprisoned within the luxurious residence, remembered the nobleman's cruelty, and wished she had acted differently.

'I don't know what's happened to me,' she said to her uncle. 'I used to be indifferent to all these things. Now I find I care deeply; I'm outraged and horrified, and filled with pity for them both.'

'Since I first set eyes on her I've been moved by Lady Shirakawa's plight,' he replied. 'It's hard not to pity her even more now.'

'What will Takeo do?' Shizuka wondered aloud.

'He will go to war,' Kenji predicted. 'And almost certainly be defeated. It may be too late for us to make peace with him.'

Shizuka saw her uncle's grief descend on him again. She was afraid he would indeed follow his daughter into death and tried to make sure he was never left alone.

Another week passed before Kondo finally returned. The weather had cleared and Shizuka had walked to the shrine to pray again to the war god to protect Takeo. She bowed to the image and stood, clapped her hands three times, asking also, helplessly, that Kaede might be rescued. As she turned to walk away Taku came shimmering out of invisibility in front of her.

'Ha!' he said in triumph. 'You didn't hear me that time!'

She was astonished, for she had neither heard him nor discerned him. 'Well done!'

Taku grinned. 'Kondo Kiichi has returned. He's waiting for you. Uncle wanted you to hear his news.'

'So make sure you don't hear it too,' she teased him.

'I like hearing things,' he replied. 'I like knowing everyone's secrets.'

He ran ahead of her up the dusty street, going invisible every time he passed from sunshine to shadow. *It's all a game to him,* she thought, *as it used to be for me. But at some point in the last year it stopped being a game. Why? What's happened to me? Is it that I learned fear? The fear of losing the people I love?*

Kondo sat with her uncle in the main room of the house. She knelt before them and greeted the man who two months earlier had wanted to marry her. She knew now, seeing him again, that she did not want him. She would make some excuse, plead ill health.

His face was thin and haggard, though his greeting was warm.

'I'm sorry I have been so delayed,' he said. 'At one point I did not think I would return at all. I was arrested as soon as I got to Inuyama. The failed attack on you had been reported to Arai, and I was recognized by the men who came with us to Shirakawa. I expected to be put to death. But then a tragedy occurred: there was an outbreak of smallpox. Arai's son died. When the mourning period was over, he sent for me and questioned me at length about you.'

'Now he is interested in your sons again,' Kenji observed.

'He declared he was in my debt, since I'd saved your life. He wished me to return to his service and offered to confirm me in the warrior rank of my mother's family and give me a stipend.'

Shizuka glanced at her uncle, but Kenji said nothing.

Kondo went on, 'I accepted. I hope that was the right

thing to do. Of course, it suits me, being at the moment masterless, but if the Muto family object . . .'

'You may be useful to us there,' Kenji said.

'Lord Arai assumed I knew where you were and asked me to give you the message that he wishes to see his sons, and you, to discuss their formal adoption.'

'Does he want our relationship to resume?' Shizuka asked.

'He wants you to move to Inuyama, as the boys' mother.' He did not actually say *and as his mistress* but Shizuka caught his meaning. Kondo gave no sign of anger or jealousy as he spoke, but the ironic look flashed across his face. Of course, if he were established in the warrior class, he could make a good marriage within it. It was only when he had been masterless that he'd seen a solution in her.

She did not know if she was more angered or amused by his pragmatism. She had no intention of sending her sons to Arai or of ever sleeping with him again or of marrying Kondo. She hoped fervently that Kenji was not going to order her to do any of them.

'All these things must be considered carefully,' her uncle said.

'Yes, of course,' Kondo replied. 'Anyway, matters have been complicated by the campaign against Otori Takeo.'

'We've been hoping for news of him,' Kenji murmured.

'Arai was enraged by the marriage. He declared it invalid immediately and sent a large contingent of men to Lord Fujiwara. Later in the summer he himself moved to Kumamoto, close enough to strike at Maruyama. The last I heard was that Lady Shirakawa was living in Lord Fujiwara's house and was married to him. She is in seclusion, virtually imprisoned.' He sniffed loudly and threw his head back. 'I know Fujiwara considered himself betrothed to her, but he should not have acted in the way he did. He had her seized by force; several of her men were killed – Amano Tenzo among them, which was a great loss. There was no need for that. Ai and Hana are hostages in Inuyama. Matters could have been negotiated without bloodshed.'

Shizuka felt a pang of sorrow for the two girls. 'Did you see them there?'

'No, it was not allowed.'

He seemed genuinely angered on Kaede's behalf and Shizuka remembered his unlikely devotion to her.

'And Takeo?' she said.

'It seems Takeo set out against Fujiwara and met Arai's army. He was forced to retreat. After that it's all very unclear. There was a huge, early typhoon in the West. Both armies were caught close to the coast. No one really knows yet what the outcome was.'

'If Arai defeats Takeo, what will he do with him?' Shizuka asked.

'That's what everyone wonders! Some say he will have him executed; some that he wouldn't dare because of Takeo's reputation; some that he'll make an alliance with him against the Otori in Hagi.'

'Close to the coast?' Kenji questioned. 'Which part exactly?'

'Near a town called Shuho, I believe. I don't know the district myself.'

'Shuho?' Kenji said. 'I've never been there but they say it has a beautiful natural blue pool which I've always wanted to visit. It's a long time since I've done any travelling. The weather is perfect for it now. You had both better come with me.'

He sounded casual, but Shizuka sensed his urgency. 'And the boys?' she asked.

'We'll take them both; it will be a good experience for them, and we may even need Taku's skills.' Kenji got to his feet. 'We must leave at once. We'll pick up horses in Yamagata.'

'What is your plan?' Kondo said. 'If I may ask, do you intend to make sure Takeo is eliminated?'

'Not exactly. I'll tell you on the road.' As Kondo bowed and left the room, Kenji murmured to Shizuka, 'Maybe we will get there in time to save his life.'

Nine

No one spoke as we rode, but the attitude of Akita and his warriors seemed courteous and respectful. I hoped I had saved my men and Hiroshi by surrendering, but I did not expect my own life to be spared. I was grateful to Arai for having me treated like an Otori lord, one of his own class, and for not humiliating me, but I imagined he would either have me executed or order me to kill myself. Despite my childhood teaching, Jo-An's words and my promise to Kaede, I knew I would have no alternative but to obey.

The typhoon had cleared the air of all humidity and the morning was bright and clear. My thinking had the same clarity: Arai had defeated me; I had surrendered; I would submit to him and obey, doing whatever he told me to do. I began to understand why the warriors had such a high regard for their code. It made life very simple.

The words of the prophecy came into my head but I put them aside. I did not want anything to distract me from the correct path. I glanced at Hiroshi riding next to me, his shoulders squared, his head high. The old horse plodded calmly along, snorting now and then with pleasure at the warmth of the sun. I thought about the upbringing that had made courage second nature to the boy. He knew instinctively how to act with honour, though I was sorry he had come to experience surrender and defeat so young.

All around us were the signs of the devastation left by the typhoon when it swept along the coast. Roofless houses, huge trees uprooted, flattened rice and flooded rivers, with drowned oxen, dogs and other animals stranded among the debris. I felt anxious briefly about my farmers at Maruyama, wondered if the defences we had built had been strong enough to preserve their fields, and what would happen to them if Kaede and I were not there to protect them. To whom did the domain belong now and who would look after it? It had been mine for one brief summer but I grieved over its loss. I had put all my energy into restoring it. No doubt the Tribe would return, too, punish those who had supplanted them and take up their cruel trade again. And no one but I could put a stop to them.

As we approached the small town of Shuho, Arai's men could be seen foraging for food. I pictured the extra hardship this huge force of men and horses was imposing on the land. Everything that had already been harvested would be taken, and what had not been harvested would have been ruined by the storm. I hoped these villagers had secret fields and hidden stores; if not, they would starve when winter came.

Shuho was famous for its many cold springs, which formed a lake of a brilliant blue colour. The water was reputed to have healing qualities and was dedicated to the goddess of good fortune. Perhaps this was what gave the place a cheerful atmosphere, despite the invasion of troops and the destruction of the storm. The brilliant day seemed to promise the return of good fortune. The townspeople were already repairing and rebuilding, calling out jokes to each other, even singing. The blows of hammers, the hiss of saws set up a lively song against the sound of water as streams ran overflowing everywhere.

We were in the main street when, to my astonishment, I heard from out of the hubbub someone shout my name.

'Takeo! Lord Otori!'

I recognized the voice though I could not immediately place it. Then the sweet smell of the fresh-cut wood brought him up to the surface of my mind: Shiro, the master carpenter from Hagi who had built the tea house and the nightingale floor for Shigeru.

I turned my head in the direction of the voice and saw him waving from a rooftop. He called again, 'Lord Otori!' and slowly the town's song stilled as one by one the men laid down their tools and turned to stare.

Their silent burning gaze fell on me in the same way that men had stared at Shigeru when he rode back from Terayama to Yamagata, angering and alarming the Tohan who accompanied us, and at me when I had been among the outcastes.

I looked forward, making no response. I did not want to anger Akita. I was, after all, a prisoner. But I heard my name repeated from mouth to mouth, like the buzz of insects around pollen.

Hiroshi whispered, 'They all know Lord Otori.'

'Say nothing,' I replied, hoping they would not be punished for it. I wondered why Shiro was here, if he had been driven from the Middle Country after Shigeru's death, and what news he had from Hagi.

Arai had set up his headquarters in a small temple on the hillside above the town. He was not accompanied by his whole army, of course; I found out later some were still in Inuyama and the rest encamped halfway between Hagi and Kumamoto.

We dismounted and I told Hiroshi to stay with the horses and see that they were fed. He looked as if he were going to protest, then lowered his head, his face suddenly full of sadness.

Sakai put his hand on the boy's shoulder and Hiroshi took Shun's bridle. I felt a pang as I watched the little bay docilely walking beside him, rubbing his head against Hiroshi's arm. He had saved my life many times and I did not want to part with him. For the first time the thought that I might not see him again lunged and hit me and I realized how deeply I did not want to die. I allowed myself to experience the sensation for a moment, then I drew up my Kikuta self like a defence around me, thankful for the dark strength of the Tribe that would sustain me now.

'Come this way,' Akita said. 'Lord Arai wants to see you immediately.'

I could already hear Arai's voice from the interior of the temple, angry and powerful.

At the veranda's edge a servant came with water and I washed my feet. I could do little about the rest of me; my armour and clothes were filthy, coated in mud and blood. I was amazed that Akita could look so spruce after the battle and the pursuit through the rain, but when he led me into the room where Arai and all his senior retainers were gathered, I saw they were all equally well dressed and clean.

Among these large men Arai was the biggest. He seemed to have grown in stature since I had last seen him at Terayama. His victories had given him the weight of power. He had shown his characteristic decisiveness in seizing control after Iida's death, and Shigeru's; he was physically brave, quick-thinking and ruthless, and he had the ability to bind men to him in loyalty. His faults were rashness and obstinacy; he was neither flexible nor patient and I felt he was greedy. Whereas Shigeru had sought power because with it he could rule with justice and in harmony with Heaven, Arai sought power for its own sake.

All this flashed through my mind as I took one quick look at the man seated on the raised section of the room, flanked by his retainers. He wore elaborate armour, resplendent in red and gold, but his head was bare. He had grown his beard and moustache and I could smell their perfume. Our eyes met for a moment but I could read nothing in them other than his anger.

The room must have served as an audience room for the temple; beyond the inner doors, which were half open, I could hear movements and whispers from the monks and priests, and the smell of incense floated in the air.

I dropped to the floor, prostrating myself.

There was a long silence, broken only by the impatient tapping of Arai's fan. I could hear the quickened breathing of the men around me, the beating of their hearts like drums, and in the distance the song of the town rebuilding itself. I thought I heard Shun whicker from the horse lines, the eager sound of a horse seeing food.

'What a fool you are, Otori,' Arai shouted into the silence. 'I command you to marry and you refuse. You disappear for months, abandoning your inheritance. You reappear and have the audacity to marry a woman under my protection without my permission. You dare to attack a nobleman, Lord Fujiwara. All this could have been avoided. We could have been allies.'

He continued in this vein for some time, punctuating

each sentence with a thwack of his fan as if he would like to beat me round the head. But his rage did not touch me, partly because I had cloaked myself in darkness, partly because I sensed that it was mostly assumed. I did not resent it; he had every right to be angry with me. I waited, face on the floor, to see what he would do next.

He ran out of rebukes and insults and another long silence ensued. Finally he grunted, 'Leave us. I will speak to Otori alone.'

Someone to his left whispered, 'Is that wise, lord? His reputation . . .'

'I am not afraid of Otori!' Arai shouted, taking rage on again immediately. I heard the men depart one by one and heard Arai stand and step down from the platform. 'Sit up,' he ordered.

I sat but kept my eyes lowered. He knelt down so we were knee to knee and could speak without being overheard.

'Well, that's out of the way,' he said, almost affably. 'Now we can talk strategy.'

'I am deeply sorry for offending Lord Arai,' I said.

'All right, all right, what's past is past. My advisors think you should be ordered to kill yourself for your insolence.' To my amazement he began to chuckle. 'Lady Shirakawa is a beautiful woman. It must be punishment enough to lose her. I think many are jealous that you went ahead and did what they wished they dared do. And you lived, which many consider a miracle, given her reputation. Women pass, though; what matters is power – power and revenge.'

I bowed again, to avoid revealing the fury his shallow words aroused in me.

He went on, 'I like boldness, Takeo. I admire what you

259

did for Shigeru. I promised him a long time ago that I would support you in the case of his death; it irks me, as it must you, that his uncles go unpunished. I did speak to the Miyoshi brothers when you sent them. Indeed, Kahei is here with my men; you can see him later. The younger one is still in Inuyama. I learned from them how you outwitted the main Otori army and how many of the clan favour you. The battle at Asagawa was well done. Nariaki had been bothering me and I was pleased to see him removed. We came through Maruyama and saw your work there and Kahei told me how you dealt with the Tribe. You learned Shigeru's lessons well. He would be proud of you.'

'I don't deserve your praise,' I said. 'I will take my own life if you desire it. Or I will retire to a monastery – Terayama, for example.'

'Yes, I can see that working,' he replied dryly. 'I'm aware of your reputation. I'd rather use it myself than have you holed up in some temple, attracting all the malcontents from the Three Countries.' He added off-handedly, 'You may take your own life if you wish. It's your right as a warrior and I won't prevent you. But I'd infinitely prefer to have you fighting with me.'

'Lord Arai.'

'The whole of the Three Countries obeys me now, apart from the Otori. I want to deal with them before winter. Their main army is still outside Yamagata. I believe they can be defeated, but they will fall back to Hagi and it is said that the town cannot be taken by siege, especially once the snows begin.'

He stared at me, studying my face. I kept my expression impassive, my eyes turned away.

'I have two questions for you, Takeo. How were you

able to identify the Tribe in Maruyama? And was your retreat to the coast deliberate? We thought we had you trapped, but you moved too quickly for us, as if it were premeditated.'

I raised my head and met his eyes briefly. 'I accept your offer of an alliance,' I said. 'I will serve you loyally. In return I understand that you recognize me as the lawful heir of the Otori clan and will support me in reclaiming my inheritance in Hagi.'

He clapped his hands and, when a servant appeared at the door, ordered wine to be brought. I did not tell him that I would never give up Kaede, and he no doubt was less than frank with me, but we drank ceremonially to our alliance. I would have preferred something to eat, even tea. The wine hit my empty stomach like fire.

'Now you may answer my questions,' Arai said.

I told him about Shigeru's records of the Tribe and how I had been given them at Terayama.

'Where are they now? At Maruyama?'

'No.'

'So where? You won't tell me?'

'They are not in my possession but I know where they are. And I carry most of the information in my head.'

'So that's how you were so successful,' he said.

'The Tribe seem eager to assassinate me,' I said. 'There were not many in Maruyama, but each one represented a threat so I had to eradicate them. I would have preferred to make use of them; I know what they can do and how useful they can be.'

'You will share those records with me?'

'If it helps us both attain our goals.'

He sat for a while brooding on my words. 'I was enraged by the part the Tribe played last year,' he said. 'I did not know they were so powerful. They took you away and managed to keep you hidden while my men scoured Yamagata for you. I suddenly realized they were like damp beneath a house or wood borers that chew away at the foundation of a huge building. I also wanted to wipe them out – but it would make more sense to control them. That brings me to something else I want to talk to you about. You remember Muto Shizuka?'

'Of course.'

'You probably know that I had two sons with her.'

I nodded. I knew their names, Zenko and Taku, and their ages.

'Do you know where they are?' Arai asked. There was a curious note in his voice: not quite pleading, but close to it.

I did know, but I was not going to tell him. 'Not exactly,' I said. 'I suppose I could guess where to start looking.'

'My son, from my marriage, died recently,' he said abruptly.

'I had not heard of it. I am very sorry.'

'It was smallpox, poor creature. His mother's health is not good and she took the loss very badly.'

'My deepest sympathy.'

'I've sent messages to Shizuka to tell her I want my sons with me. I'll recognize them and adopt them legally. But I've heard nothing from her.'

'It's your right as their father,' I said. 'But the Tribe have a way of claiming children of mixed blood who've inherited their talents.'

'What are these talents?' he said curiously. 'I know Shizuka was an unparalleled spy and I've heard all sorts of rumours about you.'

'Nothing very special,' I said. 'Everyone exaggerates them. It's mainly a question of training.'

'I wonder,' he said, staring at me. I resisted the temptation to meet his gaze. I realized suddenly that the wine and my reprieve from death had made me light-headed. I sat still and said nothing, drawing up my self-control again.

'Well, we'll talk about this again. My other question concerns your retreat to the coast. We expected you to fall back to Maruyama.'

I told him about my pact with the Terada and my plan to enter Hagi by ship and infiltrate the castle from the sea while sending an army to decoy the Otori forces and tie them up on land. He was immediately taken with the plan, as I knew he would be, and it increased his enthusiasm to tackle the Otori before Hagi was closed by winter.

'Can you bring the Terada into alliance with me?' he demanded, his eyes fiery and impatient.

'I expect they will want something in exchange.'

'Find out what it is. How soon can you reach them?'

'If the weather holds, I can get word to them in less than a day.'

'I'm trusting you with a lot, Otori. Don't let me down.' He spoke to me with the arrogance of an overlord, but I think we both knew how much power I also held in our transaction.

I bowed again and, as I sat up, said, 'May I ask you something?'

'Certainly.'

'If I had come to you in the spring and sought your permission to marry Lady Shirakawa, would you have given it?'

He smiled, his teeth white in his beard. 'The betrothal

263

had already been arranged with Lord Fujiwara. Despite my affection for Lady Shirakawa and yourself, your marriage had become impossible. I could not insult a man of Fujiwara's rank and connections. Besides,' – he leaned forward and dropped his voice – 'Fujiwara told me a secret about Iida's death that very few of us know.' He chuckled again. 'Lady Shirakawa is far too dangerous a woman to let live freely. I much prefer to have her kept in seclusion by someone like Fujiwara. Many thought she should be put to death; in a way, he has saved her life by his magnanimity.'

I did not want to hear any more about Kaede; it made me too angry. I knew my situation was still dangerous and I must not let emotion cloud my judgment. Despite Arai's friendliness and his offer of alliance, I did not completely trust him. I felt he had let me off too lightly and was holding something over me that he had not yet disclosed.

As we stood he said casually, 'I see you have Shigeru's sword. May I see it?'

I took the sword from my belt and held it out to him. He received it with reverence and drew it from its scabbard. The light fell on its gleaming blue-grey blade, showing its wave-like patterns.

'The Snake,' Arai said. 'It has a perfect feel to it.'

I could see he coveted it. I wondered if I was supposed to present it to him. I had no intention of so doing.

'I have made a vow that I would keep it till my death and hand it on to my heir,' I murmured. 'It is an Otori treasure . . .'

'Of course,' Arai replied coolly, not relinquishing the sword. 'Speaking of heirs, I will find you a more suitable bride. Lady Shirakawa has two sisters. I'm thinking of marrying the older one to Akita's nephew, but nothing is arranged yet for the younger. She's a beautiful girl, very like her sister.'

'Thank you, but I cannot consider marriage until my future is less uncertain.'

'Well, there's no hurry. The girl is only ten years old.'

He made a couple of moves with the sword, and Jato sang mournfully through the air. I would have liked to have taken it and let it slice through Arai's neck. I did not want Kaede's sister; I wanted Kaede. I knew he was playing with me now, but I did not know where he was leading.

I thought how easy it would be, as he glanced smiling at my face, to fix him with my eyes and, as he lost consciousness, take my sword . . . I would go invisible, evade the guards, escape into the country.

And then what? I would be a fugitive again and my men, Makoto, the Miyoshi brothers – Hiroshi, too, probably – would all be slaughtered.

All these thoughts flashed one after the other through my mind as Arai swung Jato over his head. It was beautiful to watch: the heavy man, his face rapt and expressionless, moving so lightly, the sword cutting through the air faster than the eye could see. I was in the presence of a master, no doubt about that, whose skills came from years of practice and discipline. I was moved to admiration and inspired to trust the man in front of me. I would act like a warrior; whatever his commands, I would obey them.

'It's an extraordinary weapon,' he said finally, finishing the exercise, but he still did not return it to me. He was breathing slightly more heavily and tiny beads of sweat had appeared on his brow. 'There's one other subject we must discuss, Takeo.'

I said nothing.

'There are many rumours about you. The most damaging and one of the most persistent is that you have some connection with the Hidden. The circumstances around Shigeru's death and Lady Maruyama's do nothing to decrease its intensity. The Tohan have always claimed that Shigeru confessed to being a believer, that he would not take the oath against the Hidden or trample on the images when Iida ordered him to. Unfortunately no reliable witnesses survived the fall of Inuyama so we will never know for certain.'

'He never spoke of it to me,' I replied truthfully. My pulse had quickened. I felt I was about to be forced into some public repudiation of my childhood beliefs, and I shrank from it. I could not imagine the choice I was to be faced with.

'Lady Maruyama had a reputation for being sympathetic towards these people. It is said that many of the sect found refuge in her domain. Did you not find evidence of them?'

'I was more concerned with tracking down the Tribe,' I replied. 'The Hidden have always seemed harmless to me.'

'Harmless?' Arai exploded into rage again. 'Theirs is the most dangerous and pernicious of beliefs. It insults all the gods; it threatens the fabric of our society. It claims that the lowest of the low – peasants, outcastes – are the equals of nobles and warriors. It dares to say that great lords will be punished after death like commoners and it denies the teachings and existence of the Enlightened One.'

He glared at me, his veins blue, his eyes three-cornered.

'I am not a believer,' I said. I spoke the truth, but I still felt a pang of regret for the teachings of my childhood and a certain remorse for my faithlessness.

Arai grunted. 'Come with me.' He swept out of the room onto the veranda. His guards immediately leaped to their feet, one of them bringing his sandals for him to step into. I followed his entourage as he walked swiftly around the side of the blue pool and past the horse lines. Shun caught sight of me and neighed. Hiroshi was standing next to him, holding a bucket. When he saw me, surrounded by guards, his face blanched. Dropping the bucket, he followed us. At that moment I was aware of a movement away to my left. I heard Makoto's voice and, turning my head, saw him ride through the lower gates of the temple area. My men were gathering outside.

A kind of hush fell. I imagine everyone thought I was going to be executed as Arai strode towards the mountain, Jato still in his hand.

Where the rocks rose, a group of prisoners were tied up; they looked like a mixture of bandits, spies, masterless warriors and the usual unfortunates who were simply in the wrong place at the wrong time. Most of them crouched silently, resigned to their fate; one or two whimpered in terror; one was keening.

Beneath their moans I could clearly hear Jo-An praying under his breath.

Arai called an order and the outcaste was pulled forward. I gazed down on him. I had gone cold. I would feel neither pity nor horror. I would simply do what Lord Arai ordered.

Arai said, 'I would ask you to trample publicly on the vile images of the Hidden, Otori, but we have none here. This thing, this outcaste, was picked up on the road last night, riding a warrior's horse. Some of my men knew him from Yamagata. There was some suspicion then that he was connected with you. He was believed to have died. Now he reappears, having absconded unlawfully from his place of dwelling and, we realize, having accompanied you in many of your battles. He makes no secret of being a believer.'

He looked down at Jo-An with an expression of distaste on his face. Then he turned to me and held out the sword. 'Let me see how Jato cuts,' he said.

I could not see Jo-An's eyes. I wanted to look deep into them, but he was trussed with his head forced down and he could not move it. He continued to whisper prayers that only I could hear, the ones the Hidden use at the moment of death. There was no time to do anything except take the sword and wield it. I knew that if I hesitated for a moment I would never be able to do it and I would throw away everything I'd struggled for.

I felt the familiar, comforting weight of Jato in my hand, prayed that it would not fail me and fixed my eyes on the exposed bones of Jo-An's neck.

The blade cut as true as ever.

You released my brother from his suffering in Yamagata. If it comes to it, will you do the same for me?

It had come to it, and I was doing what he had requested. I spared him the anguish of torture and gave him the same swift and honourable death as Shigeru. But I still regard his death as one of the worst acts of my life, and the memory of it loosens my teeth and makes me sick to my stomach.

I could show nothing of that then. Any ensuing sign of weakness or regret would have been the end of me. An outcaste's death was of less significance than a dog's. I did not look down at the severed head, the gushing blood. I checked the cutting edge of the sword; there was not a trace of blood on it. I looked at Arai.

He met my gaze for a moment before I dropped my eyes.

'There,' he said in satisfaction, looking around at his retainers, 'I knew we had nothing to worry about with Otori.' He clapped me on the shoulder, his good humour completely restored. 'We'll eat together and talk about our plans. Your men can rest here; I'll see they're fed.'

I had completely lost track of time. It must have been around midday. While we ate, the temperature began to drop and a chill wind sprang up from the north-west. The sudden onset of cold spurred Arai into action. He decided to leave at first light the next day, meet up with the rest of his army, and march at once towards Hagi. I was to take my men back to the coast, contact Terada and make arrangements for the attack by sea.

We arranged that the battle would take place at the next full moon, that of the tenth month. If I was unable to achieve the sea voyage by then, Arai would abandon the campaign, consolidate the territory he'd taken so far and retire to Inuyama, where I was to join him. Neither of us put much store by this second plan. We were determined to settle affairs before winter.

Kahei was summoned and we greeted each other with delight, both of us having feared we would never meet again. Since I could not take all my men with me by ship, I would allow them to rest for a day or two before sending them east under Kahei's command. I had not yet spoken to Makoto and was not sure whether to take him with me or send him with Kahei. I remembered he had said he had little experience of ships and the sea.

When I met up with him we were fully occupied with organizing billeting and food in a district already stretched to its limit. I was aware of something in his gaze – sympathy? compassion? – but I did not want to talk to him or to anyone. By the time everything was settled as best it could be and I returned to the pool, it was early evening. Jo-An's remains were gone. So were all the other prisoners, executed and buried with little ceremony. I wondered who had buried them. Jo-An had come with me to bury the dead but who would do the same for him?

Since I was passing the lines, I checked on my horses. Sakai and Hiroshi were there, feeding them, glad for their sake as much as their own to have an extra day or so of rest.

'Maybe you should leave with Lord Arai tomorrow,' I told Sakai. 'We seem to be on the same side as Maruyama again; you can take Hiroshi home.'

'Forgive me, Lord Otori,' he said, 'but we'd prefer to stay with you.'

'The horses are used to us now,' Hiroshi put in, patting Shun's short, muscular neck as the animal ate greedily. 'Don't send me back.'

I was too tired to argue about it and, indeed, preferred to keep both my horse and the boy with my own men. I left them and walked towards the shrine, feeling I needed to do something to mark Jo-An's death and the part I had played in it. I rinsed my mouth and hands at the cistern, asked to be cleansed from the pollution of death, and asked for the goddess's blessing, all the while wondering at myself; I seemed to believe in everything or nothing.

I sat for a while as the sun set behind the cedars, staring at the astonishing blue water of the pool. Little silver fish swam in the shallows, and a heron arrived on its great grey wings to fish. It stood in its patient, silent way, its head turned sideways, its black eye unflickering. It struck. The fish struggled briefly and was swallowed.

Smoke from the fires floated upwards, mingling with the mist that gathered over the pool. Already the first stars were appearing in a sky like pearl-grey silk. There would be no moon tonight. The wind tasted of winter. The town hummed with an evening song of many men being fed; the smell of cooking drifted towards me.

I was not hungry; in fact most of the day I'd been battling nausea. I'd forced myself to eat and drink heartily with Arai and his men and knew I should go and join them again soon, to drink more toasts to our joint victory. But I put it off, gazing instead at the pool as the colour leached from it and it became as grey as the sky.

The heron, wiser than I was, took off with a clack of wings to go to its roost.

As darkness fell, it seemed I might be able to think of Jo-An without betraying myself. Was his soul now with God, with the Secret One who sees everything and will judge us all? I did not believe such a god existed: if he did, why did he abandon his followers to the suffering the Hidden endured? If he did exist, I was surely damned to hell by now.

Your life has been brought into the open and is no longer your own. Jo-An had believed in this prophecy. *Peace comes at the price of bloodshed.* Despite the teaching of the Hidden not to kill, he had known and accepted that. I was more determined than ever to bring that peace so that his blood, shed by me, would not be wasted.

Telling myself I must not sit there and brood, I was getting to my feet when I heard Makoto's voice in the distance. Someone responded and I realized it was Shiro. In

271

one of those tricks memory plays, I had completely forgotten seeing him earlier. My meeting with Arai and what
had happened afterwards had laid too thick a layer over
it. Now it came back to me, his voice calling my name and
the hush that had fallen as I rode through the town.

Makoto called to me. 'Takeo! This man was looking
for you. He wants you to come to his house.'

Shiro grinned. 'We've only got half the roof back
on. But we've got food to spare and firewood. It'd be an
honour.'

I was grateful to him, feeling that his earthy practical-
ity was just what I needed.

Makoto said quietly to me, 'Are you all right?'

I nodded, suddenly not trusting my voice.

He said, 'I am very sorry for Jo-An's death.' It was the
second time he had used the outcaste's name.

'He did not deserve it,' I said.

'It many ways it was more than he deserved: a swift
death at your hands. It could have been far worse.'

'Let's not talk about it; it's done.' I turned to Shiro and
asked him when he had left Hagi.

'Over a year ago,' he said. 'Lord Shigeru's death saddened me, and I had no desire to serve the Otori once he
– and you – were gone. This is my home town; I was
apprenticed in Hagi as a boy of ten, over thirty years ago
now.'

'I'm surprised they let you go,' I said, for master carpenters of Shiro's skill were usually highly valued and
retained jealously by the clans.

'I paid them,' he replied, chuckling. 'The fief has no
money; they'll let anyone go if they give them enough cash
in exchange.'

'No money?' I exclaimed. 'But the Otori are one of the richest clans in the Three Countries. What happened?'

'War, mismanagement, greed. And the pirates haven't helped. Sea trade is at a standstill.'

'This is encouraging news,' Makoto said. 'Can they afford to maintain their army?'

'Barely,' Shiro said. 'The men are well equipped – most of the fief's income has been spent on armour and weapons – but food is always short and taxes are sky high. There's a lot of discontent. If Lord Takeo returns to Hagi I reckon half the army will join him.'

'Is it common knowledge that I plan to return?' I asked. I wondered what spies the Otori maintained and how soon this news would get back to them. Even if they could no longer afford to pay the Tribe, the Kikuta would no doubt work for them for free.

'It's what everyone hopes,' Shiro replied. 'And since Lord Arai did not execute you as we all thought he was going to . . .'

'I thought it too!' Makoto declared. 'It seemed I arrived to take one last look at you!'

Shiro gazed at the peaceful pool, now dark grey in the fading light. 'It would have run red,' he said quietly. 'There was more than one archer with his bow trained on Lord Arai.'

'Don't say such things,' I warned him. 'We are allies now. I have recognized him as my overlord.'

'Maybe,' Shiro grunted. 'But it was not Arai who climbed into Inuyama to avenge Lord Shigeru.'

Shiro and his family – his wife, two daughters and sons-in-law – made us comfortable in the newly repaired part of the house. We shared the evening meal with them, and then I went with Makoto to drink wine with Arai. The

273

mood was cheerful, even boisterous; Arai was obviously convinced that the last stronghold of opposition was about to fall.

And then what? I did not want to think too much about the future. Arai wanted to see me installed in Hagi, where I would bring the Otori into alliance with him and I believed he genuinely desired to see Shigeru's uncles punished. But I still hoped to get my wife back, and if I was destined to rule from sea to sea, at some stage I would have to fight Arai. Yet, I had now sworn allegiance to him . . .

I drank savagely, welcoming the sharp comfort of the wine, hoping it would numb my thoughts for a while.

It was a short night. Well before dawn, the first of Arai's troops were stirring, preparing for the long journey. By the hour of the Dragon they had all departed, leaving the town silent for a while until the sound of repairs took over again. Sakai and Hiroshi had spent the night with the horses – luckily as it turned out, for, to Hiroshi's indignation, two separate warriors had tried to make off with Shun, claiming he was theirs. It seemed his reputation had grown with mine.

I spent the day in planning. I picked all the men who could swim or who knew anything about boats and the sea: all the Otori and some locals who had joined us since we had arrived at the coast. We went through our armour and weapons and equipped the sailors with the best of them. I dispatched spearmen to the forest to cut staves and spears for the men who would march with Kahei. Anyone left over was sent to help rebuild after the storm and salvage as much as possible of the harvest. Makoto set off for the coast to make contact with Ryoma and get details of our plans to the Terada. Arai's land march would take over twice as long as our sea voyage, so we had time in hand to prepare thoroughly.

To my relief the town did have hidden stores that had escaped Arai's hungry men, and they were willing to share these with us. So many sacrifices were being made for me; so much was hanging on this desperate assault. And what about the coming winter? Would these struggles for power simply condemn thousands to starvation?

I could not think about that. I had made my decision. I had to go forward with it.

That night I sat with Shiro and his sons-in-law and talked about building. They had not only worked on Lord Shigeru's house, they had built most of the houses in Hagi and had done all the carpentry for Hagi Castle. They drew plans of the interior for me, filling out what I remembered from the day of my adoption into the Otori clan. Even better, they revealed to me the secret floors, the trap doors and the hidden compartments they had installed on Masahiro's orders.

'It looks like a Tribe house,' I said.

The carpenters looked slyly at each other. 'Well, maybe certain people had a hand in its design,' Shiro said, pouring more wine.

I lay down to sleep, thinking about the Kikuta and the Tribe's relationship with the Otori lords. Were they even now lying in wait for me in Hagi, knowing that they did not have to pursue me any more for I would come to them? It was not so many weeks since their last attempt on my life, in this area, and I slept lightly, surfacing often to hear the sounds of the autumn night and the sleeping town. I was alone in a small room at the back of the house; Shiro and his family were in the adjoining room. My own guards were outside on the veranda, and there were dogs at every house in the street. It should have been impossible for anyone to approach me. Yet, around the darkest time of night I came out of a restless doze to hear breathing in the room.

I had no doubt it was an intruder, for whoever it was breathed in the slow, almost imperceptible way I had been trained in. But there was something different about the breathing: it was light and it did not come from the height I would have expected a man's. I could see nothing in the darkness, but I went invisible at once as the intruder might have better night vision than me. I slipped silently away from the mattress and crouched in the corner of the room.

I could tell from the minute sounds and a change in the feeling of the air that he had approached the mattress. I thought I could smell him now, but it was not the full scent of a man. Had the Kikuta sent a woman or a child against me? I felt a moment of revulsion at having to kill a child, pinpointed where the nose would be, and stepped towards it.

My hands went around his throat, finding the pulse. I could have tightened them then and killed him at once, but as soon as I held the neck I realized it was indeed a child's. I loosened my grip slightly; he had tensed all his muscles to give me the illusion he was thicker built than he really was. Feeling my grip relax he swallowed and said quickly, 'Lord Takeo. The Muto want a truce.'

I held him by the arms, made him open his hands, took a knife and a garrotte from his clothes, held his nose so he had to open his mouth, and felt inside for needles or poison. I did all this in the dark and he submitted without struggling. Then I called to Shiro to bring a lamp from the kitchen.

When he saw the intruder he nearly dropped the lamp.

'How did he get in? It's impossible!' He wanted to give the boy a thrashing but I restrained him.

I turned the boy's palms over and saw the distinctive line across them. I struck him in the face. 'What are these lies about the Muto when you are marked as Kikuta?'

'I am Muto Shizuka's son,' he said quietly. 'My mother and the Muto master have come to offer you a truce.'

'So why are you here? I'm not accustomed to negotiating with brats!'

'I wanted to see if I could,' he replied, faltering a little for the first time.

'Your mother doesn't know you're here? I nearly killed you! What would have happened to the truce then?' I hit him again but not so hard. 'You little idiot!' I realized I sounded just like Kenji. 'Are you Zenko or Taku?'

'Taku,' he whispered.

The younger one, I realized. 'Where's Shizuka now?'

'Not far away. Shall I take you there?'

'At a decent hour of day, perhaps.'

'I should go back,' he said nervously. 'She'll be really angry when she finds I'm gone.'

'Serves you right. Didn't you think about that before you took off?'

'Sometimes I forget to think,' he said ruefully. 'I want to try something and I just do it.'

I repressed the urge to laugh. 'I'm going to tie you up till morning. Then we'll go and see your mother.'

I told Shiro to bring some rope and tied the boy up, instructing one of the shamefaced guards not to take his eyes off him. Taku seemed quite resigned to being a prisoner – too resigned, in fact. I thought he was sure he'd be able to escape, and I wanted to get some sleep. I told him to look at me. Somewhat reluctantly he obeyed, and almost immediately his eyes rolled back and his eyelids closed. Whatever his talents – and I had no doubt they were considerable – he had no resistance against the Kikuta sleep.

That's something I can teach him, I caught myself thinking, just before I, too, fell asleep.

He was still sleeping when I woke. I studied his face for a while. I could see no similarity to me or to the Kikuta; he resembled his mother mostly, but there was a fleeting likeness to his father. If Arai's son had fallen into my hands . . . if the Muto really wanted to make peace with me . . . It wasn't until the relief started to wash over me that I realized how deep had been my dread of a meeting with my old teacher Kenji, and its outcome.

Taku slept on and on. It did not worry me. I knew Shizuka would come looking for him sooner or later. I ate a little breakfast with Shiro and sat on the veranda with the plans of Hagi Castle, memorizing them while I waited for her.

Even though I was looking out for her, she was almost at the house before I recognized her. She'd seen me but she would have gone straight past if I had not called to her.

'Hey, you!' I did not want to name her.

She stopped and spoke without turning. 'Me, lord?'

'Come inside if you want what you're looking for.'

She approached the house, stepped out of her sandals onto the veranda, and bowed deeply to me. Saying nothing, I went inside. She followed me.

'It's been a long time, Shizuka!'

'Cousin. You'd better not have harmed him.'

'I nearly killed him, the little fool. You should look after him better.'

We glared at each other.

'I suppose I should check you for weapons,' I said. I was extraordinarily pleased to see her and tempted to embrace her, but I didn't want a knife between my ribs.

'I haven't come to harm you, Takeo. I'm here with Kenji. He wants to make peace with you. He's called off the Muto family. The Kuroda will follow, and the others, too, probably. I was to bring Taku to you to prove our good faith. I didn't know he was going to take off on his own.'

'The Tribe's record of trust with me is not high,' I said. 'Why should I believe you?'

'If my uncle comes, will you talk to him?'

'Certainly. Bring the older boy too. I'll give your sons to my men to look after while we speak together.'

'I heard you had become ruthless, Takeo,' she said.

'I was taught it by our relatives in Yamagata and Matsue. Kenji always said it was the only thing I lacked.' I called to Shiro's daughter and asked her to bring tea. 'Sit down,' I said to Shizuka. 'Your son's asleep. Have some tea and then bring Kenji and Zenko to me here.'

The tea came and she sipped at it slowly. 'I suppose you have heard of Yuki's death?' she said.

'Yes, I was deeply grieved by the news. And outraged that she should have been used like that. You know about the child?'

Shizuka nodded. 'My uncle cannot forgive the Kikuta. That's why he's prepared to defy Kotaro's edict and support you.'

'He doesn't blame me?'

'No, he blames them for their harshness and inflexibility. And himself, for many things: Shigeru's death, encouraging you and Kaede to fall in love – maybe for his daughter's death too.'

'We all blame ourselves but fate uses us,' I said in a low voice.

'It's true,' Shizuka said. 'We live in the midst of the world; we can live no other way.'

'Do you have any news of her?' I did not want to ask about Kaede. I did not want to reveal my weakness and my humiliation but I could not help it.

'She is married. She lives in total seclusion. She is alive.'

'Is there any way you can contact her?'

Shizuka's face softened slightly. 'I am on friendly terms with Fujiwara's physician, and a Muto girl is a maid in the household. So from time to time we hear about her. But there is very little we can do. I dare not make any direct contact. I don't suppose even Kaede fully realizes the danger she is in. Fujiwara has had servants, sometimes even his companions, put to death for no other reason than a dropped tray, a broken plant or some other misdemeanour.'

'Makoto says he does not sleep with her . . .'

'I believe not,' Shizuka replied. 'Generally he dislikes women, but Kaede appeals to some part of him. She is one of his treasures.'

My teeth ground in rage. I imagined penetrating his mansion at night and seeking him out. I would cut him to pieces, slowly.

'He is protected by his relationship to the emperor,' Shizuka remarked as though she could read my mind.

'The emperor! What does the emperor do for us, miles away from the capital? There might not even be an emperor. It's like a ghost story, made up to frighten children!'

'If we are speaking of guilt,' Shizuka said, ignoring my

outburst, 'I feel I am to blame. I persuaded Kaede to attract Fujiwara. But if it had not been for his support, we would all have starved at Shirakawa last winter.'

She finished her tea and bowed formally to me.

'If Lord Otori is willing I will go and fetch my uncle now.'

'I'll meet him here in a couple of hours. I have some arrangements to see to first.'

'Lord Otori.'

Being addressed thus by Shizuka had a strange effect on me, for I had only heard her use the name before to Shigeru. I realized that during the course of our meeting I had progressed from *Cousin* to *Takeo* to *Lord Otori*. Irrationally it pleased me. I felt that if Shizuka recognized my authority it must be real.

I told my guards to keep an eye on Taku and went to check out what remained of my army. The two days of rest and decent food had done wonders for both men and horses. I was anxious to move back to the coast, to hear from Fumio as soon as possible, and thought I would ride there with a small group, but I was unsure what to do with the rest of the troops. The problem as always was one of food. The Shuho people had been generous to us, but to expect them to continue to feed us was stretching their goodwill and their resources. Even if I sent the bulk of the army now, under Kahei's command, to follow Arai by the land route, I needed provisions for them.

I was mulling over these problems as I returned to Shiro's house at midday. I recalled the fisherman on the beach and the bandits he had been afraid of. A sortie against bandits might be just the thing to fill in time, keep the men from idleness, restore their fighting spirit after our retreat, please the local people and possibly obtain more

281

provisions and equipment. The idea appealed to me enormously.

A man was squatting on his heels in the shadow of the tile roof – an unremarkable man, wearing faded blue-grey clothes and carrying no visible weapon. A boy about twelve years old was beside him. They both stood up slowly when they saw me.

I made a movement with my head. 'Come up.'

Kenji stepped out of his sandals onto the veranda.

'Wait here,' I told him. 'Let the boy come with me.' I went inside with Zenko to where Taku still slept. I took Taku's own garrotte and told the guards to strangle the boys with it if any attack was made on me. Zenko said nothing and made no sign of fear. I could see how like Arai he was. Then I went back to my teacher.

Once we were inside the house, we both sat down. We studied each other for a moment, then Kenji bowed and said in his ironic way, 'Lord Otori.'

'Muto,' I replied. 'Taku is also in the next room. He and his brother will die immediately if there is any attempt made on my life.'

Kenji looked older and I saw a weariness in his face that had not been there before. His hair was beginning to grey at the temples.

'I have no desire to harm you, Takeo.' He saw my frown and amended his words somewhat impatiently. 'Lord Otori. You probably won't believe me, but I never did. I meant it that night at Shigeru's when I vowed I would protect you while I lived.'

'You have a strange way of keeping your promises,' I said.

'I think we all know what it's like to be torn between

conflicting obligations,' he said. 'Can we put that behind us now?'

'I would be glad if we were no longer enemies.' I was acting more coldly than I felt, constrained by all that had happened between my old teacher and myself. For a long time I'd held him partly responsible for Shigeru's death; now my resentment was melted by sorrow for Yuki's death, for his grief. But I was not proud of myself in relation to Yuki, and then there was the question of the child, my son, his grandson.

Kenji sighed. 'The situation's become intolerable. What's the point of wiping each other out? The reason the Kikuta claimed you in the first place was to try to preserve your talents. If anyone ever spat upwards it was them! I know you have the records that Shigeru kept. I don't doubt that you can deal a terrible blow to the Tribe.'

'I would rather work with the Tribe than destroy them,' I said. 'But their loyalty to me must be total. Can you guarantee that?'

'I can for all except the Kikuta. They will never be reconciled to you.' He said nothing for a moment, then continued bleakly, 'Nor I to them.'

I said, 'I am very sorry about your daughter. I blame myself terribly for her death. I can make no excuse. I just wish I could say that if I had my life over again, I would act differently.'

'I don't blame you,' Kenji said. 'Yuki chose you. I blame myself because I brought her up to believe she had more freedom than she really did. Ever since she brought Jato to you, the Kikuta doubted her obedience to them. They were afraid she would influence the child. He is to hate you, you understand. The Kikuta are very patient. And Yuki did not hate you and never would. She always took your part.' He smiled painfully. 'She was very angry when we took you at Inuyama. She told me it would never work out to keep you against your will.'

I felt the corners of my eyes grow hot.

'She loved you,' Kenji said. 'Perhaps you would have loved her if you had not already met Lady Shirakawa. I blame myself for that too. I actually arranged your meeting; I watched you fall in love with her during the training session. Why, I don't know. Sometimes I think we were all bewitched on that journey.'

I thought so, too, remembering the pelting rain, the intensity of my passion for Kaede, the madness of my foray into Yamagata Castle, Shigeru's journey towards death.

'I might wish things had been different, Takeo, but I don't blame you or hold any grudge against you.'

I did not pick him up on his familiarity this time. He went on, sounding more like my old teacher, 'You often act like an idiot, but fate seems to be using you for some purpose, and our lives are bound together in some way. I'm prepared to entrust Zenko and Taku to you as a sign of my good faith.'

'Let's drink to it,' I said, and called to Shiro's daughter to bring wine.

When she had poured it and gone back to the kitchen, I said, 'Do you know where my son is?' I found it hard to imagine the child, a baby, motherless.

'I've been unable to find out. But I suspect Akio may have taken him north, beyond the Three Countries. I suppose you will try to find him?'

'When all this is over.' I was tempted to tell Kenji about the prophecy, that my own son would destroy me, but in the end I kept it to myself.

'It seems that the Kikuta master, Kotaro, is in Hagi,' Kenji told me as we drank.

'Then we will meet there. I hope you will come with me.'

He promised he would and we embraced.

'What do you want to do with the boys?' Kenji said. 'Will you keep them here with you?'

'Yes. Taku seems to be very talented. Would you send him alone on a spying mission? I might have a job for him.'

'Into Hagi? That would be a bit beyond him.'

'No, just locally. I want to track down some bandits.'

'It's unknown territory to him round here. He'd probably get lost. What do you want to find out?'

'How many they are, what their stronghold's like, that sort of thing. He has invisibility, doesn't he? He wouldn't have got past my guards without it.'

Kenji nodded. 'Maybe Shizuka can go with him. But is there a local person who can accompany them at least some of the way? It would save a lot of time on the mountain.'

We asked Shiro's daughters and the younger one said she would go. She often went out to collect mushrooms and wild plants for food and medicine, and though she avoided the bandits' area, she knew the countryside all the way to the coast.

Taku woke up as we were talking. The guards called to me and Kenji and I went to see him. Zenko still sat where I had left him, unmoving.

Taku grinned at us and exclaimed, 'I saw Hachiman in a dream!'

'That's good,' I told him. 'Because you are going to war!'

He and Shizuka went out that night and returned with all the information I needed. Makoto came back from the coast just in time to accompany me as we took two hundred men and stormed the rocky hideout, with so few losses I could hardly describe it as a battle. The results were all I'd hoped for: all the bandits dead, save two who were captured alive, and their winter provisions ours. We set free a number of women who had been abducted, among them the mother and sisters of the child I had fed on the beach. Zenko came with us and fought like a man, and Taku proved invaluable: even his mother gave him a word of praise. Word spread quickly to the fishing villages that I had returned and kept my promise to the fisherman. Everyone came to offer their boats to help transport my men.

I told myself all this activity was to keep my men from idleness, but in fact it was as much for my own sake. Speaking to Shizuka about Kaede and hearing of her intolerable plight intensified my longing for her a thousandfold. I was busy enough in the day to keep my thoughts at bay, but at night they returned to torment me. All week there were small earth tremors. I had the enduring vision of her trapped in a shaking building as it collapsed and burned. I was riven by anxiety: that she should die, that she should think I had abandoned her, that I would die without telling her how much I loved her and would never love anyone but her. The knowledge that Shizuka could possibly get a message to her kept returning to me with needling intensity.

Taku and Hiroshi formed a somewhat stormy relationship, being about the same age but total opposites in upbringing and character. Hiroshi disapproved of Taku and was jealous of him. Taku teased him with Tribe tricks that infuriated him. I was too busy to mediate between them, but they followed me around most of the time, squabbling like dogs. The older boy, Zenko, kept aloof from both of them. I knew his Tribe talents were slight, but he was good with horses and already an expert with the sword. He also seemed to have been trained perfectly in obedience. I was not sure what I would do with him in the future, but he was Arai's heir and I knew I would have to come to a decision about him sooner or later.

We held a great feast to bid farewell to the people of Shuho, and then, with the food supplied by the bandits, Kahei, Makoto and my main force set out to march to Hagi. I sent Hiroshi with them, silencing his protests by telling him he could ride Shun, and hoping the horse would take as good care of him as he had of me.

It was hard to say goodbye to them all, especially to Makoto. My closest friend and I held each other in a long embrace. I wished we were going into battle together, but he had no knowledge of boats and I needed him to command the land army with Kahei.

'We will meet in Hagi,' we promised each other.

Once they were gone, I felt I needed to stay informed about their movements, about Arai's progress and about the situation in Maruyama and at Lord Fujiwara's residence. I wanted to know the nobleman's reaction to my new alliance with Arai. Now I could start using the Muto Tribe network.

Kondo Kiichi had accompanied Shizuka and Kenji to Shuho and I realized he could also be useful to me, being now in Arai's service. Arai and Fujiwara were, after all, allies, which gave Kondo an excuse to approach the nobleman directly. Shizuka told me that Kondo was essentially a pragmatic and obedient man who would serve whomever he was told to by Kenji. He seemed to have no problems with swearing allegiance to me. With Kenji's agreement, Kondo and Shizuka set out to make contact with their Muto spies in the south-west. Before they left I drew Shizuka aside and gave her a message to pass on to Kaede: that I loved her, that I would come for her soon, that she should be patient, that she must not die before I saw her again.

'It's dangerous, especially to Kaede herself,' Shizuka said. 'I'll do what I can, but I can't promise anything. But we will send messages back to you before the full moon.'

I returned to the deserted shrine on the coast and set up camp there. A week passed; the moon entered into the first quarter. We had our first message from Kondo: Arai had encountered the Otori army near Yamagata, and it was in retreat towards Hagi. Ryoma returned from Oshima to say the Terada were ready. The weather held fair, the seas calm, apart from the earthquakes which caused large swells, increasing my sense of urgency.

Two days before the full moon, at midday, we saw dark shapes in the distance coming from Oshima: it was the fleet of pirate ships. There were twelve of them, enough with the fishing boats to take all my remaining men. I lined my warriors up on the shore, ready to embark.

Fumio leaped out of the leading boat and waded through the water towards me. One of his men followed him carrying a long bundle and two smaller baskets. After we embraced he said, 'I've brought something to show you. Take me inside; I don't want everyone to see it.'

We went inside the shrine while his sailors began directing the embarkation. The man put the bundles down and went to sit on the edge of the veranda. I could already guess from the smell what one of the objects was, and I wondered why Fumio should have gone to the bother of bringing someone's head to me, and whose it was.

He unwrapped it first. 'Look at it and then we'll bury it. We took a ship a couple of weeks ago with this man on it – one of several.'

I looked at the head with distaste. The skin was white as pearl and the hair yellow like the yolk of a bird's egg. The features were large, the nose hooked.

'Is it a man or a demon?'

'It's one of the barbarians that made the seeing tube.'

'Is that what's in there?' I indicated the long bundle.

'No! Something much more interesting!' Fumio unwrapped the object and showed it to me. I took it warily.

'A weapon?' I wasn't sure how you wielded it but it had the unmistakable look of something designed to kill.

'Yes, and I think we can copy it. I've had another one made already. Not quite right – it killed the man who was testing it – but I think I know where we went wrong.' His eyes were gleaming, his face alight.

'What does it do?'

'I'll show you. Do you have someone you can dispense with?'

I thought of the two bandits we had taken. They had been pegged out on the beach, an example to anyone else who might be considering their calling, and given just enough water to keep them alive. I'd heard their groans while we were waiting for Fumio and thought I must do something about them before we left.

Fumio called to his man, who brought a pan of coals. We had the bandits, pleading and cursing, tied upright to trees. Fumio walked about fifty or sixty paces down the beach, signalling to me to go with him. He lit a cord from the coals and applied the smouldering end to one end of the tube. It had a kind of hook, like a spring. He held the tube up, squinting along it towards the prisoners. There was a sudden sharp noise, which made me jump, and a puff of smoke. The bandit gave one fierce cry. Blood was pouring from a wound in his throat. He was dead within seconds.

'Ah,' Fumio said with satisfaction. 'I'm getting the hang of it.'

'How long before you can shoot again?' I asked. The weapon was crude and ugly. It had none of the beauty of the sword, none of the majesty of the bow, but I could see that it would be more effective than either.

He went through the process again and I counted my breaths: over one hundred, a long time in the middle of a battle. The second shot hit the other bandit in the chest, tearing a sizeable hole. I guessed the ball would penetrate most armour. The possibilities of the weapon both intrigued and repelled me.

'Warriors will call it a coward's weapon,' I said to Fumio.

He laughed. 'I don't mind fighting the coward's way if it means I survive!'

'You'll bring it with you?'

'If you promise to destroy it if we lose.' He grinned. 'No one else must learn how to make them.'

'We are not going to lose. What do you call it?'

'A firearm,' he replied.

We went back inside and Fumio rewrapped the firearm. The hideous head stared with blind eyes. Flies were beginning to settle on it, and the smell seemed to permeate the whole room, nauseating me.

'Take it away,' I ordered the pirate. He looked at his master.

'I'll just show you his other things.' Fumio took the third bundle and unwrapped it. 'He wore this round his neck.'

'Prayer beads?' I said, taking the white string. The beads looked like ivory. The string unravelled and the sign the Hidden use, the cross, fell into the air before my eyes. It shocked me to see so openly displayed something that for me had always been the deepest secret. In our priest's house in Mino the windows were set so that at certain times of day the sun formed a golden cross on the wall, but that fleeting image was the only one I'd seen before.

Keeping my face impassive, I tossed the beads back to Fumio. 'Strange. Some barbarian religion?'

'You are an innocent, Takeo. This is the sign the Hidden worship.'

'How do you know?'

'I know all sorts of things,' he said impatiently. 'I'm not afraid of knowledge. I've been to the mainland. I know the world is much larger than our string of islands. The barbarians share the beliefs of the Hidden. I find that fascinating.'

'No use in battle, though!' I found it not so much fascinating as alarming, as though it were some sinister message from a god I no longer believed in.

'But what else do they have, the barbarians? Takeo, when you are established in Hagi, send me to them. Let's trade with them. Let's learn from them.'

It was hard for me to imagine that future. All I could think about was the coming struggle.

By mid afternoon the last of the men were on board. Fumio told me we had to leave to catch the evening tide. I put Taku on my shoulders and Kenji, Zenko and I waded out to Fumio's boat and were pulled over the gunwales. The fleet was already under way, the yellow sails catching the breeze. I stared at the land as it became smaller and smaller and then faded into the mist of evening. Shizuka had said she would send messages before we left, but we had heard nothing from her. Her silence added to my anxiety, for her and for Kaede.

Ten

Rieko's disposition was nervous, and she was as alarmed by the typhoon as she had been by the earthquake. It threw her into a state of near collapse. Despite the discomfort of the storm, Kaede was grateful to be free of the woman's constant attention. However, after two days the wind dropped, clear autumn weather followed, and Rieko recovered her health and strength along with her aggravating attentiveness.

She seemed to find something to do to Kaede every day, plucking her eyebrows, scrubbing her skin with rice bran, washing and combing her hair, powdering her face to an unnatural whiteness, creaming her hands and feet until they were as smooth and translucent as pearl. She selected Kaede's clothes for her and dressed her with the help of the maids. Occasionally, as a special privilege, she would read a little to her or play the lute – at which, as she let Kaede know, she was considered to be highly skilled.

Fujiwara visited once a day. Kaede was instructed by Rieko in the art of making tea and she prepared it for him, going silently through the ritual while he followed every movement, correcting her from time to time. On fine days the women sat in a room that looked out onto a small enclosed garden. Two twisted pine trees and a plum tree of extreme antiquity grew there along with azaleas and peonies.

'We will enjoy the flowers in the spring,' Rieko said, for the shrubs were a dull autumn green, and Kaede thought of the long winter that stretched ahead and after that another and another, reducing her to a lifeless treasure, seen only by Lord Fujiwara.

The garden reminded her of the one at Noguchi Castle where she had sat briefly with her father when he had been informed of the marriage arranged with Lord Otori Shigeru. He had been proud then, relieved that she was to make such a good marriage. Neither of them had known that that marriage, too, would be a sham, a trap for Shigeru. Since she had so little with which to occupy her thoughts, she went over and over the past in her mind while she gazed out on the garden, watching every minute change as the days went slowly by.

The plum tree began to drop its leaves and an old man came into the garden to pick them one by one off the moss. Kaede had to be kept out of his sight, as from all men, but she watched him from behind a screen. With infinite patience he picked up each leaf between finger and thumb so the moss would not be damaged and placed it in a bamboo basket. Then he combed the moss as if it were hair, removing every scrap of twig and grass, worm castings, birds' feathers, pieces of bark. For the rest of the day the moss looked pristine, and then slowly, imperceptibly, the world, life, began to encroach on it, and the next morning the process began again.

Green and white lichen grew on the gnarled trunk and branches of the plum tree, and Kaede found herself watching that too every day. Tiny events had the power to startle her. One morning an ivory-marbled pale pink fungus like a flower carved from flesh had erupted in the moss, and when occasionally a bird alighted on the top of one of the pine trees and let out a trill of song, her pulse stammered in response.

Running a domain had not fully occupied her restless, hungry mind; now she had so little to do she thought she would die of boredom. She tried to hear the rhythm of the household beyond the walls of her rooms but few sounds penetrated to the solitary place. Once she heard the cadence of a flute and thought it might be Makoto. She dreaded seeing him, for she was gripped with jealousy at the thought of him free to come and go, free to be with Takeo and fight alongside him; yet, she longed to see him, to have some news, any news. But she had no way of knowing if it was the young monk or not.

After the boredom, the worst thing was knowing nothing. Battles might be fought and lost, warlords might rise and fall – all news was kept from her. Her one consolation was that if Takeo were dead, she felt Fujiwara would tell her, taunting her with it, taking pleasure in his death and her suffering.

She knew Fujiwara continued to have his plays performed and wondered sometimes if he had written her own story as he had once suggested. Mamoru frequently accompanied him on his visits and was reminded to study Kaede's expressions and copy them. She was not permitted to watch the dramas but she could hear snatches of words and chanting, the sounds of the musicians, the beating of a drum. Occasionally she would catch a phrase that she was familiar with and the play it came from would take shape in her head and she would find herself suddenly moved to tears by the beauty of the words and the poignancy of the emotions.

Her own life seemed just as poignant, just as moving. Forced to contemplate the tiny details of her present existence, she began to seek ways to capture her own feelings. Words came to her one by one. Sometimes it took her all day to select them. She knew little of formal poetry, other than that which she had read in her father's books, but she collected words like golden beads and strung them together in ways that pleased her. She kept them secret inside her own heart.

She came to love above everything the silence in which the poems formed themselves, like the pillars in the sacred caves of Shirakawa, drip by drip from the limy water. She resented Rieko's chatter, a mixture of malice and self-importance expressed in commonplaces, and Fujiwara's visits, his contrived artificiality, which seemed the complete opposite of the unadorned truth that she sought. Apart from Fujiwara, the only man she saw was Ishida. The physician came every few days and she enjoyed his visits, though they hardly spoke to each other. When she started looking for words, she stopped taking the calming teas; she wanted to know her feelings, no matter what the anguish.

Next to the room that gave on to the garden was a small household shrine with statues of the Enlightened One and the all-merciful Kannon. Not even Rieko dared to prevent Kaede from praying, and she knelt there for many hours until she entered a state where prayer and poetry became one and the everyday world seemed full of holiness and significance. She meditated often on the thoughts that had disturbed her after the battle of Asagawa and Takeo's persecution of the Tribe, and wondered if this state of holiness that she brushed against might bring an answer on how to rule without resorting to violence. Then she chided herself, for she could not see how she would ever rule again, and she had to admit that if she were to wield power she would seek revenge on all those who had inflicted suffering upon her.

Lamps burned day and night before the shrine, and often Kaede lit incense and let its heavy fragrance fill her nostrils and permeate the air around her. A small bell hung from a frame, and from time to time she would feel the impulse to strike it sharply. The clear note echoed through her rooms and the maids exchanged glances, careful not to let Rieko see them. They knew something of Kaede's history, pitied her, and increasingly admired her.

One of these girls in particular interested Kaede. She knew from the records that she had copied for Takeo that several Tribe members were employed in Fujiwara's household, almost certainly unknown to him. Two men, one of them the estate steward, were paid from the capital; presumably they were spies placed there to report back to the court on the exiled nobleman's activities. There were two servants in the kitchen who sold snippets of information to whomever would pay them, and another woman, a maid, whom Kaede had tentatively identified as this girl.

She had little to go on beyond the fact that there was something indefinable about her that reminded her of Shizuka and that the girl's hands were similar in shape. Kaede had not missed Shizuka when they had first separated; her life had been completely taken up with Takeo, but now, in the company of women, she missed her acutely. She longed to hear her voice and yearned for her cheerfulness and courage.

Above all, she longed for news. The girl's name was Yumi. If anyone knew what was happening in the outside world, it would be one of the Tribe, but Kaede was never alone with her and was afraid to approach her even indirectly. At first she thought the girl might have been sent to assassinate her, for some motive of revenge or to punish Takeo, and she watched her without seeming to, not out of fear but rather with a sort of curiosity: how it would be done, what it would feel like, and if her first response would be relief or regret.

She knew the sentence of death the Tribe had passed on Takeo, made more stringent by the rigours with which he had pursued them in Maruyama. She did not expect any sympathy or support from them. And yet, there was something in the girl's demeanour that suggested she was not hostile to Kaede.

As the days grew shorter and cooler, winter garments were brought out and aired, summer ones washed, folded and put away. For two weeks Kaede wore the in-between-season robes and found herself grateful for their extra warmth. Rieko and the maids sewed and embroidered, but Kaede was not allowed to take part. She did not particularly like sewing – she had had to struggle with her left-handedness to become deft at it – but it would have helped fill the empty days. The colours of the thread appealed to her and she was enchanted by the way a flower or bird came alive against the heavy silk fabric. She gathered from Rieko that Lord Fujiwara had ordered all needles, scissors and knives to be kept from her. Even mirrors had to be brought to her only by Rieko. Kaede thought of the tiny needle-sized weapon Shizuka had fashioned for her and hidden in her sleeve hem and the use she had put it to at Inuyama. Did Fujiwara really fear that she might do the same to him?

Rieko never let Kaede out of her sight, except when Fujiwara paid his daily visit. She accompanied her to the bath house and even to the privy, where she held the heavy robes aside and afterwards washed Kaede's hands for her at the cistern. When Kaede's bleeding began, Fujiwara ceased his visits until she had been purified at the end of the week.

Time went past. The plum tree was bare. One morning the moss and the pine needles had a glimmer of frost. The onset of the cold weather brought a wave of sickness. First Kaede caught a cold; her head ached and her throat felt as if she had swallowed needles. The fever brought disturbing dreams, but after a few days she recovered, apart from a cough that troubled her at night. Ishida gave her willow bark and valerian. By that time Rieko had caught the cold; it seemed to have increased in virulence, and the older woman was far more ill than Kaede had been.

On the third evening of Rieko's illness there came a series of small earth tremors. These and the fever sent Rieko into a state of panic. She became almost uncontrollable. Alarmed, Kaede sent Yumi to fetch Ishida.

Night had fallen by the time he arrived; a silver three-quarter moon hung in an intensely black sky, and the stars were icy points of light.

Ishida told Yumi to bring hot water and he brewed a strong draught and had the sick woman drink it. Gradually her writhing lessened and her sobs quietened.

'She'll sleep for a while,' he said. 'Yumi may give her another dose if the panic returns.'

As he spoke the ground shook again. Through the open door Kaede saw the moon quiver as the floor beneath her lifted and subsided. The other maid gave a squeal of fright and ran outside.

'The ground has been shaking all day,' Kaede said. 'Is it a warning to us of a severe earthquake?'

'Who knows?' Ishida replied. 'You had better extinguish the lamps before you go to bed. I'll go home and see what my dog is doing.'

'Your dog?'

'If he's asleep under the veranda, there'll be no big quake. But if he's howling, I'll start getting worried.'

Ishida chuckled and Kaede realized it had been a long time since she'd seen him in such a good mood. He was a quiet, self-contained, conscientious man guided by his duty to Fujiwara and his calling as a doctor, but she felt something had happened to him that night to penetrate his calm exterior.

He left them, and Yumi followed Kaede into the sleeping room to help her undress.

'The doctor seems cheerful tonight,' Kaede remarked. It was so pleasant not to have Rieko listening to her every word that she felt like talking just for the sake of it. The robe slid from her shoulders, and as Yumi lifted her hair to free it, Kaede felt her breath against her ear and heard her whisper.

'That's because Muto Shizuka came to see him.'

Kaede felt the blood drain from her head. The room seemed to whirl around her, not from an earth tremor, but from her own weakness. Yumi held her to support her and lowered her onto the sleeping mat. She brought out the night robe and helped Kaede put it on.

'My lady must not get cold and fall sick again,' she murmured, taking up the comb to attend to Kaede's hair.

'What is the news?' Kaede said quietly.

'The Muto have made a truce with Lord Otori. The Muto master is with him now.'

Just hearing his name spoken made Kaede's heart bound so strongly, she thought she would vomit.

'Where is he?'

'At the coast, at Shuho. He surrendered to Lord Arai.'

She could not imagine what had been happening to him. 'Will he be safe?'

'He and Arai formed an alliance. They will attack Hagi together.'

'Another battle,' Kaede murmured. A storm of emotion raced through her, making her eyes grow hot. 'And my sisters?'

'They are well. A marriage has been arranged for Lady Ai, to Lord Akita's nephew. Please don't cry, lady. No one must ever find out that you know these things. My life depends on it. Shizuka swore to me that you would be able to conceal your feelings.'

Kaede fought to keep the tears from falling. 'My younger sister?'

'Arai wanted to betroth her to Lord Otori but he says he will not consider marriage until he has taken Hagi.'

It was as if a hidden needle had slipped into her heart. It had not occurred to her, but of course Takeo would marry again. His marriage to her had been annulled; he would be expected to take another wife. Hana was an obvious choice, sealing the alliance with Fujiwara, giving Arai another link to the Maruyama and Shirakawa domains.

'Hana is only a child,' she said dully as the comb raked through her hair. Had Takeo forgotten her already? Would he happily accept her sister who looked so much like her? The jealousy that had racked her when she'd imagined Makoto with him now returned a thousand fold. Her isolation, her imprisonment, struck

301

her with renewed force. *The day I hear he is married I will die, if I have to bite out my own tongue,* she swore silently.

'You may be sure Lord Otori has his own plans,' Yumi whispered. 'After all, he was riding to rescue you when Arai intercepted him and drove him back to the coast. Only the typhoon prevented his escape then.'

'He was coming to rescue me?' Kaede said. The jealousy abated a little, washed away by gratitude and a faint glimmer of hope.

'As soon as he heard of your abduction, he set out with over a thousand men.' Kaede could feel Yumi trembling. 'He sent Shizuka to tell you he loves you and will never give you up. Be patient. He will come for you.'

A sound came from the next room, a sort of feverish cry. Both women went still.

'Come with me to the privy,' Kaede said, as calmly as if she had said no other words all evening beyond 'Hold my robe' and 'Comb my hair'. She was all too aware of the risks Yumi took by bringing her this message, and feared for her safety.

Yumi took a warm cloak and wrapped it round her. They stepped silently onto the veranda. It was colder than ever.

'It will freeze tonight,' the girl remarked. 'Shall I order more charcoal for the braziers?'

Kaede listened. The night was still. There was no wind and no dog howling. 'Yes, let's try to stay warm.'

At the entrance to the privy she slipped the fur robe from her shoulders and gave it to Yumi to hold. Squatting in the dark recess where no one could see her, she let herself feel joy. The words were beating in her brain, the words the goddess herself had spoken to her:

Be patient. He will come for you.

The following day Rieko was a little better; she rose and dressed at her usual time, even though Kaede begged her to rest longer. The autumn wind blew more coldly from the mountain, but Kaede felt a warmth she had not known since her capture. She tried not to think about Takeo but Yumi's whispered message had brought his image intensely to the forefront of her mind. The words he had sent to her beat so loudly inside her head, she was sure someone would hear them. She was terrified of giving herself away. She did not speak to Yumi or even look at her, but she was aware of a new feeling between them, a kind of complicity. Surely Rieko with her cormorant eyes could not miss it?

Sickness made Rieko short-tempered and more malicious than ever. She found fault with everything, complained about the food, sent for three different types of tea and found all of them musty, slapped Yumi for not bringing hot water fast enough and reduced the second maid, Kumiko, to tears when she expressed her fear of earthquakes.

Kumiko was normally light-hearted and cheerful, and Rieko allowed her a certain leeway that the other maids would never have enjoyed. But this morning she sneered at her, laughing in contempt at the girl's fears, ignoring the fact that she herself shared them.

Kaede retreated from the unpleasant atmosphere and went to sit in her favourite place, looking out over the tiny garden. The sun was just barely shining into the room, but in a few weeks it would no longer clear the outer walls. Winter would be gloomy in these rooms – but surely he would come for her before winter?

She could not see the mountains, but she imagined them soaring into the blue autumn sky. They would be snow-capped by now. A bird settled suddenly on the pine tree, chirped loudly and then flew away again over the roof, a flash of green and white in its wings. It reminded her of the bird Takeo had painted so long ago. Could it be a message for her – a message that she would soon be free?

The women's voices rose behind her. Kumiko was crying. 'I can't help it. If the house starts to shake I have to run outside. I can't bear it.'

'So that's what you did last night! You left her ladyship on her own, while I was asleep?'

'Yumi was with her all the time,' Kumiko answered, weeping.

'Lord Fujiwara's orders were that there must always be two of us with her!' The sound of another slap echoed through the room.

Kaede thought of the bird's flight, the woman's tears. Her own eyes grew hot. She heard footsteps and knew Rieko stood behind her but she did not turn her head.

'So Lady Fujiwara was alone with Yumi last night. I heard you whispering. What were you talking about?'

'We whispered only so as not to disturb you,' Kaede replied. 'We spoke of nothing; the autumn wind, the brilliance of the moon perhaps. I asked her to comb my hair, accompany me to the privy.'

Rieko knelt beside her and tried to look into her face. Her heavy scent made Kaede cough.

'Don't bother me,' Kaede said, turning away. 'We are both unwell. Let us try to spend a peaceful day.'

'How ungrateful you are,' Rieko said in a voice as tiny as a mosquito's. 'And what a fool. Lord Fujiwara has done everything for you and you still dream of deceiving him.'

'You must be feverish,' Kaede said. 'You are imagining things. How could I deceive Lord Fujiwara in any way? I am completely his prisoner.'

'His *wife*,' Rieko corrected her. 'Even to use such a word as *prisoner* shows how you still rebel against your husband.'

Kaede said nothing, just gazed at the pine needles etched against the sky. She was afraid of what she might reveal to Rieko. Yumi's message had brought her hope, but the reverse side of hope was fear: for Yumi, for Shizuka, for herself.

'You seem changed in some way,' Rieko muttered. 'You think I can't read you?'

'It's true I feel a little warm,' Kaede said. 'I believe the fever has returned.'

Are they at Hagi yet? she thought. *Is he fighting now? May he be protected! May he live!*

'I am going to pray for a little while,' she told Rieko, and went to kneel before the shrine. Kumiko brought coals and Kaede lit incense. The heavy smell drifted through the rooms, bringing an uneasy peace to the women within.

A few days later Yumi went to fetch the food for the midday meal and did not return. Another maid came in her place, an older woman. She and Kumiko served the meal in silence. Kumiko's eyes were red and she sniffed miserably. When Kaede tried to find out what was wrong, Rieko snapped, 'She has caught the cold, that's all.'

'Where is Yumi?' Kaede asked.

'You are interested in her? That proves my suspicions were right.'

'What suspicions?' Kaede said. 'What can you mean? I have no feelings about her one way or the other. I simply wondered where she was.'

'You won't be seeing her again,' Rieko said coldly. Kumiko made a strangled sound as if she were muffling a sob.

Kaede felt very cold, and yet, her skin was burning. She felt as if the walls were closing in on her. By evening her head was aching fiercely; she asked Rieko if she would send for Ishida.

When he came she was appalled at his appearance. A few days earlier he had been merry; now his face was gaunt and drawn, his eyes like shrivelled coals, his skin grey. His manner was as calm as ever and he spoke to her with great kindness, but it was obvious something terrible had happened.

And Rieko knew about it; Kaede was sure of that from her pursed lips and sharp eyes. Not to be able to question the doctor was torture; not to know what was happening in the household around her or in the world outside would surely drive her mad. Ishida gave her tea brewed from willow bark and bade her goodnight with unusual intensity. She was sure she would never see him again. Despite the sedative, she spent a restless night.

In the morning she questioned Rieko again about Yumi's disappearance and Ishida's distress. When she received no other answer than veiled accusations, she decided she would appeal to Fujiwara himself. It was nearly a week since she had seen him; he had stayed away during their sickness. She could not endure the inexplicably threatening atmosphere any longer.

'Will you tell Lord Fujiwara I would like to see him?' she asked Rieko when she had finished dressing.

The woman went herself and returned to say, 'His lordship is delighted that his wife desires his company. He has arranged a special entertainment for this evening. He will see you then.'

'I would like to speak to him alone,' Kaede said.

Rieko shrugged. 'There are no special guests at present. Only Mamoru will be with him. You had better bathe, and I suppose we must wash your hair so it can be dried in the sun.'

When her hair was at last dry, Rieko insisted on oiling it heavily before she dressed it. Kaede put on the quilted winter robes, grateful for their warmth, for her wet hair had made her very cold, and though the day was sunny the air was chilly. She ate a little soup at midday, but her stomach and throat seemed to have closed against food.

'You are very white,' Rieko said. 'Lord Fujiwara admires that in a woman.' The undertone in her words made Kaede tremble. Something terrible was about to happen – was already happening; everyone knew about it but her, and they would reveal it to her when it pleased them. Her pulse quickened and she felt its rapid thump in her neck, in her belly. From outside came a dull hammering sound that seemed to echo her own heart.

She went to kneel at the shrine, but even that failed to calm her. At the end of the afternoon Mamoru came and led her to the pavilion where she had watched the first snow fall with Fujiwara at the beginning of the year. Although it was not yet dark, lanterns were already lit in the bare-branched trees, and braziers burned on the veranda. She glanced at the young man, trying to learn something from his demeanour. He was as white as she was, and she thought she detected pity in his eyes. Her alarm deepened.

It had been so long since she had seen any landscape that the scene before her, the gardens and the mountains beyond, seemed unutterably beautiful. The last rays of the sun turned the snow-capped peaks to pink and gold, and the sky was a translucent colour between blue and silver. She gazed at it, drinking it in as if it were the last sight she would see on Earth.

Mamoru wrapped a bearskin around her and murmured, 'Lord Fujiwara will be with you soon.'

Directly in front of the veranda was an area of tiny white stones raked into a swirling pattern. Two posts had been newly erected in the centre. Kaede frowned at them; they broke the pattern of the stones in a harsh, almost threatening way.

She heard the padding of feet, the rustling of robes.

'His lordship is approaching,' Rieko said behind her, and they both bowed to the ground.

Fujiwara's particular fragrance wafted over Kaede as he sat next to her. He did not speak for a long time, and when he finally told her she might sit up, she thought she heard anger in his voice. Her heart quailed. She tried to call on her courage but she had none. She was deathly afraid.

'I am glad to see you recovered,' he said with icy politeness.

Her mouth was so dry she could hardly speak. 'It is thanks to your lordship's care,' she whispered.

'Rieko said you wished to speak to me . . .'

'I always desire your lordship's company,' she began, but faltered when his mouth twisted mockingly.

Let me not be afraid, she prayed. *If he sees I am*

afraid he will know he has broken me . . . He is, after all,
only a man; he did not want me to have even a needle.
He knows what I can do. He knows I killed Iida. She
drew a deep breath.

'I feel there are things going on that I do not understand. Have I offended your lordship? Please tell me
what I have done wrong.'

'There are things going on that *I* do not understand,'
he replied. 'Almost a conspiracy, I would say. And in my
own household. I cannot believe my wife would stoop to
such infamy but Rieko told me of her suspicions and the
maid confirmed them before she died.'

'What suspicions?' Kaede asked, showing no
emotion.

'That someone brought a message to you from
Otori.'

'Rieko is lying,' Kaede said, but her voice did not
obey her.

'I don't think so. Your former companion Muto
Shizuka was seen in this district. I was surprised. If she
wanted to see you, she should have approached me. Then
I remembered that Arai had used her as a spy. The maid
confirmed that Otori sent her. That was shocking
enough, but imagine my astonishment when she was discovered in Ishida's rooms. I was devastated: Ishida, my
most trusted servant, almost my friend! How dangerous
not to be able to trust one's physician. It would be so easy
for him to poison me.'

'He is completely trustworthy,' Kaede said. 'He is
devoted to you. Even if it were true that Shizuka brought
a message to me from Lord Otori, it has nothing to do
with Dr Ishida.'

He looked at her as though she had not grasped what

he was saying. 'They were sleeping together,' he said. 'My physician has been having an affair with a woman known to be a spy.'

Kaede did not reply. She had not known of their relationship; she had been too wrapped up in her own passion to notice it. Now it seemed quite obvious. She recalled all the signs: how often Shizuka had gone to Ishida's rooms to collect medicine or tea. And now Takeo had sent Shizuka with the message for her. Shizuka and Ishida had risked seeing each other and they were to be punished for it.

The sun had set behind the mountains but it was not yet dark. Twilight lay over the garden, barely dispelled by the light of the lanterns. A crow flew overhead to its roost, cawing bitterly.

'I am very fond of Ishida,' Fujiwara said, 'and I know you had become attached to your woman. It's a tragedy but we must try to comfort each other in our grief.' He clapped his hands. 'Bring wine, Mamoru. And I think we will begin our entertainment.' He leaned towards Kaede. 'We don't have to hurry. We have all night.'

She still had not grasped his meaning. She glanced at his face, saw the cruel set of his mouth and the skin's pallor, the tiny muscle in his jaw that gave him away. His eyes turned to her and she looked away to the posts. A sudden faintness came over her; the lanterns and the white stones began to swirl around her. She took a deep breath to steady herself.

'Don't do this,' she whispered. 'It is not worthy of you.'

In the distance a dog was howling. It howled and howled without ceasing. *It is Ishida's dog*, Kaede thought, and could almost believe it was her own heart, for it expressed utterly her horror and despair.

'Disobedience and disloyalty to me must be punished,' he said, 'and in a way that will discourage others.'

'If they must die, make it swift,' she said, 'I will do anything you ask of me in return.'

'But you already should do that,' he said, almost puzzled. 'What else can you offer that a wife should not already do?'

'Be merciful,' she begged.

'I do not have a merciful nature,' he replied. 'You have run out of bargaining power, my dear wife. You thought you could use me for your own purposes. Now I will use you for mine.'

Kaede heard footsteps on the gravel. She looked towards the sound as though the power of her gaze could reach Shizuka and save her. Guards walked slowly to the posts. They were armed with swords and they carried other instruments whose appearance brought a metallic taste of fear to her mouth. Most of the men were sombre-faced but one of them was grinning with nervous excitement. Between them, Ishida and Shizuka were two small figures, weak human bodies with an immense capacity for pain.

Neither of them made a sound as they were tied to the posts, but Shizuka raised her head and looked at Kaede.

This cannot happen. They will take poison, Kaede told herself.

Fujiwara said, 'I don't think we left your woman with any way of saving herself, but it will be interesting to see.'

Kaede had no idea what Fujiwara intended to do, what torture and cruel death he had devised, but she had heard enough stories at Noguchi Castle to be able to imagine the worst. She realized she was on the edge of losing control. She half rose, in itself unthinkable in Fujiwara's presence, and tried to plead with him, but even as the words came stumbling from her there was a disturbance at the front gate. Guards called out briefly, and two men came into the garden.

One was Murita, the man who had come to escort her and had then ambushed and killed her men. He carried his sword in his left hand; his right hand was still scarred from when she had cut it. She thought she did not know the other, though there was something familiar about him. Both knelt before Fujiwara, and Murita spoke.

'Lord Fujiwara, forgive me for disturbing you, but this man says he brings an urgent message from Lord Arai.'

Kaede had sunk to the floor again, grateful for this brief respite. She turned her eyes to the other man, noticed his big hands and long arms, and realized with a shock that it was Kondo. He had dissembled his features, and when he spoke, his voice was changed too. But surely Murita and Fujiwara would know him.

'Lord Fujiwara, Lord Arai sends his greetings to you. Everything is going according to plan.'

'Is Otori dead?' the nobleman asked, glancing briefly at Kaede.

'Not yet,' the man replied. 'But in the meantime Lord Arai asks that you return Muto Shizuka to him. He has a particular personal interest in her and wishes to keep her alive.'

For a moment Kaede felt hope flood into her heart.

Fujiwara would not dare harm Shizuka if Arai wanted her back.

'What a strange request,' Fujiwara said. 'And a strange messenger.' He ordered Murita, 'Disarm him. I don't trust him.'

The dog howled with a new intensity of fear. It seemed to Kaede that there was a moment of stillness, and then as she tried to call out, as Murita stepped towards Kondo, as Kondo drew his sword, the whole world groaned and lifted. The veranda rose through the air; the trees flew and then crashed, the house behind her shook and was torn apart. More dogs were barking now, frantically. The caged birds shrieked in alarm. The air was full of dust. From the fallen buildings came the screams of women and the instant crackling of fire.

The veranda landed heavily with a thud that shook Kaede's body; the floor was slanting back towards the house, the roof splintering above her. Her eyes were full of fragments of dust and straw. For a moment she thought she was trapped, then she saw that she could climb out and began to scrabble up the strange slope the veranda had assumed. Over its edge she saw as if in a dream Shizuka slip her hands from the bindings, kick one of the guards between the legs, take his sword from him, and slash him in the neck. Kondo had already dealt Murita a blow that had almost cut him in half.

Fujiwara was lying behind Kaede, partly covered by the fallen roof. His body was twisted and he did not seem to be able to get up, but he reached out to her and took her ankle in his hand, the first time he had ever touched her. His fingers were cold and his grip inescapable. The dust was making him cough, his clothes were filthy and he smelled of sweat and urine beneath the customary fragrance; yet, when he spoke his voice was as calm as ever.

'If we are to die, let us die together,' he said.

Behind him she could hear the flames, crackling and snarling like a living creature. The smoke thickened, stinging her eyes and masking all the other smells.

She pulled and kicked against his clutching fingers.

'I just wanted to possess you,' he said. 'You were the most beautiful thing I had ever seen. I wanted you to be mine and no one else's. I wanted to intensify your love for Takeo by denying it so I could share in the tragedy of your suffering.'

'Let go of me,' she screamed. She could feel the heat of the fire now. 'Shizuka! Kondo! Help me!'

Shizuka was fully occupied with the other guards, fighting like a man. Ishida's hands were still tied to the post. Kondo killed one of the guards from behind, turned his head at Kaede's voice and then strode towards the burning house. He leaped onto the edge of the veranda.

'Lady Otori,' he said, 'I'll free you. Run to the garden, to the pools. Shizuka will look after you.' He climbed down and deliberately cut through Fujiwara's wrist. The nobleman gave one harsh scream of pain and outrage; his hand fell from Kaede's ankle.

Kondo pushed her upwards and over the edge. 'Take my sword. I know you can defend yourself.'

He thrust it into her hands and went on swiftly, 'I swore allegiance to you. I meant it. I would never let anyone hurt you while I live. But it was a crime for someone like me to kill your father. It's even more of a crime to attack a nobleman and kill him. I'm ready to pay for it.'

He gave her a look stripped of all irony and smiled. 'Run,' he said. 'Run! Your husband will come for you.'

She stepped backwards. She saw Fujiwara try to rise, the blood pouring from the stump of his arm. Kondo wound his long arms round the nobleman and held him firmly. The flames burst through the fragile walls and received them both, wrapping them, concealing them.

The heat and the screams engulfed her. *He is burning, all his treasures are burning*, she thought wildly. She thought she heard Kumiko cry out from the inferno and wanted to do something to save her, but as she started towards the house, Shizuka pulled her back.

'You are on fire!'

Kaede dropped the sword and put her hands uselessly to her head as the flames erupted on her oiled hair.

Eleven

The sun set and the moon rose over the still surface of the sea, making a silver road for our fleet to follow. It was so bright, I could see clearly the range of mountains behind the coast we were leaving. The tide rippled under the hulls and the sails flapped in the off-shore breeze. The oars splashed in a steady rhythm.

We came to Oshima in the early hours of the morning. A white mist rose from the surface of the sea, and Fumio told me it would be the same for the next few nights as the air grew colder. It was perfect for our purpose. We spent the day on the island, re-provisioning from the pirates' stores and taking on board more of Terada's men, who were armed with swords, knives and a variety of other weapons, most of which I'd never seen before.

At the end of the afternoon we went to the shrine and made offerings to Ebisu and Hachiman, praying for calm seas and the defeat of our enemies. The priests gave us conch shells for each ship and auspicious fortunes that encouraged the men, though Fumio took it all with a certain scepticism, patting his firearm and muttering, 'This is more auspicious in my opinion!' while I was happy enough to pray to any god, knowing that they were simply different faces, created by men, of one indivisible truth.

The moon, one night off full, was rising over the mountains as we set sail for Hagi. This time Kenji, Taku and I went with Ryoma in his smaller, swifter boat. I left Zenko in Fumio's care, having told him of the boy's parentage and impressing on him the importance of keeping Arai's son alive. Just before dawn the mist began to form above the water, shrouding us as we approached the sleeping city. From across the bay I could hear the first roosters crowing and the early bells from Tokoji and Daishoin.

My plan was to go straight to the castle. I had no desire to destroy my city or see the Otori clan wash blood with blood. I thought that if we could kill or capture the Otori lords right away, there was every chance the clan would side with me rather than tear itself apart. This was also the opinion of the Otori warriors who had already joined me. Many of them had begged to be allowed to accompany me and take part in the vengeance first hand. They all had experiences of ill-treatment, insults and breaches of faith. But my aim was to penetrate the castle silently and secretly. I would take only Kenji and Taku. I placed all the other men under Terada's command.

The old pirate had been alight with excitement and the anticipation of settling long-standing scores. I'd given him some instructions: the boats were to remain off-shore until daybreak. Then they were to sound the conch shells and advance through the mist. The rest was up to him. I hoped to be able to convince the city to surrender; if not, we would fight through the streets to the bridge and open it for Arai's army.

The castle was built on a promontory between the river and the sea. I knew, from my visit on the day of my adoption, that the residence was on the seaward side, where a huge wall, considered to be invulnerable, rose from the water around it.

317

Kenji and Taku had their grapples and other Tribe weapons. I was armed with throwing knives, a short sword and Jato.

The moon set and the mist grew thicker. The boat drifted silently towards the shore and nudged the sea wall with the faintest of sounds. One by one we climbed onto the wall and went invisible.

I heard footsteps above our heads and a voice called out, 'Who's there? Name yourself!'

Ryoma answered in the dialect of a Hagi fisherman, 'Only me. Got a bit lost in this dirty mist.'

'Got a bit pissed, you mean,' a second man called back. 'Get out of here! If we can see you when the fog clears, we'll put an arrow in you.'

The sound of the oar faded away. I hissed at the other two – I couldn't see either of them – and we began to climb. It was a slow process; the wall, washed twice a day by the tide, was coated in seaweed and slippery. But inch by inch we crawled up it and eventually came to its top. One last autumn cricket was chirping and it fell suddenly silent. Kenji chirped in its place. I could hear the guards talking at the far corner of the bailey. A lamp and a brazier burned beside them. Beyond them lay the residence where the Otori lords, their retainers and families would be sleeping.

I could only hear two voices, which surprised me. I'd thought there would be more but from their conversation I gathered that all available men had been posted on the bridge and along the river in anticipation of Arai's attack.

'Wish he'd get it over with,' one of them grumbled. 'It's this waiting I can't stand.'

'He must know how little food there is in the town,' the other replied. 'Probably thinks he can starve us out.'

'I suppose it's better to have him out there than in here.'

'Enjoy it while you can. If the town falls to Arai, it'll be a bloodbath. Even Takeo ran away into a typhoon rather than face Arai!'

I felt alongside me for Taku, found his shape, and pulled his head close to me. 'Go inside the wall,' I mouthed in his ear. 'Distract them while we take them from behind.'

I felt him nod and heard the tiny sound as he moved away. Kenji and I followed him over the wall. In the glow from the brazier I suddenly caught sight of a small shadow. It flitted across the ground and then divided in two, silent and ghostly.

'What was that?' one of the guards exclaimed.

They were both on their feet and staring towards Taku's two images. It was easy for us: we took one each, soundlessly.

The guards had just made tea, so we drank it while we waited for daybreak. The sky paled gradually. There was no separation between it and the water; it was all one shimmering surface. When the conch shells began to sound, the hair stood up on the back of my neck. Dogs howled in response from the shore.

I heard the household within erupt into activity: the padding of feet, not yet frantic, cries of surprise, not yet alarm. The shutters were thrown open and the doors slid apart. A group of guards rushed out, followed by Shoichi and Masahiro, still in night attire but with their swords in their hands.

They stopped dead as I walked towards them, Jato unsheathed in my hand, the mist wreathing around me. Behind me the first ships were appearing; the conch shells sang again over the water and the sound echoed back from the mountains around the bay.

Masahiro took a step back. 'Shigeru?' he gasped.

His older brother went white. They saw the man they had tried to murder; they saw the Otori sword in his hand, and they were terrified.

I said in a loud voice, 'I am Otori Takeo, grandson of Shigemori, nephew and adopted son of Shigeru. I hold you responsible for the death of the rightful heir to the Otori clan. You sent Shintaro to assassinate him, and when that failed, you conspired with Iida Sadamu to murder him. Iida has already paid with his life, and now you will!'

I was aware that Kenji stood behind me, sword drawn, and hoped Taku was still invisible. I did not take my eyes off the men in front of me.

Shoichi tried to regain his composure. 'Your adoption was illegal. You have no claim to Otori blood nor to the sword you carry. We do not recognize you.' He called to the retainers, 'Cut them down!'

Jato seemed to quiver in my hands as it came alive. I was prepared to meet the attack but no one moved. I saw Shoichi's face change as he realized he was going to have to fight me himself.

'I have no wish to split the clan,' I said. 'My only desire is for your heads.' I thought I'd given them enough warning. I could feel Jato thirsting for blood. It was as though Shigeru's spirit had taken me over and would have his revenge.

Shoichi was the closer and I knew he was the better swordsman. I would get rid of him first. They had both been good fighters, but they were now old men in their late forties and they wore no armour. I was at the height of speed and fitness, flesh and bone planed by hardship

320

and war. I killed Shoichi with a blow to the neck that cut him diagonally. Masahiro swung at me from behind but Kenji parried the stroke, and as I spun to meet my other opponent I saw fear distort his face. I pushed him back towards the wall. He avoided each stroke, weaving and parrying, but his heart was not in it. He made one last appeal to his men but still not one of them moved.

The first ships were not far off shore. Masahiro looked behind him, looked back, and saw Jato descend on him. He made a frantic, ducking movement and fell over the wall.

Furious that he had escaped me, I was about to jump after him when his son Yoshitomi, my old enemy from the fighting hall, came running from the residence, followed by a handful of his brothers and cousins. None of them was more than twenty.

'I'll fight you, sorcerer,' Yoshitomi cried. 'Let's see if you can fight like a warrior!'

I had gone into an almost supernatural state, and Jato was enraged by now and had tasted blood. It moved faster than the eye could follow. Whenever I seemed to be outnumbered, Kenji was at my side. I was sorry such young men had to die but glad that they, too, paid for the treachery of their fathers. When I was able to turn my attention back to Masahiro, I saw he had surfaced near a small boat at the front of the line of ships. It was Ryoma's. Seizing his father by his hair, the young man pulled him upwards and cut his throat with one of the knives fishermen use to gut fish. Whatever Masahiro's crimes, this was a far more terrible death than any I could have devised for him: to be killed by his own son while trying to escape in fear.

I turned to face the crowd of retainers. 'I have a huge

force of men on the ships out there and Lord Arai is in alliance with me. I have no quarrel with any of you. You may take your own lives, you may serve me or you may fight me one on one now. I have fulfilled my duty to Lord Shigeru and done what he commanded.'

I could still feel his spirit inhabiting me.

One of the older men stepped forward. I remembered his face but his name escaped me.

'I am Endo Chikara. Many of us have sons and nephews who have already joined you. We have no desire to fight our own children. You have done what was your duty and your right in a fair and honourable way. For the sake of the clan, I am prepared to serve you, Lord Otori.'

With that he knelt and one by one the others followed. Kenji and I went through the residence and placed guards on the women and children. I hoped the women would take their own lives honourably. I would decide what to do with the children later. We checked all the secret places and flushed out several spies hidden there. Some were obviously Kikuta, but neither in the residence nor the castle was there any sign of Kotaro, who Kenji had been told was in Hagi.

Endo came with me to the castle. The captain of the guard there was equally relieved to be able to surrender to me; his name was Miyoshi Satoru: he was Kahei and Gemba's father. Once the castle was secured, the boats came to shore and the men disembarked to move through the town street by street.

Taking the castle, which I had thought would be the hardest part of my plan, turned out to be the easiest. Despite its surrender and my best efforts, the town did not give in altogether peacefully. The streets were in chaos; people tried to flee but there was nowhere to go. Terada and his men had scores of their own to settle, and there were pockets of stubborn resistance that we had to overcome in fierce hand-to-hand fighting.

Finally we came to the banks of the western river, not far from the stone bridge. Judging by the sun, it must have been late afternoon. The mist had lifted long ago, but smoke from burning houses hung above the river. On the opposite bank the last of the maple leaves were brilliant red and the willows along the water's edge were yellow. The leaves were falling, drifting in the eddies. Late chrysanthemums bloomed in gardens. In the distance I could see the fish weir and the tiled walls along the bank.

My house is there, I thought. *I will sleep there tonight.*

But the river was full of men swimming and small boats loaded to the gunwales, while a long stream of soldiers pressed towards the bridge.

Kenji and Taku were still alongside me, Taku silenced by what he had seen of war. We stared at the sight: the remnants of the Otori army in defeat. I was filled with pity for them and anger at their lords who had so misled and betrayed them, leaving them to fight this desperate rearguard action while they slept comfortably in Hagi Castle.

I had been separated from Fumio but now I saw him at the bridge with a handful of his men. They seemed to be arguing with a group of Otori captains. We went over to them. Zenko was with Fumio, and he smiled briefly at his brother. They stood close to each other but did not say anything.

'This is Lord Otori Takeo,' Fumio told the men when I approached. 'The castle has surrendered to him. He'll tell you.' He turned to me. 'They want to destroy the bridge and prepare for siege. They don't believe in the alliance with Arai. They've been fighting him off for the last week.

He's right behind them. They say their only hope is to get the bridge down immediately.'

I removed my helmet so they could see my face. They immediately dropped to their knees. 'Arai has sworn to support me,' I said. 'The alliance is genuine. Once he knows the town has surrendered he will cease the attack.'

'Let's break the bridge down anyway,' their leader said.

I thought of the ghost of the stonemason entombed alive in his creation and of the inscription that Shigeru had read aloud to me: *The Otori clan welcome the just and the loyal. Let the unjust and the disloyal beware.* I did not want to destroy such a precious thing, and anyway, I could not see how they would dismantle it in time.

'No, let it stand,' I replied. 'I will answer for Lord Arai's faithfulness. Tell your men they have nothing to fear if they surrender to me and accept me as their lord.'

Endo and Miyoshi came up on horseback and I sent them to carry the message to the Otori soldiers. Little by little the confusion settled. We cleared the bridge and Endo rode to the other side to organize a more orderly return to the town. Many men were reassured enough to settle down where they were and rest, while others decided they might as well go home, and set off for their farms and houses.

Miyoshi said, 'You should be on horseback, Lord Takeo,' and gave me his horse, a good-looking black that reminded me of Aoi. I mounted, rode across the bridge to speak to the men there, causing them to break out into cheers, and then rode back with Endo. When the cheers died away I could hear the distant sound of Arai's army approaching, the tramping of horses and men.

They came down the valley, a stream of ants in the

distance, the Kumamoto and Seishuu banners unfurled. As they came closer, I recognized Arai at their head: chestnut horse, stag-antlered helmet, red-laced armour.

I leaned down to say to Kenji, 'I should go and meet him.'

Kenji frowned as he peered across the river. 'Something feels wrong,' he said quietly.

'What?'

'I don't know. Be on your guard and don't cross the bridge.'

As I urged the black forward slightly, Endo said, 'I am the senior retainer of the Otori clan. Let me take news of our surrender to you to Lord Arai.'

'Very well,' I said. 'Tell him to encamp his army on that side of the river and bring him into the town. Then we can enforce peace with no further bloodshed on either side.'

Endo rode forward onto the bridge and Arai halted and waited on the other side. Endo was almost halfway across when Arai held up his hand with the black war fan in it.

There was a moment of silence. Zenko cried at my side, 'They are arming their bows.'

The war fan dropped.

Though it was happening right in front of my eyes I could not believe it. For several moments I stared incredulous as the arrows began to fall. Endo went down at once, and the men on the bank, unarmed and unprepared, fell like deer to the hunter.

'There,' Kenji said, drawing his sword. 'That's what's wrong.'

Once before I had been so betrayed – but that had been by Kenji himself and the Tribe. This betrayal was by a warrior to whom I had sworn allegiance. Had I killed Jo-An for this? Fury and outrage turned my vision red. I had taken the impregnable castle, kept the bridge whole, pacified the men. I had handed Hagi, my town, to Arai like a ripe persimmon, and with it the Three Countries.

Dogs were howling in the distance. They sounded like my own soul.

Arai rode onto the bridge and came to a halt in the centre. He saw me and lifted off his helmet. It was a derisive gesture. He was so sure of his own strength, of victory. 'Thank you, Otori,' he called. 'What good work you did. Will you surrender now or shall we fight it out?'

'You may rule over the Three Countries,' I shouted back. 'But your falsehood will be remembered long after your death.' I knew I was about to fight my last battle, and it was, as I had known it must be, with Arai. I just had not realized it would come so quickly.

'There will be no one left to record it,' he sneered in reply, 'because I intend now to wipe out the Otori once and for all.'

I leaned down and seized Zenko, pulling him up onto the horse in front of me. I took my short sword and held it to his neck.

'I have both your sons here. Will you condemn them to death? I swear to you, I will kill Zenko now and Taku after him before you can reach me. Call off your attack!'

His face changed a little and paled. Taku stood motionless next to Kenji. Zenko did not move either. Both boys stared at the father they had not seen for years.

Then Arai's features hardened and he laughed. 'I know you, Takeo. I know your weakness. You were not raised as a warrior; let's see if you can bring yourself to kill a child.'

I should have acted immediately and ruthlessly but I did not. I hesitated. Arai laughed again.

'Let him go,' he called. 'Zenko! Come here to me.'

Fumio called in a low, clear voice, 'Takeo, shall I shoot him?'

I can't remember replying. I can't remember letting go of Zenko. I heard the muffled report from the firearm and saw Arai recoil in the saddle as the ball hit him, piercing his armour above the heart. There was a cry, of rage and horror, from the men around him and a scuffle as his horse reared; Zenko screamed, but these sounds were as nothing to the roar that followed them as the world beneath my horse's feet tore itself apart.

The maples on the far shore rose almost gracefully and began to march down the hillside. They gathered up Arai's army as they went, wrapping them in stones and soil and rolling them into the river.

My horse backed in terror, reared, and fled from the bridge, throwing me sideways onto the road. As I got to my feet, winded, the bridge groaned with a human voice. It cried out in its efforts to hold itself together and then flew apart, taking everyone on it down into the river. Then the river itself went mad. From the confluence upstream came a yellow-brown flood of water. It drained away from the bank on the town side, gathering up boats and living beings impartially, and raced over the opposite bank, where it swept away the remnants of two armies, breaking the boats like eating sticks, drowning men and horses and carrying their corpses out to sea.

The ground shook fiercely again, and from behind me I heard the crash of collapsing houses. I felt as if I'd been stunned: everything around me was hazy with dust and muffled so I could no longer hear distinct sounds. I was aware of Kenji beside me and Taku kneeling by his brother, who had also fallen when the horse reared. I saw Fumio coming towards me through the haze, the firearm still in his hand.

I was shaking from some mixture of emotions close to elation: a recognition of how puny we humans are when confronted with the great forces of nature, combined with gratitude to heaven, to the gods I'd thought I did not believe in, who once again had spared my life.

My last battle had begun and ended in a moment. There was no further thought of fighting. Our only concern now was to save the town from fire.

Much of the district around the castle burned to the ground. The castle itself was destroyed in one of the aftershocks, killing the remaining women and children who were being held there. I was relieved, for I knew I could not let them live, but I shrank from ordering their deaths. Ryoma also died then, his boat sunk by falling masonry. When his body was washed up days later I had him buried with the Otori lords at Daishoin, their name on his grave stone.

In the next few days I hardly slept or ate. With Miyoshi and Kenji's help I organized the survivors to clear the rubble, bury the dead and care for the wounded. Through the long sorrowful days of work and cooperation and grief the rifts in the clan began to heal. The earthquake was generally held to be Heaven's punishment on Arai for his treachery. Heaven clearly favoured me, I was Shigeru's adopted son and nephew by blood, I had his sword, I resembled him and I had avenged his death: the clan accepted me unreservedly as his true heir. I did not know what the situation was in the rest of the land; the earthquakes had shattered much of the Three Countries and we heard nothing from the other cities. All I was aware of was the enormity of the task that faced me in restoring peace and preventing famine in the coming winter.

I did not sleep at Shigeru's house the night of the earthquake, nor for many days following. I could not bear to go near it in case it had been destroyed. I camped with Miyoshi in what remained of his residence. But about four days after the earthquake, Kenji came to me one evening after I had eaten and told me there was someone to see me. He was grinning, and for a moment I imagined it might be Shizuka with a message from Kaede.

Instead it was the maids from Shigeru's house, Chiyo and Haruka. They looked exhausted and frail, and when they saw me I was afraid Chiyo would die from emotion. They both knelt at my feet, but I made them get up and I embraced Chiyo as tears streamed down her face. None of us could speak.

Finally Chiyo said, 'Come home, Lord Takeo. The house is waiting for you.'

'It's still standing?'

'The garden is ruined – the river swept through it, but the house is not badly damaged. We'll get it ready for you tomorrow.'

'I will come tomorrow evening,' I promised.

'You will come, too, sir?' she said to Kenji.

'Almost like old times,' he replied, smiling, though we all knew it could never be that.

The following day Kenji and I took Taku and some guards and walked down the familiar street. I did not take Zenko. The circumstances surrounding Arai's death had left his eldest son deeply disturbed. I was concerned for him, seeing his confusion and grief, but did not have time to deal with it. I suspected that he thought his father had died ignobly and blamed me for it. Maybe he even blamed or despised me for sparing his life. I myself was not sure how to treat him: as the heir to a mighty warlord or as the son of the man who had betrayed me. I thought it best for him to be kept out of my way for the time being and put him in the service of Endo Chikara's family. I still hoped his mother, Shizuka, was alive; when she returned we would discuss her son's future. Taku I had no doubts about; I would keep him with me, the first of the child spies I had dreamed of training and employing.

The district around my old house had been hardly touched by the earthquake, and birds were singing blithely in the gardens. As we walked through it I was thinking about how I used to wait for the exact moment when I heard the house's song of the river and the world, and remembering how I had first seen Kenji on the corner. The song was altered now; the stream was clogged, the waterfall dry, but the river still lapped at the dock and the wall.

Haruka found the last of the wild flowers and a few chrysanthemums to put in buckets outside the kitchen, as she always had, and their sharp autumn scent mingled with the smell of mud and decay from the river. The garden was ruined, the fish all dead, but Chiyo had washed and polished the nightingale floor, and when we stepped onto it, it sang beneath our feet.

The downstairs rooms were damaged by water and mud, and she had already started stripping them and having new mats laid, but the upstairs room was untouched. She had cleaned and polished it until it looked just as it had the first time I had seen it, when I had fallen in love with Shigeru's house and with him.

Chiyo apologized that there was no hot water for a

bath, but we washed in cold water and she managed to find enough food for an adequate meal as well as several flasks of wine. We ate in the upper room, as we so often had before, and Kenji made Taku laugh by describing my poor efforts as a student and how impossible and disobedient I had been. I was filled with an almost unbearable mixture of sorrow and joy, and smiled with tears in my eyes. But whatever my grief, I felt Shigeru's spirit was at peace. I could almost see his quiet ghost in the room with us, smiling when we smiled. His murderers were dead and Jato had come home.

Taku fell asleep at last, and Kenji and I shared one more flask of wine as we watched the gibbous moon move across the garden. It was a cold night. There would probably be a frost, and we closed the shutters before going to bed ourselves. I slept restlessly, no doubt from the wine, and woke just before dawn, thinking I had heard some unfamiliar sound.

The house lay quiet around me. I could hear Kenji and Taku breathing alongside me, and Chiyo and Haruka in the room below. We had put guards on the gate, and there were still a couple of dogs there. I thought I could hear the guards talking in low voices. Perhaps it was they who had awakened me.

I lay and listened for a while. The room began to lighten as day broke. I decided I had heard nothing unusual and would go to the privy before I tried to sleep for another hour or two. I got up quietly and crept down the stairs, slid open the door and stepped outside.

I did not bother masking my footsteps, but as soon as the floor sang I realized what it was I had heard: one light step onto the boards. Someone had tried to come into the house and had been discouraged by the floor. So where was he now?

I was thinking rapidly, *I should wake Kenji, should at least get a weapon*, when the Kikuta master, Kotaro, came out of the misty garden and stood in front of me.

Until tonight, I had seen him only in his faded blue robes, the disguise he wore when travelling. Now he was in the dark fighting clothes of the Tribe, and all the power that he usually kept hidden was revealed in his stance and in his face, the embodiment of the Tribe's hostility towards me, expert, ruthless and implacable.

He said, 'I believe your life is forfeit to me.'

'You broke faith with me by ordering Akio to kill me,' I said. 'All our bargains were annulled then. And you had no right to demand anything from me when you did not tell me that it was you who killed my father.'

He smiled in contempt. 'You're right, I did kill Isamu,' he said. 'I've learned now what it was that made him disobedient too: the Otori blood that flows in you both.' He reached into his jacket and I moved quickly to avoid the knife I thought was coming but what he held out was a small stick. 'I drew this,' he said, 'and I obeyed the orders of the Tribe, even though Isamu and I were cousins and friends, and even though he refused to defend himself. That's what obedience is.'

Kotaro's eyes were fixed on my face and I knew he was hoping to confuse me with the Kikuta sleep, but I was certain I could withstand it, though I doubted I could use it on him as I had once before, in Matsue. We held each other's gaze for several moments, neither of us able to dominate.

'You murdered him,' I said. 'You contributed to

Shigeru's death too. And what purpose did Yuki's death serve?'

He hissed impatiently in the way I remembered and with a lightning movement threw the stick to the ground and drew a knife. I dived sideways, shouting loudly. I had no illusions about my ability to take him on alone and unarmed. I would have to fight bare-handed as I had with Akio until someone came to my help.

He jumped after me, feinting at me, and then moved faster than the eye could follow in the opposite direction to take my neck in a stranglehold; but I'd anticipated the move, slipped under his grasp and kicked at him from behind. I caught him just over the kidney and heard him grunt. Then I leaped above him and with my right hand hit him in the neck.

The knife came upwards and I felt it slash deep into the side of my right hand, taking off the two smallest fingers and opening up the palm. It was my first real wound and the pain was terrible, worse than anything I'd ever experienced. I went invisible for a moment, but my blood betrayed me, spurting across the nightingale floor. I shouted again, screaming for Kenji, for the guards, and split my self. The second self rolled across the floor while I drove my left hand into Kotaro's eyes.

His head snapped sideways as he avoided the blow, and I kicked at the hand that held the knife. He leaped away with unbelievable speed and then seemed to fly back at my head. I ducked just before he could kick me in the head and leaped into the air as he landed, all this time fighting off shock and pain, knowing that if I gave in to them for a moment, I would die. I was about to try to kick him in a similar way when I heard the upstairs window open and a small invisible object came hurtling out.

Kotaro was not expecting it and he heard it a second after I did. By then I had perceived it to be Taku. I leaped to break his fall, but he seemed almost to fly down onto Kotaro, distracting him momentarily. I turned my leap into a kick and rammed my foot hard into Kotaro's neck.

As I landed, Kenji shouted from above. 'Takeo! Here!' and threw Jato down to me.

I caught my sword in my left hand. Kotaro grabbed Taku, swung him above his head, and hurled him into the garden. I heard the boy gasp as he landed. I swung Jato above my head but my right hand was pouring blood and the blade descended crookedly. Kotaro went invisible as I missed him. But now that I was armed he was more wary of me. I had a moment's breathing space. I tore off my sash and wound it around my palm.

Kenji leaped from the upstairs window, landed on his feet like a cat, and immediately went invisible. I could discern the two masters faintly and they could obviously see each other. I had fought alongside Kenji before and I knew if anyone did how truly dangerous he was, but I realized I had never seen him in action against anyone who had a fraction of his skills. He had a sword a little longer than Kotaro's knife and it gave him a slight advantage, but Kotaro was both brilliant and desperate. They drove each other up and down the floor and it cried out under their feet. Kotaro seemed to stumble, but as Kenji closed in on him, he recovered and kicked him in the ribs. They both split their images. I lunged at Kotaro's second self as Kenji somersaulted away from him. Kotaro turned to deal with me and I heard the whistling sound of throwing knives. Kenji had hurled them at his neck. The first blade penetrated and I saw Kotaro's vision begin to waver. His eyes were fixed on my face. He made one last vain thrust with his knife but Jato seemed to anticipate it and found its way into his throat. He tried to curse me as he died, but his windpipe was slashed and only blood came bubbling out, obscuring the words.

By now the sun had risen; when we gazed down on Kotaro's broken, bleeding body in its pale light, it was hard to believe that such a fragile human being had wielded so much power. Kenji and I had only just managed to overcome him between us and he had left me with a ruined hand, Kenji with terrible bruises and, we found out later, broken ribs. Taku was winded and shaken, lucky to be still alive. The guards who had come running at my shouts were as shocked as if a demon had attacked us. The dogs' hackles rose when they sniffed around the body, and they showed their teeth in uneasy snarls.

My fingers were gone, my palm was torn open. Once the terror and thrill of the fight had subsided the pain truly made itself felt, turning me faint.

Kenji said, 'The knife blade was probably poisoned. We should take your hand off at the elbow to save your life.' I was light-headed with shock and at first thought he was joking, but his face was serious and his voice alarmed me. I made him promise he would not do it. I would rather be dead than lose what was left of my right hand. As it was, I thought I would never hold a sword or a brush again.

He washed the wound at once, told Chiyo to bring coals, and, while the guards knelt on me to hold me still, seared the stumps of the fingers and the edges of the wound and then bound it with what he said he hoped was an antidote.

The blade was indeed poisoned and I fell into hell, a

335

confusion of pain and fever and despair. As the long tormented days passed, I was aware that everyone thought I was dying. I did not believe I would die but I could not speak to reassure the living. Instead I lay in the upstairs room, thrashing and sweating and babbling to the dead.

They filed past me, those I had killed, those who had died for me, those I had avenged: my family in Mino; the Hidden at Yamagata; Shigeru; Ichiro; the men I had murdered on the Tribe's orders; Yuki; Amano; Jiro; Jo-An.

I longed for them to be alive again, I longed to see them in the flesh and hear their living voices; one by one they bade me farewell and left me, desolate and alone. I wanted to follow them, but I could not find the road they had taken.

At the worst point of the fever, I opened my eyes and saw a man in the room. I had never seen him before but I knew he was my father. He wore peasant's clothes like the men of my village and he carried no weapons. The walls faded away and I was in Mino again; the village was unburned and the rice fields were brilliant green. I watched my father working in the fields, absorbed and peaceful. I followed him up the mountain path and into the forest and I knew how much he loved to roam there among its animals and plants, for it was what I loved too.

I saw him turn his head and listen in the familiar Kikuta way as he caught some distant noise. In a moment he would recognize the step: his cousin and friend who was coming to execute him. I saw Kotaro appear on the path in front of him.

He was dressed in the dark fighting clothes of the Tribe, as he had been when he came for me. The two men stood as if frozen before me, each with their distinctive stance: my father, who had taken a vow never to kill again, and the future Kikuta master, who lived by the trade of death and terror.

As Kotaro drew his knife I screamed out a warning. I tried to rise but hands held me back. The vision faded, leaving me in anguish. I knew that I could not change the past but I was aware, with the intensity of fever, that the conflict was still unresolved. However much men craved an end to violence, it seemed they could not escape it. It would go on and on for ever unless I found a middle way, a way to bring peace, and the only way I could think of was to reserve all violence to myself, in the name of my country and my people. I would have to continue on my violent path so that everyone else could live free of it, just as I had to believe in nothing so everyone else was free to believe in what they wanted. I did not want that. I wanted to follow my father and forswear killing, living in the way my mother had taught me. The darkness rose around me and I knew that if I surrendered to it I could go after my father and the conflict would be ended for me. The thinnest of veils separated me from the next world, but a voice was echoing through the shadows.

Your life is not your own. Peace comes at the price of bloodshed.

Behind the holy woman's words I heard Makoto calling my name. I did not know if he was dead or alive. I wanted to explain to him what I had learned and how I could not bear to act as I knew I would have to and so I was leaving with my father, but when I tried to speak, my swollen tongue would not frame the words. They came out as nonsense and I writhed in frustration, thinking we would be parted before I could talk to him.

He was holding my hands firmly. He leaned close and spoke clearly to me. 'Takeo! I know. I understand. It's all right. We will have peace. But only you can bring it. You must not die. Stay with us! You have to stay with us for the sake of peace.'

He talked to me like this for the rest of the night, his voice keeping the ghosts at bay and linking my spirit with this world. Dawn came and the fever broke. I slept deeply, and when I awoke lucidity had returned. Makoto was still there and I wept for joy that he was alive. My hand still throbbed but with the ordinary pain of healing, not with the ferocious agony of the poison. Kenji told me later he thought something must have come from my father, some immunity in the master poisoner's blood that protected me. It was then that I repeated to him the words of the prophecy, how my own son was destined to kill me and how I did not believe I would die before then. He was silent for a long time.

'Well,' he said finally. 'That must lie a long way in the future. We will deal with it when it comes.'

My son was Kenji's grandson. The prophecy seemed even more unbearably cruel to me. I was still weak and tears came easily. My body's frailty infuriated me. It was seven days before I could walk outside to the privy, fifteen before I could get on a horse again. The full moon of the eleventh month came and went. Soon it would be the solstice and then the year would turn, the snows would come. My hand began to heal: the wide, ugly scar almost obliterated both the silvery mark, from the burn I received the day Shigeru saved my life, and the straight line of the Kikuta.

Makoto sat with me day and night but said little to me. I felt he was keeping something from me and that Kenji also knew what it was. Once they brought Hiroshi to see me and I was relieved that the boy lived. He seemed cheerful, telling me about their journey, how they had escaped the worst of the earthquake and had come upon the pathetic remnants of Arai's once mighty army, and how marvellous Shun had been, but I thought he was partly pretending. Sometimes Taku, who had aged years in a month, came to sit by me; like Hiroshi, he acted cheerful, but his face was pale and strained. As my strength returned, I realised we should have heard from Shizuka. Obviously everyone feared the worst; but I did not believe she was dead. Nor was Kaede, for neither of them had visited me in my delirium.

Finally one evening Makoto said to me, 'We have had news from the south. The damage from the earthquake was even more severe there. At Lord Fujiwara's there was a terrible fire . . .' He took my hand. 'I'm sorry, Takeo. It seems no one survived.'

'Fujiwara is dead?'

'Yes, his death is confirmed.' He paused and added quietly, 'Kondo Kiichi died there.'

Kondo, whom I had sent with Shizuka . . .

'And your friend?' I asked.

'He also. Poor Mamoru. I think he would almost have welcomed it.'

I said nothing for a few moments. Makoto said gently, 'They have not found her body but . . .'

'I must know for sure,' I said. 'Will you go there for me?'

He agreed to leave the next morning. I spent the night anguishing over what I would do if Kaede was dead. My only desire would be to follow her; yet, how could I desert all those who had stayed so loyally by me? By dawn I'd recognized the truth of Jo-An's words, and Makoto's. My life was not my own. Only I could bring peace. I was condemned to live.

During the night something else occurred to me, and I asked to see Makoto before he left. I was worried about the records that Kaede had taken to Shirakawa with her. If I was to live, I wanted to have them back in my possession before winter began. For I had to spend the long months in planning the summer's strategy; those of my enemies who remained would not hesitate to use the Tribe against me. I felt I would have to leave Hagi in the spring and impose my rule over the Three Countries, maybe even set up my headquarters in Inuyama and make it my capital. It made me smile half bitterly, for its name means Dog Mountain, and it was as if it had been waiting for me.

I told Makoto to take Hiroshi with him. The boy would show him where the records were hidden. I could not suppress the fluttering hope that Kaede would be at Shirakawa – that Makoto would somehow bring her back to me.

They returned on a bitterly cold day nearly two weeks later. I saw they were alone, and disappointment nearly overcame me. They were also empty-handed.

'The old woman who guards the shrine would give the records to no one but you,' Makoto said. 'I'm sorry, I could not persuade her otherwise.'

Hiroshi said eagerly, 'We will go back. I will go with Lord Otori.'

'Yes, Lord Otori must go,' Makoto said. He seemed to be going to speak again but then fell silent.

'What?' I prompted him.

He was looking at me with a strange expression of compassion and pure affection. 'We will all go,' he said.

'We will learn once and for all if there is any news of Lady Otori.'

I longed to go yet feared it would be a useless journey and that it was too late in the year. 'We run the risk of being caught by the snow,' I said. 'I had planned to winter in Hagi.'

'If the worst comes to the worst, you can stay in Terayama. I am going there on the way back. I will be staying there, for I can see my time with you is drawing to a close.'

'You are going to leave me? Why?'

'I feel I have other work to do. You have achieved all that I set out to help you with. I am being called back to the temple.'

I was devastated. Was I to lose everyone I loved? I turned away to hide my feelings.

'When I thought you were dying, I made a vow,' Makoto went on. 'I promised the Enlightened One that if you lived, I would devote my life to your cause in a different way. I've fought and killed alongside you and I would do it gladly all over again. Except that it solves nothing, in the end. Like the weasel's dance, the cycle of violence goes on and on.'

His words rang in my ears. They were exactly what had pounded in my brain while I was delirious.

'You talked in your fever about your father and about the command of the Hidden, to take no one's life. As a warrior, it's hard for me to understand, but as a monk it is a command that I feel I must try and follow. I vowed that night that I would never kill again. Instead, I will seek peace through prayer and meditation. I left my flutes at Terayama to take up weapons. I will leave my weapons here and go back for them.'

He smiled slightly. 'When I speak the words, they sound like madness. I am taking the first step only on a long and difficult journey, but it is one I must make.'

I said nothing in reply. I pictured the temple at Terayama where Shigeru and Takeshi were buried, where I had been sheltered and nurtured, where Kaede and I had been married. It lay in the centre of the Three Countries, the physical and spiritual heart of my land and my life. And from now on Makoto would be there, praying for the peace I longed for, always upholding my cause. He would be one person, like a tiny splash of dye in a huge vat, but I could see the colour spreading over the years, the blue-green colour that the word *peace* always summoned up for me. Under Makoto's influence the temple would become a place of peace, as its founder had intended it to be.

'I am not leaving you,' he said gently. 'I will be with you in a different way.'

I had no words to express my gratitude: he had understood my conflict completely and in this way was taking the first steps to resolve it. All I could do was thank him and let him go.

Kenji, supported tacitly by Chiyo, argued strongly against my decision to travel, saying I was asking for trouble by undertaking such a journey before I was fully recovered. I felt better every day and my hand had mostly healed, though it still pained me and I still felt my phantom fingers. I grieved for the loss of all my dexterity and tried to accustom my left hand to the sword and the brush, but at least I held a horse's reins in that hand and I thought I was well enough to ride. My main concern was that I was needed in the reconstruction of Hagi, but Miyoshi Kahei and his father assured me they could manage without me. Kahei and the rest of my army had been delayed with Makoto by the earthquake but were unharmed by it. Their arrival had greatly increased our forces and hastened the town's recovery. I told Kahei to send messages as soon as possible to Shuho, to invite the master carpenter Shiro and his family back to the clan.

In the end Kenji gave in and said, despite the considerable pain of his broken ribs, he would of course accompany me, since I'd shown myself unable to deal with Kotaro alone. I forgave him his sarcasm, glad to have him with me, and we took Taku as well, not wanting to leave him behind while he was so low in spirits. He and Hiroshi squabbled as usual, but Hiroshi had grown more patient and Taku less arrogant and I could see a true friendship was developing between them. I also took as many men as we could spare from the town and left them in groups along the road to help rebuild the stricken villages and farms. The earthquake had cut a swathe from north to south and we followed its line. It was close to midwinter; despite the loss and destruction, people were getting ready for the New Year's celebration; their lives were starting again.

The days were frosty but clear, the landscape bare and wintering. Snipe called from the marshes, and the colours were grey and muted. We rode directly south and in the evenings the sun sank red in the west, the only colour in a dulled world. The nights were intensely cold with huge stars, and every morning was white with frost.

I knew Makoto was keeping some secret from me, but could not tell if it was to be a happy one or not. Every day he seemed to shine more with some inner anticipation. My own spirits were still volatile. I was pleased to be riding Shun again, but the cold and the hardship of the journey, together with the pain and disability in my hand, were more draining than I had thought they would be, and at night the task in front of me seemed too immense for me ever to achieve, especially if I was to attempt it without Kaede.

On the seventh day we came to Shirakawa. The sky had clouded over and the whole world seemed grey. Kaede's home was in ruins and deserted. The house had burned and there was nothing left of it but charred beams and ashes. It looked unutterably mournful; I imagined Fujiwara's residence would look the same. I had a serious premonition that she was dead and that Makoto was taking me to her grave. A shrike scolded us from the burned trunk of a tree by the gate and in the rice fields two crested ibises were feeding, their pink plumage glowing in the forlorn landscape. However, as we rode away past the water meadows Hiroshi called to me. 'Lord Otori! Look!'

Two brown mares were trotting towards us, whinnying to our horses. They both had foals at foot, three months old, I reckoned, their brown baby hair just beginning to give way to grey. They had manes and tails as black as lacquer.

'They are Raku's colts!' Hiroshi said. 'Amano told me that the Shirakawa mares were in foal to him.'

I could not stop looking at them. They seemed like an inexpressibly precious gift from Heaven, from life itself, a promise of renewal and rebirth.

'One of them will be yours,' I said to Hiroshi. 'You deserve it for your loyalty to me.'

'Can the other one go to Taku?' Hiroshi begged.

'Of course!'

The boys yelped with delight. I told the grooms to bring the mares with us and the foals gambolled after them, cheering me enormously as we followed Hiroshi's lead, riding on along the Shirakawa to the sacred caves.

I had never been there before and was unprepared for the size of the cavern from which the river flowed. The mountain loomed above, already snow-capped, reflected in the still black water of the winter river. Here if anywhere I could see, drawn by the hand of nature, the truth that it was all one. Earth, water and sky lay together in unbroken harmony. It was like the moment at Terayama when I had been given a glimpse into the heart of truth; now I saw Heaven's nature revealed by Earth.

There was a small cottage at the river's edge just before the gates of the shrine. An old man came out at the sound of the horses, smiled in recognition at Makoto and Hiroshi, and bowed to us.

'Welcome, sit down, I'll make you some tea. Then I'll call my wife.'

'Lord Otori has come to collect the chests we left here,' Hiroshi said importantly, and grinned at Makoto.

'Yes, yes. I'll let them know. No man may go inside, but the women will come out to us.'

While he poured us tea, another man came out from the cottage and greeted us. He was middle aged, kind, and intelligent looking; I had no idea who he was though I felt he knew me. He introduced himself to us as Ishida and I gathered he was a doctor. While he talked to us about the history of the caves and the healing properties of the water, the old man went nimbly towards the entrance to the caves, jumping from boulder to boulder. A little way from it a bronze bell hung from a wooden post. He swung the clapper against it and its hollow note boomed over the water, echoing and reverberating from inside the mountain.

I watched the old man and drank the steaming tea. He seemed to be peering and listening. After a few moments he turned and called, 'Let Lord Otori only come thus far.'

I put down the bowl and stood up. The sun was just disappearing behind the western slope and the shadow of the mountain fell on the water. As I followed the old man's steps and jumped from rock to rock, I thought I could feel something – someone – drawing towards me.

I stood next to the old man, next to the bell. He looked up at me and grinned, a smile of such openness and warmth it nearly brought tears to my eyes.

'Here comes my wife,' he said. 'She'll bring the chests.' He chuckled and went on, 'They've been waiting for you.'

I could see now into the gloom of the cavern. I could see the old shrine woman, dressed in white. I could hear her footsteps on the wet rock and the tread of the women following her. My blood was pounding in my ears.

As they stepped out into the light, the old woman bowed to the ground and placed the chest at my feet. Shizuka was just behind her, carrying a second chest.

'Lord Otori,' she murmured.

I hardly heard her. I did not look at either of them. I was staring past them at Kaede.

I knew it was her by the shape of her outline, but there was something changed about her. I did not recognize her. She had a cloth over her head and as she came towards me she let it fall to her shoulders.

Her hair was gone, her head shorn.

Her eyes were fixed on mine. Her face was unscarred and as beautiful as ever, but I hardly saw it. I gazed into her eyes, saw what she had suffered, and saw how it had refined and strengthened her. The Kikuta sleep would never touch her again.

Still without speaking, she turned and pulled the cloth from her shoulders. The nape of her neck, which had been so perfect, so white, was layered with scars of red and purple where her hair had burned her flesh.

I placed my damaged hand over it, covering her scars with my own.

We stood like that for a long time. I heard the harsh cry of the heron as it flew to its roost, the endless song of the water, and the quick beating of Kaede's heart. We were sheltered under the overhang of the rock, and I did not notice that it had started snowing.

When I looked out onto the landscape it was already turning white as the first snow of winter drifted down upon it.

On the banks of the river the colts were snorting in amazement at the snow, the first they had seen. By the time the snow melted and spring came their coats would be grey, like Raku's.

I prayed that spring would also bring healing, to our scarred bodies, to our marriage and to our land. And that spring would see the *houou*, the sacred bird of legend, return once more to the Three Countries.

Afterword

The Three Countries have enjoyed nearly fifteen years of peace and prosperity. Trade with the mainland and with the barbarians has made us rich. Inuyama, Yamagata and Hagi have palaces and castles unequalled in the Eight Islands. The court of the Otori, they say, rivals that of the emperor in splendour.

There are always threats – powerful individuals like Arai Zenko within our borders, warlords beyond the Three Countries, the barbarians who would like to have a greater share of our wealth, even the emperor and his court who fear our rivalry – but until now, the thirty-second year of my life, the fourteenth of my rule, we have been able to control all these with a mixture of strength and diplomacy.

The Kikuta, led by Akio, never gave up their campaign against me, and my body now bears the record of their attempts to kill me. Our struggle against them goes on; we will never eradicate them completely but the spies I maintain under Kenji and Taku keep them under control.

Both Taku and Zenko are married and have children of their own. Zenko I married to my sister-in-law Hana, in an only partially successful attempt to bind him closer to me in alliance. His father's death lies between us and I know he will overthrow me if he can.

Hiroshi lived in my household until he was twenty and

then returned to Maruyama where he holds the domain in trust for my eldest daughter who will inherit it from her mother.

Kaede and I have three daughters: the oldest is now thirteen, her twin sisters, eleven. Our first child looks exactly like her mother and shows no sign of any Tribe skills. The twin girls are identical, even to the Kikuta lines on their palms. People are afraid of them, with reason.

Kenji located my son ten years ago when the boy was five. Since then we keep an eye on him, but I will not allow anyone to harm him. I have thought long and often about the prophecy and have come to the conclusion that if this is to be my destiny I cannot avoid it, and if it is not – for prophecies, like prayers, fulfil themselves in unexpected ways – then the least I try to do about it the better. And I cannot deny that, as the physical pain I suffer increases and as I remember how I gave my adopted father, Shigeru, the swift and honourable death of a warrior, wiping out the insult and humiliation he had undergone at the hands of Iida Sadamu, the thought often comes to me that my son will bring me release, that death at his hands may be welcome to me.

But my death is another tale of the Otori, and one that cannot be told by me.

Acknowledgments

I would like to thank the Asialink Foundation who awarded me a fellowship in 1999 to spend three months in Japan, the Australia Council, the Department of Foreign Affairs and Trade and the Australian Embassy in Tokyo, and ArtsSA, the South Australian Government Arts Department. In Japan I was sponsored by Yamaguchi Prefecture's Akiyoshidai International Arts Village whose staff gave me invaluable help in exploring the landscape and the history of Western Honshuu. I would particularly like to thank Mr Kori Yoshinori, Ms Matsunaga Yayoi and Ms Matsubara Manami. I am especially grateful to Mrs Tokoriki Masako for showing me the Sesshu paintings and gardens and to her husband, Professor Tokoriki, for information on horses in the mediaeval period.

Spending time in Japan with two theatre companies gave me many insights — deepest thanks to Kazenoko in Tokyo and Kyushuu and Gekidan Urinko in Nagoya, and to Ms Kimura Miyo, a wonderful travelling companion, who accompanied me to Kanazawa and the Nakasendo and who has answered many questions for me about language and literature.

I thank Mr Mogi Masaru and Mrs Mogi Akiko for their help with research, their suggestions for names and, above all, their on-going friendship.

In Australia I would like to thank my two Japanese

teachers, Mrs Thuy Coombs and Mrs Etsuko Wilson, Simon Higgins who made many invaluable suggestions, my agents, Jenny Darling, Joe Regal and Sarah Lutyens, my son Matt, my first reader on all three books, and the rest of my family for not only putting up with but sharing my obsessions.

In 2002 I spent a further three months in Japan in the Shuho-cho Cultural Exchange House. Much of my research during this period helped in the final rewrite of *Brilliance of the Moon*. My thanks to the people of Shuho-cho, in particular Ms Santo Yuko and Mark Brachmann, and to Maxine McArthur. Also again deepest thanks to ArtsSA for a Mid-Career Fellowship.

Calligraphy was drawn for me by Ms Sugiyama Kazuko and Etsuko Wilson. I am immensely grateful to them.